# TOMORROW'S CONSTANT HOPE

---

## HISTORICAL CHRISTIAN ROMANCE

## NAOMI RAWLINGS

TEXAS PROMISE BOOK #3

*To the Pandemic Survivors,*

*When I penned the first words of this book, I never imagined we would soon be in the midst of a world-wide pandemic. Thank you to everyone for coming together and finding ways to get through the pandemic. Some of you worked as first responders, who went out and dealt with stressful and life threatening situations on a daily basis. Some of you worked as mothers and suddenly found yourself homeschooling and trying to shepherd your children through stress-filled and unpredictable times. And some of you were grandparents, who were restricted from seeing family and friends in an effort to stay safe and healthy.*

*Thank you to everyone who changed their schedules and their lives in an attempt to see fewer deaths. You are all wonderful, strong, beautiful people. Because of people like you—coming together and each doing what you could—we are looking at the pandemic with the lowest death rate in the world's history.*

# DESCRIPTION

*The last thing a woman on the run needs is to find herself married to the richest rancher in Texas...*

*Keely O'Brien has spent the past five months on the run, but no matter what she does, she can't seem to evade the ring of dangerous criminals that killed her brother in Chicago. When she spots an ad for a wife from the owner of a small ranch on a remote stretch of Texan desert, she knows she's found the perfect hiding spot. The Wolf Point Ring might be searching far and wide for her, but they wouldn't think to look in tiny, sun-scorched town of Twin Rivers, Texas. Now if she can just keep her new husband from finding out why she really married him...*

*Agamemnon "Wes" Westin's feet might be firmly planted in West Texas soil, but his heart is running... Running from the loss of his first wife and stillborn daughter, and running from the fear of suffering loss again. Unfortunately, he has little choice about needing to marry, but he does have a choice about who he marries. If he has to share his roof with someone, he wants a woman who works hard and doesn't complain. That's why he decides to run an ad for a bride, claiming that he owns a small ranch, rather than the sprawling cattle empire he inherited from his father. After all, what woman is going to be upset when she finds out her husband is one of the richest men in Texas?*

*When Wes discovers Keely is hiding from criminals who want her dead, he can't help but protect her—even if she's irate with him for lying about the size of his ranch. When danger arrives in Twin Rivers, both Wes and Keely find themselves facing their deepest fears. Will they let their pain and past losses ruin their dreams? Or will Wes and Keely find a way to forge a new life together?*

# PROLOGUE

**San, Antonio, Texas; September 1885**

I t was all too much—the music, the dancing, the laughter. Agamemnon Westin VI—"Wes" to those who knew him—looked around the ornate ballroom, filled with people and decorated floor-to-ceiling in pink and white swaths of fabric. The fabric matched the pink and white flower arrangements that had been plopped on every flat surface inside the gargantuan room, which matched the dresses that the twelve bridesmaids wore as they twirled around the dance-floor in time with the music from the string ensemble that filled every last corner of the room.

Wes stuck a finger in the collar of his shirt and tugged. His sister Charlotte didn't feel comfortable trussed up in glittering jewels and shimmering fabrics, but these kinds of situations had never grated on him before.

But tonight?

He'd rather be in the horse barn, mucking out stalls.

He pressed a hand to his temple, which pounded in time

with the beat of the waltz. Fifteen more minutes. Then he'd have stayed at the wedding reception long enough to not be rude. He'd go upstairs to his room and pray that the music wouldn't travel all the way to the east wing of the house. Maybe then his headache would subside.

"Agamemnon, there you are." Thomas Ross, a banker and one of his father's friends, came up beside him, his large girth making the already claustrophobic room seem even smaller. "Was hoping to see you tonight."

Pity, he'd been planning to stay mostly hidden for the next fifteen minutes. But little about his night so far had worked as he'd planned. This was the first time in two hours he'd gotten a break from the dance floor, and only because he'd found a little alcove tucked behind a pillar and a potted tree.

"What did you want to see me about?" Wes took a sip of the sickeningly sweet punch in his hand.

The banker eyed him. "Heard you sold thirty thousand head of cattle at auction earlier this week."

Wes clenched his jaw, but that only increased the pounding in his temples. "Seems as though the whole of San Antonio heard that."

Ross's laugh boomed across the ballroom. "Must not feel like you have much of a ranch left."

"I have plenty of ranch." And as of that afternoon, a lot of railroad. Unfortunately.

"You talk to Captain King over there yet?" Ross nudged him with his elbow, then pointed. "Bet he has the biggest ranch in Texas now that he bought up half the cattle you sold."

"It's not a competition," Wes mumbled.

Ross cackled. "Sure it ain't. Just go tell that to Richard King, will you?"

"I already talked to King."

To be honest, the only thing surprising about Captain Richard King having a larger ranch was that it had taken him selling off half his herd to accomplish it. The King Ranch was located near Brownsville, Texas, which had things like rain and creeks and rivers and grass that actually turned green rather than staying brown all year. The terrain near Brownsville was prime Texas cattle land, nothing like the dry, arid desert where the A Bar W was located.

When they'd spoken earlier, King had shaken his hand, apologized about the loss of his father, and commented how surprised he was at the selling of the cattle.

Wes would have told King the reason for selling off so many cattle—that before his death, his father had agreed to an astronomical railroad investment, and he now owned five percent of the Southern Pacific railroad track being laid between Houston and San Diego—but Mrs. Frampton had chosen that moment to appear at his arm, wanting to introduce him to her oh-so-delightful niece who painted watercolors lovely enough to be in an art gallery, played the piano well enough to accompany the Houston Philharmonic Orchestra, and sang with the voice of an angel.

Oh, and as fate would have it, her niece was also single and in need of a dance partner.

"You know you can come to me if you need a loan." Ross sipped his champagne, the sour scent of the large man's body odor drifting to him.

"I don't," Wes quipped a bit too forcefully.

"I know your father wasn't a fan of loans, but that has to be better than selling off so much of your herd."

"I can hardly go back and unsell the cattle at this point." Besides, he wasn't fool enough to take a loan out for an investment, even one that seemed as secure as the railroad.

"You could take out a loan for some yearlings."

He'd already toyed with the idea. It would be the fastest way to rebuild. But did he want to owe money on something that could be killed off by drought or disease?

Wes slanted the man a glance, but movement past Ross caught his eye. A middle-aged woman was coming toward him, her hand clutching the elbow of a girl—she was certainly too young to be called a woman—in a hideous orange gown with sleeves so puffy they swallowed her shoulders and neck.

Wes reached into his pocket, his hand sliding over the envelope there. It was an automatic reaction at this point in the evening. He wouldn't be able to count the number of times he'd touched it even if he tried, just like he couldn't say what had possessed him to slip it into his pocket before the wedding.

The envelope contained the most recent letter he'd gotten from Keely McBryan. Keely knew him only as Wes, owner of what she thought to be a small ranch in the desert. She didn't know about his money. She didn't know about the size of the A Bar W or his railroad holdings or the socialites who thronged him with dollar signs in their eyes whenever he visited a city.

All she wanted was a roof over her head and food on the table. And he was thinking awfully hard about giving it to her —along with his last name.

"Mr. Westin, how lovely to see you again!" The screeching tone of the woman's voice gave him the sudden desire to wince.

"It's nice to see you too." He had no idea who this woman was. Had they been introduced before, or was that a ploy?

"This is my daughter Eva."

He surveyed the poor girl in front of him, young, slender, and too timid to even lift her head and meet his eyes. He raised an eyebrow at her mother. "Is she in need of a partner for the next dance?"

"However did you know?" The woman pressed a hand to her chest as though surprised at his offer.

Behind him, Mr. Ross chuckled, then covered the sound with a cough.

"Just a hunch I had." He extended his hand to Eva. "Shall we?"

The girl's face flushed red, and she mumbled something he couldn't make out against the noise of the room. But she reached out a slender hand and placed it in his palm.

He led her to the dance floor amid a flurry of swaying skirts and glittering jewels and took his position for the waltz. Then he froze. There, three people over in a dark purple dress, was Lydia Hootler.

He shuddered, his heart starting to pound against his ribcage.

"Mr. Westin, are you all right?"

Wes snapped his gaze back to his dance partner, only to realize the music had started. He settled a hand on her waist and guided her around the floor. She took shy, timid steps that required he readjust his gait lest he end up trampling her.

A quick glance over his shoulder at the smile on Lydia's face told him she was having fun being twirled around the floor.

Hopefully her dance partner didn't have much money. Either that, or he actually wouldn't mind being married to Lydia. Did the poor fellow she was dancing with realize just how far she was willing to go to procure a husband?

Wes tried to focus on the small woman in front of him, tried to listen to the music and stay aware of what the dancers around him were doing, but he couldn't quite keep his mind from drifting back to the house party his father had thrown in July. Lydia had asked him to take her on a walk numerous times. When he'd finally given in, he'd found himself locked inside an old bunkhouse with her.

Fortunately, his sister had been out riding and seen them go into the bunkhouse. She'd figured out what was afoot and unlocked the door within seconds, dragging Lydia back outside. A few minutes later, Lydia's mother and sister had appeared, also out on a "walk" and thoroughly disappointed to find he and Lydia hadn't been alone in a secluded place for any length of time.

It had been what prompted him to place an ad for a wife in several newspapers in the Midwest—an ad that had deliberately left out any mention of his money.

The dance came to an end, and Wes offered Eva a small smile. "Thank you for dancing with me."

When he tried to release Eva's hand, she didn't let go, but she did find the courage to at least raise her head and meet his eyes. "I'm... I'm feeling rather hot. Perhaps we could take a walk in the garden... to ah... to cool off. Just... just the two of us."

A walk.

In the garden.

Just the two of them.

He could only imagine how that would turn out. But unlike when he'd gone on that blasted walk with Lydia, his sister wasn't around to rescue him tonight.

"I'm afraid I'll have to pass. Is there anything else your mother told you to say to me?"

She jolted, her eyes coming back to meet his for a second time. "How did you know it was my mother?"

"Must be smarter than I look," he muttered.

Her brow creased together in confusion, but then her sense of manners must have kicked in, because she gave a dainty curtsy. "Thank you for the dance."

*The pleasure was all mine.* They were the proper words to say, and yet he couldn't force them over his tongue.

Eva left his side just as the first of two mothers reached him, dragging her daughter behind her, and smiling in a sickeningly sweet way.

It took three additional dances and a full half hour before he could thread his way out of the ballroom and escape up the stairs to his room.

Wes nodded at the servant in the hallway who stood with a tea tray in her hand, softly knocking on a door, and headed two doors down. His head pounded as he turned the knob and pushed the heavy wood open.

And then he froze. Right in the middle of the doorway. Because there was a woman.

In his room.

Sitting on his bed.

"Out!" he bellowed.

"Mr. Westin." The woman stood, and only then did he realize she was wearing a corset and drawers. No gown over it, no chemise, nothing besides her underthings.

He took as step back into the hallway. "Hadley!"

Wasn't that the name of the servant who had shown him to his room and unpacked his things? Or had it been Hartford? Or Harold?

The woman from the bed pulled a wrapper over her shoulders as she hurried toward him. "What are you doing? You're going to make a scene."

"A scene? If you don't want a scene, don't enter my bedchamber and undress."

Hang it all! What had made the woman think he wanted to come to his room and find her there? He didn't even recognize her from earlier in the evening. And there was no way anything he'd done could somehow be construed into an invitation to his bed.

"There must be some kind of misunderstanding. I was only—"

"What are you doing in my daughter's room?" A feminine voice screeched from down the hallway.

Wes turned to find a plump woman, also in a wrapper, storming toward him with an irate look on her face.

"Of all the improper things! Lucille, my poor dear, are you all right?" She hugged the younger woman, then turned to glare at Wes. "I suppose the two of you shall have to marry now."

"Because your daughter came into my room and undressed? I think not."

"Your room?" The mother's cheeks grew pink. "This is her room, the one the servant showed us when we arrived earlier. Isn't it, Lucille?"

Lucille nodded.

Wes sucked in a breath. This was not happening. All he wanted was his headache to go away and a good night's sleep.

No. Never mind that bit about sleep. At that exact moment, he wanted to be back in Twin Rivers, married to a woman who actually might be grateful for his wealth rather than think she was somehow entitled to it. And he wanted to never need to worry about something like this happening again.

"You must be mistaken." Wes's voice rumbled from his chest, loud enough to fill the hallway. "This is the room Hadley showed me to, which I can prove by the presence of my valise being by that chair." He pointed at the overstuffed chair where he'd left his single bag earlier that afternoon.

"Agamemnon, is there a problem?"

Wes turned to find Edward Bradford headed toward him. Several others had gathered in the hallway. Most of them were servants, but there were just enough wedding guests to ensure that every little thing that transpired would be dutifully reported in the ballroom in a matter of minutes.

"Sorry, Edward. I didn't mean to interrupt Polly's wedding reception." But since Edward owned the house and it was his daughter's wedding, he was probably the best person to deal with the situation. "When I came upstairs, I found a woman in my room. They're claiming we had some sort of mix up, and we were both somehow put into the same room? Perhaps she arrived after I did and didn't notice my bag."

He didn't buy the story, not for a second, but at least going with that explanation would let Lucille out of the situation with her dignity intact—which was probably more than the woman or her mother deserved.

"He was in the room alone with my daughter while she was undressed." The mother clutched her daughter to her, her face still red with feigned rage. "Clearly they have to marry."

"I never stepped foot inside the room," Wes gritted. "As soon as I opened the door and saw Lucille, I called for Hadley."

Lucille stepped forward and latched onto his arm, her lashes fluttering as she smiled up at him. "Oh, Wes, don't tell fibs just to save my reputation. We both know you were alone in here with me."

Wes yanked his arm away, his blood turning suddenly hot as he faced Bradford. "She's lying."

Lucille's mother—he still didn't know her name—made a screeching sound and pressed her hand to her chest." The audacity! You think you can ruin my daughter and then walk away as though nothing happened?"

"If you don't want your daughter ruined, I suggest you teach her to stop going into strange men's bedchambers and undressing."

"Just a minute here." Bradford turned to where a cluster of servants stood. "Who showed Miss Inverly to her room earlier?"

A servant stepped forward. "It was me, sir."

"Did you show her to this specific room, or was it another one?"

The maid looked between her employer and Miss Inverly, her brow furrowing. "I showed several people to their rooms, sir. I thought I put Miss Inverly in the one across the hall, but I might have put her in this one. I don't quite remember. I just matched her name to the room on the list."

"Miss Hanover has a list of the room assignments," one of the male servants said. "We all followed it."

Another servant stepped forward to stand beside the first

one. Wes recognized her as the servant who'd been in the hallway when he'd passed by earlier. In fact, she was still holding the tea service from before. "Mr. Westin never went inside the room. As soon as he opened the door and saw Miss Inverly, he shouted for Hadley, and he stayed in the hall the entire time, even when Miss Inverly started talking to him."

"I see." Bradford narrowed his eyes at the Inverlys.

"Surely you don't intend to take the word of a servant over the word of my daughter," Mrs. Inverly gasped.

"No, but I will take the word of my friend, especially when his story matches that of a servant."

The woman clutched her hand to her chest again, and Lucille covered her mouth, tears springing to her eyes.

Wes turned his back on them both and stared at Bradford. "Send Hadley up to gather my things. I'm not stepping foot inside that room."

His host's bushy gray eyebrows disappeared beneath his hairline. "You're leaving? At this hour of the night?"

"Yes."

"But it's nearly eleven. Surely a little misunderstanding—"

"I wouldn't call this misunderstanding *little*." Staying another minute was too risky, let alone eight more hours. Did Lucille have a key to his room? Would she appear in his bed in the middle of the night?

That situation would be compromising enough that he wouldn't be able to wriggle out of it.

He was leaving. Tonight. Even if he did nothing more than get outside the city before he climbed into his bedroll. The sooner he got back to Twin Rivers, the sooner he could marry Keely McBryan.

She would solve his biggest problem—the need for a wife. And he would solve hers—the need for food and a roof.

He wouldn't tell her who he was until after the wedding, after he knew for certain she wasn't part of some scheme or trick. After he knew she was marrying him for some reason other than his money.

And then, when she learned how large his ranch was and that her days would be filled with more leisure than work, he'd make her the happiest woman in Texas.

# 1

Twin Rivers, Texas; October 1885

I t was about to begin. The first day of the rest of her life. Keely McBryan drew in a nervous breath and peeked through the crack in the door of the pastor's office where she stood. There were an awful lot of people in the sanctuary. Not necessarily what she'd been hoping for when all she needed was a pastor and two witnesses for her marriage to be legal. But she wasn't going to complain, not when this marriage would solve her biggest problem and put the mess of what had happened in Chicago behind her for good.

She forced her shoulders to relax. The large number of people would be fine—as long as a tall, wide-shouldered man with a pair of blue eyes as cold as ice didn't pull open the door of the church and walk inside.

The door at the back of the sanctuary opened, and a shadow filled the space.

She froze, just for a second, but she couldn't help the way her breath clogged in her chest and her lungs refused to draw air. Then the man entered and took a seat in one of the back pews.

The breath involuntarily released from her lungs, rushing out of her in a giant whoosh. Not Lester Mears or anyone that worked for him.

Why had she even thought it was him in the first place? It had been eight months since she'd fled from Chicago. Eight months that she'd stayed hidden. Mears couldn't have followed her here. He hadn't even been able to track her to Springfield, Missouri, where she'd been hiding for the past four months—and she hadn't had any papers to prove her false identity when she'd fled to Springfield.

Now she had identification claiming she was Keely McBryan, and her name was about to change again—legally and permanently.

So why had she thought of Lester Mears when the door opened?

It had to be nerves. Pledging the rest of her life to a man was a big decision.

But it was also the best way to let herself live again. She was tired of running. She was tired of hiding. She was tired of looking over her shoulder and jumping at shadows.

This marriage would give her a new name and a place to belong.

Which was why she couldn't be too upset about all the people filling the sanctuary of the little church or the dinner that was to follow. If she was going to start anew in Twin Rivers, Texas as the wife of a local rancher, then it seemed having a big wedding followed by a dinner was the expected thing to do.

"Are you ready?" the pastor's wife said from behind her.

Keely turned to face the dark-haired woman that wasn't quite old enough to be her mother.

*Was she ready?*

Was marrying a stranger something a woman could ever be ready for?

She drew in a breath and urged a smile onto her face. "I suppose I am."

"Excellent," the other woman said. "As soon as the music starts, we'll step out the side door here and head around to the back of the church so you can walk up the aisle."

"All right." Keely glanced out the crack in the door to the sanctuary one more time, then pressed her hands over her stomach to clamp down on the sudden bout of nerves.

"I can do this," she whispered to herself.

Then the piano began playing, and she followed the pastor's wife outside.

This was the first day of the rest of her life. She was determined to make it not just a good day, but a good life.

~.~.~.~.~

WHAT IF HE was making a mistake?

Wes stood at the front of the church, holding the gloved hands of the woman who was becoming closer to being his wife with each word that Preacher Russell spoke.

No, this couldn't be a mistake. Not after what had happened last month in San Antonio with Lucille Inverly. Not after what had happened last summer with Lydia Hootler.

So why did he have the sudden urge to drop Keely's hands and tell the preacher to wait?

He'd been over his options too many times to count. He had to get married, plain and simple. And if he didn't take some initiative and choose a wife for himself, a woman he couldn't stand was going to trap him into a marriage he'd hate. He'd gotten a handful of letters for the ad he'd placed for a wife, and Keely McBryan had seemed like the best fit.

But the plan he'd formed after Lucille Inverly had snuck into his room in San Antonio seemed far different now that he was standing here in front of half the town, pretending that getting married was something to celebrate.

He didn't feel like celebrating. Taking his new wife home, showing her the ranch, and explaining who he really was, yes. But celebrating?

There wasn't all that much to celebrate this time around. Now, last time...

Wes bit the inside of his cheek hard enough he tasted blood. Nothing good would come of thinking about the day he'd stood in this very spot, pledging his life to a woman he'd loved wholly and completely.

"Um, Wes?" Keely whispered, then squeezed his hands harder.

He looked down at her. She was staring at him with wide green eyes, eyes that quickly narrowed. She pressed her lips together and glanced at Preacher Russell.

Only then did he realize the preacher had stopped talking. He looked in the preacher's direction. The man stared back at him, a hint of consternation creasing his brow.

Something told him if he looked out at the packed church, he'd find every single eye pinned to him too.

"Say 'I do,'" she gritted.

Were they at that part already?

Wes swallowed, but the words stuck in his throat, and he couldn't seem to move his lips.

Keely gripped his hands even tighter.

"I do." The words that finally sputtered out of his mouth were loud enough they could probably be heard at the newspaper office across town.

Preacher Russell cleared his throat. "And Keely, do you take this man to be your lawfully wedded husband?"

"I do." Her words sounded just as bold as his, but something flashed in her eyes, and she kept her grip on his hands just hard enough he had trouble thinking about Abigail again.

At least until it came time to recite his vows. Then he couldn't quite stop himself from remembering how Abigail had looked in her wedding finery the last time he'd promised to honor and cherish a woman for the rest of his life...

Or until she died.

Wes swallowed. He had to stop this. Now. He'd known whomever he married wouldn't be able to fill the hole in his heart Abigail had left. It shouldn't surprise him that his petite new wife with curly red hair and green eyes looked nothing like Abigail either. Hopefully their differences in appearance meant he wouldn't be remembering his late wife every time he glimpsed his new one around the ranch.

"I now pronounce you man and wife." Preacher Russell's words rang through the church, causing Wes to suck in a breath. "What God has joined together, let no man put asunder. You may now kiss the bride."

Wes lifted the small, gauzy veil over Keely's face. Their eyes met, and he was struck by the intensity in them—and was that a glimmer of hope too?

Hope in what? Not in some kind of love match or true marriage between them. He'd been clear he wasn't looking for that in his letters. He'd told her he'd wanted a woman who was willing to work around the ranch, and she had agreed to take on housekeeping duties.

So what was the hope for?

Preacher Russell cleared his throat and muttered, "Kiss your bride, Wes."

Wes slammed his eyes shut and brushed his lips against

Keely's so briefly he wasn't actually sure they'd touched. Then he turned her to face the crowd.

Keely's grip on his hand turned to stone, and she stared at a figure at the back of the church.

"Is that a camera?" Her voice was soft enough that others couldn't hear, but there was nothing soft about the words themselves. "What is that man doing?"

"That's Glen from the newspaper. I assume he took a picture or two of us during the wedding." The newspaper had come out and taken one of him and Abigail standing at the front of the church when they'd been married, then had sold the picture to bigger papers in the city after it had been developed. Wes had bought a copy of the picture from the paper himself and still had it tucked away in the drawer of his nightstand.

"The paper!" Keely squeaked, loud enough for others to hear this time.

"We need to walk down the aisle. Everyone is staring." He tugged on her hand, but the movement did no good. She just stood at the front of the church, shooting death glares at Glen.

If people were going to stare, he might as well give them something to stare at. Wes turned and scooped her up into his arms.

He'd known his new wife was small when she'd stepped out of the carriage and the top of her head hadn't even reached his chin. But he wasn't quite prepared for how delicate she felt in his arms, like one of her bones might snap if he held her too tightly.

But he had to hold her tightly, because she started to squirm.

"What are you doing?" she whispered. "People are staring."

"They were staring before too. When you refused to walk down the aisle."

"Put me down. I don't want all this attention."

He glanced around the church. Every eye was pinned to them, but everyone had smiles in their eyes and laugh lines around their mouths. "They'll only think this odder if I put you down halfway down the aisle. Besides, I can't be the first man to carry his wife out of the church after their wedding."

She gave a small huff. "Fine."

He strode the rest of the way down the church, holding her like he might if they were in love and he was about to carry her over the threshold of their house. They passed through the wooden doors of the church, and he carried her down the steps. Most of the food for the dinner had already been set up on the table in the yard, so Wes turned that direction, then set her down.

"I need to find the man with the camera," she blurted, scanning the churchyard.

"I'm right here," Glen said from behind them. "Gotta say, that was brilliant, Wes. Never seen a man carry his wife out of church like that before. The town will love it. It'll be on the front page of the paper come Wednesday."

"Front page?" Keely strode straight to Glen and plopped her hands on her hips. "There will be no front-page news story and certainly no picture. Now give me the camera plate from the wedding."

"You want both of them?"

She scowled. "Just how many pictures did you take while we were standing up there?"

Glen shrugged. "Three or four. You stand in the same spot for most of the ceremony. I took as many as I could, hoping one wouldn't be blurry."

"Keely," Wes stepped forward. "I asked the paper to send a reporter to our wedding. I figured you'd want an announcement. Most weddings around here get a full article." And theirs was sure to be on the front page, seeing how he was owner of the second largest ranch in Texas.

"I don't want any mention of the wedding. I never said I did. The only thing I want is those camera plates." Keely turned to him.

He opened his mouth, but something about the look on her face stopped him from speaking. Her face had drained of color, and was that a flicker of fear in her eyes?

He scratched the side of his head. Most women would be tickled pink by the notion of pictures of their actual wedding.

"Does this mean you won't pose for a picture before the meal starts?" Glen asked.

"Absolutely not." Keely shot a death glare at the reporter.

"Sorry, Glen." Wes offered him an apologetic smile. "Looks like we'll have to pass."

The reporter pressed his lips into a flat line, then withdrew a notepad and pencil from his shirt pocket. "Fine then, any comments for the paper about the wedding?"

"I said no article!" Keely screeched.

"Is everything all right here?" Daniel Harding, one of Wes's closest friends, came up to them.

Past Daniel, the churchyard had filled with people, and it seemed like every one of them was staring at him and Keely. Again.

"We were just having a little..." Wes's voice faltered as he glanced at Keely. Her face was even whiter now than it had been a moment ago.

"You were saying?" Daniel crossed his arms over his wide chest, the tin star of his sheriff's badge glinting in the sunlight.

Keely took a couple steps to the side, putting Wes between Daniel and her.

Did his friend have to act so all-fired intimidating? Daniel *wasn't* intimidating once you got to know him. But given the wide breadth of his shoulders and the way he towered over most people in town, he could certainly look frightening.

"Mrs. Westin was about to try telling me what I can and

cannot put in the paper. But last I checked, she doesn't own the paper, so she doesn't have any say over what goes in it. Good day, Sheriff." Glen turned on his heel and stalked off.

Daniel raised an eyebrow at him. "What'd you do to set Glen off?"

He wasn't sure. Or more to the point, he wasn't sure what had set his new wife off. Even now he could feel her behind him, standing so close the heat from her shoulder radiated into his back.

"Good grief, Daniel." Anna Mae—Daniel's sister and the one who'd done most of the planning work for the dinner—came up to them. "It's your best friend's wedding. Would it kill you to smile?"

"Best friend?" Keely's question from behind him was so soft Wes barely heard it.

"I've been smiling." Daniel held up his hands.

"Then why is Wes's new bride cowering behind him?" Anna Mae quipped. "Looks as though you've scared her silly, and on her wedding day, no less."

"I didn't scare her," Daniel protested.

But Anna Mae was already tugging Keely out from behind him. "It's Keely, right? I'm Anna Mae Harding."

Anna Mae drew Keely straight into a hug, a wide smile plastered to her face.

Wes bit back a laugh. His new wife looked stiff as a fence post in Anna Mae's arms, but given the way Anna Mae was smiling, she was too taken with the notion of making a new friend to notice.

"Don't you worry about my brother none. The oaf doesn't realize how intimidating he can be. Now come on." Anna Mae tucked one of Keely's hands in hers. "The women are still getting the food ready, and there are some people you need to meet now that you're an official part of Twin Rivers. I'll deliver you back to Wes before the meal starts."

Wes raised an eyebrow at Keely and opened his mouth to ask if she wanted to go off with Anna Mae, but Keely was already nodding her head, a small smile inching onto her face.

It was the first time he'd seen her smile since arriving, and it looked downright cute.

"Don't let Anna Mae talk you into anything too crazy," he warned.

That was all the invitation Anna Mae needed to steer Keely into the crowd. Wes watched them for a few seconds, his wife's small form and green dress almost unnoticeable beside Anna Mae's full curves and brightly colored skirt.

"I feel like I'm supposed to say congratulations." Daniel turned to him, the tiny creases around his mouth serious. "But part of me can't believe you went through with it, not when you're still grieving Abigail."

Wes shoved a hand through his hair. If they'd been over this once, they'd been over it a thousand times. "If not Keely, I'd be stuck marrying Lucille Inverly or someone of her ilk. I've only known Keely for two hours, and I can already tell she'll be a much better choice."

Of the letters he'd gotten, she'd been the only person who made him smile. She hadn't asked how big his house was or how many cattle he had. And there hadn't been dollar signs in her eyes when she'd gotten off the stage either.

Daniel watched him, his keen blue eyes assessing far too much. "I just hope this isn't a mistake."

"It's not." The words came out just a little too quickly.

"Well, well, looks like the wedded bliss afforded most newly married folks has somehow escaped Wes." Sam Owens sauntered up beside him, a thatch of reddish-brown hair hanging over his brow. "Why am I not surprised you look this serious on your wedding day?"

Wes glared at the auburn-haired man who had been his friend for over two decades. "Stow it."

Sam only grinned, the smile spreading across his face making him look more like a fourteen-year-old than a grown man with a family of his own. "Seeing how she married you, I assume she was pretty happy when you told her how big your ranch is."

"I haven't told her yet."

"What? Why not?" The grin dropped from Sam's face. "You know you're not going to be able to keep who you are a secret once she has a look at your ranch."

"That's how I plan to tell her. I figured I'd explain once she saw everything." Wes shifted. It was a sound idea, wasn't it? "Not even sure how to bring it up in a conversation, really. What am I supposed to say? 'I know the ad I placed said I owned a small ranch, but it's really the second largest ranch in Texas.'"

"Sounds better than keeping secrets from your wife," Sam retorted.

"It's not a secret. It's just... I needed to make sure she wanted to marry me for something other than my money. You know how much time and work my father, Charlotte, and I have put into the ranch."

And yet he had that sudden urge to scratch the place he couldn't quite reach between his shoulder blades. Should he have told her about his wealth before the wedding?

If he had, how would he know that she'd married him because she wanted to and not for the size of his bank account?

Sam rubbed the back of his neck. "I see what you're saying, but I've been in your situation before. Trust me, you're better off being completely open with your wife. If you try keeping things from her, it will only cause problems."

"I'm one of the richest men in Texas. How is that going to cause a problem?"

"I don't know." Daniel slung an arm around his shoulders and grinned. "I seem to remember you standing in front of the general store eight months ago, telling Sam he couldn't marry his mail-order bride because she was sure to poison him for his land."

Sam guffawed. "Forgot all about that. Yeah, Wes, how do you know Keely won't decide to poison you when she sees how big your ranch is?"

Wes rolled his eyes. "I may have overreacted when I said that."

More laugher broke from Sam. "You think?"

Daniel gave his shoulder a crushing squeeze, then let him go. "In all seriousness, if something goes wrong once you get Keely home, you can always fill out a petition for an annulment."

"An annulment?"

"Can a judge grant an annulment on the grounds of sheer stupidity?" Sam gave Wes a little shove.

"No, but a judge can grant one on the grounds of fraud," Daniel said.

Wes blinked, then looked around at the three of them. "No one here is committing fraud."

"Ah... well..." Daniel winced. "Technically, you concealed information from your wife before the wedding, leading her to believe you're someone different than you truly are. That's considered fraud in Texas."

Sam let out a bellow, then slapped him in the shoulder. "Looky there. If your new wife tries to poison you for your ranch, you got a way out of your marriage. Don't you feel lucky?"

Wes's lungs filled with laughter, Daniel and Sam joining in.

A bride he didn't know, a ranch she didn't know about, and the option for an annulment because he had too much money. Had there ever been a more unconventional way to start a marriage?

## 2

Her new husband was friends with the sheriff. Keely drew in a breath and tried to focus on the plate in front of her, piled high with meat that Wes had called brisket. It was better than watching the sheriff.

At least no one seemed to be avoiding him as he walked around talking to the wedding guests. Hopefully that meant he was a trustworthy lawman.

The sheriff in Springfield had seemed upstanding too. But it wasn't as though she could vouch for the man personally.

Now the chief of police in Chicago...

"Sorry if this is all a bit overwhelming." Wes took a drink of water from where he sat beside her at the table.

"If what's overwhelming?" *Being friends with the sheriff?* How could he know that was going to be a problem?

Her husband made a circular motion with his fork to encompass the church yard. Most of the townsfolk were either standing in line to get food or making their way down the long table filled with meat, potatoes, beans, squash, and just about every other food imaginable.

"The size of the wedding," Wes speared another bite of

meat with his fork. "The dinner right now, all the people. I imagine it's a bit intimidating to come to a new town and have a bunch of people you don't know celebrate your wedding."

"I don't mind."

"Really?" He paused his fork halfway to his mouth. "I intended for things to be a bit smaller than this, but Anna Mae loves a good party, and once she found out about the wedding, it was hard for me to say no to inviting the town and having a dinner afterward."

"I don't mind. It's a good chance to meet people." Not that she'd be able to remember everyone, but some of the names and faces were already starting to stick. "Anna Mae and the sheriff are brother and sister?"

She already knew the answer, of course. But if she could get her new husband talking about the Harding family, maybe she'd learn some useful information about the sheriff—like if they were best friends who saw each other a few times a year or if they visited every day.

"Sure are. That's their pa over there." Wes jabbed his fork toward where a man sat in a wheelchair on the far side of the churchyard. "He lost his leg to a band of outlaws seven years ago, and Daniel got elected sheriff shortly afterward."

Keely forked some potatoes into her mouth and chewed slowly. If outlaws had been shooting at the sheriff, that proved the law hadn't been in cahoots with them. Yet another good sign. "Seems like you know the Hardings well."

Wes shrugged. "Daniel and I have been friends since the cradle, and both our parents were friends before that."

The potatoes turned to dust in her mouth. If Wes and the sheriff were that good of friends, then what if Daniel thought it his duty to look into the past of Wes's new bride? What if he found out she wasn't really Keely McBryan? Or her true reason for coming to Twin Rivers?

She'd already known that if she wanted to start a new life,

she'd need to destroy the evidence she had about the Wolf Point Ring. But now it looked like she'd need to burn anything with her real name on it too.

Because if Wes found her true name, he'd probably tell the sheriff, and if the sheriff decided to contact the police in Chicago...

She bit her lip. She needed to calm down. It had been months since she'd seen a man in a red bowler hat, months since she'd read anything in the Chicago papers that indicated a criminal ring was controlling most of Chicago's business and politics. Mayor Grisdale wasn't even running for reelection next month.

She didn't know if the Wolf Point Ring was still smuggling opium into the country, but she'd already evaded them for eight months. Now it was time for her to assume a completely new identity and start a new life in a place where they would never, ever find her...

But that could only happen if no one from Twin Rivers learned who she was.

When she cooked supper later, the papers were going in the stove's fire. Every last one of them. Then there would be no way for Wes or the sheriff or anyone in Twin Rivers to discover what had happened that spring. No way for them to learn she used to go by the name Nora O'Leary. No way for them to tie her to Chicago.

"Wes, good grief. What have you done now?"

Keely jerked her head up to find Anna Mae and two other women coming toward the table.

Wes scowled at Anna Mae. "I don't know what you're yammering on about."

Anna Mae stopped in front of the table, reminding Keely of just how beautiful she was. Her simple attire of a Mexican shirtwaist with wide shoulders and a scooped neckline, paired with a full, patterned skirt, only made her glossy black hair and brown eyes stand out against her porcelain skin.

Anna Mae set her plate of untouched food down and glared at Wes. "Your new wife looks terrified. Again."

Wes turned to her, and the intensity of his dark eyes made her want to squirm. "We weren't talking about anything terrifying. I was just telling her about the townsfolk."

"I'm Charlotte Harding." The tall woman beside Anna Mae stuck out her hand to shake. "I'm Wes's sister."

Keely reached out and took Charlotte's hand. "Nice to meet you."

Had she said her last name was Harding too? As in, Sheriff *Harding*? Keely shoved another bite of into her mouth and chewed. Maybe it wasn't as bad as all that. Wes's sister could be married to a different Harding and not necessarily the sheriff.

"My husband's the sheriff," Charlotte announced, almost as though she could read her thoughts. "Have you met him yet?"

Keely nearly choked.

"And I'm Ellie Owens." The last woman in the group spoke. Her hair was a brighter color than Keely's own red tresses, and freckles scattered across her face and down her arms. "Seems you and I have a lot in common. I moved here from Michigan last spring to marry my husband and help with his ranch. I would have dragged him over here to meet you, but the twins are in a mood today and won't stop fighting."

Ellie pointed toward a blanket that had been spread not too far away from where the man in the wheelchair sat. "That's him over there with the brown cowboy hat."

She saw the man in the brown hat, but five other children were crowded onto the blanket happily eating.

Keely looked back at the rounded bump peeking out from Ellie's skirt that could only indicate a coming baby. "Just how many children do you have?"

Ellie laughed, the sound full and hearty. "No children of my own yet, though that's set to change this spring. But I did bring eight siblings with me when I moved here."

"And your husband took them all in?" Keely couldn't quite keep the squeak from her voice.

A smile wreathed Ellie's face. "Did I mention I married the most wonderful man in the state of Texas?"

"I suppose you did," Keely muttered.

"The three of us actually came to eat with you, if that's all right." Ellie set her plate down beside Anna Mae's.

"You two sit together so you can talk." Anna Mae walked around the side of the table and switched her plate with Ellie. "You already have a lot in common, and I'm sure Keely has questions about the desert."

"I'll sit by my brother and make sure he behaves." Charlotte moved her plate to the opposite side of Wes.

Ellie sat, then reached out and gripped Keely's hand. "Don't be nervous. You're doing great, though I'm sure all this is rather intimidating."

It was, but not for the reasons Ellie thought. Keely scooped a bite of brisket onto her fork. "Did you feel intimidated when you married Sam?"

"I did, and like you, I hadn't met him before our wedding day, though we had been writing each other for over a year." Ellie slanted a glance Wes's direction. "And there were some differences in our situation, wasn't there, Wes?"

Wes muttered something under his breath that Keely couldn't quite make out, but Charlotte and Anna Mae both burst into giggles.

"I'm just glad everything worked out for Ellie and Sam." Wes's voice held a seriousness that contrasted with the bright smiles the women shared.

"Me too," Ellie said.

Keely glanced around the churchyard, which was now filled with people contentedly eating their food. Hopefully things would work out as well for her and Wes as they had for Sam and Keely.

But that meant the sheriff couldn't learn she was really from Chicago, not Springfield, Missouri—or the true reason she'd left her home.

~.~.~.~.~

"YOU EXPECT me to climb on top of that thing?"

Wes slanted a glance at his new wife. She stood staring up at Hestia as though the medium-sized mare was about to breathe fire on her. "How else do you plan to get back to the ranch?"

"Don't you have a wagon?" She looked around the road.

"I had one of my cow hands drive it back to the ranch with your trunk."

"Oh... well... I don't... um..." She twisted her hands together. "I don't know how to ride a horse."

And here he'd brought a pair of their prized Arabians to impress his new wife.

"West Texas is too spread out to go anywhere on foot." He untied Hestia's reins from the hitching posed and secured them to Ares, then swung up into the saddle. "You'll need to learn to ride, but for this evening, you can ride with me."

Keely stared up at him. "I don't suppose we could... um, ride the smaller one?"

His wife wasn't actually scared of horses, was she? It was one thing to not know how to ride. It was another thing to protest getting onto a horse at all, especially a twenty-thousand-dollar Arabian like Ares.

"My stallion's size means he'll be able to handle two riders better than Hestia." He held out his hand for her. "I'll make sure you don't fall."

She bit the side of her lip, then placed her palm in his. He stilled. Her skin certainly wasn't smooth or uncalloused like a socialite's, but it felt small and dainty in his hold.

She cleared her throat and looked around. "Um, what next?"

"The stirrup." He moved his own foot out of the leather strap hanging by the horse's side and jutted his chin toward it. "Place your foot in there and lift yourself up. I'll help you the rest of the way."

She did as he instructed, and he lifted her up, settling her sideways before he kicked Ares into a trot.

"This is... ah... a bit different." Keely kept her back as straight as a board as Ares moved over the uneven desert.

Wes chuckled, then nestled her a little more securely between his arm and chest. "I don't suggest being so stiff for one. But we can get some split skirts if you feel more comfortable riding astride."

"How much farther to the ranch?"

"About two miles."

She winced. "I can't sit like this for two miles."

"All right." He tried repositioning her so that more of her weight was centered over the horse than on his arm. "You can swing your leg over the saddle if you want, though your dress will come up a bit on your legs."

Two bright splotches of red appeared on her cheeks. "Maybe I'll stay here after all."

She eased her weight back against his arm, and more silence descended on them, filled with an awkward heaviness Wes didn't know how to break.

Keely kept her gaze pinned on the yellow, rock-strewn terrain of the Chihuahuan Desert, and he scanned the landscape too, trying to see it like a newcomer might. But the desert was the only thing he'd ever known, so the brown scrubby bushes, dull green cacti, and rocky yellow ground didn't seem all that strange.

Wes nearly opened his mouth to ask what she thought of it. If she could see herself being content in a place like Twin Rivers. But what if she said no?

He shook his head. She'd ridden from San Antonio to Twin Rivers on the stage. If she'd thought the terrain would be a problem, she wouldn't have married him.

The silence still hung between them, making that spot between his shoulder blades itch again. "Do you have any questions about the ranch before we get there?"

She sank her teeth into the side of her lip. "I know you said in your letters this was to be a marriage in name only, but I don't know how big the house is. Is there... will we... Are there separate rooms for each of us?"

Boy howdy, was she going to be surprised when she saw the hacienda. They could have five bedrooms a piece and still not have to worry about sharing. "There will be plenty of space. My ranch isn't exactly as small as I made it sound in the ad."

"Oh..." Her brow drew down, and lines etched her forehead. "So it's big?"

"Yes. At least that's one way to put it."

She turned, her elbow digging into his leg as she repositioned herself to better see him. "Why'd you lie about the size of your ranch?"

He grimaced, and only half because of the bruise forming on his leg. "I wouldn't say I lied."

Why didn't she look excited over the fact that his ranch was bigger than she'd thought?

"You just admitted your statement about the ranch being small wasn't true." Her voice emerged short and clipped. "I'm pretty sure that means you lied."

"I... ah..." He rubbed the back of his neck. "The ranch was

supposed to be a surprise. I figured you'd be happy to learn I wasn't struggling to put food on the table or that your room would be separate from mine. Good grief. I even hired a dressmaker to come from Austin and make you some clothes that will keep you cool on the desert."

He blew out a breath. "I suppose I didn't give you the specifics about my ranch because life on the desert can be hard, and not many women would be happy living somewhere so isolated. You saw for yourself on the stage trip here, it takes two weeks of travel to get to a city from Twin Rivers. Plus, ranching means hard work, and I needed a woman who understood that, not someone who would sit around and expect to be waited on hand and foot."

"Waited on? You mean by servants?" Her fingers dug into his arm.

"I don't have much by way of servants." His housekeeper Consuela would have qualified as a servant before she left, even though he'd always considered her more of a mother than anything else. "I have ranch hands, of course. But as for the house, I just have a cook, a scullery maid to assist him, and some help that comes in from Mexico to clean a couple days a week. Like I said in my letters, I need you to be in charge of keeping house."

"I see."

*I see?* That was all she was going to say? He'd just told her he had a cook and maids. Not too many ranchers in Texas had that. Sam certainly didn't.

Did she not understand what he was trying to say? Or was she angry with him?

With the way she kept her back stiff and her face turned away, he couldn't tell. "I'm sorry. I suppose I should have told you about the size of my ranch sooner, before the wedding."

Though then he'd never have known she was willing to marry him without his money.

"Maybe I overreacted." She turned to face him again, their eyes meeting as the wind off the desert toyed with the red curls about her face. "The two of us barely know each other. There's a lot I need to learn about you yet, and a lot you don't know about me. To be honest, it's a bit of a relief to know putting food on the table won't be a struggle for you. Thank you for your honesty. Maybe next time—

"Wait. *That's* your ranch?" She stiffened, her eyes rivetted to the hacienda now visible partway up the mountain and the three large barns in front of it.

Ares chose that moment to pick up his pace, moving toward the yard at a brisk trot.

"Yes. The A Bar W. It's... um... it's rather famous in these parts."

"Is that the house? Please tell me that's not the house."

What was wrong with the house? He surveyed it, but it looked just as it always did, clean and well kept, with large windows to let in the sunlight and a grand arch to mark where the front door was. Flowering shrubs and green plants that had to be watered regularly even grew by the front of the house.

Perhaps she thought the shape made it look more like a business than a home? "I know most houses aren't square, but this is called a hacienda, after the Spanish style of—"

"It's huge! It could fit four of the orphanages where I used to work."

She'd worked at an orphanage? He didn't recall her mentioning that in any of her letters.

Ares reached the yard and slowed in front of the barn where the horses were stabled, and several of his cowhands filed out of the barn's doorway, where they'd probably been waiting for his arrival.

Instead of asking for an introduction, Keely turned to him and jabbed a finger into his chest. "You said it wasn't small," she hissed in a voice low enough that only he could hear. "But this?"

Dobbs approached and took Ares's reins. He grinned up at them from beneath his dusty cowboy hat, revealing a large gap between his two front teeth. "Welcome to the A Bar W, ma'am. The second largest ranch in Texas."

## 3

"The second largest..."

Keely's voice trailed off. She couldn't speak—not that she wanted to. All she wanted to do was snap her fingers and be back in Springfield.

No. That wasn't correct. First, she wanted to wrap her hands around her husband's neck and squeeze. Then she wanted to snap her fingers and be back in Missouri, where she hopefully wouldn't be caught for murdering him.

"Keely, this here is Dobbs," Wes said from behind her. "He's been on the ranch longer than anyone else and knows everything there is to know about the A Bar W. That's Jeb. He's the foreman and lives in the foreman house behind the barn there. Then you have Gunther, Bruce, Handy, Melvin..."

Wes kept listing names and pointing to the men that had come into the yard, but she couldn't concentrate enough to listen, let alone try to learn what name went with which man. She couldn't even suck a full breath of air into her lungs. All she could do was stare at the giant mansion in front of her. She'd asked if the ranch was big a few minutes ago. He should have told her that it was huge. Or at least, the house was, and while she didn't know a whole lot about ranching, she knew enough to understand that a house like that wasn't going to belong to a modest-sized ranch with only a handful of cowpokes.

"Keely, are you all right?" Wes squeezed her shoulders.

No. Nothing was right. She wasn't sure whether she wanted to scream or cry, but her heart pounded against her ribcage, and her lungs refused to draw breath.

"Keely?" Wes gave her a gentle shake.

She didn't meet his gaze, just stared at the ranch hands—over a dozen of them, then back up at the house.

"What's wrong with her, boss?" someone asked.

"Was it something we did?" another man said.

"It's probably the heat." Wes's voice rumbled in his chest as he answered the men.

"But it's not even hot."

"I'm going to hand her down to you, Dobbs." Wes repositioned his arms so that one braced her back and another slipped beneath her knees. "Let's get her inside."

"I can stand," she croaked. Or rather, she hoped she could stand. But with the way the sun was beating down on her and her head was spinning, she just might faint. And that was the last thing she wanted to do in front of all of Wes's cowhands.

*Calm down, Keely. All you need to do is walk into the house.*

And then what?

She didn't rightly know, but whatever was going to happen next, she didn't want it to be in front of fifteen men. "Can you ask them to go away first?"

"Them? You mean the cowhands?" Wes's gaze shot up to his men. "All right, everyone, back to work."

The men scattered, boot steps crunching on the rocky ground, each of them seeming to know exactly where to go and what to do.

Wes shifted her, then picked her up beneath her arms and lowered her until her feet touched the dirt.

Her stomach churned with the movement, and blackness crept into the edges of her vision. She reached out to steady herself against the horse.

Wes swung down from the giant beast, then swept her into his arms and started carrying her toward the house without so much as a word.

"What are you doing?" She gripped his shirt to help keep her balance.

"You looked like you were about to fall over."

She grimaced. "I think I was."

The blackness was already receding from her vision, and there was something comforting about having her husband's arms wrapped around her. It made her feel safe in a way she hadn't felt since her brother had died.

Wes carried her to the house, his boots echoing on the massive stone steps that looked to have been newly swept free of dust. The large wooden doors stood open, and he kept her tucked in his arms as they moved beneath a towering arch that seemed more like the entrance to a castle than a house.

Once inside, she could immediately see the desert straight in front of her.

But it made no sense. The house was huge. There was no way she could be outside again in thirty steps.

Wes passed a grand staircase that looked fit for a palace from a fairytale, carrying her straight toward the desert again. At the last moment he turned. She would have said they were in a hallway. The trouble was, one side of the hallway was entirely open to outside. The open hallway wrapped around the entire inside of the house in a giant square, while the ceiling above was held up by a series of giant arches like the one they'd passed through when coming inside.

"What is that?" She pointed to the square in the middle of

the house that displayed a series of flowers and small, leafy trees far more colorful than anything she'd seen growing naturally in the desert.

Wes slowed for a moment, though he didn't put her down. "The courtyard?"

Courtyard. Maybe her husband really did live in a castle. Turrets were the only thing the massive building was missing.

He turned and carried her through another archway into a large room that looked just as fancy as the staircase.

The furniture alternated between being either dark orange or navy blue, and cushions with bright colors and patterns rested on the furniture in a perfect display. The children from the orphanage would have loved this house—the mixture of colors, the shiny mirror and lights, the pillars and arches for them to hide behind.

"Are you sure you're all right?" Wes finally lay her down on the navy-blue sofa and crouched in front of her. "Do you still feel faint?"

Keely drew in a breath and raised her eyes to the ceiling, only to discover the ceiling wasn't made of plaster and beams, but had an intricate arrangement of tiny, rust-colored tiles covering it.

As though the house wasn't already fancy enough.

She closed her eyes, starting to feel like she just might faint even though she was already lying down. "You lied to me. Twice."

He sat back on his haunches. "What?"

"This ranch isn't just a little bit bigger than what you said in your ad. This is an empire, and you rule the entire thing from your grand castle." She spread her arms to encompass the ridiculously ornate room.

"It's a hacienda. Not a castle. And I'm hardly the only rancher to own one."

"The man outside said the A Bar W is the second largest ranch in Texas. Just how much land do you own?"

"About seven hundred thousand acres."

She blinked. She had no idea how big an acre was, let alone seven hundred thousand of them.

Still, seven hundred thousand was a lot of anything.

Was it even legal for one person to own that much land? "How many cattle do you have?"

"At the moment? Only about forty thousand head on this property. I've got about six hundred thousand acres of the ranch that are grazable, so the ranch here reaches capacity around seventy thousand head."

Had he just said forty *thousand* head of cattle? She couldn't imagine what it would look like to have that many cattle all together in one place.

"I have another property in East Texas with around thirty thousand head. The land there is better for grazing, so the ranch itself is quite a bit smaller. I have a manager who runs it, and I make trips there two or three times a year."

So he owned seventy thousand cattle, not forty? She was going to faint just trying to imagine a number that large. "How much money do you have?"

"At the moment? Not nearly enough of it."

"What's that supposed to mean?"

He shook his head. "That's a conversation for another day."

How could a person own seventy thousand cattle and say he didn't have enough money? Even if each cow was only worth a dollar, that meant her husband owned $70,000 worth of cattle. And she was betting each cow was worth more than a buck. "Is it true what the one ranch hand said about this being the second largest ranch in Texas?"

"Used to be the largest until about six weeks ago."

She stared at him, but he only shrugged.

"I just had to sell off thirty thousand head. Now the rancher who bought my stock is the largest. And the Willis Cattle Company out of North Dakota just bought up five hundred thousand acres north of here. They've got backers in Boston and New York, and I expect their Texas outfit will be the largest ranch in the state within the next five years. A ranch with a single owner isn't going to be able to keep pace with an investor-backed corporation with holdings in multiple states."

She couldn't care less what type of ranch would be able to claim the title of biggest ranch or who wanted to fight for it. Only one thing mattered at the moment, and she had a sick feeling she already knew the answer. "So if I go to San Antonio or Austin or Dallas or any other city in Texas and I say your name, everyone will know who you are, that you own the second largest ranch in the state."

"Well, probably not everyone, but—"

She leveled him with a glare.

"Most people will recognize it, yes."

The ad, the letters, her trip here, her hope of starting a new life in a place the Wolf Point Ring would never think to look for her. It had all been for nothing.

Heat pricked the backs of her eyes, but she wasn't about to cry, at least not in front of her oaf of a husband. Instead, she jammed her finger into his chest again. "First thing tomorrow, you march yourself down to the newspaper office and you get every last camera plate and picture that blasted reporter used for the wedding. Get any other evidence there might be of the pictures too. You bring it all back here and you burn it. Do you understand me?"

"Keely—"

"Don't. You owe me that much, especially after you lied about who you are." She stood and swept past him, stalking out of the room.

The echo of the door slamming behind her reverberated down the stone hallway and out into the courtyard, but she only got two steps away from the door before she stopped. She had every intention of going to her room, but she didn't have the first clue where it was.

She looked down the hall one direction, then the other, and finally at the courtyard. As far as she could tell, the house was empty of anyone besides her and her lying husband.

Where did she find servants in a house such as this? The kitchen? That would probably be located at the back of the house. She turned to walk past the parlor door, but it opened.

"Going somewhere?" Wes watched her with flat, unreadable eyes.

"To my room, thank you."

"It's the other direction."

"I'm sure I can find a servant to show me."

"I already told you. I don't have much by way of servants, and the only ones who live here are the cook and the cook's niece who works as a scullery maid."

She nearly toppled over. He'd lied to her about the size of the ranch and misled her about who he was. But he'd decided to tell the truth about not having servants?

This house was gargantuan. He'd said something about help coming from Mexico a couple times a week. Was that for cleaning, or was she going to need to clean the entire house by herself?

Did it even matter? Wes had told her in his letters he expected her to keep house, and she'd agreed. He'd also told her he wanted to marry a woman who wasn't afraid to work. Whether she had help or not, she'd certainly have to work to take care of this house, so much so that she'd probably never get any sleep.

And why was she wasting energy thinking about this when she couldn't stay in Twin Rivers?

She turned and started walking back toward the stairs. Her bedroom was probably upstairs, and if she had to open every door on the second floor to find the room that held her trunk, then that's what she'd do.

Footsteps sounded behind her. "Do you know where you're going?"

"I can figure it out on my own, thank you." She started up the staircase, ignoring the intricate tile patterns that decorated the rise of each step.

Wes followed her up the stairs, then came up beside her. "This way. The other direction holds the ballroom."

Of course the house would have a ballroom. The mention of yet another fancy, ornate room made her want to scream.

"I said I can find my room on my own." She looked down the hallway and instantly spotted her satchel sitting outside the door to one of the rooms. "I'd prefer to be alone right now, thank you."

Instead of leaving, he walked down the hallway with her. "I really am sorry. I meant this whole thing as a surprise. I didn't imagine my, um... financial situation would be a problem for you."

"Well, it is."

He stayed quiet beside her, and his steps slowed to a stop in front of her room.

She chanced a look in his direction. His forehead was furrowed, and the corners of his mouth were drawn down. He seemed genuinely baffled by her statement.

She really couldn't blame him. Most women who traveled west to marry would be thrilled to find they'd wed a wealthy man—one who could certainly afford to have a full household staff, even if he didn't want one.

If not for Mears, if not for what happened in Chicago, she'd be thrilled as well.

But she simply couldn't stay married to someone as well-known as Agamemnon Westin. Mears would find her, and then...

Nausea churned in her belly, and she closed her eyes. But she still couldn't prevent Cynthia's image from rising in her mind, her body crumpled on their doorstep and—

"Keely?" Strong hands reached out and gripped her shoulders.

She opened her eyes and found herself staring into two warm brown pools that seemed far too kind. And suddenly, she didn't want to leave, didn't want to go somewhere else and make a new home. She could see herself being happy here, married to this serious man with his strong chin and immaculately combed brown hair.

She could see herself becoming friends with Anna Mae and Charlotte and Ellie. She could see herself volunteering at church or making cookies for the school children.

When she'd stepped off the stage, she'd thought this was going to be the first day of the rest of her life. That life felt so close she could reach out and touch it, and part of her wanted the life that was spread out before her rather desperately.

But she wanted to stay alive more. And that meant she'd have to move to two or three more towns before she could be certain Lester Mears hadn't tracked her to Twin Rivers and the famous husband she'd accidentally married. There would have to be drably appointed hotel rooms and boarding houses, and train rides with her bonnet pulled low over her face so none of the other passengers noticed anything recognizable about her.

Keely drew in a breath and met her husband's gaze. "I shouldn't be here. I never would have agreed to come had I known who you really were."

He dropped his hands from her shoulders, and the tenderness vanished from his face. "I'm sorry that I inconvenienced you by having you come here and marry me. We can go to the courthouse and file for an annulment in the morning."

"Annulment?

"Think of it as having the marriage canceled. Since I didn't tell you who I was before we wed, we can file a petition on the grounds that I committed fraud."

She scowled. Fraud seemed a little harsh. Maybe her husband had technically committed some kind of fraud, but there was no ill intent behind what he'd done. If not for what had happened in Chicago, she'd be thrilled to realize she'd married one of the wealthiest men in the state.

But if Wes could file for an annulment, then nothing prevented him from turning around and placing another ad for a bride. In a few more months, he'd be married to a woman who would be ecstatic when she learned who her new husband really was.

"I'll pay for your trip back to Springfield after the annulment is granted," Wes said, his voice brisk and businesslike. "I'll also pay you for your time. You must have quit your job to come here, and I'm sure it will take time to find new work once you return to Springfield."

Something in her chest started to ache. Her husband really was a good man, wasn't he? But she couldn't think about that.

She straightened her back and tried to clear her face of every last bit of emotion like Wes had. "Sounds like you should go to the courthouse in the morning and get started on the annulment then."

He took a step away from her. "Right."

"Good night, Mr. Westin." She swallowed the thick lump that had lodged in her throat, then opened the door to her room and slipped inside. But even as she wandered about the beautifully decorated room and readied herself for an early bedtime, she couldn't seem to wipe her husband's stricken look from her mind.

The life she'd thought she could have was disappearing on her faster than smoke from a fire.

So much for this being the first day of the rest of her life.

# 4

He couldn't afford for anything to go wrong. Wes stared at the column of numbers on the desk in front of him and scrubbed a hand over his face. He had enough funds to live on and pay his cowhands through to next year's cattle drive, but if something went wrong, he was going to be in trouble.

*I just need one year, God. One good year. No drought. No disease. No rustlers.*

They'd already got a decent amount of rain this year—at least for the desert. And he'd not heard of any diseases infecting cattle in the West.

That just left the rustlers to worry about.

They hadn't been active since summer, but that didn't mean they wouldn't decide to target his ranch tomorrow, and the A Bar W had already lost two thousand head to the rustling ring last spring.

Wes pushed his chair back from his desk and raked a hand through his hair.

Maybe he should have taken out a loan like Thomas Ross had suggested.

Maybe he should have sold more cattle to Richard King.

But the more cattle he sold, the harder it would be to rebuild. And loan payments would put him in a similar situation. Next year the prime stock that he'd been breeding would be ready for market. He anticipated a thirty-seven percent increase in the selling price for those cattle.

Of course, he could have sold some of the herd this year, but a man didn't spend four years breeding superior cattle only to sell them off a year before they were ready to go to market.

The door to his office swung open, and Wes's head jerked up.

In stepped Daniel, the sheriff's badge glinting on his hat, and a mug of steaming coffee in his hand.

Wes scowled. "When are you going to learn to knock?"

"I did. When are you going to hire a housekeeper to answer your door?"

Wes sat back in his chair. "As soon as I find where Consuela went and offer her job back."

Yet another thing his father had messed up right before his death. The man, in his illness, had managed to run off the woman who had held the ranch together for the decade and a half since Wes's ma and baby brother had died.

Daniel settled himself in the upholstered armchair in front of the desk. "How long have you been working this morning?"

Who knew? "Since three or four, I suppose." Whatever time he'd gotten tired of tossing and turning while trying to push thoughts of Keely from his mind.

"And how are things with your new wife?" Daniel leaned back in his chair and clasped his hands over his chest.

"They're fine. She's staying in Charlotte's old room."

"Have you seen her yet this morning?"

He shrugged. "No, but it's a hard journey just from here to San Antonio. Coming all the way from Springfield has to be grueling, so she's probably still resting."

Daniel's lips twitched into a smile. "You don't have the first clue where your wife is, do you?"

"Of course I do. She's in bed."

"Why don't you go check and see, then let me know how that turns out. I'll sit here and wait." Daniel settled even deeper into the chair, looking almost comfortable enough to take a nap.

Wes narrowed his eyes at his friend. "What are you playing at?"

"Oh, you'll figure it out soon enough. Go check on your wife." Daniel waved his hand toward the door.

Wes stood and strode out of the office, his legs eating up the steps of the tile corridor as he headed to the dining room to make sure she wasn't eating breakfast. A quick peek inside the large room told him the buffet had been set with a delicious breakfast, but the food looked untouched.

He headed for the staircase. She was probably in bed, just as he'd told Daniel.

He still couldn't figure out what had gone so wrong between them last night. He'd been trying to do a good thing by surprising Keely with the size of his ranch. How had it all gone sour?

What kind of woman actually complained that her husband had too much money?

It didn't make any sense. But like he'd told Daniel, the trip to Twin Rivers was long and grueling. Maybe Keely had been too tired to be thinking straight. After a good night's rest, she just might change her mind about the annulment and agree to stay in Twin Rivers.

And why did he want her to stay so much?

He barely knew her, and their marriage had been more of a business arrangement than anything else. He'd be able to find another woman who was willing to take his name in exchange for a place to live and food on the table, even if she had to move to the middle of the desert.

But something about Keely niggled at him. Maybe it was the sadness she carried in her cactus-green eyes, or the way her shoulders seemed perpetually slumped with an invisible weight. Maybe it was the way she'd gone head-to-head with Glen yesterday about not having her picture printed in the paper, or the way she'd lectured him for lying after he told her just how wealthy he was.

She had a streak of fire in her.

And she needed help. He'd bet his stallion, Ares, on it. He didn't know why or exactly what kind of help she needed. Only that she needed... well, something.

And he probably had the means to help, even if his money was a little tight at the moment.

He stopped in front of her door and knocked. "Keely?"

No answer.

He waited a moment, then knocked again before twisting the door handle. It opened smoothly.

"Keely?" He didn't need to take a full step inside to know she was gone. Not gone as in away from her room. Gone entirely. He could feel it in the emptiness that radiated from the window seat and perfectly made bed.

He moved to the bed, where a lone sheet of paper lay atop the diamond-patterned spread.

*Dear Mr. Westin,*

Mr. Westin? He was her husband—even if she didn't plan to keep it that way for very long.

*I'm sorry to leave you so suddenly, but I realized last night as you explained more about yourself and your ranching situation that I simply cannot stay in Twin Rivers. You have my full permission to proceed with an annulment on whatever grounds you wish, my abandonment included.*

*I regret I cannot take my trunk with me on this next leg of my journey. I have taken what I need out of it, and I would be ever so grateful if you could give what remains to another woman of my height and size whom you think might benefit from some extra clothing.*

*Please do forgive my abrupt departure.*

*Sincerely,*

*Keely*

His fist tightened around the paper, and he whirled from the room and stalked back down to his office.

He was missing something here. No one walked away from a marriage because her husband was too wealthy.

He strode into his office and waved the note in Daniel's direction. "She's gone, along with the belongings she could carry."

Daniel took a sip of coffee. "I'm aware."

"If you're aware of so much, then where on earth is she?"

"At my house. She arrived in town this morning carrying a carpetbag and satchel and asking what time the stage left."

"The stage only comes once a week."

"I think she's used to how they run things in a bigger town, where they have multiple trains a day departing for the same location."

He shook his head. "I don't understand. I was trying to surprise her with how big the ranch is, but now that she knows who I am, she wants nothing to do with me."

He looked down at the letter. "She told me last night she wanted an annulment, and this letter says the same. I just didn't realize she planned to leave so quickly."

"Well, if she takes the stage, it will be another six days before she leaves." Daniel drained the last bit of coffee from his mug, then stood. "That's plenty of time to sort this business out. Let's get over to my place."

"My thoughts exactly." Wes beat Daniel through the door, and rather than walking down the corridor, he stalked straight across the courtyard to the hacienda's front door. He paused long enough to grab his hat off the hook in the entry, then strode outside into the sunshine. The echo of footsteps behind him told him Daniel was keeping pace as he headed toward the barn that held the horses.

When he entered, Dobbs looked up from where he stood brushing one of the quarter horses. "You need something, boss?"

"Just Ares. I can saddle him myself."

He headed down the aisle lined with stalls on either side, toward where the ranch's rare breed of Arabian horses were stabled at the back of the barn. The mixed scents of hay and leather and horseflesh usually calmed him, but not today.

"Hey, boy." He let himself into Ares's stall, then looked back toward the entrance. Except for the extra stalls, every single one had a horse in it.

But if all his horses were here, how had his wife left the A Bar W?

He hefted his saddle over Ares's back, cinched it, then slipped the bit and reins over his head, working as quickly as possible.

The moment he led Ares out of the barn, he called to Daniel, who was already seated atop his appaloosa. "How did you say Keely got to town?"

"She walked."

His stomach churned. It was a long enough walk from the hacienda to town during the day, but to do it in the dark? "The walk must have taken most of the night."

"At least there was a full moon so she could see the trail."

His gut cramped for a second time as he swung up onto Ares. "Thank God she didn't step on a rattler."

She probably didn't even know to look for them. He certainly hadn't warned her about them last night, and most people didn't realize just how common the poisonous snake was on the Chihuahuan Desert.

"Hadn't even thought about that." Daniel's eyes were serious as he turned Blaze toward his house and urged the horse into a trot. "She's running from something, Wes."

Was she? He shifted. "That makes sense, seeing how she thought she was coming here to marry a dirt-poor rancher. I suppose a woman would need to be in rather dire straits for that."

"Dire straits aren't what concerns me." Daniel's jaw seemed to get harder with each step Blaze took closer to his house.

"What has you so all-fired worried, then?"

"That she might be running from the law."

The words slammed into him, stealing his breath and sending a flash of pain into his chest. Keely was certainly hiding something, but that didn't mean she was a criminal...

Did it?

## 5

"So there they were, running through town in nothing but their soaking-wet drawers." Anna Mae's eyes danced with laughter from across the table from where Keely sat beside Charlotte. "You should have seen the look on Ma's face when they rushed into the kitchen. I was there making tortillas with her, and I remember it like it was yesterday."

Keely laughed. She couldn't help it. She might be trapped in a strange house, forced to depend on a sheriff she didn't quite trust to return and explain his plan to get her out of Twin Rivers, but she couldn't help laughing at the image that popped into her head of four thirteen-year-old boys running through town in their unmentionables.

If the orphans would have pulled a trick like that, the head-mistress would have made them scrub dishes after every meal for a month straight.

"We never found out who took their clothes either." Charlotte spoke, her voice soft and regal. She reached for another biscuit off the platter in the middle of the table. "Probably whichever of the other boys in town they'd teased most recently and happened upon them swimming in the river."

"My money's on Preacher Russell." Anna Mae sent her a wink.

Charlotte coughed. "You think the preacher stole their clothes?"

"He's got just enough of a mischievous streak in him to do it. Especially since they were supposed to be scrubbing the floor of the church and school that afternoon. That's one way to teach a group of hooligans a lesson."

Charlotte cut her biscuit open and spread butter over it, the simple action somehow seeming refined and elegant. "Could be. Didn't the clothes show up on the porch outside your father's office the next morning?"

"They did," Anna Mae said. "Every last one of them. Pa found them when he went to work."

"Well, at least the boys didn't lose them permanently." Keely reached for a large crumb sitting on her plate beside her mostly uneaten biscuit. Rather than put the bite of food in her mouth, she squeezed it until it broke into a half dozen smaller crumbs. "How much longer do you think the sheriff will be?"

Anna Mae reached across the table and patted her hand. "It shouldn't be long now."

Hopefully Anna Mae was right. The sheriff had seemed sincere when he'd offered to help her find a way out of Twin Rivers, but maybe she'd been wrong to trust him.

Keely drew her hand away from Anna Mae's and looked around the tastefully decorated room. The house where Wes's sister lived didn't begin to compare to the A Bar W's grand hacienda, but the room was large enough to encompass the kitchen, table, and a parlor area without feeling cramped. The bold colors of the upholstered furniture and southwestern-style pattern on the blanket folded over the back of the sofa all reminded her of how the hacienda was decorated.

Sheriff Harding obviously didn't have anywhere near the same level of wealth as Wes, but Charlotte had done well with the space, and even more, she seemed content with both the smaller home and the sheriff.

"Would you like a croissant?" Charlotte asked, glancing at the crumbled biscuit. "I know I'm not the best at making biscuits just yet, but I have some croissants from Marceau's kitchen up at the big house. You won't find a better pastry in all of Texas."

"Actually, I need to leave. I've been here over an hour, and I best be on my way." She scooted her chair back and stood. "Can one of you draw me a map of how to get to the nearest train station?"

Anna Mae bolted up from her chair. "Leave? By yourself? The nearest train station is in Midland, over two hundred and fifty miles away."

Keely swallowed. She hadn't realized getting to a train would be that difficult.

"You've never even been to the desert before," Anna Mae continued, "let alone traveled across it. And I'm not talking about your journey here on the stage, with arranged stopping points for food and water."

"Even if we could somehow draw you a map that would take you to enough watering holes to make it to Midland, what do you intend to do about a horse?" Charlotte's gaze met hers. "And what would you do for food? If I gave you a gun, could you shoot and cook a jackrabbit?"

Keely rubbed her temple. Why hadn't she thought to ask Wes about transportation to and from Twin Rivers before she'd agreed to marry him?

*Because you were trying to go somewhere forgotten and out of the way, you dolt. The harder it is to get to Twin Rivers, the smaller the chance Mears will find you.*

But she'd failed to take into consideration what would happen if she accidentally married the richest man in Texas.

Oh, if she ever saw Wes again, she'd—

"Is marriage to my brother really that bad?"

Keely swung around to look at Charlotte, who was still sitting at the table, her face white while her hands gripped the teacup in front of her.

"I know he can be a bit stern at times, but I promise you he's a good man."

Keely swallowed. She couldn't let herself forget she was in the house of her husband's sister—no matter how worried she was about Mears finding her. "I never meant to imply there's something wrong with Wes. I know it might seem hard to believe, but this has nothing to do with your brother. I simply—"

The door opened, and the sheriff entered.

Keely let out a giant breath. Now she'd be able to get moving before...

"What's he doing here?" She stared at Wes, who stood in the doorway Sheriff Harding had just walked through.

"He's here to take you home," the sheriff answered.

She clenched her hands into fists at her sides. Looked like her instincts yesterday after the wedding had been right. She had no business trusting a lawman after all. "You said you were going to find someone who could take me to the nearest train station!"

"No," the sheriff spoke in an even voice. "I said I knew of someone who could take you where you needed to go. Since your husband wasn't even aware you'd left his house, that's not the nearest train station."

"Yes, it is," she gritted.

"No, it's not." Sheriff Harding crossed his arms over his impossibly broad chest and glowered down at her, looking more like a supernatural giant who'd been tasked with guarding the door behind him than a normal human being.

"Don't try telling me where I need to go." She stalked toward him, stopping only when the front of her shoes touched the tips of his boots. "You don't know the first thing about my life or why I need to leave."

She jammed a finger into his chest, then grimaced at the hard muscle she felt beneath his shirt.

He thrust her finger away. "You need to go home with your husband. You're a married woman."

"Not for long!" She whirled to glare at Wes. "He didn't tell me who he was. That means we can get an annulment on the grounds that he committed fraud."

A gasp sounded in the direction of the kitchen, and Keely glanced over her shoulder to find Charlotte staring at her. She held a kettle of hot water suspended above a teapot but seemed to have forgotten how to pour water into the pot.

"You might have a point about an annulment." The sheriff's words cut through the room. "But I have a suspicion you weren't completely honest with Wes before your wedding either."

"I certainly didn't make him think I have no money when I have wagonloads of it," she shot back.

"Just like you didn't explain your real reason for coming to Texas."

She stilled. Had the sheriff discovered something about her? So quickly? He hadn't somehow seen the papers inside her satchel...

Had he?

"I told you she was running from something." The sheriff turned to Wes. "It could well be the law. It's the best reason a person would need to leave Twin Rivers so quickly after arriving. Once she found out how well known you were, she realized she couldn't hide here like she'd planned."

So he didn't know why she was running. Keely drew in a breath, then opened her mouth to argue. Except, technically, she was running from the law—or at least from certain parts of it.

Just not for the reasons they thought.

"Keely?" Wes came a few steps closer, his eyes searching her face. Unlike the anger and accusations radiating from Daniel, he looked genuinely concerned. "What's going on? Why do you need to leave Twin Rivers? And don't tell me it's because of my money."

"It is because of your money. I promise you that. Now please just find someone who can take me to Midland. Today."

"Why today? Why not wait for the stage that will take you back to San Antonio in another week?"

She shifted from one foot to the other. "Because that's too long. He might... that is, I can't... I can't stay a full week."

"I just want to know why." Wes kept his eyes on her, his gaze still soft and questioning. "I've told you the truth, about who I am, about why I claimed to be the owner of a small ranch in the ad. Now it's your turn to tell me the truth. You said in your letters that your family had died, and you were looking for a new place to settle down. Is that true?"

It was, but it was hardly the whole of it. She ran her tongue over her lips again, which seemed to be drying out faster than she could lick them. "Please stop asking questions and let me leave."

"If she doesn't want to be around us, and she doesn't want to tell us anything, then get one of your cowhands to take her to Midland and let her go." Anna Mae picked up her satchel from where it sat propped against a chair. "We're probably better off without her anyway."

Keely couldn't say why the words stung, not when she'd barely known Anna Mae a day.

Anna Mae thrust the satchel toward her, the brisk movement causing a paper to flutter to the ground.

Keely stared at the paper for a moment, the breath clogging in her chest. Was that...?

She lunged for it, but Anna Mae, who'd only been standing a couple steps from the paper, beat her to it.

*Dear God, please don't let that be one of my birth certificates.*

But she already knew it was, just by the square shape of it. She'd pulled one out of the hidden compartment that held her other papers last night and had placed it in a front pocket, thinking she'd go by the name Amelia McCullough next.

Anna Mae glanced at the paper, then at her. "I... I don't understand. Is this your real name?"

"Let me see that." Daniel strode to his sister, peering at the birth certificate over her shoulder. Then his eyes came up to meet hers, steely and cold. "Care to explain just what you're doing with Amelia McCullough's birth certificate?"

"I..." Heat crept up her neck and onto her cheeks. "Um..."

"Is your real name even Keely McBryan?" Anna Mae asked.

Another flush, this one hot enough to scorch the skin off her cheeks.

"What else are you hiding from us?" Daniel demanded.

She looked down at the floor. How was she even supposed to answer that?

"Let's search the bag," Daniel said to his sister.

"No!" She lunged for her satchel, but before she could take a full step, strong arms reached out and grabbed her, pulling her back against a chest that felt entirely too muscular.

"Let me go." She struggled against Wes's hold.

"Not before you tell us what's going on," Wes said against her ear. "You still haven't said if your real name is Keely McBryan."

She clamped her mouth shut and tried to lunge away from her husband.

It took Daniel and Anna Mae only a matter of minutes to find the hidden pocket at the bottom of her satchel. Daniel pulled out the thick stack of papers, which he split between him and Anna Mae.

"Don't pay any attention to those," she rasped. "They need to be burned is all."

They would have been burned last night, had her husband actually been the owner of a small ranch like he'd said. Then she would have had access to a cookstove.

Silence descended on the room as Daniel and Anna Mae each scanned the papers. She didn't know how long she stood there, her chest heaving as she tried to get out of Wes's hold. But the stubborn man was determined to keep her in place.

Finally, Anna Mae held up a paper. "I think she's involved in a smuggling ring."

"A smuggling ring?" Wes asked. "Springfield is in the middle of the country, completely landlocked. What could possibly be smuggled into or out of Springfield, Missouri?"

"Not Springfield. Chicago." Anna Mae handed the paper to Daniel.

"No! Don't give those to him." Keely tried to lunge for the papers again, only to be pulled back against Wes, his hold even stronger.

"Please don't give that to him," she pleaded. "He might be your brother, but he's also the sheriff. You can't trust him."

The sheriff looked up from his own stack of papers, his eyes flashing. "If you weren't breaking the law, then you'd have nothing to fear from me."

He looked down at the top of the papers in his hand, then snapped his gaze back to her. "You're... smuggling vases from Asia?"

"I'm not smuggling anything! Your sister's mistaken. All I have is evidence of the smuggling ring. That's not supposed to be a crime."

And now she'd said too much.

She closed her eyes and drew in a breath, but she could still feel the weight of everyone's gazes on her. It was probably useless to ask Wes to take her to the train station again before he made her explain everything.

The trouble was, none of them realized how much danger the truth could put them in.

At least they hadn't figured out the full extent of what was in the papers. Maybe she could only explain part of it, then find a way to get out of Twin Rivers while also protecting them from the worst of things. A woman as beautiful as Anna Mae didn't need the likes of Lester Mears after her. And the sheriff had no idea how powerful the Wolf Point Ring was.

Her brother hadn't known it either—until it was too late.

"I don't think vases are the thing that's being smuggled." Anna Mae held up another sheet of paper, and this time Keely felt the hot sting of tears well behind her eyes.

How had Anna Mae found it? There were nearly a hundred papers stuffed into the secret compartment of that carpetbag, and the Harding siblings had somehow not only discovered the compartment, but honed in on the one paper that proved everything.

"Don't," she rasped. "Whatever you think you know, just pretend you didn't see it. Put it back and walk away before it's too late."

"It's opium." Anna Mae didn't even spare her a glance as she handed the incriminating piece of paper over to the sheriff. "I wonder if it's hidden inside the vases. The first papers here all catalogue things like vases and teapots, but this paper here shows the funds received from opium shipments. And this signature keeps showing up on the bottom of a lot of the pages."

The sheriff took the paper, then stepped closer to her and pointed to the signature at the bottom. "Who is this man?"

Keely shook her head. "You don't want to know who he is. I promise. Please just let me go. Give me back my papers and let me leave in peace."

"Hey."

Despite Wes's arms still clamped around her middle, a warm hand settled on her shoulder. Keely looked over to find Charlotte had left the kitchen and now stood beside her.

"Seems like you've been through quite an ordeal. You have proof of an opium smuggling ring, and rather than go to the police, you ran clear down to Texas. I'm betting there are some very bad men trying to find you."

"I've been hiding for eight months. I thought that was long enough, but now I'm afraid it wasn't." Her voice emerged as little more than a whisper.

"We might be able to help, especially with all the resources Wes has." Charlotte sent him a small smile. "But first we need to know more. Why don't you sit down here at the table, I'll get you another cup of tea, and you can start by telling us how you learned about the opium ring."

Keely swallowed. It wasn't what she wanted to do. She'd give anything to go back thirty minutes in time, before Daniel had ever pulled those papers from her satchel. She'd give anything to stuff her secrets back down into the dark place inside her heart.

But now that the truth was out, she had little choice but to explain it—and pray no one in the room ended up dead.

~.~.~.~.~

WES PACED from one side of the kitchen to the other, his head down while Keely sat at the table telling Charlotte what had happened in Chicago.

Her brother, James, had been an accountant for the mayor's office, but the longer he held his job, the more he sensed the mayor's lavish personal spending didn't match his salary from the city, not even after that salary was combined with profits from the shipping company he owned twenty-five percent of.

Then one day James had discovered a couple errant documents in the financial records he'd been working on. The papers had a very precise list of the number of teapots that had come in on a series of sailing vessels over the previous three months, and the price of each teapot listed was astronomically high.

The next sheet of paper had a list of people's names and a dollar figure for what they had been paid from the total sale of the teapots. The people included not just the mayor but the harbormaster, chief of police, two town councilmen, and two prominent Chicago business owners.

James assumed the paper was probably supposed to go to whoever was doing accounting for the mayor's shipping company but had been mistakenly put in the stack of city financial records.

But the price of the teapots and the list of people getting money—people who weren't owners in the shipping company alongside the mayor—made James suspicious.

Wes gave his head a small shake as he continued pacing in front of the sofa. A better husband would probably sit beside his wife, hold her hand, and whisper encouraging words while she shared her story. But he couldn't sit as the details poured from her lips. Anna Mae had moved closer to the table, but she hadn't sat down yet either.

Daniel stood against the wall by the door, his eyes riveted to Keely. Normally Daniel would have plopped himself down at the table and taken over the questioning. But Wes had a feeling if Daniel tried that, Keely would either start arguing with him or shut down completely and refuse to talk.

And his quiet, reserved sister, of all people, was the one wheedling information out of her.

"So finally, after several months of searching for extra documents and requesting old records from the courthouse, James went to the U.S. Marshal's office in Chicago." Keely's soft, quivering voice filled the otherwise silent house. "We both assumed once he turned over proof of the opium smuggling, arrests would be made. But no one was ever arrested, and two days later, they... they killed Cynthia."

She stared down at her hands.

"Remind us who Cynthia is again," Charlotte asked gently. "I don't think I recall."

Charlotte didn't recall because Keely hadn't yet explained her connection. But the subtle question caused more words to tumble from Keely's lips.

"James's fiancée. They left her on our doorstep, without... without any clothes. Whoever killed her had..."

"Did they touch you too, Keely?" Everything inside Wes turned rigid. "Did they hurt you in some way?"

She looked over her shoulder at him, her cheeks bright with embarrassment, then slowly shook her head. "No. I left right after they killed James. But if they ever find me, find the evidence I have, I'll die the same way Cynthia did. Or maybe... maybe they'll find worse things to do before they let me die."

*Before they let me die.* The way she said it, as though death would somehow be a mercy, made blood roar through his veins.

Wes stalked around the couch in four giant steps and slid onto the bench beside her. He reached out and took her by her shoulders, his grip probably tighter than it should be. "Nobody is going to lay a hand on you. You're my wife now, and you're under my protection. I won't let any of those men touch you, not ever. Do you understand?"

"I don't know if they've stopped looking for me," she whispered. "I thought I was ready to stop hiding, that I could assume a false name, then come to the middle of the desert and marry you and never need to worry about being found. But the Wolf Point Ring knows I'm the only person who could possibly have the evidence James collected. That's why I have to destroy it."

"I thought you said James turned all his evidence into the U.S. Marshal Service," Daniel spoke from where he still stood by the door.

Keely's face turned instantly hard, and Wes could feel her shoulders tighten beneath his grip. "He's just asking. It's a logical question."

"And I'm sure you have an explanation," Charlotte added. "Just like you've had an explanation for everything else."

Keely looked at the stack of evidence sitting on the table, almost all of it comprised of the carbon paper used in roller presses. "It doesn't make much sense, does it? Funny how I never questioned it before. James made it sound like as soon as he turned everything into the Marshals, the opium ring would be dealt with. But he must have suspected something would go wrong, because he was careful to go to the courthouse and have the office boy make duplicates of the information he collected all along. And even that is a bit odd, now that I think about it, because the mayor's office had a letter press, and he could have had the office boy there make copies just as easily as he could at the courthouse. But he always went to the courthouse."

"Because he didn't want word to get out that he was duplicating documents reaching the mayor," Daniel explained. "Your brother knew what he was about, even if he downplayed the risks to you."

"He didn't know what they would do to Cynthia." She absently picked up a piece of biscuit from the plate in front of her, then crumbled it to dust. "He was beside himself with grief, and he blamed himself. Cynthia's family thought it was some random attack. That's what the police report said. But James and I knew the truth."

"What happened to James?" Wes could already guess the answer, but he still needed to ask.

"He didn't return from work one day, so I took the papers and left town, just like he told me to do. He said I'd need to keep them safe, that the Marshal's office in Chicago might be in league with the Wolf Point Ring. That if anything happened to him, I'd need to find a lawman that wasn't corrupt to give the papers to." Her throat muscles worked overly hard as she swallowed. "It all happened so fast. The children don't even know why I left. I didn't have a chance to tell them goodbye."

"The children?"

"At the orphanage. I worked there."

Wes ran his eyes down his wife, her thin dress, her slumped shoulders. This was the second time she'd mentioned an orphanage. She'd not written of one in her letters, but the pain creasing her face only proved how much the children there had meant to her.

"I tried to watch the newspapers as I traveled south, first out of the city and then out of Illinois." She fiddled with the cloth napkin on her lap. "I wanted to know what the paper said about his death, but I must have missed the day they ran the article."

"Didn't you say the chief of police was getting payments from the smuggled opium?" Daniel asked.

Keely gestured to the stack of papers still sitting on the table. "That's what the ledgers indicate, yes."

Daniel took a few steps closer to the table. "Then the police could have made his body disappear in such a way that news of your brother's death never reached the paper, especially if you were gone and couldn't call attention to his disappearance."

"I've thought about that too." Keely wrapped her arms around herself in a lonely sort of hug.

Wes settled one of his hands on top of hers. It was a gentle touch, just enough to remind her she wasn't alone anymore. "So you ran. First to Springfield Missouri, and then here."

"I needed to find somewhere to hide. Somewhere with enough people I could blend in, but not so big that Mears would send men looking for me."

"And who is Mears?" Daniel asked.

"Lester Mears. The harbormaster's righthand man. Or at least that's who I thought he was. He worked at the harbor, but James said he was always at the mayor's office dropping off reports and having meetings. Now I think he's the Wolf Point Ring's henchman, the one responsible for what happened to Cynthia and James."

"The Wolf Point Ring?" Daniel asked.

"That's what they call themselves. It's named after Wolf Point in Chicago." Keely picked up another piece of biscuit, only to pinch it until it turned to dust once more on her plate. "Mears followed me out of Chicago. I was mostly able to keep ahead of him, but he arrived in Peoria a few hours before my train was scheduled to leave. I had to head north back toward Chicago rather than west to St. Louis as I had planned. I knew he'd have his men searching the trains, but he wasn't smart enough to have them search the one headed to Joliet that departed a half hour after his arrival. From Joliet I had to go to Cedar Rapids, Iowa, and then down to St. Louis."

The names of the places fell off her tongue with ease, but something inside Wes's belly grew tighter with each location she listed. Just how many places had she gone before finding somewhere safe to stay?

"I thought for sure I'd see Mears or one of his men at the train station in St. Louis," Keely went on. "But no. I made my way to Springfield from there, taking stages rather than trains. And that's where I've been for the last four months, working in the general store and trying to blend in. But I didn't have my fake birth certificates when I moved there, and I'd wondered if I could still be traced. I was ready to stop running, but I wasn't sure if Springfield was safe enough for me to stay."

"That's where you saw my ad in the paper." Wes edged the cup of tea Charlotte had brewed closer to Keely. Maybe a sip or two would help calm her nerves.

"Yes. I knew Mears wouldn't be able to find me in Twin Rivers. Or at least that's what I thought until I saw the size of your ranch." There was no anger or desperation in her voice when she said it, just a simple weariness.

Wes had the sudden urge to swallow, even though he hadn't taken a sip of tea. But he couldn't quite bring himself to apologize. If she hadn't come to Twin Rivers, where would she have gone next? To another medium-sized town where she hoped the Wolf Point Ring wouldn't find her?

Then what? When did she plan on turning the evidence she had in to the authorities? And who would protect her until everyone implicated in the opium ring was arrested and in jail?

"Is there any chance you could have been followed from Springfield down here?" Daniel asked.

"No. The Wolf Point Ring never even followed me to Springfield. That's why I thought I would be safe here, especially with my new birth certificate."

"This Mears character, what does he look like?" Daniel reached into his shirt pocket and retrieved the small notepad and pencil he kept there.

"He's tall with wide shoulders. Almost like you, but a little stockier. He has black hair and brown eyes, and he wears a red bowler with a black sash."

A red bowler? Most bowlers were black or brown or gray. Wes had never seen a red one. "With a hat like that, it's almost like he wants people to recognize him from a distance."

Keely's forehead creased with worried lines. "Maybe that's the point. He's so big that it's not as though he could ever hide well in a crowd. Although I'm hardly one to talk. I can't exactly hide in a crowd with my ridiculous hair."

"Your hair isn't ridiculous." It was kind of pretty, really, with errant red curls that hung down by her cheeks and the curvy way her hair spilled from the top of her updo. He knew women in Austin who spent hours with their lady's maids and a hot iron to achieve that curly effect.

"When I first left Chicago, I wondered if Mears could trace my steps simply by asking if a short woman with curly red hair had passed through." Keely reached up and tugged on one of the curls that hung by her ear. "It's not like there are a lot of us. But he never found me."

"So after you left Chicago, your first plan was to hide, which you've done." Anna Mae took a sip of tea. At some point she'd sat down at the table, though Wes couldn't say when. "But now you want to burn this evidence rather than turn it in? Don't you want justice for your brother? For Cynthia?"

Keely stared down at her teacup. "There was a time when I did, but I've come to realize it just isn't possible. The chief of police in Chicago was working for the Wolf Point Ring. It's not like I could have given my file to the sheriff in Springfield, even though he seemed honest. This needs to go to a lawman with national jurisdiction, like a U.S. Marshal. But going to the Marshal service is what got Cynthia and James killed, which makes me think the Wolf Point Ring must have a snitch. I don't know how to turn in the evidence and stay alive." She sniffled, then blew out a breath. "I've thought about mailing it and hoping for the best, but the postmark would give my location away."

Daniel plopped himself down at the head of the table and met Keely's eyes. "You need to stay in Twin Rivers and let me have the evidence. You might not like me very much, but I'm not going to take the information you shared and wire Chicago to tell the chief of police or do anything else that will put you in danger. And just in case you're right about the marshals and news spreads that you turned in evidence, you'll be safer on the A Bar W than anywhere else."

Keely's jaw trembled.

Wes wiped a wayward curl away from her face and tucked it behind her ear. "It's time to stop running."

She looked at Daniel. "If I agree to stay here and give you the evidence, what will you do with it?"

"There are several agents at the marshal's office in San Antonio that I know and trust," Daniel answered. "I would send for one of them, and I would use the roller press at the courthouse to copy as many of your documents as possible. What we can't copy with the press, I can have the copyist finish. I would keep the copies at the sheriff's office, then we would give the marshal what you have. I don't think we'll have the trouble with corruption at the San Antonio office that your brother had with the Chicago office. But having a copy of your evidence won't hurt anything."

"But someone inside the marshals' office is corrupt. What if they find out about the evidence turned in at the San Antonio office and tell the mayor of Chicago?" Keely twisted her hands together on the table. "Even if your Texas marshals could somehow manage to keep this quiet, whoever goes in to arrest the mayor would need to arrest everyone on my list at the same time. If even one person from the smuggling ring escapes arrest, I'm a dead woman."

"If they know where you are. And if they can get to you." Wes rested his hand over hers on the table and waited until she turned to look up at him. "I won't make getting to you easy."

She licked her lips. "I... I don't know what to say."

"You went through great lengths to come all the way here carrying that evidence. What do you think should come next?" His voice emerged soft against the quietness of the room.

She looked at him, a pained look filling her face.

The breath stopped in his chest. He couldn't imagine letting her leave, not now that he knew why she was running, but it wasn't as though he could force her to stay.

*Dear God, make her want to stay, please. Give me a way to help her.*

"I want criminals to be held accountable under the law, and justice for James and Cynthia." The crease on Keely's forehead looked so painfully deep it was all he could do not to reach out and soothe it away with his thumb. "And... and I want to be done hiding. I want life to be normal again—as normal as it ever can be now that my brother's dead and I'm two thousand miles from home."

*Thank you, God.*

He squeezed her hands, which were still resting beneath his on the table. "Then that's what we'll give you."

He only hoped he could live up to his promise.

## 6

She felt too slender in his arms, almost like she would break if he held her too tightly.

From his position atop Ares, Wes drew his gaze away from Keely's porcelain face with her eyes closed in slumber and looked out over the desert. Everything seemed normal. The sun burned brightly overhead, and yellow prairie grass filled the landscape, interspersed every so often with a scraggly bush or pile of boulders.

But could the valley on the other side of the hill hold the men Keely was hiding from? Had they somehow tracked her to West Texas?

Or even worse, maybe there was a bounty on Keely's head, and every outlaw between Chicago and Twin Rivers was on the lookout for her.

Ares crested the hill, and Wes pulled him to a stop, then looked down to study the valley below. Cattle drank from the stream that snaked between the bottom of this hill and the next one, and a javelina rutted around near a shrub, but there wasn't a person in sight, not even a ranch hand.

But what about the pile of boulders just on the other side of the creek? The trail led right past it, and it was large enough for a couple men to hide behind.

Wes shifted both the reins and the bulk of Keely's weight into his left arm and rested his palm on the hilt of his pistol. He nudged Ares into movement again. The horse trotted the familiar trail as though nothing was wrong, as though they were just riding between Daniel's house and the hacienda like they did numerous times each week.

But Wes's heart beat loudly in his ears, and his lungs worked harder than normal to draw breath.

He edged Ares around the pile of rocks, his hand still resting on his pistol.

Nothing. No person. No animal. Just a sparse patch of desert grass growing in the thin shade.

He let out a breath. Here he'd known about Keely's troubles for an hour, and he was seeing threats around every corner.

But he would be a fool not to see some threats, wouldn't he? The smuggling ring Keely had proof of held both money and power. They wouldn't fall easily, and they'd already proven they weren't afraid to kill—in as brutal a manner as possible.

Wes looked down at Keely's innocent face and tried to put from his mind what she'd said about finding her brother's fiancée on their doorstep. But he could almost see bruises form on Keely's own features, almost imagine her body being cold and lifeless in his arms.

He had to stop thinking this way. His wife was in danger, yes, but he needed a plan, something he could do to make sure she stayed safe.

He could hire some extra men, as Charlotte had said. Daniel was making sure that the newspaper destroyed any pictures of him and Keely, but he'd ride into town later just to double-check that a picture of Keely wouldn't end up getting printed.

He'd move her bedroom closer to his too. No more of her sleeping on the other side of the house.

He'd call a meeting with his hands that bunked near the house and tell them to keep an eye out for anything unusual. He wanted to know about any man trespassing on his land. He'd tell Dobbs to stick close to the house for the time being too.

And he'd start looking for guards immediately. If he had any luck, he'd be able to hire some men who knew how to handle themselves both around cattle and in a gunfight.

That was going to cost money, but he'd find a way to come up with the funds.

Ares trotted through the gate posts marking the official entrance to the A Bar W, and the horse naturally picked up its gait until he reached the yard.

A moment later, Dobbs appeared from around the corner of the barn. "Howdy, boss."

Wes waved him over. "Can you hold Keely for a minute?"

"She all right?" Dobbs frowned as his boots crunched over the yard.

"Just tired. She didn't sleep well last night."

Dobbs reached up, and he shifted Keely's subtle weight into the cowhand's arms before swinging down. The second his feet reached the ground, he scooped her back against his chest.

*Where she belongs.*

He blinked. Where had that thought come from?

"You sure everything's all right?" Dobbs eyed him.

It was so far from all right, and he didn't know where to start. "Leave the saddle on Ares and put him in the corral. I need to head to town in a bit."

He walked across the yard and up the stone steps to the house, but rather than go upstairs to her room, he headed into the corridor and turned right. Call him crazy, but he wasn't too keen on putting her all the way upstairs when no one else was around. He laid her on the couch in the parlor—the very one she'd claimed was too fancy yesterday before storming out of the room—and tried not to think about how empty his arms felt after he stepped away from her. Tried not to think about how fragile and slender she looked lying there against the plush cushions.

He huffed out a breath, then turned and forced himself to leave the parlor. He had enough things to do without standing there ruminating over the confusing woman he'd somehow pledged his life to.

He'd work in his office for an hour or so before he went into town. Just in case Keely woke up and needed something.

He headed down the corridor, then turned, skirting the courtyard until he came to his office door.

His *open* office door.

Had he left it that way?

He'd been in a hurry when he left with Daniel, so maybe he'd forgotten to close it.

Wes opened it all the way and stepped inside, only to find a familiar form seated behind his desk, pouring over a stack of papers.

"You came." Wes couldn't help the smile that spread across his face. If anyone could get him out of the mess his father had left behind, Harrison Rutherford could. "I didn't figure you'd be here until after Christmas."

Harrison looked up from the papers, the dark brown of his eyes gleaming with memories of fishing expeditions along the Rio Grande and ghost stories told around campfires. The massive mahogany desk where he sat had always dwarfed Sam and Daniel, but Harrison had a way of commanding it. That must be what happened when a man moved to the city and made a name for himself as a hoity-toity lawyer. He learned how to look important and powerful.

"Of course I came. You need help, and it's not the sort of

thing that should wait." Harrison gestured to the papers spread across the desktop. "I know you sent me copies, but the original contract was sitting here. I just need a minute to finish reviewing it."

"Go right ahead."

Harrison's gaze dropped back to the railroad contract Pa had signed shortly before his death.

Wes walked over to the bookshelf and perused the titles, even though he well knew what was there. At least it gave him something to do while Harrison studied the contract. Of all his childhood friends, he and Harrison had grown up in the most similar situations. Harrison's father had always been wealthy, and his ma had died when he was young, leaving only his father to raise him.

The difference was his own father had never been as cruel and ruthless as Harrison's.

"Your father know you're in town yet?" Wes asked.

Harrison set the stack of papers down and grimaced. "I was hoping to delay that visit a little longer. Can I stay here?"

"Of course." Wes waved his hand absently at the ceiling. "Take your pick of the rooms upstairs, except for the one right next to mine. I'm going to have Keely moved there."

"Keely?"

"My wife."

Harrison sat back in the chair and folded his arms across his chest, still looking entirely too comfortable behind the desk. "You went through with it? I could hardly believe it when I received Sam and Ellie's letter saying you'd placed an ad for a bride."

"Keely arrived yesterday."

Harrison raised his eyebrows. "You sure have an interesting way of starting a marriage."

Harrison didn't know the half of it, but that was a story for after they'd discussed the contracts.

"What about you? Any women in Austin take your fancy?" Wes sank down into the high-back chair across from the desk.

"Why? You trying to imagine how I'd look with a shaved head?"

Wes shrugged, a grin tilting his lips. Years ago, the five of them had made a marriage pact of sorts. He, Daniel, and Sam had all promised to marry before they were thirty, and Harrison and Cain had sworn not to marry until after thirty—if at all. "At least one of us should end up with a shaved head out of that deal."

That had been the agreement, made with an abundance of twelve-year-old wisdom. Anyone who broke the pact got his head shaved. "I thought sure it was going to be Daniel, but then he up and married Charlie a few months before his thirtieth birthday."

Harrison smirked. "Maybe Cain will be the one who gets his head shaved."

Wes choked. "Cain? You think Cain is going to get married at all, let alone before he's thirty?" An image popped up in his mind of Cain with his wavy blond hair that fell past his shoulders and his devil-may-care attitude. The man would die a bachelor and be proud of it. "He hasn't changed a bit since the day we made that pact. If anything, he's become harder."

"You don't need to tell me that. He stops by whenever he's in Austin, usually stays with me for a few weeks if he's got work at the Ranger headquarters."

Wes scratched the back of his head. How hadn't he known that? He'd assumed that because Cain had hightailed it out of Twin Rivers seven years ago and not come back until this summer, he'd not had any contact with Harrison.

"Cain is about as likely to fall head over his heels for a woman as you are to have snow in Twin Rivers on Christmas Day," Harrison said.

Wes snorted. He only remembered it snowing once, just a

sprinkle of fluffy white stuff one February night, and it had all been melted by the time the sun crested the mountains in the morning. "The way I see it, you've always been the one most likely to break the pact."

"Me?" Harrison chuckled. "You just said you expected Daniel to be the one who broke the pact."

"Yes, but for a different reason. He was determined not to marry unless he found the right woman. You, on the other hand, have gone through your entire life claiming you don't need a family when it's probably one of the things you want most in this world."

Harrison narrowed his gaze. "Families are too much drama. Too many emotions. That's why I'm surprised you remarried. You have even less of a tolerance for drama and emotions than I do."

"I remarried to avoid drama." And yet, it didn't appear his plan had worked.

But he couldn't be sorry for it, not now that he knew how much help Keely needed.

Harrison steepled his fingers and tapped them together beneath his chin. "I might start pursuing a wife of my own in another year or so, after I turn thirty. Her name is Adeline."

Wes laughed. "You might start pursuing her in a year? What do you think this is, a chess match? If you can wait a year to begin courting her, it doesn't sound like she's turned your head all that much."

"She hasn't. She's vapid and insipid, but she's also beautiful and comes from a wealthy family. I'm to the age where I need a wife, and she's exactly the kind of woman everyone expects a man like me to marry."

"You criticize me for marrying a woman I don't know to escape all the vapid, insipid socialites, and here you are contemplating marrying a woman you know for certain you won't like?"

Harrison shrugged. "My house is big enough, I'll barely have to see her. And unlike here, Austin has plenty of activities and charities and ladies' societies to keep her busy."

"You're a fool."

"Perhaps. But I daresay my reasons make as much sense to me as yours make to you." Harrison rubbed the back of his neck, then looked down at the stack of papers sitting in front of him and grimaced. "Let's talk about this contract. I can't see a way out of it."

A sinking sensation filled Wes's belly. "I don't want to be a railroad owner."

"You already are."

"Do you know how many cattle I had to sell to buy into the railroad?"

Harrison didn't so much as blink. "Raise more. That's what your father did."

"My father never took this ranch backward."

"He did at the end, when he signed the contract with the railroad. He knew you'd have to sell cattle to finance it. But I bet he also knew the railroad would be a good investment." Harrison shifted in his chair, leaning back before steepling his fingers together beneath his chin again. "Had I known the Southern Pacific was taking more investors, I would have jumped at that opportunity, and so would a couple dozen of my acquaintances in Austin. I don't know how your father whee-dled his way into this deal with the railroad so close to being finished, but you should be thankful. You'll be getting quarterly dividends in another year, and those checks aren't going to be small."

"Maybe." But it had galled, having the King Ranch purchase his cattle and become the largest ranch in Texas—a title his father had worked tirelessly for.

Wes stood and walked to the window, looking out over the hazy peaks of the Bofecillos Mountains. Harrison had a way of making the railroad investment sound rational, but none of that changed the fact he'd rather expand the ranch than be a railroad owner. There was something about sitting in a saddle with the sun beating down on his back, or riding the fence, or cutting the herd and branding calves.

Cattle ran in his blood, not transportation methods.

"The railroad is over budget," he said. "That's why the Southern Pacific took on another investor when the line is only months away from being completed. I don't know if Pa was aware of the money trouble when he signed the contract. But even if he was, he was too sick to be thinking clearly."

Harrison came up beside him, his brown eyes sharp and attentive. "I'll buy half your shares."

"Can I sell it?"

"From what I see, yes."

That would give him easy money to hire guards for Keely, though if he moved some funds around and didn't hire a couple of the hands he'd planned to for the north part of the property, he might be able to get by without selling any railroad shares. "Let me run some figures, but I might take you up on that."

"But my buying your shares isn't going to get you out of the second contract with the Mortimers."

Wes sighed. There was a bit of merit in buying into the railroad. He could see some of his father's logic behind signing that contract. But the second contract? The one that had nothing to do with the railroad and everything to do with his personal life? It said that if he died without an heir, the entirety of the A Bar W and all his other holdings, including the Southern Pacific Railroad, would go to Andrew Mortimer's oldest son. And in the absence of a son, Mortimer's eldest daughter.

Wes pressed his eyes shut. To be fair, his father hadn't been completely crazy when he'd signed the contract. He'd been certain that Charlotte would marry the Mortimer heir, Andrew, and the contract had been Pa's way of protecting the ranch and making sure it didn't get divided up among a litany of relatives.

But Charlotte had married Daniel instead of Andrew Mortimer, and now all of his holdings would one day go to the offspring of a man he barely knew.

"There has to be a way out," Wes rasped.

Harrison raised an eyebrow. "You're a married man. Get your wife with child."

Wes clenched his teeth together. "That's not going to work."

"Why not? It's the normal way of things, and certainly the best solution here... unless your wife can't bear a child for some reason?"

"Keely and I don't have that kind of marriage."

Harrison narrowed his eyes, his expensive, tailored suit making him look all that more intimidating as he stared. "Don't have *what* kind of marriage?"

"The kind where I take her to bed."

"Then what kind of marriage do you have?"

"One where I give her food and lodging and she shares my last name in return."

"Are you insane? What kind of man doesn't share his bed with his wife?"

*The kind who doesn't want his wife to die in childbirth.* Wes swallowed. His friend knew that Abigail had died and how it had happened, but they saw each other a couple times per year at best. He wouldn't know everything, and Wes didn't plan on sharing. Instead, he raised his eyes back to the mountaintops. "You wouldn't understand."

Harrison leaned against the trim that lined the window, the gold from his pocket watch catching the sun and blinking out at the room. "You're a man, and she's a woman. Take her to bed tonight and get yourself an heir. Problem solved."

And if Keely died during childbirth like Abigail had?

Wes felt suddenly hot.

He'd never so much as kiss a woman again, not even if he and Keely were married for fifty years.

It wasn't worth the risk of having not just one, but two wives buried in the family cemetery.

~.~.~.~.~

AN OPIUM SMUGGLING RING.

Daniel stared down at the top of his desk, where the glass plates and two developed photographs he'd gotten from the newspaper rested.

As sheriff of Twin Rivers, Daniel had thought a lot of things when he'd laid eyes on Keely Westin—or was it Nora O'Leary? —for the first time. That she was small. That she had a mane of unforgettable red hair. That she seemed scared of something.

But he'd attributed her skittishness at the wedding to being overwhelmed with all the people that had shown up.

He hadn't put together that she might be on the run until Anna Mae had brought her to his house that morning.

But even after he'd realized she was on the run, he hadn't come close to guessing she might be running from a band of powerful criminals.

Ones that would spare no mercy in torturing her if she was caught.

Daniel rubbed the side of his head where the bone fell away to form a small hole only covered by skin and hair. After his run-in with the rustlers last summer, he was lucky to be alive.

But the band of rustlers hadn't been caught yet, and while that responsibility lay more with the rangers than on him, he still couldn't ignore the weight of it. His county had been ravaged. His friends had lost cattle. And his life had almost been forfeited.

What if the opium ring somehow learned Nora O'Leary was in Twin Rivers? He had three deputies to help him cover a county that spanned over a thousand square miles. Would he have a prayer of stopping the outlaws?

Had his father ever needed to help a woman hide before? He'd been sheriff of Twin Rivers for over twenty years. Surely there'd been a woman trying to escape an abusive husband or some other such situation over the years.

Daniel stood from behind his desk and strode to the back door. He pushed it open to reveal the little alley that ran behind the row of businesses that lined the town's main road, and the houses on the next road over.

A few steps and he'd be at the back door of his parents' house. Ma was sure to be inside cooking lunch, but instead of walking into the kitchen, Daniel headed around the front of their house, where Pa was more likely to be.

He knocked twice, then pushed the door open.

"Daniel." Pa looked up from where he sat in the parlor at the writing desk. A smile lit his face. "I wasn't expecting you until lunch. Look what came in the mail."

Pa rolled backward in his wheelchair, then held out a letter.

Daniel scanned the letterhead. "Western Theological Seminary?"

"Go on, read it."

He did. It was some kind of acceptance letter for the spring term starting in January.

"I can see by the look on your face you don't think it's a good idea," Pa said.

"Think what's a good idea? I don't understand."

"I'm thinking about me going to seminary next year."

Daniel stilled, every muscle in his body tensing. The scent of meat and chiles and beans floated from the hallway that led to the back of the house, and the sound of a neighbor whistling outside filtered through the window. But all Daniel could do was stare at his father.

Pa wanted to go to seminary?

On the other side of the state?

"It's just that, well..." Pa looked down, then gave his head a small shake. "I may have lost my leg seven years ago, but I didn't lose my brain—or my desire to help people. You know I've been meeting with Preacher Russell and going through Bible studies."

"Yes," Daniel agreed. Preacher Russell even let Pa sermonize for church every now and then.

"Preacher Russell thinks I should go to seminary."

"But this seminary's clear over in..." Daniel checked the letterhead at the top of the page. "Houston?"

"It would just be for a few years. Then we would come back."

"We? Are you planning to take Ma and Anna Mae?"

"Well, yes to your ma. She's even more excited about it than I am. But as for Anna Mae, the choice would be up to her."

Daniel's hair suddenly felt too tight for his head. "Is Preacher Russell planning to leave in a few years?"

Pa rubbed the back of his head. "I can't rightly confirm that part. He and Emmaline like Twin Rivers well enough."

"But if you go to seminary, you'll want your own church when you finish school, and it will probably be somewhere other than Twin Rivers."

His crippled father, who'd lived in Twin Rivers his entire life, was thinking about moving clear across the state and never coming back. Forget his hair feeling too tight. He wanted to go outside and yell until his lungs burned.

Pa looked down. "The truth is, I'd need to sell the house to pay for seminary."

"Sell the..." Daniel couldn't finish. His father might claim that losing his leg didn't mean he'd lost his mind, but he would beg to differ. Clearly his father had lost every last bit of rational thought, or he wouldn't be talking about selling the house he and Ma had lived in for thirty years.

"The trouble is Anna Mae," Pa continued. "I can't imagine that girl being happy anywhere other than Twin Rivers, but if we sell the house, where will she live? What will she do for work?"

"I don't—"

"I always figured she'd marry, you see. But here she is, twenty-two, and I can't think of a single man who's ever caught her eye." Pa sighed, then looked at the letter Daniel still held. "Maybe this is all just foolish talk. Your ma and I can't just up and leave your sister without a place to live. She doesn't even have a job."

*Charlotte and I could add a room on. Anna Mae could stay with us.*

But he couldn't make himself form the words—and not because he needed to talk to Charlotte.

"If this is what God really wants for your life, then He'll have a way of working everything out." Daniel had to force his tongue to form the words inside his mouth. They were the right words, the kind of thing Preacher Russell would say. But his mouth protested each sound that he formed.

"Do you..." Pa's voice had gone soft, and he stared down at his hands, his shoulders hunched. "Do you think I'm a fool, wanting something more for my life than to be an invalid?"

Daniel pressed his eyes shut. "I don't think you're a fool, Pa. I think it's right honorable that you want to help people spiritually, seeing how you can't help them physically anymore. I just..."

He looked around the four familiar walls of the parlor. He'd envisioned watching his son or daughter toddle around this very room while Anna Mae played something on the piano and his parents looked on with smiles on their faces. Not that Charlotte was pregnant, but one day they hoped to have children, and he'd always thought his parents would be part of that.

Always thought his father would be here to give advice on sheriffing.

Always thought his ma would be the first person to volunteer when something needed doing at church.

Always thought his parents would be part of his everyday life.

Daniel swallowed. His eyes grew glassy. "I think you'll be missed an awful lot if you leave."

## 7

H arrison shifted in his saddle, the sun beating down on his back as he studied the massive adobe structure in the valley below. His task was simple. Get in and see if anyone remembered a man named Hernando Padilla. Or if not Hernando, then men named Carlos Arroyo or Diego Lopez.

If he was lucky, he'd be able to get out before anyone realized who he was or that he was there—especially his father.

A steady stream of traders trickled in and out of the entrance to Fort Ashton, which was guarded by a burly man whose size would deter anyone with nefarious intentions from entering.

But no one with a lick of sense would enter in the first place.

A stone ball formed in Harrison's stomach, heavy and sour.

His father had done many things over the course of his life. Few of them had been honorable, but nearly all of them had made money.

Which was why his father now owned the trading post that had once belonged to the Ashton family.

The notion made bile churn around the stone lodged in his stomach.

Nothing Father had done in acquiring the fort had been illegal, but that almost made the situation worse. His father's actions had been calculated, thought-out, patient. Perfectly legal yet utterly ruthless.

The guard at the entrance turned his way, and not for the first time. If he stayed here any longer, Father would probably send men out to question him about why he was watching the fort, and even though he hadn't seen his father for three years, one of them was bound to recognize him.

Harrison urged his horse forward, giving him his head as he picked his way down the mountain.

He'd already noticed one change with the fort. It used to be maybe a quarter of the men traveling the trail from Mexico sold their wares at the trading post located just inside the American border instead of continuing on to San Antonio. But in the time he'd been watching, he hadn't seen a single Mexican continue on the trail. Every one of them was entering the fort.

The guard he'd seen from the mountain stood at the large wooden gates, talking to each person before they entered. Noise rose from the walls behind him, and Harrison ran his eyes along the thick adobe barricade that served as a trading post, hotel, restaurant—and even his father's home.

"You got goods to trade?" the guard barked at him.

"Something like that," Harrison answered.

The man looked him over. "Where?"

Harrison scratched the side of his head beneath his hat brim. "In my saddlebag."

It wasn't a complete lie. He had a few things in there from Austin he could give his father if needed.

The guard glared at him but gave a slight nod of his head to indicate he could enter.

Harrison nudged his horse, Toronto, through the tunnel

and into the corral. Mexican and American traders alike milled about, watering, feeding, and stabling their livestock. Dust from the constant movement of hooves filled the space, and the sounds of lowing oxen, snorting horses, and constant conversation made it nearly impossible to discern what anyone was saying, either in Spanish or English.

The layout was the same as he remembered from visiting the fort when the Ashtons had owned it, but he never remembered so many people or so much noise. Whatever changes his father had made, they seemed to be working in terms of business.

He had to wait behind two others to water Toronto. Harrison used the time to ask if anyone knew a man named Hernando Padilla. They hadn't. Nor had they heard of Carlos Arroyo or Diego Lopez.

And why would they? The people he spoke with were nothing more than travelers like Hernando, Carlos, and Diego. Most of them would be at the fort for a few hours. A handful might spend the night, but they'd have no reason to know of travelers who had come through a month ago or better.

After watering Toronto, Harrison tied his horse in one of the shaded places beneath an ocotillo mat, then he crossed the corral and entered the archway that led to the courtyard.

It was only slightly less busy than the corral. People milled about, most heading toward or coming from the southeastern corner, where the trading post had always been.

Harrison stepped forward and approached a man with a wife and two young children. "Excuse me, but I'm looking for a man named Hernando Padilla. He's twenty-one, about five foot seven."

The man shook his head. "*Lo siento.* I don't know him."

"Don't suppose you were at this trading post about a month ago?"

The man shook his head again. "I must be going. We have a long journey ahead."

"So then you're continuing on the trail to San Antonio?"

The man's eyes grew large. "Never. I have a wife and two children to think of. We are going back to Mexico." The man took his wife's hand and stepped around him, heading straight for the corral.

He approached a man standing by himself next, but the Mexican didn't know Hernando, Carlos, or Diego either, nor was he continuing to San Antonio. The man after that hadn't heard of the three Mexicans either, but he came straight out and said the trail to San Antonio was too dangerous to travel.

The Chihuahuan Trail hadn't seemed overly dangerous to Harrison when he'd traveled it, and he'd taken it from southwest of Austin to Twin Rivers. He hadn't seen any bandits, and he'd hardly been the only person on the trail.

So why did the Mexicans seem to think the trail dangerous? Was that why Hernando, Carlos, and Diego were all missing? Had danger befallen them on the trail?

He looked around. If he wanted to find out, he needed to question the workers who were likely to have seen Hernando or the others.

He started toward the entrance to the kitchen, but one of the guards stationed along the edge of the courtyard stepped forward. Harrison didn't recognize him, but the man was watching him awful closely.

Had he given himself away by talking to the travelers?

Oh, if Jonas Redding were here, he'd give the man an earful. How many times had he tried telling the marshal he wouldn't make a good spy? But the man had been insistent he was the best person to get information from inside Fort Ashton.

He'd tried explaining that he and his father barely talked, that he would be nothing but noticeable inside the fort, but it hadn't changed Jonas's mind.

Harrison sauntered closer to the trading post, as though that's where he'd been headed all along. The guard watched him until two other men caught his attention. Their faces were red and movements jerky as they shouted at each other in Spanish.

The guard stalked toward the men, and Harrison used the distraction to slip through the door of the servant's staircase beside the kitchen. Maybe he could find a maid away from the eyes of a guard on one of the upper floors.

He headed up the first flight of stairs, then opened the door to the second floor. He didn't see a guard anywhere in the corridor, but a woman stood beside the first door to his left. She faced away from him, but the white apron strings tied at the back of her waist and her plain blue dress told him that she worked at the fort.

*Thank you, God.*

He headed straight toward her. "Excuse me, miss."

She jumped at the sound of his voice, turning around as her eyes went wide.

*Crash!*

The tray he hadn't realized she'd been holding fell to the ground, and the set of what looked to be silver tea service and fine crystal shattered against the tile.

Harrison hurried forward to help clean up the mess, but the door to the room jerked open, revealing an angry yet familiar form.

So much for remaining undiscovered.

"What's going on out here?" Rooster snarled. The hulking guard leveled the full power of his glare at the woman.

"*Lo siento,*" she muttered in Spanish. "I dropped Mr. Rutherford's tray."

The woman sank to her knees and began scooping the mess back onto the polished silver tray.

Rooster didn't look at him, and probably wasn't even aware

he was present as he stared down at the servant. A snarl twisted his face, almost as though he was getting ready to either spit on her or kick her.

Harrison stepped forward. "It was my fault. I startled her."

Rooster's gaze shot up to meet his, still as menacing and cold as he remembered. Harrison suddenly felt like he was twelve again and sneaking around his father's house just to avoid accidentally running into his father's longstanding henchman.

"Your father know you're here?" Rooster was still large and well-muscled, big enough that most people would naturally shrink from him. The constant scowl he carried on his face hadn't changed either.

"Who is it?" A Mexican man appeared beside Rooster. He wasn't as tall or hulking as the guard, but there was something dark and dangerous about him.

"Just a kitchen maid, one who can't keep her wits about her. The price of that crystal will come out of your pay. Do you hear me?" Rooster nudged the woman with the toe of his boot, and not in a gentle way.

She still knelt on the floor, frantically scooping the broken glass up with her fingers.

The Mexican looked down at her bent head, and a strange look passed over his face. Harrison couldn't quite name it. Recognition, most likely, but there was something more, something almost cruel about the way he looked at her.

A sharp gasp sounded from the floor, and Harrison looked down to see a line of blood springing up from the woman's palm.

"Go fetch a broom and dustpan," Harrison said, making his voice gentle. "You'll only injure yourself trying to clean up that way."

"Probably deserves to get cut," the Mexican spat. "Now we'll have to wait longer for our food."

Harrison narrowed his eyes at the man. "And you are?"

"Not your concern."

"This is Harrison Rutherford, Mr. Rutherford's son," Rooster said.

He heard another quick intake of breath from the floor, and the woman looked up at him with accusing eyes.

The look in the Mexican man's eyes changed too. He stuck out a hand, his hard demeanor now replaced with business-like calculation. "Pleased to make your acquaintance."

"Hurry up with that mess, then go tell Mr. Rutherford his son is here." Rooster nudged the woman with his boot again.

She still hadn't left to get a broom, and blood now covered the lower part of her hand.

"Here, use this." Harrison plucked a handkerchief out of his pocket and handed it to her.

He'd meant for her to staunch the bleeding, but instead she wrapped it around her entire hand as a protective layer, then used her hand to brush the remaining bits of glass onto the tray.

A few moments later, she stood with the tray, keeping her head bent the entire time. She muttered *"lo siento"* once more before scurrying off.

Rooster and the Mexican watched her go, and Harrison used the few seconds to look past them. A group of Mexicans sat inside a room that had been set up like a parlor, their dusty clothes surely making a mess of the lavish upholstery. Looked like the lot of them had just come off the trail.

Rooster shifted, moving into his line of sight. "I'll show you to your father's office."

"Maybe I should meet my father's friends first," Harrison murmured, then moved his eyes to the Mexican man who now stood shoulder-to-shoulder with Rooster so that his view inside the room was completely blocked. "You haven't told me your name."

"If Mr. Rutherford wants you to meet, he'll make the introductions himself," Rooster snapped.

"I see." Would the Mexicans know something about Hernando's disappearance? Would Rooster? If so, they weren't likely to tell him. And asking would only give away his true purpose for coming.

His best option was to talk to the woman with the tea service, but that would have to wait until after he met with his father.

Rooster stepped into the corridor, giving Harrison one last glimpse inside the room before the Mexican closed the door in his face. "This way."

Harrison followed Rooster down the corridor until he stopped in front of the first door on the south wall. He opened it to reveal a room with a magnificent view of the green Rio Grande Valley and the mountains beyond.

"Your father should be here shortly," Rooster said, then closed the door, leaving Harrison alone in the room.

He moved straight to his father's desk and pulled open the top drawer.

*Please don't let there be anything about Hernando, Carlos, or Diego.*

He wouldn't call his father's business practices fair or generous, but his father had never before been involved in a person's disappearance.

But he still needed to check.

The drawers were all painfully neat, with stamps and pens more plentiful than papers. The few papers he found tended to be lists of supplies or workers' pay rates.

He put the contents back in the desk, then turned and scanned the books on the shelf behind it. He stopped when he reached a set of similar-looking books that had dates inked on their bindings. Did his father keep records of who passed through the fort? Or maybe of things that happened? Hernando had sent a letter from Twin Rivers on September 6, mentioning that he was staying the night at Fort Ashton. That was the last correspondence his mother had from him.

The dates on the spines weren't that recent. The last book stopped at the end of July. Harrison pulled it out, along with the first book that was dated three years ago, shortly after his father had assumed ownership of the fort. He opened the earliest one.

A ledger.

Harrison ran his finger down the column of numbers on the right side. Fifty cents apiece for three rugs, twenty cents apiece for pottery, and on the list went.

The prices all seemed about what he would expect for three years ago, though the cost of Mexican wares in Austin had certainly gone up since then.

Harrison opened the most recent ledger and flipped to the final page, then frowned. It had the price for seven rugs recorded at seventy cents total, meaning his father had only paid ten cents for each of the rugs?

How had that happened? Especially considering the rugs were selling for a dollar and a half or more in the city. Three years ago those same rugs would have sold for just under a dollar, and the ledger said his father had paid fifty cents for them.

Something moved near the corner of his vision, and he jumped, slamming the book closed and dropping it onto the desk before he fully looked up.

The woman from earlier stood just inside the door. "Sorry if I startled you, *señor*. Your father says he will be up in a few minutes. He has some business downstairs he needs to finish."

Harrison took a quick step away from the desk. Did she know he'd been snooping?

"Do you want me to bring you something from the kitchen while you wait? Some coffee, perhaps? And a piece of pie?"

Harrison gave his head a small shake. He needed to stop acting so nervous. Rooster had brought him here and a worker was offering him pie. No one thought it odd that he be in his father's office examining ledgers—except maybe his father, who knew he wanted nothing to do with the fort.

He replaced the ledgers on the bookshelf, then walked around the desk. "I don't need any food, but there was a man who passed through here about a month and a half ago. His name was Hernando Padilla. He was about five-foot-seven with brown eyes and black hair. Do you remember him?"

She shook her head. "There are so many travelers that come through, it's impossible to remember them all."

"He stayed the night, probably ate a meal or two here?"

"Hernando Padilla," she repeated to herself, then pressed her lips together, clearly thinking. After a few moments, she gave her head another shake. "I remember a man who came through about that time, but he had his wife with him and several children. He made a scene in the courtyard, accused your father of stealing from the Mexicans and keeping heaps of money for himself. The guards escorted him out of the fort immediately and said he wasn't allowed back. No one else from about that time sticks out to me."

The breath he hadn't realized he'd been holding rushed out of his chest, his shoulders deflating along with it. If a worker didn't remember Hernando, then what hope did he have of finding someone who would, let alone learning what had happened to him?

"Do you know him?" the woman asked. "Is he a friend of yours?"

"My cook's son. He went missing somewhere between here and Austin."

The woman's eyes came up to meet his, wide and brown

and a little too vulnerable. "Do you think bandits got him on the trail?"

"His body hasn't been found." But that meant little in a vast, dry desert filled with any number of places for bandits to hide or a dead body to be dragged. "What about the names Carlos Arroyo or Diego Lopez? They passed through here at the end of August."

"Both Mexican? With brown eyes and black hair?"

He wished he could say one of them had blond hair or green eyes or anything that would make them stand out. "Yes, and both about five-foot-seven or eight."

She shook her head for the third time.

"Thank you for trying."

"I'm only sorry I can't help more. I can't imagine how I would feel if something happened to Gabriella. It must be awful to have someone you know disappear." She looked at him again, her eyes filled with compassion. "I really hope you find them and that they are all right."

"Me too."

She glanced at the door. "If there's nothing more, I best get back to the kitchen."

"Actually, I'd like to see your hand." It was still wrapped in his handkerchief, and a thin line of red seeped through it.

Her gaze dipped down to her palm, then she tucked it behind her back. "It'll be fine."

"I just want to make sure it will heal properly."

She stared up at him for a moment, that vulnerability back in her expressive eyes. What was she doing away from her family, and working for his father, no less? She seemed far too innocent to be putting up with the likes of Rooster and the rest of the guards.

"It looks as though the handkerchief still hasn't staunched the blood." His voice rumbled from his chest, deep and gravelly. "I want to see how bad the injury is."

She slowly drew her hand out from behind her back and held it out, watching as he unwound the strip of cloth. Just as he suspected, a gash that looked to be quite deep ran along the side of her palm. Several smaller cuts marred her skin as well.

"You should have gotten the broom."

"It seemed best to pick up the mess as quickly as possible, but I can tend it later. I really do need to get back to work."

"This is deep enough to invite infection. Let me get some brandy." He turned toward the liquor cabinet that sat behind the desk to the right.

"No!"

He looked over his shoulder at her.

"Don't take any liquor, please. If one of the bottles is opened or gone, they'll blame me, and I already need to pay for the crystal."

"I'll let my father know I'm responsible for the brandy." The liquor cabinet was locked, but Harrison pulled out the first book on the bookshelf closest to the keyhole, then reached to the back of the empty slot. Sure enough, the key to the cabinet hung on a nail.

His father was nothing if not predictable.

Harrison opened the cabinet, removed a half-filled bottle of brandy, and uncorked it before returning to where the woman stood. "Let me see your hand again."

She took a step back, placing herself against the wall. "You're sure I won't get in trouble for using the brandy?"

Was his father really cruel enough to charge an injured woman for the mouthful of brandy that would be used cleaning her wound?

Harrison almost opened his mouth to offer her a job working for him in Austin, just to get her away from this place. He forced himself to answer her question instead. "You won't get in trouble. I always take a glass of brandy when I visit my father's office."

He fished a clean handkerchief out of his pocket, then held her hand open. "This is going to sting for a moment."

He dripped brandy onto the smaller cuts first, then poured a few drops into the gash.

She hissed and pressed her eyes shut, her hand involuntarily trying to close on him. He tightened his grip to keep it open so that the brandy would reach the deepest parts of the wound.

Her lips moved silently in what he assumed was a prayer, but a few words floated to him about the crystal and money. If he wasn't mistaken, she also mentioned Gabriella.

He dribbled more brandy onto her hand, and she stopped praying to whimper, scrunching her eyelids together even harder.

"The worst of it should be over." He wrapped the clean handkerchief around her hand, then stepped back.

"Thank you," she said, her eyes slowly opening, though she still stood with her muscles tense, clearly needing a distraction from the pain.

"Who's Gabriella?" he asked.

But rather than relax at his question like he'd hoped, her face turned a shade paler.

Which only made him more curious. About Gabriella. And about the woman standing in front of him.

"You said her name when I was asking about Hernando, then again when you were praying. I just wondered who she was."

She drew in a breath. "My sister."

"Do you send her money? Is that why breaking the crystal is such a problem?" It would also explain why she'd taken a job at Fort Ashton when she seemed so ill-suited to work here.

She stiffened. "I don't owe you any explanation."

He reached into his pocket and pulled out his billfold. "Let me pay you for the crystal. Had I not startled you, I'm sure you wouldn't have…"

*What?*

What had she been doing standing beside the door with the tray? He replayed the first few moments of him emerging from the stairway in his mind. He'd assumed she was performing one of her duties, but what kind of duty required her to stand outside a door with a tray while a conversation took place behind it?

"Were you eavesdropping earlier?"

Her shoulders turned rigid. "I don't know what you're talking about."

"In the corridor, when I came up from behind and scared you. Were you eavesdropping?"

"I don't know what you think you saw, but I was taking the tray to the men and you startled me. That's how I dropped it."

"What's your name?"

Her lips pressed together in a firm line, and her chin came up.

"If you refuse to tell me, I'll just ask my father or Rooster."

She let out a huff. "Alejandra."

"Alejandra," he repeated. A beautiful name. "I'm sorry for how the men treated you earlier."

"Don't apologize for Rooster and Raul," she spat. "It's clear you're not like them."

"Raul? Is that the man who came to the door with Rooster? You know him?"

"I really must be going."

"Not before I pay you." He opened the billfold.

"You want to pay me for the crystal…" Her brows drew down. "In exchange for what?"

He frowned. "In exchange for the fact it's my fault you dropped it. I'm the one who startled you, remember?" He held a handful of bills toward her.

Rather than take it, she crossed her arms over her chest. "If I take your money, what will you expect from me in return?"

What would he expect? Nothing.

She just stared at him, her eyes hard and posture stiff, all semblance of the vulnerable, compassionate woman from earlier gone.

Wait. Did she think that... that he was *propositioning* her?

Heat climbed up the back of his neck. He took his money and tucked in the fold where one of her hands rested on her crossed arm.

"You don't owe me anything for this, do you understand?" His throat felt dry and raspy. "I'm staying with a friend, not at Fort Ashton, and I'll be going back to Austin in a few days. The next time I return to Twin Rivers, you'll probably have moved on from here."

She uncrossed her arms and looked down at the bills, then shook her head. "The crystal won't cost this much."

"No, but I wouldn't put it past Rooster to inflate the price and pocket the extra."

She held the money out to him. "I still can't take it."

"What will happen if you don't? Something that affects your sister, I assume."

Two bright spots of red sprouted on her cheeks. "You don't know that."

"Call it a guess then. Am I right?"

She opened her mouth, but the door swung open.

"Well, well, I see the prodigal son has returned." Father stepped inside the room, his shrewd brown eyes sweeping slowly down Harrison's form.

He didn't even seem to notice Alejandra, and when Harrison glanced back toward the door, she was gone along with the money. "I'm hardly a prodigal, proven by the fact that I'm not here to grovel for money to replace my squandered inheritance."

"No, you're here to learn how to run Fort Ashton."

Harrison clenched his teeth together. How many times had his father written, asking him to return and take over his business?

And how many times had he responded that he wasn't interested in leaving Austin? But if pretending to learn the business gave him an excuse to spend more time inside the fort and learn what had happened to Hernando, then that's what he'd have to do.

His father raised his hands to encompass the fort. "What do you think of this place?"

*It feels wrong standing here, having you own this.* He swallowed back the answer. "You've done well for yourself."

"I'm glad you're here to help. Blasted Mexican traders always think their goods are worth more than their true value."

"That's strange. I'd think the goods would be valuable considering the cost of things like woven rugs, baskets, and pottery has risen ridiculously high in Austin."

Something sharp and knowing flashed in his father's eyes. "Has it now? And here everyone's saying the cost of goods will go down as soon as the railroad opens."

"Reckon we'll have to see what happens after the track's finished."

Father turned to face the window, affording him a view of the majestic wall of mountains jutting up on the Mexican side of the river. "Dinner is at seven."

"I'm staying with Wes."

His father turned sharply. "I thought you were here to learn how to run this place."

He didn't want to. Even if his father had been the one to start this trading post, he still wouldn't want to live here, on the backside of the desert, brokering deals for plates and rugs every day.

But for the sake of the missing Mexicans, he could pretend for a few days.

He forced a smile onto his face. "I'll be here during the day to learn, but I'm staying with Wes, and I return to Austin in two weeks."

Hopefully that would be enough to get the information he needed.

## 8

K nock. *Knock. Knock.*

Wes looked up from the stack of papers on his desk. Rosa, one of the three Mexican women who worked as a maid three days, a week peeked her head in, then stepped inside. Benita, the other maid, stood just behind her.

"Hola, Rosa. Don't suppose you have any news of Consuela?" He spoke in Spanish, the words rolling easily off his tongue. One didn't grow up on the Mexican border without learning Spanish right along with English.

She shook her head. "No. I asked a few more people, but I still don't have any idea where she went. No one in Ojinaga does."

His shoulders slumped. He'd spent the past four months since his housekeeper had left trying to find where she'd gone in Mexico. He was running out of ways to find her short of hiring a private investigator.

"All right. Thank you." He gave her a dismissive nod of the head.

"Actually, sir, I didn't come to bring you news of Consuela. I was wondering if you wanted us to clean today."

"Of course." Why wouldn't he have them clean? The women came every Monday, Wednesday, and Friday, and it was Friday. And since he'd gotten married on Tuesday, he'd asked the maids not to come Wednesday to give Keely a few days to learn her way around the hacienda. The house would be especially dirty today.

"What do you want us to clean then?" Rosa asked.

Wes blinked at her. Consuela had hired Rosa five years ago. Why was she asking what to clean? "The entire house. Like usual."

A crease formed on Rosa's brow. "But the house is already clean."

"Did you hire someone else to clean on the days we're not here?" Benita bunched the side of her skirt in her hand. "Was our work not good enough?"

Wes stood and walked around his desk toward the women. "No. I didn't hire anyone else. And the house should be filthy." It took dust all of twenty minutes to accumulate in the desert.

He looked down at the floor, intending to scuff the layer of fine desert dust coating the tiles. But there wasn't any. He frowned, then scanned the wide expanse of his desk. There wasn't any dust on the glossy surface, nor did there look to be any on the thick adobe surrounding the windows.

"Where's my wife?"

Rosa shrugged. "I know you got married, but I haven't seen another woman around, and we've been here for a half hour."

"It took us that long to walk through all the rooms and see they were already clean," Benita added.

"*All* the rooms are clean?"

"Well, Marisol is sweeping the terrace." Rosa jutted a thumb over her shoulder in the direction of the terrace on the west side of the house. "That can always use a good sweeping."

Wes scratched the side of his head. He'd told Keely he expected her to oversee housekeeping duties, not become his maid. But even if she'd decided to take some of the cleaning on herself, that didn't explain the entire house being clean.

Had she hired more maids without talking to him? He was fairly certain he'd told her that he had three maids who came from Mexico to clean several times a week, but a lot had happened since their wedding. Maybe she'd forgotten.

"Let's find Mrs. Westin." He stepped out into the corridor. It looked like even that had been swept and mopped already. But he hadn't seen Keely with either a mop or a broom. In fact, he hadn't seen her at all today.

Yesterday he'd seen her in passing a time or two, but she'd not even sat down to dinner with him and Harrison.

And the same was true of Wednesday. He'd laid her in the parlor after bringing her back to the ranch, and he'd made a point of introducing her to Harrison that afternoon after she'd woken up. But he'd not seen her again after that.

Where could she be? Certainly not outside. He'd told her that he wanted her to let him know if she went outside so he could have someone go with her for protection.

But her face had turned pale at the notion of venturing into the desert, and she'd said the house was big enough that she wouldn't have any trouble staying indoors.

Wes headed toward the staircase at the front of the house, the footsteps behind him indicating that both Rosa and Benita were following. He'd start by checking her room.

The stairs were just as clean as the downstairs corridor, and the upstairs corridor was the same. Surely if Keely had hired more help, he would have seen the maids cleaning. The only other explanation was that Keely had cleaned it herself. But when?

He opened the door to her room only to find it empty. And dusty.

He turned to Benita. "You can start in here."

He stepped aside to let Benita enter, then retraced his steps to his own bedroom with Rosa following close behind. He opened the door to a spotless room without so much of a speck of dust on the floor, let alone on any other surface.

"Rosa, check the rooms downstairs for Keely, please. I'll look up here." Wes followed the maid back into the corridor.

All the doors to the guestrooms looked to be shut up tight, so he walked to the first one, then the second and the third. All were empty, but all were extremely clean.

He checked the rooms on the east side of the house, then rounded the corner to the back of the house and started on the rooms that opened into the north corridor.

He found her in the third room from the end. She had shimmied the top half of herself under the bed, leaving her backside sticking up to greet him.

"What on earth are you doing?"

A thump sounded, causing the bedframe to move the slightest bit, and a string of muffled muttering to sound from underneath.

Keely inched herself backward, crawling on her knees while the top half of her still remained under the bed. The movements were so ridiculous he would have laughed—if he hadn't just found his wife crawling on the floor like an urchin.

"Wes? Is that you?" She finally pulled her head out from under the frame and pushed herself to a stand, holding a blue shirt out with enough pride to match that of a fisherman who'd just caught a prize fish on the Rio Grande. "There was a shirt under there."

"I see that. It's covered in dust... right along with you."

She glanced around. "These rooms are filthy. What do you expect?"

"Um... I expect my wife to look like my wife? You look like a parlor maid who just lost a war with a dust devil." He glanced around the room. "Why are you cleaning? And these rooms, of all places?"

"Because you told me to," Keely answered, wrinkles creasing her forehead. "You said in your letters it was the main reason you wanted a wife."

"I said I wanted you to work as the housekeeper."

She looked from him to the dusty shirt and back again. "I am being your housekeeper."

"No, you're being a parlor maid. The housekeeper oversees the running of the house. She makes sure rooms are being cleaned, bedlinens and dishes are getting replaced as they get worn out, laundry is getting done. But she doesn't do any of the work herself."

Keely's brows wrinkled into deep groves again. "Then what does she do?"

"I just told you. She oversees everything."

But would Keely know that? She hadn't come from wealth in Chicago, so she probably didn't know how a household of this size worked.

"So you expect me to be the housekeeper, but not do any work?"

Wes rubbed his temple. "You're supposed to *manage* the work."

"*Señor* Westin?" Rosa peeked her head into the room, then continued in Spanish. "I didn't find Mrs. Westin downstairs but..."

She trailed off as her gaze landed on Keely.

Wes stepped to the side so that both women could clearly see each other, then almost stepped back in front of Keely when he once again noticed how dusty she was. If the dust wasn't bad enough, her hair hung in two braids by her ears like she was a child still wearing pinafores rather than a grown woman. A grown, *married* woman.

It also didn't help that she was wearing a shapeless, gingham dress that was too loose in the shoulders and had certainly been purchased in a store rather than made by a seamstress to fit Keely's exact size. He had a dressmaker coming on Monday, but it would probably be a week before his wife had a suitable dress to wear.

Rosa, on the other hand, appeared fresh and clean. Her traditional Mexican shirtwaist with a scooped neck and wide ruffle around the collar looked much more stylish than anything he'd seen Keely wear.

He could only imagine the stories that would be swirling in Rosa's village when she returned to Mexico later.

"Keely, this is Rosa. She's one of the maids who comes over from Mexico three days a week. She's been working here the longest and has been in charge of the other maids since my previous housekeeper, Consuela, left."

"It's nice to meet you. I'm Keely." She stuck out her hand, probably expecting Rosa to shake it.

Rosa sent him a questioning look.

In the five years Rosa had been working at the A Bar W, he'd never once shaken her hand. It wasn't something an employer did when dealing with the staff. But Keely obviously didn't know that.

Finally, Rosa reached out and shook Keely's hand, then turned back to him, speaking in Spanish. "Now that you found your wife, what do you want us to clean for the rest of the day?"

"Do any of your maids speak English?" Keely looked between the two of them. "I don't know Spanish. How am I supposed to—"

"They speak English, right, Rosa?"

"Yes, we all speak English." The maid's words came out clear, with only the slightest accent. "Everyone on the border knows both languages."

"I see," Keely said, her voice short and clipped. "These rooms all need to be cleaned today. Every one of them is covered in dust." Keely held the shirt up for Rosa to see. "I found this under the bed, and it looks like it's been crammed there for months."

"That's because we only use these guest rooms once a year," Wes answered. "Once the maids tidy up after our house party every summer, we don't bother cleaning the rooms again until they are needed at the end of June."

She stared at him for a moment, her mouth opening, then snapping shut, then opening again. "You mean you didn't want all these rooms cleaned? Why didn't you tell me that before?"

"Maybe because I didn't know you were cleaning them. I wish you would have asked me about it."

"What was there to ask?" She threw her hands up in the air and started pacing, her determined steps scattering little plumes of dust across the floor. "You told me my job was to keep house, so I did. Now you're saying you didn't really mean for me to keep house, you just meant for me to be the house-keeper. As though there's some difference, and as though any of that let me know you didn't want the rooms at the back of the house cleaned."

He pressed two fingers to his temple, where he could feel a headache starting to form. It wasn't his fault she'd decided to play maid this morning and tried cleaning the entire hacienda by herself.

Wait. Had she cleaned like this yesterday too? And the day before?

Just how much time had she spent cleaning since he'd brought her home from Charlotte and Daniel's?

"What have you been doing for the past three days?" he barked.

"Cleaning. This place was a mess. Do you realize how quickly the floor gets dusty?"

He couldn't help the small smile that tipped the corner of his mouth. "I've lived on the desert my entire life, darling. I know how dusty it gets." But that didn't change the fact that he shouldn't have left her to herself for the past day and a half. When she hadn't come to him asking any questions, he'd assumed she'd contented herself in the library or studying the plants in the courtyard or cross-stitching. "I don't expect you to keep up with the dust. No one on the desert keeps up with it in a normal size house, let alone in a place this big."

Beside him, Rosa let out a giggle. He sent her a glare, but even that didn't stop a small smile from tilting the corners of her lips.

He'd be the talk of the town in Mexico tonight. And the talk of it in Twin Rivers tomorrow night, because this story was definitely going to make it back over the border. At this point, he'd be lucky if it didn't reach Austin. He could almost see the headlines plastered across the top of the society section in the newspaper: *Richest Rancher in Texas Makes New Wife Clean Mansion.*

Or *Westin Heir Says he Expects Wife to Work for her Place in his Household.*

"Come on." He put his hands on Keely's shoulders and steered her toward the door. He had to get her out of here before she gave Rosa more rumor fodder. "Rosa will finish cleaning in here, then make sure the rest of the rooms are shut up."

He looked over his shoulder at the maid, who wasn't even attempting to hide her grin anymore. "Once you, Benita, and Marisol finish with your tasks, take the rest of the day off. The three of you can resume your usual duties on Monday."

"Where are we going?" Keely asked as he led her into the corridor.

"Somewhere with lots of dust, and no broom or dustpan for you to try cleaning it up."

~.~.~.~.~

Wes had been right. Riding through the desert was incredibly dusty. Over the past three days, she'd discovered sitting atop a horse wasn't nearly as scary as she'd thought—except when Wes took her up a rather steep slope, like he was doing now.

Keely's hands gripped the reins of her horse, her legs tightening on the saddle as she tried not to look at how narrow the trail was or how far below the valley lay.

"Try to relax in the saddle." Wes had stopped his horse on the trail ahead of her and looked over his shoulder. "A horse can sense if you're nervous."

Relax, right. "I wouldn't be nearly so nervous if we were closer to the ground."

He chuckled. "The ground is right beneath us. What do you think the horse is walking on?"

"The ground isn't very close over there." She would have pointed at the valley that dropped away from the mountainside a few feet from the trail, but taking her hands off the reins seemed too dangerous, so she jutted her chin that direction.

"Do heights make you nervous? We can turn around and take another trail."

She swallowed. The only thing worse than going up the trail on a horse would be going down on one. At least now she had to deliberately look over the side of the trail to see how high she was. She'd not be able to avoid looking at the cliff and the valley far beneath it on the way down.

"Most people enjoy the views. I had no intention of frightening you." Wes dug his heels into his horse's side, which caused the beast to start trotting forward, even though Wes was still turned in the saddle looking back at her.

Keely clutched her reigns tighter. What if his horse walked off the trail and ended up going over the cliff? "I'm sure I'd enjoy these views too, if I handled myself in a saddle the way you do."

"Guess I didn't think about that either. Charlie was the last person I taught to ride a horse, and she was about four. Riding is just a way of life out here."

Riding, speaking Spanish, having a housekeeper who didn't keep house. The list of differences between Texas and the Midwest just kept growing.

"You seem like you're a quick study, though. I led Charlie around the paddock for two weeks before I took her on her first trail."

"I thought you said she was four?"

A smile spread across his lips. A real, true smile. It climbed from his mouth to his bunched-up cheeks to the faint lines around his eyes.

And it took her breath away. Her husband was too handsome. And that smile was going to haunt her dreams.

Or make her try goading him into more smiles.

Which was completely foolish. She didn't even know if she'd be able to stay in Twin Rivers.

"You never said whether you want to turn around."

Keely forced her gaze away from him and up the trail. "How much farther to the top?"

"Not much, maybe a quarter mile at most. But if you're miserable, we can find another trail."

"Let's keep going."

He sent her another smile, not as big as before, but it still caused a strange sensation to flutter in her stomach. Then he faced forward and led his horse higher up the slope.

He ended up being right. The view from the top of the mountain was so breathtaking that she forgot she was even sitting atop a horse. Mountain peak after mountain peak filled her view to the north and west.

"It's the most beautiful thing I've ever seen." And that was saying something, considering she'd spent most of her life near the blue water and sandy beaches of Lake Michigan.

"It's my favorite place to come." Wes tethered his horse to a shrub, then came toward her. "My sister likes the view from one of the ridges that drops down into a valley below. You can see quite a few mountain peaks from there too, but not as many as here. This makes me feel like I'm standing at the top of the world."

"It does." The sky was vast above them, going for miles and miles above the jagged mountains.

"Here, let's get you down."

There was probably some proper way to dismount, but Wes simply wrapped his hands around her waist, plucked her off the horse, and set her down again. He quickly ran his gaze down the length of her dress, then met her eyes. "I have a dressmaker from Austin scheduled to come on Monday. She'll bring different dresses with her and stay for about a week to alter them."

She glanced down at the dress she wore. "I already have several dresses. I really don't need more."

"You will when we go to Austin in the spring. Besides, once you see the dresses, I'm sure you'll find several that you like."

"I don't need anything fancy. You said you wanted me to be your housekeeper, remember?"

"Are Charlotte's dresses too fancy?"

Keely thought back to what Wes's sister had worn both for their wedding and the morning she'd gone to her house. "No."

"This is the same dressmaker that outfits Charlotte. If she can find suitable dresses for Twin Rivers, then I'm sure you can too."

But hadn't Charlotte said something about Wes not having money? Or maybe Wes had been the one to say that. So why spend money on something she didn't need?

Seemingly satisfied with the conversation, Wes turned and

led her horse—she didn't even remember its name—over to the same shrub as his and tethered it.

He returned with a blanket, which he then spread on the ground before going back to get a small basket. She couldn't help but watch him. His movements were effortless. He went from one task to the next to the next with smooth, fluid motions.

She hadn't known much about him when she'd gotten on the train in Springfield, but she'd not expected him to be so attractive. From his dark hair and high cheekbones to the confident manner in which he carried himself to the way he always had a smart, quick answer on the tip of his tongue. It was fine most of the time, when he was locked in his office working or spending time with Harrison. But when it was just the two of them, and she had nothing better to do than watch him...

He looked up for a moment, and their gazes met, causing the breath in her chest to still. *No romantic entanglements.* He'd laid that out right from the very first letter. So why was her heart suddenly playing traitor on her?

"Come and sit." Wes patted the blanket beside him. "Do you like ham?"

"I didn't realize we were having a picnic." She dropped to the blanket beside him, trying to ignore her leg muscles, aching from the ride in the saddle.

"Figured we'd be gone past lunch. It's not a short ride out here."

She picked up the sandwich, then moved her gaze back to the mountains. "How much of this do you own?"

"In that direction?" Wes shrugged. "All of it."

"You own all the mountains?" She couldn't stop the squeak in her voice. She hadn't known it was possible to own one mountain, let alone a dozen of them.

"Don't look that impressed. Rock-strewn mountains don't make for good cattle grazing. Now the valleys in between, especially if they have streams, can do nicely, but there's nothing all that great about having mountains on a ranch."

"It's like an empire."

"It's an empire full of headaches at the moment." He took a bite of the sandwich and chewed, completely oblivious to the stray crumb that lingered on his lower lip.

She drew in a breath, then looked away. Was she really so starved for company that she'd go and develop feelings for the first man who took her on a picnic?

But he wasn't the first man to ever take her on a picnic, just the first one to do so since she'd left Chicago. Surely that had something to do with the butterflies that had once again filled her stomach and the sudden warmth in her cheeks. It wasn't an attraction to Wes that was causing this reaction. It had just been too long since she'd done something so utterly normal.

Wes took a sip from his canteen. "When have you been cleaning my office?"

She shrugged. "You use it every morning, and you're usually awake just after dawn, so I clean it first thing. There're enough lamps in there that I don't need to wait until the sun is up."

"So this morning you cleaned it before dawn?"

She nodded, still chewing her bite of sandwich.

"Did you clean it yesterday too?"

She nodded and picked up a small round cookie of sorts. It looked as though it had some type of cream in the middle, but the entire thing was a faint pink color, even the cookie part.

"And when did you clean the corridor?"

"After I cleaned the parlor." She took a bite of the cookie.

It was like a piece of heaven exploded in her mouth. The cookie wasn't a cookie at all. The flavor in her mouth was light and airy, almost like taking a bite of a cloud. The entire thing, even the filling, was flavored like a berry. Strawberry, maybe. Or raspberry. She'd never eaten anything so delicious.

"Keely?"

She looked up to find Wes staring as though he expected another answer from her.

She quickly chewed the rest of her bite, though doing so felt wrong. The flavors in her mouth deserved to be savored. "I'm sorry. Did you say something?"

Wes glanced down at the cookie, then back up at her. "You like the macarons, I see."

"Is that what they're called? They're so light."

"They're some kind of French confectionary. Our chef says it's his grandmother's recipe."

"They are delicious."

"Here, try one of the lemon." He held one out to her. "And then you can tell me when you swept the corridor this morning."

Was that what he'd asked earlier? Why did he suddenly care about her cleaning? "After you were in your office and before Mr. Rutherford was awake."

He took his own bite of a brown macaron, staring out over the desert as he chewed. "I'm sorry I didn't explain what I expected of you as the housekeeper. Please know that I never intended for you to do any cleaning, just to oversee it. I don't want you up before dawn. I'm not sure what your schedule at the orphanage was, but you're in Twin Rivers now, and there's no need for you to keep a candle burning at all hours of the night."

"But you do."

A small smile curved the corners of his mouth. "I'm a poor example. I'll not have my wife working as much as I do. It's not healthy."

She tilted her head to the side. "Then why do you work so much?"

"At the moment? There's no choice. My father passed away in August, which left much to do in terms of settling the estate. But Father was ailing for nearly a year before that, and he made a mess of the ranch during that time. I'm still trying to dig my way out."

She ran her finger along the edge of the lemon macaron. "I don't mind cleaning. I can see you're horrified that I would spend my time doing it, though I don't have the faintest notion why. Everything needs to be cleaned at one point or another, and there's no shame in that. You told me you wanted a wife to make your life easier. And that's what I fully intended to do. But now that you know about the smuggling ring, it seems like I ended up making things more complicated instead. So don't feel bad about the cleaning. It gave me something to do to keep my mind off everything else."

Mostly. It had still been far too easy to think about Lester Mears while dusting. "Chances are, I won't be an obligation you'll have for very long, because I won't be able to stay."

Wes scowled. "Don't say that."

"It's the truth. You're too famous. Mears is bound to find me."

"Not if we get the law to find him first."

"I hope that's how it happens." And she did. Not just because she wanted justice for James and Cynthia. Not just because she was tired of running. But because sitting on the mountaintop with Wes, staring out at boulder-filled peaks in the distance, was almost peaceful.

She hadn't married Wes for love, but for the first time since she'd fled Chicago, she could see herself settling down and having a home in Twin Rivers.

She could see herself being content.

And somewhere deep inside, she wanted that more than anything else.

## 9

"Goodbye! Come again soon." Keely couldn't keep the smile off her face as she stood on the steps of the hacienda and waved to Anna Mae, Charlotte, and Ellie. Evidently Wes had sent word that she needed some company, and the three women had arrived after lunch to visit.

They'd sat in the ridiculously fancy parlor and drank tea and eaten cookies—though none of them had been as delicious as the macarons from the picnic yesterday. Anna Mae was full of stories. From ridiculous things Wes and Daniel and Sam had done as boys to hilarious kitchen mishaps, she kept everyone's attention as she talked. And then there was Charlotte's dry humor and Ellie's kindness and practicality. Combined together, the three women could lift anyone's mood—they'd even made her forget about Mears for a bit.

"See you tomorrow at church." Anna Mae looked over her shoulder and gave a final wave before swinging up onto her horse.

"Church?" She hadn't even thought of attending. She'd not been to church since she left Chicago. The fewer people who saw her around town, the better. But it would be awfully nice to hear a sermon and visit with her friends.

She bit the side of her cheek. Maybe Wes wasn't planning to go to church, and she wouldn't need to worry about making a decision.

He hadn't said anything one way or the other. In fact, she'd barely seen him since their horseback ride yesterday. He'd either been holed up in his office or out working the ranch.

At the moment, he was in his office. She wasn't quite sure why, but somehow she could tell when he was in the house. He had a way of filling the massive space, even when he was in a different room.

She headed down the corridor and knocked softly.

No one answered, so she turned the door handle and peeked inside.

Wes sat at his desk, shoulders slumped and head bent. His fingers rubbed little circles over his temples, like he was trying to scrub a headache away.

She moved to close the door, thinking she'd just return later, but he raised his head.

"Keely? Did you need something?"

"I can come back."

"I'm not busy, just in need of some willow bark tea." He gestured toward one of the empty chairs in front of his desk. "Come in."

She couldn't stop her fingers from twisting together as she came forward and slid into the chair. "I was wondering about church tomorrow. Are you planning to attend? Anna Mae is expecting me to go, but I'm not sure if I should."

"Yes, I usually attend. Pastor Russell is a good man. Does a lot to serve the town, and he preaches a good sermon too. Do you have a reason for not wanting to go?"

"No, no. I'd love to go. I haven't been in so very long. But with the Wolf Point Ring looking for me, and you being so well known, I'm not sure how much I should be seen."

"There will be a smaller crowd for church than there was for our wedding."

"Oh, I hadn't thought of that. I suppose just about everyone in town has already seen me... but... well..." Her fingers started twisting themselves again. "People might not remember me too well if they've only seen me once, but if I go to church every week..."

"If you don't go, that will make everyone more curious about you. People all across the county know that I've married. If I show up at church without my new wife, you'll get more questions than you ever would by going." Wes pressed his eyes shut and grimaced, then moved his fingers back to his temple, where he started rubbing again.

Keely jumped up from the chair. "I'm sorry. I'm making your headache worse, aren't I? Don't give church another thought. I can figure out what to do."

Wes gave his head a small shake, then winced, as though the movement had caused him more pain. "Don't apologize. These headaches have nothing to do with you and everything to do with my father."

"Your father... and the mess he left when he died?"

"Exactly." He didn't even open his eyes to look at her when he spoke.

"Is there something I can do to help with your paperwork?"

"No." Again he kept his eyes shut, his fingers pressed to his temple.

"Really, I don't mind helping. I don't have much else to do, and I'm more than willing to work. Charlotte said tonight that you sold cattle to buy into a railroad in a business deal your father arranged. I have quite a head for numbers. Maybe if I—"

"If I don't have a child, then when I die, the A Bar W and all our shares in the railroad won't go to Charlotte or our other sister, Mariah." He looked at her, a weary resignation in his eyes. "Instead, everything I own will go to Andrew Mortimer's offspring."

"Oh." She took a step back. Wes needed to have an heir? That wasn't the type of help she'd had in mind.

She didn't recall meeting anyone named Andrew or Mortimer. Why would he get the ranch if Wes didn't have an heir?

Wes was back to having his eyes closed, his fingers still rubbing his temples.

"Well, then maybe you should... ah..." She felt her face flushing. But they were married, if her husband needed an heir, there was only one logical way to get one...

And it involved her.

She nearly recoiled at the idea. She barely knew Wes. But she was still his wife, and it would be downright cruel to deny him the chance to keep his ranch and railroad holdings in the family.

Why had he said he didn't want any romantic entanglements in his letters? Had he not known he needed an heir when he started writing her? A child would bind them permanently together.

If Mears found her and she needed to leave Twin Rivers, walking away from Wes alone wouldn't pose near as much of a problem as walking away from a child.

Could she do it? Desert her own flesh and blood in order to stay alive?

Oh, she was getting ahead of herself. There was no sign that anyone from Chicago was on her trail, and the sheriff seemed to think the Wolf Point Ring could be caught.

"Your bedroom or mine?" she asked.

"What?" Wes blinked at her.

"Do you want to go to your bedroom or mine to... ah... for the... the child?"

He slammed his hand on the desk. "I am not having a child with you."

"But I thought you said—"

"What I said, is that I'm not having a child with you." His voice was so frosty, she could almost feel it seep into her skin and turn her blood to ice.

"Forgive me," she whispered, taking another step away from him. "I thought..." Her tongue came out to moisten her lips.

Wes's gaze remained dark and impenetrable.

"Never mind," she squeaked, then turned and fled the room.

~.~.~.~.~.~

HE WAS A MONSTER. An utter and complete monster. What had he been thinking to snap at Keely that way? Of course she'd run from him. He couldn't have sounded like more of a brute had he stayed up all night thinking of boorish things to say.

Wes looked down at the silver tea tray in his hand, set with tea, cream, sugar, and four raspberry macarons. Marceau had thrown a fit when he'd drug him away from the feast the cook had been preparing for dinner and told him to get the macarons ready that he'd started the previous day, but Wes had been insistent he have another batch of the airy cookies before he went and talked to Keely. Of course, the delicacies wouldn't make up for how he'd treated her, but hopefully they would at least make her willing to listen.

He knocked on the door.

No answer.

He opened it and stepped inside.

"Leave." Keely sat on the bed, arms crossed over her chest as she stared out the window.

"Er... I brought you tea."

"I said leave."

"And raspberry macarons. Marceau just put the finishing touches on them."

She picked a pencil up from her bedside table and hurled it. It hit him smack in the forehead, reigniting a bit of the headache the willow bark tea had calmed.

He set the tray atop her dresser before he dropped his mother's favorite china.

"That's not leaving." She shot off the bed and stalked toward him, her back rigid. "I said I want you gone. That means not here in my bedroom. That means not anywhere I can see you. I may be married to you, but I don't have to like you or spend time with you or talk to you."

She pushed at his chest, and he took a step back. Something told him that even Charlotte and Abigail, who were both taller and larger, didn't have the strength to push him with such force.

Keely reached out to shove him again, but he captured her hands with his own and held her still.

"My first wife died in childbirth, the baby with her." He blurted the words in a rush. Not smooth, not polished, not anything like the conversation he'd practiced in his head the entire time Marceau had been making the macarons. "Abigail died, and at her funeral, I promised myself I'd never do that to another woman again."

Keely stopped struggling to yank her hands away and look up at him. "Never do what again?"

"Get a woman with child."

Her tongue came out to moisten her lips. "Oh."

"I'm sorry for being so terse when I spoke earlier. I should have explained myself better, or maybe explained my position before now. I know Charlotte has told you some things about the ranch, but it doesn't appear anyone told you how my first wife died."

She shook her head.

"I want you to know that me not taking you to bed—not wanting to be a husband to you in the traditional sense—it has nothing to do with you." He pursed his lips. Everything was coming out wrong. "Or maybe it has everything to do with you, but not for the reason you think. I like you, Keely. I want you to live a long, happy life here on the A Bar W, which means I won't do anything to harm you, and I certainly won't get you with child."

"Because you think getting me with child will harm me?"

"Having a child..." his voice broke, and his eyes suddenly seemed to burn. "It killed Abigail."

"But you need a child to keep the ranch in the family." Her voice was soft, barely a whisper against the stillness of the room.

"I already have the death of one woman on my conscience. I'll not risk the life of another because my father put a draconian clause into a business contract. I'm working with Harrison to get myself out of it, mainly because I'd like to leave the ranch to Charlotte and Daniel and the children I'm sure they'll have one day."

She looked away from him and wrapped her arms around herself. "Thank you for explaining."

The hug looked so lonely and forlorn he had the unexplainable urge to wrap her in his own arms. Instead, he turned and headed for the door.

"Your letters said you wanted to marry me because you needed help around the ranch," she called from behind him.

He paused a few steps from the opening and turned back to her.

She still stood in front of the window with her arms

wrapped around herself. "You don't need my help, not really. And you don't intend to ever make me your wife in truth or have a child with me. So why did you marry me when you're still in love with your late wife?"

The burning sensation returned to his eyes, and his chest suddenly ached. "Abigail was my other half, my better half in every sense. I don't expect that to ever stop or fade."

"That doesn't tell me why you placed an ad for a wife."

"Because I had to have one."

Her brow furrowed, and he sighed. If the two of them were going to live together for the next forty years, then he needed to put effort into making things work for Keely, not just for himself.

He came back inside the room, sinking onto her bed and resting his elbows on his knees. "As you've already pointed out, I'm too wealthy and well-known for my own good. Abigail and I were young when we married. Before that, I went to parties in San Antonio and Austin and Houston when I traveled with my father on business, but I never paid much mind to the socialites who saw me as a potential husband, and I don't think anyone from the city expected me to get married so young. It all changed after Abigail died. It was like someone had taken an ad out in every newspaper in Texas. 'Wealthy bachelor looking for a wife. Any woman desiring a life of luxury and comfort may apply.'"

Keely snorted. "Clearly the people taking out that ad don't know you very well."

"Exactly." He closed his eyes as he continued speaking, allowing himself to remember his father's house party in July when Lydia had tried trapping him in the old bunkhouse and Charlotte had just happened to see them. Then he told Keely of San Antonio at the end of the cattle drive and Lucille showing up in his room.

"Those two women, Lydia and Lucille, they really did that

to you?" Keely had sat down beside him at some point, and one of her hands reached out to cover his on the bed.

"I'd decided to place an ad for a bride last summer after Lydia and the bunkhouse. By the time Lucille showed up in my bedroom, I was already writing you. In fact, I'd slipped your most recent letter in my pocket before the wedding."

"You had?"

He nodded, feeling heat creep up his neck. "Something in your letters resonated with me. You made me laugh rather than asked how many cattle I owned or if I had enough means to indulge in a feast at Christmas."

She blinked. "It never occurred to me to ask such things."

"Of course not, you were too busy trying to stay alive to worry about how big of a dinner we'd have over the holidays." He raked a hand through his hair. "Look, I know I haven't been the perfect husband. I forgot to explain that I didn't want you cleaning, and it's not that I mean to ignore you, but I can get quite distracted with work sometimes. But despite all that, I want you to understand that when I said my vows to you, I had every intention of honoring them until my death."

She looked up at him, her green eyes wide in the sunlight slanting through the window. "Except for the part about having and holding me, you mean."

He swallowed. "It conflicts with the part about loving and cherishing you. A person doesn't take someone he cherishes and put them in a position where they could get harmed."

He felt her go stiff beside him, but she remained silent.

Keely was staring down at her hands again. A lock of her curly red hair had fallen down, hiding most of her cheek from view.

He reached out and brushed the lock of hair over her shoulder, then waited for her gaze to meet his. "Placing an ad for a hardworking wife was unconventional, sure, but by going that route, I knew I'd be helping a woman who needed a home. Like

I said earlier, I'm not sorry for anything about our situation. God knew you needed help, and He knew I'd be able to provide it, as would Daniel. Even if I don't see myself ever sharing this bed with you, I see you as a gift from God to me. So we'll get this business with the Wolf Point Ring taken care of, and you can live a long, happy life here on the desert."

But even as he said the words, something about them felt empty.

A long happy life on the desert... living like strangers under the same roof?

Was that possible?

## 10

"This has been the most wonderful day." Keely slipped her hand into Wes's as the wagon jostled and bumped its way over the desert back toward the ranch. "I couldn't believe it when the Hardings invited us over for dinner. Mrs. Harding is so sweet, and she's beautiful, just like Anna Mae. Now I know where Anna Mae gets her loveliness from. I've never tasted such good Mexican food either. Well, truth be told, I don't suppose I've ever tasted Mexican food at all, but I'm sure what I just had was some of the best. I can still feel some of the flavors on my tongue. And I never imagined..."

She broke off when she noticed Wes was grinning at her. Grinning. Meaning his smile was so big it took up half of his face.

Something fluttered inside her stomach.

Her husband shouldn't be allowed to smile like that. It made him look far too handsome. "Why are you smiling?"

"You've barely stopped talking since we left town."

"That's because this was the most wonderful day I've had in eight months. The weather is perfect, I had church and a visit with friends all in one morning, and for a few minutes, I even forgot Mears is looking for me."

Wes turned his hand under hers and gave it a gentle squeeze. "I wish you would forget about Mears more often."

She sighed. "At least after this morning, I have reason to be of good courage. I know I've heard Deuteronomy 31:6 before, but I can't quite explain how comforting it is to be reminded that God won't fail or forsake me."

In fact, she still had the verse going through her head. *Be strong and of a good courage, fear not, nor be afraid of them: for the LORD thy God, he it is that doth go with thee; he will not fail thee, nor forsake thee. And the LORD, he it is that doth go before thee; he will be with thee, he will not fail thee, neither forsake thee: fear not, neither be dismayed.*

She couldn't say why the sermon impacted her so much. Maybe it was being out of church for eight months and hearing any sermon would have seemed wonderful, or maybe God had known just what she needed to hear that morning.

Wes gave her hand another squeeze. "You're safe in Twin Rivers, Keely. I sent for some guards last week. They should be here to help look after you by the beginning of November."

Guards. As in, a team of men to protect her? Wes had mentioned doing something like that, but hiring a bunch of extra men couldn't be cheap, and he'd already had to sell off cattle because of the business predicament his father had left him in. "I hope we don't need them for long."

Wes didn't say anything, just stared out over the desert. His face gave no hint to what he was thinking, other than that it was serious.

"Do you think we can go to church together again next week?"

The question drew his gaze back to her. "I make a habit of going every Sunday, and I have a standing invitation for dinner at the Hardings' afterward."

"Every week?" Her words came out more as a squeal than a question.

A ghost of a smile tilted the corners of his mouth. "Do simple things always make you so happy?"

"I don't know. Maybe." Going to church and having dinner with friends was probably simple, but her life had been so far from normal that anything other than running and hiding and looking over her shoulder felt like a treat.

The wagon crested the top of a hill, and the gateposts to the A Bar W came into view. A few more minutes and their lovely morning would end. "Is there anything you want me to do after we get back to the ranch?"

Wes slanted her a look. "Stop sweeping everything so the maids have something to clean tomorrow."

"It all gets so dusty!" She'd tried not to clean too much, but what was a woman supposed to do when there was a layer of dust on the floor and a perfectly good broom in the closet?

"It won't hurt you to take an afternoon off." Wes loosened his grip on the reins, letting the horses follow the familiar path to the barn. "This is supposed to be a day of rest, remember? Maybe read one of the books from the library or do some cross-stitching."

"So you're going to rest?"

"I have work."

"You always have work." She stared at the barn ahead. Each bump and jostle of the wagon brought Wes nearer to the point where he would disappear into his office for the rest of the day. Some ridiculous, romantic part of her didn't want him to. "Have a picnic with me tonight. You can work for a few hours this afternoon, but for supper, why don't we ride out to that mountain you love? We can make a habit of doing it every Sunday evening."

"A picnic?" The inflection in his voice made it sound as

though he'd never heard of such a thing. Never mind that their first picnic together had been his idea.

"Please. Didn't you say that mountain was your favorite place on the ranch? And it will be nice to get away from the house after you work for a bit."

He sighed, his shoulders rising and falling with the puff of breath. "All right. We can go on a picnic."

"Can we go on one next week too? And the week after that?"

He narrowed his eyes at her. "Has anyone ever told you that your persistence can get rather annoying?"

She laughed. "Only my brother and my father and my friends and the workers at the orphanage and just about anyone who knew me back in Chicago."

"We can try for a picnic on Sunday nights, but sometimes I might have to work."

"Thank you." Her heart felt ridiculously light as they crested the final hill and the yard came into view.

While she waited until it was time for the picnic, she'd do some reading like Wes had suggested. He had shelves and shelves of books on cattle breeding and grazing management. It wouldn't hurt to learn a thing or two about running a ranch.

Wes held her hand until he needed it to slow the reins for the wagon. Once they stopped, he walked around the side to help her down. When his hands wrapped around her waist, another swarm of butterflies took flight in her stomach, but if Wes felt anything strange, he didn't show it as he tucked her arm into his and led her across the yard.

They were partway to the house when he paused, a frown on his face.

"What's wrong?"

"Do you hear that? It sounds like something's crying."

She listened and could just make out a faint wail. "Where do you suppose it's coming from?"

He looked around. "Not the barn. We just came from that direction."

"The house, maybe? It could be a baby. Someone probably stopped for a visit."

"Maybe." But the frown stayed on his face. Sure enough, the closer he led her to the house, the louder the crying grew. "None of my friends have babies."

"Perhaps it's someone you're not that close to. An acquaintance that came from the city on business or something." They climbed the steps together. There was no question about where the wailing was coming from now. It sounded like there was a babe just inside the door—a rather upset babe.

Wes let go of her hand and pushed on the large wooden door, then stepped aside so she could enter first. A new round of wailing assaulted her ears. The chef stood on the other side of the door, still wearing an apron and a white hat. A brightly colored Mexican basket sat at his feet, and inside it lay a swaddled babe with a face red from constant hollering.

"What are you doing with a baby?" Wes had to shout at Marceau to be heard over the noise.

The Frenchmen shook his head, then shouted back, "It isn't mine. I don't know where it came from, but the crying was so loud I could hear it in the kitchen."

"Where are its parents?" Wes shouted.

"If I knew that, I wouldn't be standing here having my ears injured by that horrid sound." The man threw up his hands, then started muttering in French.

Keely sidled up to the basket. One look at the child's bunched up, angry face, and she felt like she was back in Chicago, working at the orphanage. She bent down and scooped the baby up, and a flood of warmth surged through her.

Yes, exactly like the orphanage.

She was small in her arms, but not quite a newborn. She'd guess her to be about four weeks old or so.

She gave the child a few bounces, and the wailing quieted but didn't stop completely. "There, there. Don't cry. Your mama will be back shortly."

"There's a letter," Wes said over the mewling.

Keely looked back at the basket. Sure enough, an envelope lay there with *Mr. Westin* printed clearly on the front of it.

He picked it up, then tore it open.

The babe chose that moment to start hollering again.

"There's no need for that." Keely patted her back. "Your mama will be here soon."

"No, she won't," Wes said.

"I beg your pardon?" Keely stuck the tip of her pinky in the child's mouth, and the babe began sucking fiercely.

"It doesn't appear that the child's mother will be returning anytime soon. She seems quite confident that we can care for him."

A baby? In the house with her and Wes?

She slanted a glance at her husband. His face had turned stark white, but his eyes flashed with fire. Did that mean he was angry or terrified?

Yesterday he had told her why he was so afraid to get a woman with child, but what if the birthing had already taken place and the child was alive and healthy? Was he opposed to having a babe in the house then?

The babe chose that moment to stop sucking on her finger and let out an ear-piercing wail.

Both the chef and Wes winced.

"Do you have a bottle?" She had to step closer to Wes to be heard above the noise.

It shouldn't be possible for her husband's face to get any whiter, but it did. He suddenly looked like he wanted to run outside retch into the shrubs. "Maybe. I... I think there are a couple in the attic."

"Then go get one and wash it. She's not going to calm down until she's fed."

"He."

"What?"

"It's a boy. The letter says his name is Leo."

She moved Leo up to her shoulder and gave him a few pats, but that served no purpose except to bring the screaming closer to her ear.

"Go find me a bottle, Wes. And Marceau, I'm going to need some warm milk."

~.~.~.~.~

WES RAN his hand down the rear flank of one of his longhorn cows, the feel of her muscles smooth yet strong beneath his hands. He moved his hand to her stomach next, which was already beginning to swell with the weight of the calf she carried.

"You feeling all right?" he crooned. "You getting enough to eat and drink?"

He'd specifically chosen her for breeding because of her medium build and desire to stay near the stream and eat grass in easy-to-find places. She didn't roam while grazing like some of his other cows. In fact, she was downright lazy.

The cow beside her was the same way, as was the one standing beneath the cottonwood tree. All the cattle in the valley where he stood had been chosen for their modest-sized builds and lazy qualities.

He was banking on that laziness producing tender, flavorful beef.

Wes raised his eyes to encompass the herd of nearly four thousand cattle he'd spent the last four years breeding. It seemed like a piddly amount of cattle compared to the seventy thousand head he owned, and yet he'd poured hours upon hours into selecting the cattle he wanted to breed, making sure the cows were impregnated, and ensuring the herd had some of the best grazing his property could offer.

By this time next year, he'd know whether his labor was worth it.

Most ranchers bred their largest bulls with their largest cows. After all, the more a heifer or steer weighed, the better price it brought at market. But the largest heifers and steers rarely produced the best beef, and for years his family had butchered the medium-sized, lazy cattle for their own food. The less a beast used its muscles, the softer those muscles were, leading to a more tender cut of meat.

To his knowledge, not a single rancher anywhere in the West had tried to breed cattle to produce a superior quality of beef. Everyone was interested in size and weight.

But if the beef that came from the prime herd tasted as good as the beef his family ate, he anticipated charging thirty-seven percent more per pound than he did for his other cattle.

And he fully expected the wealthy set in cities like Austin and San Antonio would pay for it.

He'd had ten steers butchered this year and had sold the meat directly to business acquaintances and restaurants when he'd been in San Antonio. He'd already gotten over a dozen letters from people asking if they could purchase more beef directly from him.

"There you are."

Wes jumped, then turned to find Harrison approaching on his horse.

"A man has to cross half your ranch to find you these days."

Wes ran a hand along the backbone of the cow closest to him. "Didn't realize you were looking for me."

"There's a baby in your house."

"I'm aware." It was what had driven him out here.

He'd tried to work in his office, but his mind had been too busy replaying the sight of Leo lying in that basket for him to focus. Then when it was time for the picnic, he'd gone to get Keely, only to find her frazzled and trying to comfort a wailing Leo. She'd said it wasn't a good night for an outing.

Wes had hoped getting out of the house would help clear his mind, but even riding out to check his herd hadn't been able to make him forget the writhing, crying infant Keely had scooped out of that basket.

Or the terrible feeling in his gut as he'd gone to the attic and rummaged around for the bottles Abigail had bought when she was expecting.

He'd gotten the baby clothes that had been in the attic too. Abigail had sewn most of the outfits, and he hadn't been able to get rid of them after her death, just like he hadn't been able to get rid of the majority of Abigail's things. They were all stored away and had been nearly forgotten.

Until Leo.

Wes scrubbed a hand over his face. How could he look at another baby wearing clothes that had been meant for his own child?

How could he watch Keely feed him with a bottle that had never touched the lips of his stillborn daughter?

"You all right?" Harrison asked.

Wes blinked, then turned to find Harrison had tethered his horse and now stood beside him.

"Fine." Or he would be once Leo's mother returned. "Is there something you wanted?"

"I had an idea about that contract with the Mortimers."

The Mortimers. Yes, perfect. That discussion might actually prove a worthy distraction. "What did you come up with?"

"Have you tried talking to them about the contract? Seeing if they'll let you out of it since Charlotte didn't marry Andrew?"

Wes grimaced. "I met with Charles Mortimer when I went to San Antonio for the cattle drive. He laughed when I brought it up, then told me a contract was a contract. It couldn't be broken."

"Can't say I'm surprised." Harrison readjusted his hat on his head. "I imagine Mortimer relishes the thought of one day seeing his son own the A Bar W."

"Andrew wouldn't know what to do with it."

"That's probably true." Harrison reached out and rubbed the nose of the cow nearest him. "I've thought of a couple different ways to approach this. It involves filing a lawsuit."

Wes bit back a groan. Just how much money would that cost? "Are you sure that's our only option?"

"Quite sure. There's no loophole I can find in the contract itself, and though one would expect to find a clause in the contract that declares it void if Charlotte and Andrew don't marry, there's nothing about what happens if the marriage doesn't take place."

Wes looked at his friend. "So what would this lawsuit claim?"

"That your father was too impaired at the time the contract was signed to realize what he was doing."

"He was." Wes scrubbed a hand over his face. If only he'd realized how sick his father had been. If only he'd realized just what the business negotiations his father had been working on entailed. But instead of barging into the office and demanding details, he'd busied himself with his prime herd and other goings on about the ranch. "What's the other option for the lawsuit?"

"We claim there was an unwritten understanding that

Charlotte would marry Andrew Mortimer and be part of the Mortimer family when the contract was signed."

"That's true as well, but is something that was unwritten submissible in court?"

"It is if you can prove it. Did you ever hear your father say Charlotte and Andrew were going to marry?"

"I did, as did Charlotte and numerous others. It was pretty much all Father talked about before his death."

"Then I'll add both arguments to the lawsuit, but I suspect Charles Mortimer will make it a long, drawn-out battle."

Wes rubbed his head. "If that's the case, I best sell you a couple shares of railroad stock."

Harrison grew silent beside him. "Are you that hard-pressed for money?"

"For cash, yes." Especially after hiring guards for Keely. That had wiped out every last bit of extra money he had, and it would put him down two ranch hands on the northern part of the property. "I sold as few cattle as I could to pay for the railroad, but I knew things would be tight for the next year or so. If I take more cattle to market this late, I won't get a good price for them. I'd rather sell a percentage of the railroad."

"I'll draw up a contract for that when I get back to the ranch, and I should be able to have a bank draft to you within a couple weeks."

"Good." Wes gave a sharp nod. "Now tell me more about the lawsuit."

"Our biggest obstacle to claiming your father was too ill to make a rational judgment will likely be the railroad contract. Mortimer's lawyer will argue that deal shows your father was still competent, since it's a good investment for your family."

"Do you think there's any chance they'll let the contract go once we start legal proceedings?" Wes shifted on his feet. "If at all possible, I'd like to settle this out of the courtroom."

Harrison shrugged. "The Mortimers have a lot to gain by

keeping the contract as is, but you could try sending Andrew a letter and seeing what he has to say."

"You think that will do any good after his father laughed me off?"

"The contract is pretty one-sided and seeks to circumvent well-established inheritance law." Harrison's voice took on an edge as he spoke. "Perhaps Andrew Mortimer isn't so fond of his father's way of doing business."

Of course Harrison would say that. He certainly wasn't going to be running Fort Ashton after his father died. "I'll write to Andrew, but even if he agrees I should be released from the contract, his father is still going to want it kept intact."

"Having Andrew on your side will all but guarantee a judge will rule in your favor, which Charles Mortimer's lawyer is sure to know. If you want this settled quickly and cheaply, your best bet is to sway Andrew. And if you can't bring Andrew over to your side, he still might say something in his letter to you that will prove useful in court."

He'd write the letter that night. It certainly wouldn't hurt to see what Andrew had to say. "When will the legal documents be filed?"

"As soon as I get back to Austin."

Wes raised his eyes to scan the cattle, then the peaks of the small yet jagged mountains surrounding them. "When I stand here and look at the cattle and the land, I can't imagine it going to someone who isn't part of the family."

"You mean Charlotte?"

"I'm not about to leave the ranch to Mariah," he quipped.

Harrison chuckled.

Mariah lived in Austin with her husband. Harrison saw them often enough and was more than familiar with the endless parties and social events and garish displays of wealth that Mariah loved.

"I wasn't talking about Mariah." Harrison's dark gaze bored into him. "I meant you and Keely."

Wes grew still. "I thought I already explained we won't be having children."

"But what if—"

"Don't," he rasped, then swallowed the lump that had stuck in his throat. "I just... not right now, all right?"

There were some things he just couldn't bring himself to talk about...

At least not while there was a baby in his house, drinking out of his daughter's bottles and wearing clothes from her layette.

## 11

**K**eely woke to silence. Utter complete silence.

A quick glance at the cradle beside her bed told her little Leo slept peacefully. But for how long? He'd screamed most of the night, and a bottle had only satisfied him half the time.

Poor thing. She reached down to stroke a hand over the downy tuft of hair growing on his head, then looked at the bedside table, where the letter from his mother sat.

From her position on her stomach, she could just make out the words.

*Dear Mr. Westin,*

*I was told you could care for my son Leo. If I am able, I will return for him. If not, I know he will be in good hands.*

Something hard formed in Keely's stomach.

Though she'd worked at the orphanage in Chicago, most of those children's parents had died. What would possess a mother with a healthy babe to give her child to complete strangers?

The mother's situation must be grave.

But was it any graver than her own? If she had a child,

would she not have found someone to care for it when she fled Chicago? In fact, part of why she'd left Chicago so quickly was because she hadn't wanted the Wolf Point Ring to turn its attention to the orphanage. If they were willing to harm Cynthia in an attempt to intimidate James, what would stop them from harming the children?

Keely laid back in her bed and stared at the ceiling. Yes, if she'd had a child, she would have left him behind in Chicago. Being separated would be hard, but nowhere near as unbearable as seeing her child killed because he'd stayed with her.

*Dear God, I don't know what situation Leo's mother is in, but please protect her. Please bring her back safely to her child.*

Whoever Leo's mother was, she'd probably looked at the A Bar W, saw Wes atop his fine horse and dressed in his expensive clothes, and assumed he'd have no trouble caring for a child.

But each time Wes had seen her with little Leo yesterday, he'd grown pale and left the room.

When he'd gone to the attic, he'd brought down not just bottles, but clothes that had clearly been hand-sewn and little toy animal figures that had been hand whittled...

By Wes?

Keely reached for the horse she'd placed on the table next to the letter, and a weight settled over her chest. The horse was perfect, an exact replica of Ares running over the desert.

How long had it taken Wes to carve such a toy?

And what was it costing him to give it to another child?

~.~.~.~.~

"THAT WAS FAST." At the sight of Daniel entering the dining room, Wes set his croissant down and gestured to the buffet laden with scrambled eggs, bacon, and croissants. "Have something to eat."

Harrison frowned at him from across the table. "There's no way Dobbs made it into town that fast."

Daniel, who still stood in the doorway, looked between the two of them. "I have no idea what you two are talking about. Was I supposed to talk to Dobbs?"

"You mean you didn't?" Wes straightened in his chair. He'd sent Dobbs into town to tell Daniel about the baby. "Then why are you here?"

"Because Jonas arrived." Daniel took a couple steps inside the room, revealing another figure standing behind him.

He was tall, with reddish-brown stubble covering his jaw and clear green eyes that seemed to take in everything about the room in a single glance. Wes had seen the face a time or two before and knew the man was a U.S. Marshal, but he couldn't have given his name.

"Marshal, hello." Wes stood and shook the man's hand. A bit of dust clung to his clothes, but he certainly looked like he'd changed and shaved before heading out to the ranch. "Have you had breakfast?"

"I had a bite or two at the sheriff's office, but those croissants look mighty good, as does the bacon."

"Help yourself." Wes gestured to the food.

The marshal headed to the buffet and filled his plate.

Daniel moved to the buffet behind the marshal but only poured himself a cup of coffee. "We came here as soon as Jonas arrived so he could talk to Keely."

"Talk to Keely about what?" Harrison said.

"So you're not here about the baby?" Wes spoke at the same time.

"Baby?" Daniel's brows drew down. "What baby?"

"The one that was left here while we were at church yesterday," Wes plopped back into his chair.

"It's true." Harrison shoveled another bite of food into his mouth. "There's a baby here, all right. His name is Leo."

"Do you have any idea where it came from?" Daniel leaned back against the buffet, his eyes narrowed and coffee cup forgotten.

"I wish I did. There was a note asking us to care of him until the mother returns, and that was it." Wes took another bite of croissant.

"Where's the baby now?"

"With Keely," he muttered. It was all he could do to keep an image of his wife from rising in his mind, her arms gently cradling the infant as she tried to quiet his squalling.

"And that's a bad thing?" Daniel asked.

*Yes.* But he wasn't about to explain why. "What are we supposed to do with him? Does he need to go to an orphanage while we search for his mother? Are we allowed to keep him here? The note said we should, but I don't know what's legal."

"Not sure." Daniel rubbed the back of his neck, looking right comfortable from where he still leaned against the buffet. "Let me check on that."

"If the child was given to you, and you have a note to prove it, then no, it doesn't need to go to an orphanage." The marshal left the buffet and walked around the table to sit beside Harrison.

"He's right." Harrison speared a clump of eggs with his fork. "The note means you effectively have permission from the parent to care for it."

"For how long?" And why hadn't Harrison thought to tell him this last night?

"Until either the mother returns or eighteen months have passed. If the child goes eighteen months without contact from his mother, then it's considered legal abandonment. You can petition the court to have the mother's parental rights terminated and adopt the child." Harrison put the forkful of eggs into his mouth and chewed.

"How can we have parental rights terminated if we don't know who the mother is?" Wes leaned forward over the table.

Harrison shrugged, then swallowed his bite of food. "Abandonment is abandonment. You don't need to know the mother's name to have it proved in a court of law. In fact, had the baby been dropped off at an orphanage rather than a private residence, the mother's parental rights would already be considered terminated."

Eighteen months. Wes thrummed his fingers on the tabletop. He couldn't keep the child that long. Every time Leo cried, he couldn't help but remember how he'd never gotten to hear the sound of his daughter crying.

"Looks like y'all are having a party and forgot to invite me," a lazy voice drawled from the doorway.

Wes turned to find his childhood friend, Cain Ramos Whitelaw, standing in the entrance to the dining room. The Texas Ranger had been gone from Twin Rivers for three months, and he looked like he'd spent every last bit of it on the trail. He was covered in dust from the top of his hat down to the tips of his boots, he hadn't shaved in several days, and the wavy blond hair that had been far too long before he'd left now fell to the middle of his back.

He wore guns on both hips rather than just his right one like most men, and he stepped into the room with his trademark saunter, making him look both careless and dangerous at the same time.

"Harrison," Cain nodded his direction, then jutted his chin toward the marshal, who was now eating one of Marceau's legendary croissants. "Jonas."

If Cain was surprised to see either one of the men, he didn't show it. He paused beside Daniel at the buffet, gave him a long, slow perusal, then slapped him on the back.

"Looks like you're recovered. Glad to see it." Cain took a plate and began heaping food onto it, not that Wes could blame him. Cain and the men he commanded had probably been living on jerky and hardtack for the last several days.

"Did you find the rustlers?" Daniel set down the coffee he'd been nursing and grabbed a plate from the buffet.

Cain snorted as he piled bacon onto his plate. "In a manner of speaking. There's a few less rustlers to contend with, but the ring itself isn't gone, if that's what you mean. My men and I were called back to Austin for a few weeks. That's part of why we've been gone so long."

Daniel followed Cain down the buffet, serving himself a much more reasonable portion of eggs and a single croissant. "So what's the plan?"

"To meet Wes's new wife." Cain left the buffet and walked around the table, setting his plate down beside the marshal's. "Heard she has a head of curly red hair."

"You came out here to meet Keely?" Wes slanted a glance at Cain. "Since when do you care about my family affairs?"

"Came as soon as I heard about her hair. Was curious to see if she looked anything like this." Cain handed him a rolled-up piece of paper that had been tucked into his gun belt. "Been carrying it in my saddlebag since Austin."

Wes rolled out the unusually large paper, glanced at it, then froze.

The word "Wanted" was printed in large, bold type on the top of the poster, but just beneath it...

No. It couldn't be.

His heart pounded against his chest, and sweat dampened his hairline. There had to be some mistake.

He squeezed his eyes shut, but doing so didn't erase the image of Keely staring back at him from beneath the word "Wanted."

"That's his wife?" The marshal asked, standing to get a

better look at the poster from the opposite side of the table. "The woman who's been on all the posters?"

"That's what I'm here to find out." Cain scooped a mound of eggs onto his fork and shoveled it into his mouth. "Part of the job an' all."

"What's she wanted for?" Daniel stepped up beside him, the scent of his bacon making Wes's stomach curdle.

Wes forced himself to read the small print at the bottom of the poster. "It says double murder in Chicago."

He'd believed her story about the Wolf Point Ring, smuggling, and fleeing for her life. Had she'd been lying? Had her elaborate story been a cover so she could run from a crime she'd actually committed?

Wes drew in a breath, trying to regain a semblance of calm.

No. It wasn't possible. Not from the woman who begged him to go on picnics, cleaned his entire house without a word of complaint, and was right now upstairs cuddling a baby that wasn't hers.

Besides, she had a mountain of papers to back up her claims about the Wolf Point Ring.

"She didn't do it." His voice was so hard it echoed off the walls.

"But the woman in that picture is your wife." Cain met his gaze across the table.

"No."

"Yes." Daniel answered at the same time.

"I'm not saying she doesn't look like my wife, but..." Wes glanced at the image again. Could Keely have a sister she hadn't mentioned? "It can't be her. It just can't."

"Turns out the woman on the poster has a fondness for arsenic, and I'm wondering if your wife has the same." Cain leaned back in his chair, shoved another forkful of eggs into his mouth, then spoke around his food. "Where is she, if you don't mind my asking?"

"Would it kill you to have a little sympathy?" Daniel growled. "Wes is right. This situation isn't what you think. The poster says the murders were committed in Chicago on August twenty-fourth. But Keely was in Springfield by that time, wasn't she?" Daniel nudged him. "Don't you have letters from her postmarked from Springfield at the end of August?"

Wes dragged another breath into his lungs, though the fresh bout of air only seemed to make his chest burn. "I do. Let me get them."

He stood and started for the door, but Keely chose that moment to step into the room, holding a quiet Leo snuggled against her chest.

Of all the times for her to appear. Couldn't she have waited a half hour or so? Given him and Daniel time to tell Cain and the marshal about the Wolf Point Ring?

"Oh, goodness." She looked around the room, then her gaze sought his. "I didn't realize you had company. I'll come back later."

"I... uh..."

"Actually, why don't you sit down." Daniel stood and scooted out a chair for her. "We were just discussing something that concerns you."

Keely's gaze flew to Daniel, and she stiffened. "You're here about the baby, aren't you? I'm not giving him away to anyone but his mother."

Harrison chuckled, and the marshal raised an eyebrow.

"As you can see, Daniel and my wife aren't exactly best friends." Wes wrapped an arm around Keely's shoulders, then glanced at the doorway. He could still steer her out of the room and call her back later. Daniel, Cain, and the marshal would probably be livid, but it was his house and she was his wife.

Wes drew in a breath, forcing himself to stay calm. The men at the table just had questions for her, much like he did. Sure, his blood had half a mind to start boiling on him. But it wasn't his face on the wanted poster, and he was confident Keely hadn't poisoned two elderly women with arsenic. That meant he needed to control himself for Keely's sake.

He guided her farther into the room, his arm still wrapped tightly around her shoulders. "Keely, this is Mr. Jonas Redding. He's a U.S. Marshal out of the San Antonio office."

"I see." Keely had been stiff before, but at the mention of the marshal, her entire body turned to stone, her grip on the baby going from tender to tense. He'd give the child about twenty seconds before he started squalling, and Keely didn't even know about the wanted poster yet.

A distraction was in order. Wes used the arm on her shoulders to turn her toward the buffet. "Have you eaten? Marceau made croissants."

"I'm not hungry."

"You need to keep your strength up if you're going to care for Leo. Here, let me hold him while you fix yourself a plate."

Not that he wanted to hold the baby, but he didn't want to look ridiculous trying to avoid Leo either.

She handed him the babe without further comment and dished a few things onto her plate.

Good. He'd get some food in her, they'd talk about the Wolf Point Ring, and then—after Cain realized that there was a group of dangerous men searching for Keely—they could discuss the wanted poster.

But when Keely turned from the buffet, her eyes locked with Cain's. "Who's the outlaw, and why is he sitting here with a marshal and a sheriff?"

Harrison burst into laughter. "You hear that, Cain? Better cut that hair of yours. Everyone thinks you're on the wrong side of the law."

"Maybe I want it that way," Cain drawled.

"He's the law, Keely," Wes answered. "Not an outlaw, a Texas Ranger. Cain Whitelaw."

Her gaze jerked to his. "You called in the rangers too?"

"Not for you. He's here for the rustling."

"Rustling?" She plopped herself into an empty chair, then picked up her croissant.

Wes slid into the chair beside her, with little Leo tucked against his chest. The child wasn't sleeping quite yet, but Leo seemed downright content burrowed in the crook of his shoulder. "Earlier this year we discovered a rustling operation that was taking cattle across the border into Mexico, where they can't be recovered. They had quite a large outfit, and Cain has been in and out of Twin Rivers trying to track down the rustlers since summer."

"Were any of your cattle stolen?"

"About two thousand head, yes."

"Two thousand? But..." She turned toward Cain, her eyes narrowed. "Did you catch the men who took my husband's cattle, Mr. Whitelaw?"

Cain tilted his head to the side, studying Keely in a way that made a hard ball form in Wes's stomach.

Wes sent Cain a tight smile. "Actually, Keely, why don't we talk to the marshal before—"

"Haven't caught 'em yet. But I will." Cain smirked. "Now it's my turn to ask questions, darlin'. You ever spent the night in jail?"

"What kind of a question is that? Of course I haven't spent the night in jail." She took a bite of her croissant.

"Then maybe you'd care to explain why your face is on a wanted poster with the name Nora O'Leary beside it."

"Stop," Wes snapped. "This is no way to ask her about the poster. Your questions'll be answered better if you let her talk to Jonas first."

"My name's on a wanted poster?" Keely whispered.

"Take a breath." Wes ran his free hand along the top of her shoulder, but it did little to soften her tense muscles.

"What does it say? Why am I on there?"

"Like I said, let's talk to the marshal first, then we can—"

"It says you killed two women with arsenic poisoning at the end of August." Cain spoke over him.

"Arsenic? Me?" Panic creeped into her voice. "With my real name? I wasn't using my real name at the end of August, and I've never purchased arsenic before. I wouldn't know how to get some if I wanted it."

Wes gave Keely's shoulder a gentle squeeze. "No one in this room thinks you committed murder."

"We don't?" Cain drawled.

He shot Cain another warning glance, but the look that would have most people in Twin Rivers searching for a place to hide was lost on him.

"I think the Wolf Point Ring is trying to flush you out." Daniel pulled out the chair beside Keely and sat, never mind his coffee was on Wes's opposite side. "They don't know where you went, and they hope if they plaster your face on a bunch of posters, someone will report where you are."

"They're going to find me, aren't they?" She pressed her eyes shut, her face turning pale.

"No, they're not." Wes gave her shoulder another squeeze, but it felt about like trying to crush a rock with his bare fist.

"Two questions." Cain leaned back in his chair and crunched off a piece of bacon, not bothering to finish chewing before he spoke again. "Who's the Wolf Point Ring, and why do they want to find you?"

"I can answer that." The marshal pulled a familiar-looking stack of papers out of his satchel. "It's a smuggling gang that's bringing opium into Chicago illegally, evading the tariffs. The U.S. Marshal's office has suspected smuggling activity on Lake Michigan for some time, but our last break in the case was two years ago, when we uncovered an arm of the ring led by Warren Sinclair, a wealthy businessman who had been set to inherit a shipping company. After that, our information went dark... until Keely's brother came to us with proof of who was involved."

"You already knew about the ring?" Keely had been pushing eggs around on her plate, but when the marshal stopped talking, she looked up.

"Vaguely, yes. I've seen the file at the headquarters in Austin before because it's been a particularly difficult case for the Chicago office. There was a bulletin sent out sometime last spring asking the other marshals' offices if they might have any information pertaining to the Wolf Point Ring." He riffled through the stack of papers, then handed one to Cain. "Here's the list of people we expect are involved. We only know this thanks to Keely's brother James."

Cain let out a low whistle. "The chief of police and the mayor? That's not an easy group to take on."

Keely looked down. "I just want them to answer for their crimes, for what they did to Cynthia and my brother."

"And this Wolf Point Ring knows you have information against them?" If Cain wondered who Cynthia was or what had happened to Keely's brother, he gave no hint of it.

"They must. Why else would they have tried following me when I left Chicago? But it's been so long, I'd thought they'd given up looking for me."

"Not if there are wanted posters of you plastered in every major city from here to Chicago." Cain gave his head a curt nod.

"There's that many posters?" Keely's hand tightened around her water glass.

"Yes, so many of them that I became suspicious of the posters themselves. One usually doesn't find that number of posters of a wanted person, especially of someone who's committed a crime so far away from Texas."

"We don't have any in Twin Rivers yet," Daniel said. "But it's been about six weeks since I got my last mailing of posters. I'm due for a new shipment any day, and yours will probably be in it."

"No, I didn't spot posters in any of the small towns between here and Austin, just in the cities," Cain answered.

"Can I see it?" Keely's voice was so quiet, Wes could barely make it out.

Cain drew up the poster from where it had been on the floor near his chair and slowly unrolled it. A fairly good semblance of Keely stared back at them, curly hair and all.

She let out a little gasp, then looked away, a tear streaking down her cheek. "They're going to find me. There's no help for it."

"Don't say that." Wes reached out and settled a hand on her cheek, then turned her head and waited until she brought her gaze up to his.

Tears brimmed, but beyond the watery film, her normally bright green eyes were dull and resigned.

He tucked a strand of hair behind her ear. "We'll protect you. I promise."

"Everyone in town knows what I look like." Her tongue slid out to lick her lips. "Half the county showed up for our wedding, and I was at church yesterday."

"Daniel's not going to let any of those posters get hung around Twin Rivers. And if someone from town sees a poster somewhere else and reports you, I've already told you I hired guards to pose as cowhands. If we need to hire Pinkerton agents to dig up more information in Chicago, I'll do that too. Trust me, Keely. Please."

A hint of color climbed into her cheeks, turning them the loveliest shade of pink. She looked at him without blinking, her eyes wide and large. It was all he could do to not lean forward and rest his forehead against hers, or scoop her into his lap and hold her there until her worries melted.

"I don't think the posters pose a big threat to you." Daniel's voice sounded like it came from far away.

But at the sound of it, Keely jerked away from him and glanced at Daniel, then ran her gaze slowly around the table.

Wes sent his friend a glare. Couldn't Daniel see he'd been trying to calm Keely down? That he'd been succeeding until he'd been interrupted? Now Keely was back to being as tight and prickly as the barbed wire that ran the perimeter of his ranch.

"At least, I don't think the posters are much of a threat at the moment," Daniel continued. "Cain here says these posters were all around the city, but cities are so crowded and there are so many wanted posters hanging everywhere that most people don't even take notice of them. As long as the local sheriffs who get sent posters don't hang the ones of you up, I doubt anyone from Austin or San Antonio will remember your poster by the time they get to Twin Rivers."

"But what if the sheriffs around here hang the posters of me?" Keely dabbed at the corner of her eye with a handkerchief.

"I doubt they will. I get far more posters than what I can hang sent to me. I put up the ones with crimes committed in West Texas. Every once in a while, I'll hang a poster for someone wanted in East Texas or New Mexico. But I'd never bother hanging a poster from Illinois, nor would any of the other sheriffs that I know around these parts."

"All right." She dabbed at the corner of her eye again and let out a small sniffle.

"Nora, or Keely, or whatever you'd prefer to be called, I need to ask you questions about some of these papers." The marshal sifted through the file Keely had turned over to Daniel. "I could be misremembering, but I think you have more evidence here than what we have in Austin. Do you know where this page came from?"

She glanced at the page Jonas held out, then shook her head. "From the same place as everything else. James got ahold of it somehow."

"And where is James?"

"Dead, of course. Like Cynthia."

"I didn't think his body had been found."

She shook her head. "I don't know that it has been, but if the Chicago chief of police can frame me for two counts of murder that I didn't commit, then he can kill James and make his body disappear."

"Do you have questions about something besides her brother?" Wes's words came out harsher than he intended, but he saw little point in rehashing the circumstances of her brother's death.

"I do, as a matter of fact." Jonas repositioned himself in his chair.

And then they started, one question after another after another. Sometimes Cain jumped in with a question of his own, every once in while Daniel asked for clarification of some sort, and Harrison offered legal advice once or twice.

The life slowly drained from Keely. He could see it with each question that she answered. Her shoulders slumped, and the rest of her body seemed ready to melt into the chair. Her words turned to whispers, and she didn't raise her bent head once to meet the eyes of the three lawmen surrounding her.

Wes wanted to make it stop. To spirit her away from the questions and painful memories. To wipe away all that had happened in Chicago.

But he just sat there, jostling Leo if he started to awaken, gripping Keely's hand under the table when she looked ready to burst into tears...

And trying to hold together the ramshackle family he'd been given.

## 12

Harrison rolled his shoulders and tugged on his horse's reigns as Toronto trotted over the desert. Normally he wouldn't complain about Toronto's brisk pace, but he was in no mood to visit his father today. Just like he hadn't been in a mood to visit his father yesterday, or the day before that, or the one before that.

Yet he'd gone every day since arriving in Twin Rivers, hoping to find information on any of the three Mexican men who had disappeared so he could hand it over to the very marshal that had sat at Wes's dining room table that morning.

Since none of his friends knew the true reason he'd come to Twin Rivers, he'd opted for passing Jonas a note and some papers he'd collected before he left the A Bar W rather than trying to have a conversation. The fewer people who knew he was spying on his father, the better.

Harrison sighed and scanned the desert as Toronto ambled along the rocky path. There were things he missed about Twin Rivers. The slower pace of small-town living, the way every person he met had a smile for him, the time he could spend with his friends...

The desert itself.

Part of him had always loved the wide-open space, the craggy mountains that boasted more shrubs than trees, and the fertileness of the Rio Grande Valley. Austin was far too crowded and hurried. He could count only a handful of times he'd enjoyed himself in the city, and most of those were when Sam or Wes or Cain had come to visit.

But he'd wanted to put space between him and his father and earn a living for himself, and that had meant leaving the town he'd grown up in.

Now three more days was all the longer he could afford to stay in Twin Rivers.

Toronto crested a small hill, and Harrison looked down to find a familiar figure atop a horse in the valley. Jonas.

He dug his heels into Toronto's side.

"Harrison." Jonas gave him a nod as he approached. "Headed to Fort Ashton, I see."

"Did you have a chance to look at the papers?" he asked.

"All they had was proof of the price of Mexican goods being devalued in Twin Rivers and rumors about the trail being dangerous." Jonas repositioned his hat over his head, the ruddy stubble on his chin making him look half outlaw. "There wasn't anything about the missing men."

"That's because I haven't uncovered anything. That fort sees so many people in and out that no one remembers who was there the day before, let alone a month ago. I've been going there every day. My pa thinks he's convincing me to take over the fort in a few years." Harrison didn't even try to disguise the disgust in his voice.

"Why aren't you staying at the fort?"

"Have you ever met my father?"

Jonas didn't so much as frown. His lips remained flat, his eyes void of any emotion. "Seems like you'd have a better idea what's going on if you were staying there."

Maybe, but he wasn't trained to collect information on people the way a lawman was. "Send a marshal to stay inside the fort. He can pretend to be a trader."

"It won't be the same."

Harrison rubbed the back of his neck. "I'm going to give myself away. This pretending to do one thing while really trying to do another, it's just not me. I want to find Hernando as much as anyone, but—"

"No, you want to find out what happened to Hernando. It's been six weeks since his mother reported he didn't return from his trip. You're not looking for a missing person. You're looking for something that will lead us to his body. The same with Carlos and Diego."

His gut churned. He'd wanted to do more for Inez. When he'd agreed to come to Twin Rivers, part of him had actually thought he'd be returning with his cook's only son at his side. But after a week and a half of being here... "Going back to the fort feels pointless. I won't find anything I haven't already uncovered."

"I'm going to assume the men disappearing has something to do with why most Mexicans are afraid to take the trail, even though the papers you gave me don't come straight out and say it," Jonas said.

Harrison raised his shoulders and let them fall in a shrug. "I haven't heard anything about disappearances. I feel like the Mexicans are afraid they'll be robbed and lose everything, but I don't know that they fear being killed. Though their fears don't make much sense to me. I didn't have any problems while traveling the trail, did you?"

"No." Jonas drew his horse a few steps closer. "But outlaws could be targeting the Mexican travelers and leaving the American ones alone."

"Why? Wouldn't Americans have just as many valuables on them as the Mexicans, if not more?"

"Could be because it's harder to get the law to pay attention to crimes again non-citizens who are passing through. If not for Inez, would you have ever known about Hernando?"

The man had a point. "So the fear of the trail and Hernando's disappearance could be connected. Outlaws could be robbing and murdering Mexicans, then hiding the bodies."

"Based on the information you've given me, that's certainly a possibility. And these outlaws' existence would greatly benefit your father, enabling him to pay less for the goods he trades at Fort Ashton. In fact, your father has so much to gain from the situation, that I can't help but wonder if there's a connection to the outlaws and Fort Ashton."

Harrison met Jonas's gaze without flinching. "I detest my father. I detest what he did to the Ashton family, and I detest how he swindles and manipulates. But he's never been involved in anything close to murder."

"Then maybe someone else at Fort Ashton is."

A sudden lump rose in his throat. "These bandits, if they exist, might not be connected to the fort."

"Every piece of information I have points to Fort Ashton. It was the last place Hernando, Carlos, and Diego were all seen alive. The price it's paying for goods has changed dramatically, everyone there seems afraid of the Chihuahuan Trail."

"Then go in and arrest someone."

"Who? And based on what evidence? The desert can be brutal and take a man's life all on its own. I need proof of the outlaws. I need someone who actually witnessed an attack on the trail... Either that, or I need a dead body with a bullet hole in it." Jonas turned his gaze southwest, in the direction of Fort Ashton. "That's why I need you to move into the fort."

Harrison shifted in his saddle. "I'll only be here through the end of the week. I need to get back to Austin."

"That's three days. Could be you'll learn something staying

inside the fort that you'd never have learned if you kept sleeping at your friend's."

He wanted to open his mouth and refuse. The idea of Father and his guards looking over his shoulder every minute of the day made him suddenly feel itchy. But he couldn't say no, not when peoples' lives could be at stake. "I should have been at the fort ten minutes ago. I need to go meet my father, but I'll come back tonight, collect my things, and let Wes know I'll be leaving."

Jonas's eyes met his. "I know you don't see it, but you really are the best person for this job."

Harrison gave a small nod then urged Toronto down the trail.

If only he was as confident about things as Jonas.

~.~.~.~.~

IT HAD BEEN HEART-WRENCHING. Even now, as Keely sat atop Hestia with the cool breeze toying with her hair and a desert valley splayed before her, she could still hear the marshal's questions ringing through her head.

*Why did you run from Chicago instead of going to the marshal's office?*

*Why didn't you turn your evidence over to the sheriff in Springfield?*

*Are you sure you don't have any proof of your brother's death?*

And on and on the questions had gone. Marshal Redding had interviewed her for over an hour, with Cain, Harrison, and Daniel all looking on.

Wes had tried to comfort her. He'd reached out and taken

her hand a time or two, patted her shoulder, even stroked her arm and prodded her to eat some breakfast.

She hadn't been able to manage a bite.

"Keely, are you all right?"

"Huh?" She looked up to find Wes had turned Ares around and was coming back to where Hestia had stopped on the trail. Leo was snuggled up against his chest, tied there with a long strip of cloth that Wes said Mexican women used to carry their babies.

She wasn't sure why he'd decided to take her on another picnic, not when he hadn't wanted to touch the baby yesterday. But when Marshal Redding had questioned her earlier, he'd taken the babe without a word of complaint. Now he held Leo again, and he didn't seem to mind overmuch.

"Was there a reason you stopped?" Wes asked.

"I... I didn't realize that I had." Oh goodness. She sounded like a halfwit. "I'm sorry. I guess I just got lost in my own thoughts."

She looked out over the valley where they rode. A stream ran through it, filling this section of the ranch with more green than she'd seen since arriving in Twin Rivers. Cattle wandered around the pasture, their long horns making the beasts look ferocious, even when they did something simple like drink from the stream.

"What do you think?" Wes asked.

She blinked. "About what?"

He gestured to the cattle in front of him, grazing in a creek bed. "My stock."

"Oh, um..." Wes had spent the better part of their ride chatting about the cattle and how he was breeding some of his stock a certain way, hoping to be able to sell his beef for colossal prices in places like Austin and San Antonio one day.

She forced herself to focus on the cattle. "They're... they're magnificent."

And they were. She didn't know much about cattle, but even she could see the beasts before her were of excellent quality. The glossy hair and well-defined muscles made them look like they belonged in a king's pasture, not tucked into a valley in the middle of a brown, scraggly desert.

"I'll be able to butcher the first of the herd next year, and I already have buyers lined up. If the beef tastes like I'm expecting, I won't be able to keep up with the demand, and that's just selling to restaurants and in Texas."

"So even though there's a large cattle company going in north of here, your beef will be better?" she asked.

"The beef from this herd, yes. My regular stock will be comparable to what the Willis outfit produces."

"But if you can focus on growing this herd and producing superior beef, your ranch will be fine in spite of what the competition is doing."

Wes winked at her, then sent her one of his devastatingly handsome smiles. "I'll make a good rancher out of you yet, Keely Westin."

Something fluttered in her stomach.

"Come on. There's a perfect spot for a picnic down by the creek, and I'm pretty sure Marceau packed macarons." Wes started for the far corner of the field, where a cotton tree grew next to the water.

She prodded Hestia into a trot, allowing the horse to weave her way between the cattle until Wes stopped. This picnic spot wasn't as magnificent as the last one, but there was something charming about sitting beneath a tree on a sunny October day.

She dismounted without Wes's help, and he sent her another grin as he loosened the picnic basket from where it had been strapped to his saddle. "You're looking more and more natural on a horse."

"Thank you." She took the blanket from him and spread it on the ground, then sat.

Wes sat beside her and pulled a couple sandwiches from the basket.

Did he realize how close they were sitting? That she could feel the heat from his body seeping into her? That she could smell the bergamot he put on every morning, and the way it mixed with the leather from the chair in his office and the scent of sunshine and wind from being outside?

She forced her gaze away from Wes and onto the cattle— anything to distract her from her traitorous heart. "I was wondering, is there something I can do to help?"

"I don't think I need assistance getting the food out of the basket, if that's what you're asking." He handed a sandwich to her.

She gave her head a little shake. "No, I wasn't asking about help with the picnic, I meant with the ranch. I know you say I need to be the housekeeper, but since that job doesn't involve any cleaning, well, I don't have much to do."

Wes adjusted the cloth strap over his shoulder. It held little Leo, who still slept soundly against his back. "Charlotte rode the ranch a lot. She would look for signs of cattle in trouble or trespassers or broken fences."

"I think I need to get a little better at riding before I try something like that."

"Yes, and you'd need to have at least one guard with you until this business with the Wolf Point Ring is settled."

"Of course." She sucked in a deep breath, then forced the air out in a giant whoosh. Would she ever see the day when she could make decisions based on what she wanted and not what the Wolf Point Ring might try doing to her?

"I was thinking I could look at some of the figures you're always going over. I have a head for numbers, and I'm good at planning. I did all the bookkeeping at the orphanage, and I was in the process of putting together a business plan when I had to leave."

Their eyes met. "That's the second time you've asked about helping with the paperwork. Are you sure you want to?"

"I think I'd be good at it, and it would give me something to do besides clean."

"I need you to care for Leo, Keely. At least until his mother can be found."

"I know. But hopefully his mother will come for him soon. Even if she doesn't, I should still have time to help you when he's napping."

"All right. If that's what you want. I'll show you around the office when we get back." Wes took a bite of his sandwich and chewed. "Just so you know, I've sent men down into Mexico, as well as to the towns east and west of here along the border. I intend to find Leo's mother and see what kind of trouble she's in. Maybe it's something I can help with."

She drew in a breath and tried to put a few more inches between her and Wes without being too obvious. Just far enough away she couldn't smell the bergamot and leather on his skin.

First, he took her in and helped her with the Wolf Point Ring, then he took in Leo despite the obvious pain having a baby in the house caused him. Now he was spending resources to locate Leo's mother, whom he would certainly help the moment he found.

If only he wasn't quite so caring and kind, then maybe being married to a man who never intended to make her his wife in truth would be easier.

"You're a good man, Agamemnon," she whispered.

"I'm not, Keely. And you more than anyone should understand why."

How was she supposed to answer that? His expectations of her as his wife didn't mean he was bad, it meant he was terrified. There was a difference.

He handed her a cluster of grapes, then popped one into his

mouth. Silence spread between them, not the awkward kind, but the calm, comfortable sort. Or rather, it would be comfortable if she could stop noticing the way the heat from his body radiated into her right side, or if she could make herself look away from him for long enough to forget the fascinating ring of dark brown that lined the outside of his light brown eyes.

Wes looked over the desert, seemingly unbothered by both the quiet and their nearness. She could almost swear he'd moved closer to her at some point.

The lowing of cattle echoed through the field, and the creek filled the air with a steady gurgle. It really was a perfect day for a picnic. Now if she could just keep her heart from playing traitor on her, she might be able to enjoy herself.

"I'm sorry about all the questions the marshal asked earlier today." Wes turned to her, and their gazes met, the ring of brown around his irises seeming to grow more intense as he spoke. "I know it was hard going back and reliving what happened in Chicago and the tactics you used to hide from the Wolf Point Ring, but you handled yourself amazingly well."

The warmth she'd felt just moments earlier drained away. "My face is on a wanted poster."

"We'll make sure it doesn't get shown around Twin Rivers."

She looked down at where her hands sat numbly in her lap, her appetite for the grapes beside them suddenly gone. "That's not the point. I've done nothing wrong. And now that I'm trying to make sure criminals answer to the law, those criminals turned around and made me into the criminal instead."

That had been the worst part of the morning. Not remembering James, not recalling Cynthia's lifeless body slumped on their doorstep, not the painstaking detail she'd gone into as she recounted each place she'd traveled while trying to stay hidden. The worst part was realizing the people who had killed those she loved and destroyed her life in Chicago had the power to destroy it everywhere—even in Twin Rivers.

If she was wanted for murder, would she be able to testify against the Wolf Point Ring in court? Or would she be considered too unreliable of a witness to even bring an accusation against them? Tears filled her eyes, and she was helpless to blink them away.

"Hey there, don't do that." Wes reached out and wrapped an arm around her shoulders, tugging her against his chest.

Part of her knew she should resist him, that nothing good would come of being so close. But she melted into him anyway, letting her tears fall.

"I'm sorry," she muttered, his familiar scent surrounding her even more.

"Don't be." He stroked a hand up and down her arm in a soothing motion.

Despite the heaviness in her heart, a sense of warmth flooded her. Wes was only holding her with one arm, and yet his grip felt so incredibly strong, so incredibly safe.

"I'm not one of those women who cries constantly, I swear. It's just..." She sniffled.

"You don't need to explain." His breath ruffled the hair on the side of her head as he spoke, and his hand made that soothing motion on her arm again.

"I suppose that poster is worth it if it means bringing the Wolf Point Ring to justice, but do you have any idea what it's like to see your face on a public announcement that's accusing you of a crime you didn't commit?"

His chin moved against her hair as he shook his head. "I don't, no. But I do know that you've already suffered enough, and through no fault of your own. I don't want to see you suffer more while you're here under my care."

She stared up into his eyes, and for a moment, one brief, sweet moment, she could almost imagine herself raising her head and brushing her lips against his.

Why, she couldn't say. She'd never been kissed before, let

alone been the one to initiate a kiss. But something about the way he held her, the way he looked into her eyes and murmured soothing words in her ear, was almost enough to make her forget the rest of their situation.

Almost. But not entirely.

She pulled away from him. A sudden emptiness filled her, but that only caused her to scoot farther back on the blanket. He'd married her under specific conditions, and she didn't even know if she'd be able to stay in Twin Rivers.

She couldn't let any feelings develop between her and Wes...

But what if she couldn't stop them?

S taying at Fort Ashton hadn't helped. Harrison looked around the adobe room. It was immaculately appointed with a grand bed and tiled ceiling above, and large windows offered a sprawling view of Twin Rivers and the desert beyond. But it all felt stiff and formal, and he was ready to be done.

His bags were packed at the foot of the bed and ready for him to head out at first light. He'd stayed two days longer than planned, all in hopes of uncovering what had happened to Hernando, Carlos, or Diego. All in hopes of discovering if there was something that connected the three men's disappearances, or any other disappearances he hadn't yet learned about, to Fort Ashton.

Now when he left, he'd head straight north to Midland and catch the train. It was out of the way, but still the quickest route for a man in a hurry to get to Austin since the second half of the journey could be done via rail.

Harrison opened the door to his room and peeked down the quickly darkening corridor. No light shown from under the door to his father's office. He'd try looking in there one more time for any clues, just in case he'd missed something. At this point he'd been in the office so much with his father that no one would think his presence there unusual.

The cool of night surrounded him when he stepped outside. The courtyard below was lit, and the sound of voices rose from it. He headed toward his father's office, only three doors down from the guestroom where he stayed. Of a sudden, the door next to the office opened, and a blur of dark hair and white apron flew out, holding a tray with a pitcher and snacks. Alejandra. He'd seen her several times since he'd taken a room at the fort, but they'd not spoken since that first day.

Her eyes were down, her feet moving too fast as she rushed over the tile floor. She would have run into him again had he not reached his hands out to stop her.

He let out a grunt as he caught her, using one hand to steady the tray that would have gone careening to the floor again, and the other hand to grip her shoulder and keep her from stumbling.

"I'm so sorry!" She gushed in Spanish, her head bent so she couldn't see his eyes.

Did she even know who she'd stumbled into—again?

"I didn't see you there."

"It's all right."

At the sound of his voice, her head snapped up. "Mr. Rutherford, I didn't realize it was you."

Yes, she would have been required to look at where she was going in order to know that. He opened his mouth to say something to that effect, then paused. Even in the dim light from the courtyard, he could see red rimmed her eyes and tears streaked her cheeks.

"What happened?"

"Nothing."

He glanced at the door she'd bolted out of. It was open a

crack, letting a sliver of light spill into the corridor. Almost on cue, a chorus of male laughter rose from the room.

"Who's in there?"

"Raul and his friends arrived this evening. I was told to bring them food, that's all. I was only doing my job."

"Then why are you crying?"

She shook her head, causing a strand of glossy black hair to fall across her cheek. "No reason."

"Did they say something cruel?"

Her chin quivered, then a tear crested and spilled down her cheek.

"Come to Austin with me." He didn't know what possessed him to say it. The words spilled out before he could stop them, but he wasn't sorry. It was the perfect solution.

She reared back, the hurt in her eyes replaced with a fiery anger. "I told you before, I'm not that kind of woman. You'd best look elsewhere for your entertainment."

He released her shoulder and the tray and held his hands up in a gesture of innocence. "That's not what I meant. Come to Austin and work in my house as a servant. I've need of another parlor maid, and you would do nicely."

It was a lie. Unless Millie had somehow quit while he was gone, he didn't need another maid, but he'd find a position for her. Something about leaving her here with the likes of Rooster and Raul and his father made his gut cramp.

She shook her head. "I still can't go, not even for a reason such as that."

"Why? You're not treated well here. You work constantly, yet you eat meals by yourself rather than with the staff, and Rooster and Raul have a singular hatred for you."

She shrank back against the railing that lined the side of the corridor open to the courtyard below. "You've observed all that."

"I have." He'd seen her eating alone more than once. While

he'd been curious, it hadn't seemed that odd to him at the time. But now that he saw her leaving Raul and his men, now that he thought back on the cruelty Rooster had shown her the last time he'd seen them together, something seemed terribly wrong.

"You need to leave this place, Alejandra."

"I can't."

And here they were, back to the same answer they'd started with. He nearly opened his mouth to tell her that she could, that all she needed to do was leave with him in the morning. But her eyes were a well of emotion, part hope, part resolve, part desperation. "Why not?"

"You already know."

He shook his head. "No, I don't."

She looked away from him and swiped an errant strand of hair from her face. "For the same reason I couldn't afford to pay for the broken dishes."

He thought back to the first time he'd met her, to why she'd been so worried when Rooster had said her pay would be docked.

"Gabriella." He shifted from one foot to the other, the night-time November air carrying a hit of coolness. "She can come too."

Alejandra pressed her eyes shut, her jaw quivering as she drew in a breath. "If only it was as easy as you say. But this is... we shouldn't... I can't talk about this. Now if you'll excuse me." She opened her eyes, ready to dash down the corridor again, but he stepped in front of her.

"Here, take this." He reached into his pocket and pulled out his billfold, then peeled off several large bills. Enough to get both her and her sister to Austin.

Her jaw dropped open. "What... what are you doing?"

"Three-nineteen Enderfield Street. Can you remember that?"

"Why?"

"That's my address, and this is enough money for two tickets to Austin." He tucked the bills on the tray beneath the pitcher of water. With both her hands holding the tray up, she had no way to try giving the money back to him.

Still, her eyes shot fire at him. "Take it back. I'll not be joining you, and once you leave, I'll have no way of giving the money back."

"It's already yours. Save it in case you find a way to leave. And if the opportunity never presents itself, then take it with you when you finally get yourself free of this place. Use it to start again somewhere new."

He stepped to the side, and she swept past him in a huff. Yet he couldn't help but stare after her, even after she disappeared down the stairs.

He may have uncovered little of use for the marshals, but something told him if he could find a way to help Alejandra, his time in Twin Rivers would still be well spent.

## 14

Wind from the desert ruffled his shirt as Wes stared at the small circle on the ground filled with ash. Someone had definitely camped there, but who? Rustlers? The Wolf Point Ring?

He straightened and looked at the thin form of Raymond Sloan, the head guard he'd hired from the Pinkerton Agency. "How thoroughly have your men searched the area?"

"Our initial search yielded just this campsite and those tracks." The man pointed at where a series of prints from four horses led away from the space where the bedrolls had clearly been spread. "They cross the ranch south of here and head into Mexico."

"Do you have men following them?"

"Two." The man scratched the side of his droopy mustache, then scanned the desert with wizened eyes that said this was hardly his first assignment by the Pinkerton Agency. "Should probably point out that the contract we signed was for work in Texas alone. Didn't realize we'd be crossing the border."

"I'll pay extra. Just find out who made the tracks."

"Probably travelers passing through," Raymond drawled.

"There's no sign these people approached any cattle, and I can't think either rustlers or opium smugglers looking for information about the ranch would set up camp on it."

Wes agreed. If he were with the Wolf Point Ring and searching for Keely, the last place he'd camp was on the A Bar W where he might draw attention to himself. Plus, the campsite was just off one of the main trails through his property, not even close to being hidden. More than likely, whoever had used it thought they were on an actual road. It wouldn't be the first time travelers had mistakenly wandered onto the ranch on their way either to or from Mexico.

"Keep a man on guard out here for the next few nights, just to make sure no outlaws pass through."

"Already planning on it." Raymond twirled the end of his droopy mustache with his finger.

"Didn't know we were having a party on the trail today," a familiar voice called.

Wes turned to find Sam approaching on his horse.

"Came to tell you there was a trail leading into Mexico through my property." Sam brought his horse to a stop in front of them. "I decided to trace it for a bit on my way to tell you, but it looks like you've already discovered things."

"We've got men in Mexico trying to find out who was here." Wes jutted his chin south toward the border.

Sam scanned the campsite. "My guess is travelers passing through. Maybe they were trying to avoid the Chihuahuan Trail for some reason."

"I agree about the travelers, but I'm also not taking any chances. The guards here will find out who camped on my property and why, right, Raymond?"

The wiry little guard gave a slow nod. "Got the rest of my men doing a more thorough search of the surrounding area too."

"You headed back to the ranch soon, Wes?" Sam shifted in his saddle. "I'll ride with you."

Wes clamped a hand on Raymond's shoulder. "I assume your men can handle things here?"

"Yes, sir. I'll give you a report when our search is done."

"Perfect." Wes headed over to where Ares stood tethered to a shrub and swung up onto the Arabian.

Sam guided his horse around the campsite, then let the beast have its head on the familiar trail.

As soon as they were out of earshot, Wes looked at his friend. "You discover something else about those tracks you didn't want the guards to know?"

Sam had seemed to want to get away from the Pinkerton agent rather quickly.

"Not at all. I came to ask about the babe."

Wes raised an eyebrow. "You've got eight young'uns in that house plus one on the way. Don't tell me you're looking to take on another one."

Sam's jaw went hard, an unusual look for his gangly, easy-going friend. "Quite the opposite. How hard are you searching for his mother?"

"I sent Handy down to Mexico three different times last week. He came back with nothing each time."

"Send him again. Or better, send Bruce down with him. Or maybe some of your Pinkerton agents. Aren't they trained to find this sort of thing?"

Wes rubbed the back of his neck. "I hired the guards to keep my wife safe, not find Leo's mother. Keely comes first. But trust me. If there was a woman living on the border who was pregnant a few weeks ago and now doesn't have a child, then no one is willing to speak of her."

"You can't give up that easily."

Wes slowed Ares to a stop and looked over at his friend. His back was straighter than a fence post, his hands were clenching his horse's reigns, and his lips were pressed into a thin white line. "Why is this so important to you?"

"Because... because it is. The child should be with his mother. Don't you understand?"

He did, or at least he thought he did. But what he understood didn't come close to justifying why Sam was so upset. "Why don't you explain it."

Sam threw up his hands. "You don't know why his mother left him. You don't know what's wrong. Leo could have siblings, a sister or a brother. He could... he could..." Sam sucked in a sharp breath and raised his eyes to the south, where the Sierra Madres cast their shadow over the Rio Grande Valley. "Look, I'd give anything to know who my mother is, all right? Anything to know if I have a brother or sister out there somewhere. Anything to know why my ma gave me up. I was dropped off at an orphanage and that was it. No note. No explanation. I wasn't even given a last name."

Wes sat back in the saddle. He didn't know what it was like, to not have roots, to not have a family. But he'd understood from the moment he'd met Sam, round about the age of eight, that the one thing Sam wanted more than anything else was a family.

"Hang it all, Wes. All it would have taken was one person when I was a babe. One person to look into how I got to the orphanage. One person to go looking for my mother. Maybe— if someone would have done that, if someone would have cared enough—maybe things would have been different. Maybe all my ma needed was a few dollars, or a job, or a roof over her head. Maybe... maybe I could have had a family all those years, if only someone would have cared enough to look for my ma."

"All right, all right." Wes held up his hands. "I understand."

"Do you?" Sam looked up sharply. "You have money. If that's what Leo's ma needs, you can give her some. If it's a job, I know you could find a place for her on the ranch. If it's something else..." He shook his head. "I'd give the woman my horse and a few acres of my ranch if it meant she'd have the ability to raise her own child."

"I hadn't thought of it like that." He had more resources to help Leo's ma than anyone else in Twin Rivers. But Keely had done such a good job caring for Leo that he'd not done much to find the babe's ma besides send a ranch hand out to ask questions. "I'll go into Mexico myself tomorrow."

"Take Keely and Leo with you."

Wes raised an eyebrow. "You're telling me to take my wife, whom we think is being tracked by smugglers, into a country where we know outlaws are hiding?"

"I'm just saying, it's one thing for people to tell a strange man they don't know anything about a baby's mother. It's another thing to look at the baby's face and deny knowing something. If the mother's living in Ojinaga or one of the other border towns, she's not going to be able to look at Leo without giving herself away."

Wes sighed. It made sense, in a strange sort of way. He'd been making Keely stick close to the ranch, but no sign of those wanted posters from the city had shown up in Twin Rivers over the past weeks, and there was even less of a chance of them being in Mexico. Besides, Mexicans and Americans were across the border constantly. A day trip to a few towns with Keely should be safe.

"As long as the guards can prove whoever camped on my property last night didn't mean any harm, I'll take Keely and the babe with me tomorrow."

"Thank you." Sam gave him a little nod. "You're a good man, Wes. Most people in your situation wouldn't care a whit about Leo or Keely or even me. But you've always cared. I want you to know I count you as more of a brother than a friend."

"You're welcome." A lump formed in his throat, but he

spoke past it. "You're more brother than friend to me too, and it's an honor to know you."

The trouble was, when it came to being a husband to Keely and a temporary father to Leo, he didn't feel like he was nearly as good as Sam made him out to be.

~.~.~.~.~

KEELY CLUTCHED the shawl around her as a shiver traveled up her spine. Her legs and back ached from hours of sitting in a saddle, and now her head was starting to pound.

"Are you all right?" Wes paused his horse on the mountain trail in front of her and turned with little Leo on his back, tied in the Mexican style of carrying a babe. "Do we need to stop?"

She shivered again. "No need for that. I'm just cold."

"Do you want the blanket from my saddlebag?"

She didn't want a blanket. She wanted to be curled up in front of a fire with a steaming mug of tea. "How much farther until home?"

He winced. "At least an hour, maybe closer to two."

Keely surveyed the sky to her west. Clouds blocked the sun for one of the first times she could remember since coming to Twin Rivers, but the mountain peaks towering around them prevented her from seeing most of the sky. "Will we make it home before dark?"

"It's going to be close. Let me get the blanket." Wes reached down and undid the top strap of his bag, then pulled out a brightly colored blanket and turned Ares carefully around on the narrow trail. He stopped when he was beside her and draped the thickly woven wool over her shoulders.

"Is that better?"

Another shiver traveled through her, but not nearly as large as the last two had been. "Yes, thank you."

"I'm sorry. We should have turned around sooner."

"I wanted to go to Cantarrecio just as much as you did."

They'd left the A Bar W early that morning, stopping first in the Mexican town of Ojinaga, just across the border from Twin Rivers. When no one in Ojinaga offered helpful information about Leo's mother, they'd traveled west to Tierras Nuevas and La Esmerelda. Those stops had proven just as futile as their time in Ojinaga, so they'd traveled east to La Estacion. There they met an older widow who remembered a pregnant woman from the town of Cantarrecio, which was the next town south and over the mountain pass.

It turned out that the pregnant woman from Cantarrecio wasn't Leo's mother. She had safely delivered her own baby boy two weeks ago and had been proud to show him off.

Keely couldn't be sorry that they'd gone to Cantarrecio or any of the other towns, even though they were still over an hour from home, even though she longed for a hot bath and a warm mug of tea. She was only sorry that their efforts hadn't yielded any results.

Wes had gone ahead of her on the trail again, and Keely dug her heels into Hestia's sides. In maybe a quarter mile the trail turned, and they'd crest the final rise of the Sierra Madres before descending down the mountains and making their way into the flat Rio Grande Valley.

"Just a little longer," she whispered to herself. Her stomach cramped with hunger, and her fingers grew numb on the reigns. She'd realized during her first week in Twin Rivers that the desert could get cold when the sun went down, but she hadn't known the desert could cool quite this quickly.

Another blast of cold air hit her, and she shivered beneath the blanket. Ahead, Wes's horse disappeared around a bend in the trail.

She urged Hestia to follow, but the second she turned around the side of the mountain, a gust of cold wind blasted her, followed by a flash of light.

"Turn around—!"

A crack of thunder cut off the rest of Wes's words, but he was turning Ares around in the small space the trail afforded.

Another slash of lightning lit the sky, and Keely surveyed the wide expanse that now spread before her. The clouds to their west were a formidable shade of dark gray, menacing enough to make her shiver without another blast of wind.

"Keely, can you turn Hestia?" Wes shouted. "Or do you need me to do it for you?"

She looked down at her horse, who simply stood in the middle of the trail, almost as though she was too stunned by the sight of the angry sky to move.

"I think so." She pulled the reigns to the side, turning Hestia's head closest to the wall of rock rather than the side of the mountain where the trail dropped off. Hestia dutifully turned, then started back down the path.

"We passed a cave about halfway down the mountain." A gust of wind carried Wes's voice her direction, followed by a cry from Leo. "Hurry, I'd like to beat the rain."

Keely dug her heels into Hestia's side and urged the beast to go as quickly as possible, but it wasn't fast enough. Rain had begun falling in earnest by the time they reached the small cave Wes had spotted, and Leo's screams tore through the pass.

The cave wasn't very big, just deep enough to shield the three of them considering how the wind was blowing the rain sideways.

Keely jumped off her horse and turned to tether her, but Wes was already at her side, handing her the sling that held a screaming Leo. "Get him inside."

"You're both soaked." She'd be wet too if not for the blanket. The water hadn't fully absorbed into the thick wool.

"Just get into the cave." Wes waved her away, then turned and busied himself with the horses.

Keely scooted inside, the low ceiling and cramped space only making Leo's crying louder. "There, there. No need to fuss. Wes is getting you a bottle."

At least she hoped that's one of the things he was doing. They'd fed Leo in several of the small towns that day, purchasing milk directly from farmers. Before leaving Cantar-recio, she'd insisted they fill up two bottles just in case Leo got hungry on the trip home.

"Let's get you out of these wet clothes." She stripped him of his frock, then wrapped him in the edge of the blanket that was still draped over her. Lifting him to her shoulder, she bounced him in the small space of the cave, but her actions did little to calm the babe.

Wes crawled inside a few minutes later. He handed her both bottles, three diapers, and the extra frock she'd packed for Leo.

She changed his diaper as quickly as she could, then dressed him in the dry frock. The moment she pressed the bottle's nipple to Leo's mouth, he quieted.

Only then did she hear the low chattering of Wes's teeth.

She looked over at him to find water practically dripped from his clothes. "You're freezing."

"I'll warm up."

"How? Do you have a blanket?"

"I only packed the one."

"Then we'd better share." She scooted over to make room for him beside her, which meant her opposite side was nearly touching the cool side of the cave.

Wes gave his head a shake. "I-I'm n-n-n-o-t going to sit beside you. I'll get you w-wet."

"Leo already got me wet."

"Not that w-w-wet."

She raised her chin. "Either you can share the blanket and get me wet, or you can have the blanket entirely, but you have to warm up."

"F-fine." He scooted close and took one end of the blanket, then wrapped it tightly around him. "We shouldn't have gone to Cantarrecio."

"Don't say that. At least now we know that Leo's mother isn't there, and you couldn't have known a storm would crop up."

Another shiver wracked his body, followed by a small cough. "We'll have to spend the night here, and this is all we have for food." He held out a few pieces of jerky and hard tack. "I only packed one saddlebag with supplies."

"We'll be fine."

His gaze settled on the side of her face, though he didn't speak until his teeth had stopped chattering. "Has anyone ever told you how strong you are?"

She had the sudden urge to squirm. "I'm five-foot-two and a hundred and fifteen pounds. I'm not strong."

"I just told you that we were spending the night in a cold cave with a wet blanket and hardly any food. And all you have to say is, 'We'll be fine.'"

She shrugged. "It's not the hardest thing I've ever faced in my life."

Silence descended on the cave, making the ping of rain pelting the ground the only sound to fill the space. She repositioned Leo in her arms and tilted his bottle further upright.

"Tell me about your parents." Wes shifted a little closer, causing the heat from his body to radiate into her, along with dampness from his clothes. "I know how you lost James, and I know you're alone, but I was thinking the other day that I've barely heard you mention your parents."

She stared out into the gray abyss of the storm. "They came over from Ireland before either James or I were born. That's why I don't have an accent, but I have an Irish name."

"Did they settle in Chicago?"

"They did. There's a rather large Irish population in the city."

"What did your father do for work?"

"He worked in a factory, as did my mother. Factory work makes for a hard life. But it gave us enough to live on, and allowed James and I to go to school. One winter my mother fell ill with a fever, and she never recovered."

That kind of death was rather common in factories. It seemed that the work itself drained so much life from the workers that they didn't have the strength to fight off something as simple as an illness. "An accident at the factory took my pa two years later."

Wes's hand covered hers beneath the blanket. "I'm sorry."

"Me too, though..." She stared at a flat rock just outside the opening of the cave, the water on its surface reflecting the flash of lightning from the sky. "I can't say they loved each other. It was more like they made a life side by side. My father never attended my mother the way Daniel tends to Charlotte or Sam to Ellie. I think they'd lost so much in Ireland that they were both too afraid to really care about anything here in America."

Wes was silent beside her, but his warmth seeped into her. He was probably getting her wet, but all she could feel was the heat of his body near hers.

"Did you have siblings that died before your parents came to America?" he asked softly.

She shook her head. "My parents both survived the potato famine as children, and more people died during that than lived, including all but one of my grandparents. Most of my aunts and uncles—all children during the famine—died. That kind of loss, it can have a way of never leaving a person."

"I understand."

She looked over at him, and heat climbed into her cheeks.

What had she been thinking to say such a thing? All she'd done was set her husband's mind on the pain of losing Abigail.

A shutter wracked Wes's body, followed by another small cough.

"You're shivering again."

"C-can't seem to get warm with these w-w-wet clothes." His teeth started chattering.

"Take your shirt off."

He looked at her as his body fought off another shiver. "You w-want me to take off my c-clothes?"

"I won't have you catch your death from pneumonia on account of me. We may not be... intimate the way most married couples are, but I assure you, I've seen a man bare chested before."

"Have you now?" His voice turned low and deep. "And who, sweet wife, have you s-s-seen without a shirt on?"

"Well, James for one. But he liked boxing, and he took me to several boxing matches. The men in the ring don't wear shirts."

"Boxers and your b-b-b-brother?" He unwound the blanket from his shoulders and scooted a few feet away from her.

"Yes."

"I suppose I can live with that." His hands reached for the top button of his shirt.

Keely looked down and readjusted Leo's bottle. The milk was nearly gone, and he was starting to doze. "He feels cold too," she murmured, pulling the scratchy blanket even tighter around him.

Wes crawled back beside her, his sopping shirt discarded on the cave's floor. "Take his frock off and let me have him."

"He's cold, and you want me to take his clothes *off*?"

"I'll hold him against my chest, let my body heat keep him warm. It's the best way to keep him from being cold."

She looked between the two of them. The heat from another person's body was probably the best way to warm Leo, but it seemed terribly odd to undress a person who was already cold. Were she at home, she would cover him in more clothes and blankets, but what choice did she have at the moment?

She carefully undid the buttons on the back of his frock, then handed him over to Wes.

Wes held him against his shoulder, their bare chests touching, then wrapped the end of the blanket around the two of them.

Keely couldn't tear her gaze away. Did Wes realize how gentle he was with Leo? He might claim to never want children of his own, but he'd make a good father.

He used his thumb to wipe a droplet of water from Leo's cheek. "I can already feel him getting warmer."

"I'm sure you can," she rasped. She couldn't say what was so sweet about the image of her husband holding a nearly naked baby to his skin. But no matter how long she lived or how far she traveled, she'd never forget the sight.

She swallowed and dropped her gaze, but that only meant her eyes traveled along the edge of the blanket as it fell farther down Wes's chest. Defined, well-sculpted muscles peeked out from beneath the coarse wool.

She'd already admitted that she'd seen men without shirts on, but it had never felt intimate or personal before. But this? Stuck together in a cave with a babe to care for? She couldn't let herself be attracted to her husband, nor could she let her mind wander in the direction of home and family.

Wes had been clear with her from the beginning. She could even repeat the proposal he'd written in his letter.

*I'm not looking for romance or any romantic type of entanglement. I believe we can become first companions and then friends, working together side by side to grow my ranch. If this situation interests you, please respond to this letter, and I'll send funds for your trip to Twin Rivers.*

When she'd read the letter, Wes's desire for no romance had

sounded like a good idea. She didn't want to arrive in Texas and have a near stranger take her to his room on her first night in town. But she also hadn't realized that Wes meant there would be no chance of romance ever. She'd just assumed that if they suited well enough, if love grew between them, that...

Well, that they'd one day become a normal family.

But she hadn't known then how Abigail had died, or why Wes was so opposed to any type of romance between them.

And yet, as she sat beside him in the dank cave, she couldn't seem to stop her heart from beating faster than it should or the warmth from where their shoulders and hips touched from spreading to the rest of her body.

## 15

Burning, there was a burning sensation somewhere deep in his chest. Wes turned, rustling the sheets around him, and pressed a hand to his ribs.

It did little to relieve the pain.

"Wes?" A hand rested on his brow, slender and cool. "Can you hear me?"

His eyes fluttered open, expecting to find cactus green eyes and curly red hair hovering above him.

Instead, he found the clear blue gaze of his sister.

"Charlotte." Even rasping her name made his chest hurt. *Where's Keely?*

She'd been here, hadn't she? He remembered her palm against his forehead, her gentle hum filling the room, her hands touching his cheek, his neck, his...

*Chest?*

Had Keely bathed his chest?

He shifted and looked down at himself, only to find his chest wrapped in a cloth, and what he assumed was a poultice underneath it.

"It seems as though your fever has broken." Charlotte

pulled her hand away from his forehead and settled it on the top of his bare shoulder.

"I had a fever? For how long?"

"Five days."

Was that how long Keely had been caring for him? He only remembered snippets of seeing her in his room, just like he remembered snippets of waking up in the cave during the night, shivering uncontrollably while his body curled around Keely's, trying to keep her and Leo warm. Then a cough had wracked his chest, followed by another.

He remembered trying to ride Ares off the mountain, coughing so hard he could barely stay in his saddle. Cain and Sam had shown up at some point with a couple of Rangers.

Evidently when he hadn't returned to the A Bar W, Dobbs had gone to town and rounded up a posse, not knowing what had befallen them in Mexico.

"How are Keely and Leo?" A small cough rattled his chest. "Did they get sick?"

"Only you. Keely said she and Leo were able to stay fairly dry, but you got soaked."

*Thank you, Father.*

He looked around the room again, but it was empty of anyone save his sister. "Where's Keely?"

Hadn't he asked that already? Or had he only thought about asking it?

Either way, his sister hadn't answered.

"I sent her to bed." Charlotte moved to the table beside his bed, where she poured steaming liquid from a teapot into a cup. "The poor woman hasn't slept for days."

Wes repositioned himself against the pillow and stared up at the ceiling. His eyelids were heavy, and yet they'd only been open a matter of minutes. "Why not? I thought you said she didn't get sick."

His sister gave him a look, one that he should probably be able to read, but he was too tired to try understanding.

"Maybe because she's been too busy trying to care for you, or Leo, or both at the same time to get any sleep." Charlotte adjusted his pillows so that he sat higher on the bed. "Maybe because she's been working through the stack of papers you left on the desk in your office."

"I never said she needed to work on my papers."

"She said you gave her permission to help the other week, and let me tell you, that woman is a fiend with numbers. She can add things in her head faster than she can with an arithmometer."

She could?

"Here, sit up." Charlotte returned to the bed and patted his shoulder, then started propping up pillows behind him. "Doc Grubbins wants you to drink six cups of tea per day. Says it's supposed to help your lungs breathe better."

Wes pushed himself into a sitting position, only to have a cough wrack his body, causing the burning sensation to return to his chest.

"Did I give you much of a scare?" he wheezed.

"Only when the doc started talking about pneumonia." She handed him the cup of tea.

"I was a little sick before taking Keely and Leo into Mexico. Had a few sniffles and a slight cough, but it wasn't slowing me down." He took a sip from the cup, then grimaced as the bitter liquid slid down his throat.

"Keely told us."

He blinked. "She told you I was sick before? I didn't say anything to her."

"She must have noticed on her own. I think she pays more attention to you than you realize."

"I tried to stay dry, but once I got cold and wet, I couldn't stop coughing or shivering." He took another sip of tea, then leaned his head back against the pillow. He could still see the way Keely had looked at him in the cave when he'd snuggled Leo against his chest. Still feel the weight of her head on his arm as they'd curled their bodies together and tried to sleep on the hard, cold floor. Still see the worry on her brow when she'd woken to discover he was sick.

He wanted her here with him, in his room. Wanted to see her, to talk to her. To reach out and hold her slender hand with his.

Another cough rumbled his chest, and he set his tea down on the table before the coughing overtook him completely. Why was he suddenly thinking of Keely so much? He'd been too sick to check in on the ranch for five whole days, shouldn't he be thinking about that instead of a woman who was more friend to him than wife?

"Have the Pinkerton guards found any more signs of tres-passers?"

Charlotte shook her head. "No."

"What about Leo's mom? Has she been found?"

Again Charlotte shook her head. "Manny's gone back to Mexico twice, but whoever his mother is, she's not living along the border."

"And the ranch? Anything happen while I was sick?"

She rolled her eyes. "This place can survive a handful of days without you. The only thing interesting that happened is Keely found this." Charlotte crossed the room to his dresser, then held up a small stack of papers that had been placed atop the polished wood. "She found it while she was working on some kind of business projection."

He couldn't quite make out the words printed across the top from where his sister stood on the other side of the room.

"You're suing the Mortimers? And you want to leave the ranch to me? Since when?"

Ah. That. "I won't have this ranch going to Andrew's

offspring. I expect that you and Daniel will have children, and I fully intend to leave the ranch to them."

"To my children." Her words were flat, maybe even harsh. And was that a spark of anger in her eyes?

Why would she be mad about him leaving the A Bar W to her children? "If I die soon, then I'll just leave the ranch to you and let you sort it out."

"What about leaving it to your *wife*?" Charlotte's voice pitched higher.

"I have no intention of leaving Keely unprovided for. I've allotted her money and other assets in my will, but she doesn't know how to run the ranch."

"She might one day. After she's been here a few years."

He gave his head a small shake against the pillow. "You're getting ahead of yourself. I can always rewrite my will if it looks as though Keely will be the best person to take possession of the ranch. It's the contract I need to get out of first."

His sister stayed silent, the only sound the ticking of the clock that hung on the wall. But this time he could read the questions in her eyes, could see the direction of her thoughts.

"I know you and Daniel are happy with your new life together. I know when you look at your future, you see love and contentment and a passel of young'uns. But Keely and I aren't a love match. I proposed a marriage without any romantic entanglements, and Keely agreed."

"But what if she wants romantic entanglements? What if she wants to have a family?"

He stilled, the question causing his chest to burn, and not because of an impending cough. "Has she said anything to make you think that?"

"She was so devoted while you were sick. You should have seen how she cared for you."

"I'm sure she made the very best nurse." He rubbed a hand

over his face, trying to find the words he needed to help his sister understand. "She's a hard worker, dedicated, determined. I can't imagine her doing anything other than taking excellent care of me, but that doesn't mean she has feelings for me."

Charlotte licked her lips. "I suppose I just assumed that the two of you, living in this house together, well, that you'd..."

"Develop feelings for each other?"

A blush crept up Charlotte's cheeks.

"You're looking at your own happiness with Daniel and assuming that Keely and I feel the same. We don't, nor do we know that Keely can stay here."

She bit the side of her lip. "I suppose you're right. It's just... you're certainly trying your best to keep Keely here, what with the guards you've hired and everything. I assumed that meant..."

"Like I said, I've seen nothing from Keely that makes me think she has feelings for me, let alone that she wants children with me."

But even as he said the words, he couldn't get the hopeful way Keely looked at him in the cave out of his mind, or the contentment he'd felt when she'd snuggled against his chest.

What if Charlotte was right, and Keely wanted a normal family with him?

~.~.~.~.~

DANIEL PUSHED through the door of the telegraph office and out into the bright sunshine. He'd walked over to the telegraph office just to make sure a telegram hadn't gotten missed, but nothing had been waiting for him. Again.

Jonas Redding had left Twin Rivers exactly four weeks ago. He'd said he would send word when he knew something about the Wolf Point Ring, but Daniel hadn't heard a thing from him in twenty-eight days.

What should he do next? It seemed the entirety of his sheriff duties could be summed up in one phrase: sit around and wait. First with Cain catching the rustlers, and now with the marshals catching the Wolf Point Ring.

Was there something more he should be doing? He could tell Wes to hire a private investigator in Chicago, but if the Wolf Point Ring was as well connected as Keely said, they might realize someone was looking into them and then trace the investigator back to Twin Rivers. It seemed like an unnecessary risk when the marshals should be able to handle the band of criminals.

A flash of red caught his eye, and he paused, scanning the road near where it met the Chihuahuan Trail. He swore he'd seen a red bowler hat atop a man's head—just like Keely had said the henchman leading the search for her wore.

He took a few steps down the road, scanning carefully. Another flash of red, but it was a plume of dyed ostrich feathers in the top of Mrs. Grubbins's hat, not a bowler.

He blew out a breath. All this talk of rustlers and smugglers had him seeing things that weren't so.

He headed back to his office, shoving open the door a little more forcefully than he should have. Both Cain and Wes were inside waiting for him.

"I see you're feeling better." He ran his eyes down Wes, who looked a bit pale. He'd not seen his friend since he'd been caught in the storm over two weeks ago.

"Do you have any news from the marshal?" Wes let out a small cough, then took a step toward him. "Are they going to arrest the Wolf Point Ring soon? It's been four weeks."

Daniel raised his hands. "I was just at the telegraph office, checking to see if Jonas sent word."

"And?"

He shook his head. "As soon as I learn something, I'll ride out and tell you."

"What if you don't hear something for another month?" Wes crossed his arms over his chest.

"These things take time." Cain leaned back against Daniel's desk and crossed one foot over the other. "Especially if the criminals are well connected and organized. Look at how many months I've spent trying to bring down the rustlers, and they're right under our noses."

Wes pressed a hand to his chest and loosed another small cough, then glared at Cain. "Keely's been running for long enough. Don't tell me there's nothing more we can do."

Daniel felt the same, but if there was nothing he could do as sheriff, then there was even less for Wes to do. "How are things between you and Keely?"

Wes looked at him. "What do you mean?"

Daniel was tempted to roll his eyes. "She lost her brother and friend earlier this year, moved across the country, and is being hunted by powerful men. How is she doing with all of it? And how are things between the two of you?"

"She's fine. We're... fine."

Was that red creeping up the back of Wes's neck? Maybe something more was developing between Wes and Keely than her working as his housekeeper. "What about the baby? Is he doing okay?"

A half smile tilted the corners of Wes's mouth. "Keely's a natural with him. She'll make a good mother one day."

Daniel raised his eyebrows, waiting for Wes to realize that if Keely did, in fact, become a mother, it would mean she was the mother of his children.

"I'm sure you've heard, but I'm having no luck finding his

mother," Wes went on, the notion of Keely one day baring his children seeming to elude him. "I have inquiries out to several towns along the border, but that's gone about as well as my search for Consuela."

"Seems to me if a woman is going through that much trouble not to be found, it's probably best to leave her be," Cain drawled.

"She could be in danger." Wes headed to the back table that held the coffee and poured himself a cup. "Her note indicated it wasn't safe for her to keep the baby."

Cain inclined his head. "Exactly. She knows where her baby is, so if she wants to be found, she'll come to the A Bar W."

"But what if I can help her?" Wes grabbed a muffin off the table.

"Sounds like you already are by taking in her babe." Cain pulled a piece of paper out of his pocket and held it out for both of them to see. "Not to change the subject, but have either of you seen this woman?"

Daniel took the paper and raised his eyebrows. It was a good sketch, capturing not just the woman's likeness, but a bit of emotion about her too. "You draw this?"

"Didn't see no professional artist around to do it."

A Mexican woman stared back at him with dark eyes. Her dark hair and bronze skin made her undistinguishable from most other Mexican women, but she had a square jaw and a broad forehead, and her eyes were set wide apart on her head. "How tall is she?"

"Medium height. Not as tall as Charlotte, but certainly taller than Anna Mae. You see her?"

Daniel shook his head, then handed the paper to Wes, who'd come over to the desk for a look.

"Nope. Sorry." Wes shoved a bite of muffin into his mouth.

"You can keep that copy in your desk and ask your deputies," Cain jutted his chin toward the sketch. "But don't go showing it around town. Can't have the rustlers learn I'm looking for her."

Daniel slid the paper into his top desk drawer. "You think she can help you find the rustlers?"

Cain shifted. "Maybe. I've got some reliable informants in Mexico now, so I get word as soon as the rustlers start to move. But my informants can't tell me what they'll do next or when they plan to do it."

"And this woman..."

The door to his office opened, and Daniel clamped his mouth shut.

"Hi there, Sheriff." A short, scrawny man stepped inside, his shirt and trousers covered in a layer of dust. He glanced at Cain and Wes, then headed to the desk. "Have some wanted posters for you."

Daniel frowned. "The latest batch just arrived in yesterday's post. And you have more? Hand delivered?"

"Just one poster, really, but the police up in Chicago would like several copies hung around town. This particular criminal is wanted for double murder."

*Chicago.*

*Double murder.*

Daniel glanced at Wes. His friend was already staring a hole through the dusty traveler, but Cain at least had the sense to grip Wes's shoulder and pull him back a step.

The man took one of the posters from his satchel and handed it to Daniel.

He only unrolled it partway, just long enough to see the familiar curly hair and eyes of his best friends' wife.

Daniel narrowed his eyes at the traveler. Was he a member of the Wolf Point Ring?

If so, he couldn't give any indication that Keely was in Twin Rivers, but he also couldn't let any posters of her be shown. Too many people had seen her at the wedding.

"Got one of these a few weeks back," Daniel said. "But I'll keep this copy too."

The man looked around the office, pausing when his gaze landed on the two posters Daniel had up near the door. "It's not hanging with those others."

"The crime was committed clear up in Illinois. I tend to keep the posters I display limited to crimes from Texas or New Mexico. You come down here clear from Chicago looking for this woman?"

"Naw, I'm from Houston. Someone's paying me a hundred dollars to travel through all the small towns like this, hanging up posters. Got a bunch of them in my wagon. If I catch the woman, there's a five-hundred-dollar reward."

"I see." Daniel watched the man closely. Was he lying? Could he still be part of the Wolf Point Ring? His accent sounded Texan, but that didn't necessarily mean he was innocent. "Five hundred dollars seems like quite a reward."

"Sounds like the authorities in Chicago are looking for her pretty hard." The man rubbed his chin and shifted from one foot to the other. "I have more posters. Don't suppose it will be a problem if I post them around town."

"Leave a stack with me, and I'll send my deputies out later. We'll see that they're posted not just here, but in all the towns in Twin Rivers County this afternoon." Daniel forced the words out of his mouth, though even he could hear the coldness seeping into his tone. "That should save you some time. I'm sure you have several more stops to make before sundown."

But how many of those stops were places where people from Twin Rivers might travel and see posters of Keely? He had jurisdiction over all the towns in Twin Rivers County, but he'd have to contact the sheriffs in the bordering counties if he wanted those posters taken down.

He nearly cursed. He'd assumed the wanted posters would be limited to cities, and there were so many posters and so many people in places like Austin and Houston a single poster did little good.

But if multiple posters of Keely were hanging in every town along the Chihuahuan Trail, someone would be sure to recognize her.

"Thanks, Sheriff. I'll take you up on that offer." The man rubbed the back of his neck again. "Let me go out to the wagon and get you a stack."

"I'll come with you." Daniel followed the man out into the sunshine, only to find a wagon loaded with mounds and mounds of rolled up posters.

The stranger helped Daniel load as many posters as he could manage into his arms, then the man climbed onto the wagon seat.

"Thank you again, Sheriff." He tipped his hat in Daniel's direction and gave the reigns a flick. "Good day."

Daniel trudged up the stairs to his office and nudged the partially open door far enough that he could walk inside.

Wes stalked straight over to him. "What are you thinking? You can't let him go on to the next town! Those posters are a lie."

"Keep your voice down." Daniel dumped the posters onto his desk, where three of them proceeded to roll onto the floor.

"Why didn't you arrest him?"

"He hasn't committed a crime."

"That you know of," Wes gritted, his jaw hard. "What if he's part of the Wolf Point Ring?"

"He hasn't committed a crime that I can *prove*. I can't just go around arresting people because I don't like them—but I can have them followed, see if that turns something up. And I also stopped him from hanging posters of your wife around town. You could try thanking me."

"Why? All someone needs to do is see one of those posters in the next county for Keely to be turned in." Wes started pacing again, five steps one direction, a whirl, and then five steps in the other. "You both made it sound like the posters were going to stay in the cities. How did it get to the point where there are about to be fake wanted posters of my wife in every small town in the state?"

"They're not fake." This from Cain, who had gone to the table at the back of the office for another cup of coffee.

"What?" Wes stopped pacing long enough to glare at Cain.

"Daniel here looked into it. The posters are real."

Wes spun back around, and Daniel swallowed. Leave it to Cain to up and tell Wes something like this when his temper was already high. "I made some inquiries when I saw that first poster a month ago. There's an open investigation in Chicago and a police report to go with it."

The red that had tinged Wes's face and neck drained away, leaving him suddenly pale. "What does the report say?"

Daniel opened his top desk drawer and pulled out an envelope, then handed it to Wes. "I had my sheriff friend in St. Louis telegram Chicago and ask for the report, then he mailed it to me. If the Chicago police department is as corrupt as Keely says, I didn't want to do anything that might draw their attention to Twin Rivers. I would have told you sooner, but you were sick."

That, and he'd known Wes wouldn't be happy.

"You can't actually think Keely..." Wes stared down at the report, the muscles of his throat working.

"No. But I think two women died in Chicago, possibly of arsenic poisoning, though that part could be fabricated. The part that's not fabricated is the bodies. They exist, and so the chief of police found a way to blame Keely for their deaths, hoping it would lead to a national hunt for her."

"That's sick. Who would blame an innocent woman for something like this?" Wes clamped his jaw shut, but a sheen of moisture glinted in his eyes.

"People who stand to lose tens of thousands of dollars a year in illegal opium trade," Cain said. "Those are the kind of people who'd frame an innocent woman. They'll get caught eventually, but you have to be patient. Like I said earlier, something this big is going to take time."

"And we need to be careful. We can't do anything that might make whoever's controlling things in Chicago look too closely at Twin Rivers." That was the most frustrating part of Keely's situation. Normally, as a lawman, Daniel would be able to ask questions, find information, and make arrests, but not when it came to the Wolf Point Ring and Keely.

"You want one of my men to follow the man with the posters?" Cain jabbed his thumb over his shoulder in the direction of the road. "Or are you going to send one of your deputies?"

Daniel rubbed his jaw. "I've got a mind to send my deputies to the neighboring counties and ask those sheriffs either to pull the posters or to stop them from going up. If you have a man to spare, I'd appreciate help following the wagon."

"Will do." Cain repositioned his hat on his head, then headed for the door.

Wes waited until the door closed behind Cain to look up at him. His usually dark eyes were filled with a raw sort of emotion. "Whatever it takes, Daniel. Do you hear me? I don't care if you need money or a team of Pinkerton agents or an army of outlaws. I'll do whatever it takes to bring these people down. Just let me know what you need."

Daniel met Wes's gaze and swallowed. Standing there, in his familiar office, with his oldest friend in all the world, he wished he could promise Wes what he wanted—wished he could promise the Wolf Point Ring would be caught and Keely would be safe.

But he couldn't. "Keely's well protected on your ranch, and

criminals always mess up sooner or later. All it takes is one mistake for them to get caught."

"I hope you're right," Wes rasped.

He hoped he was right too. Because if something happened to Keely, he wasn't sure Wes would ever forgive him...

And he wasn't sure he'd be able to forgive himself either.

## 16

Daniel swung off Blaze and rolled his overly tight, aching shoulders as he headed toward the door of his house. First, he'd had to deal with the stranger wanting to hang up posters of Keely, then he'd had an unexpected chase over the desert to catch an outlaw who'd robbed the haberdashery, followed by another conversation with his father about seminary. He was ready to fall into bed, and the sun hadn't even sunk below the horizon yet.

He opened the door to the scent of cooking meat.

"Daniel." Charlotte rose from the couch where she'd been sitting, took one look at him, and sighed. "Was it that long of a day?"

He held his arms out, and she came into his embrace, never mind his clothes were covered in dust and his skin coated in a layer of sweat.

"What's wrong?"

He gathered her even closer. "Nothing. Everything. I stopped by Ma and Pa's before coming home. He's more determined than ever to go to seminary, and as much as I want to be happy for him, all I can think about is what I'll miss once he's gone."

Charlotte leaned back just far enough to stroke hair back from his brow. "Has he told Anna Mae yet?"

"No. I think he's waiting. For what, I don't know. My blessing, maybe?"

A furrow marred the skin between her eyebrows. "He doesn't need your blessing to go to seminary."

"I know, but... well, it's the same as you wanting your father's blessing for our marriage, love. These kinds of things matter."

"I suppose they do."

She rested her head on his chest, and he placed a kiss atop her head, content to simply hold her while the sounds of night on the desert crept through the open window.

"I went into town to visit Anna Mae today and get a few things from the general store," she spoke into his chest.

"All right."

"I stopped by your office. You were gone, but... there was a paper that had rolled behind your desk. I picked it up, but when I did..." She pushed back enough to peer into his face. "Is Keely really wanted for double murder in Chicago?"

Daniel dropped his arms from around her. "Is she wanted for it? Yes. Did she do it? No."

He hadn't told anyone, even Charlotte, about the poster Cain had brought to town four weeks earlier. Like Cain and Wes, he'd been hoping Twin Rivers was remote enough to avoid having any posters other than the one that had been sent to him.

"Daniel, what is going on? I thought you said Keely would be safe in Twin Rivers."

He groaned, the weight of the day pressing down on his chest until he almost forgot how to draw breath. "I thought she would be too. But the Wolf Point Ring is determined to flush her out."

Charlotte took a step back from him. "How long have you known about the posters?"

"A few weeks, right around the time Leo came to live with them."

Another furrow formed on her brow. "Why didn't you say anything?"

"Didn't want you to worry. Or Anna Mae. Or Ellie." He didn't want anyone to worry about anything. In a world that was just and fair, a woman like Keely Westin would have no reason to look over her shoulder.

Charlotte turned toward the kitchen. "Are you hungry? I made dinner."

Was she upset with him for not telling her about the posters earlier? He couldn't quite tell, not with the reserved way she held herself as she headed toward the stove.

"I should probably be starved, but..." He covered the distance between them in three steps, swooped her up in his arms, then walked to the couch and settled down with her in his lap. "I just want to hold you for a bit longer."

"All right." She leaned her head against his chest and curled into him. They probably looked a bit ridiculous, seeing that his lap was far too small for someone as tall as Charlotte. But he didn't care.

He wasn't sure how long they sat there, her head resting against his chest, his arms wrapped tightly about her, neither of them speaking as night crept into the corners of their house. When he finally raised his head to look around, he noticed the table had been set with candles, and a vase held a handful of green shrubs.

"Are we celebrating something special tonight?"

"I, um..." Charlotte bit her lip. "We don't have to, not if you're tired. It can wait for another night."

"What can wait?" It wasn't their anniversary, not of either their first date or first kiss, and certainly not of their marriage.

Her teeth sunk into her lip again. "Wes isn't going to be happy."

He raised an eyebrow. "We're celebrating your brother not being happy?"

"That's not what I mean. I... um..." Her hand crept onto her belly, cradling it.

He couldn't help but stare down at her flat stomach, at what her hand covering it might mean. "Tell me, love."

A smile broke across her face. "We're going to have a child."

He let out a bark of laugher, then squeezed her tight. "Nothing could make me happier."

"I think it will come mid-summer. Probably July."

He crushed her against him, the smile splitting his face so large it drew his skin tight. "That's the best news I could hope for."

Much might be wrong in Twin Rivers, with the rustlers and the Wolf Point Ring and his father wanting to leave. Daniel couldn't begin to promise he could make everything right again. But between his wife and the babe she'd bear next summer, he was a man blessed twice over, and he fully planned to take comfort in that.

~.~.~.~.~

WES OPENED the door of his office, then stopped. After a morning spent riding the ranch with a couple of his hands, he'd been intending to get paperwork done. But afternoon sunlight filtered through the window, casting Keely in a spray of light as she sat at his desk, pouring over a stack of papers.

Again.

He'd found her there more times than he could count in the past two weeks since he'd recovered from being sick.

She hadn't been lying when she said she had a head for numbers. She'd spent all of last week looking at every report he had from the Southern Pacific Railroad and trying to figure out how much profit he would get when the railroad became operational. She'd also given him an entire report of her own making that showed when she expected the railroad to be completed and why it would take that long based on how long completion had taken for other sections of the track.

What was she working on now?

Whatever it was, it had her full attention. She had stacks of ledgers piled on the desk, along with a mess of papers.

The cradle beside the desk rocked ever so slightly, and a fist appeared above the wooden edge.

Wes swept into the room and lifted Leo out of the cradle before he started crying. He expected Keely to look up and notice him, but she kept her head down, her eyes fixed on a column of numbers that she was adding. The arithmometer sat on the desk beside her, but she didn't appear the least bit interested in using it.

A lone curl had fallen by her cheek, the soft red color contrasting with the creamy hue of her skin. She looked fine and dainty as she sat there, nearly swallowed by his giant desk, yet the gentle yellow color of her dress made her stand out against the polished mahogany.

Wes swallowed. When had his wife become so beautiful? He'd realized she was attractive when he first saw her step out of the stage. But it had been a passing observation, nothing more. Yet now as she sat there, her lips pressed together in concentration, he found himself wanting to reach out and run his fingers along the soft curve of her cheek, to smooth the wayward curl behind her ear.

Leo let out a small cry, and Keely looked up, her gaze landing on him.

"Oh, Wes. I didn't realize you were there...and with Leo. Is he fussy? Do you want me to hold him?" She scooted the chair that was far too big for her back a few inches.

Wes glanced down at the babe, who had snuggled back against his chest with droopy eyelids. He was probably trying to decide whether to go back to sleep or wake up. "I can hold him while you finish tallying your numbers."

"Oh." Her eyes moved from his face to Leo's and back again. "Thank you."

She scooted her chair back in and bent her head over the ledger she'd been using once more. A moment later, the steady scratch of her pencil filled the room.

Wes turned away, studying the books on the shelf behind his desk. Better to do that than stare at Keely. He couldn't so much as look at her without thinking of the gentle curve of her neck or the pink tint of her lips. Even last night, when they'd sat in the parlor talking—as they'd started doing most nights after Leo went to bed—he couldn't stop himself from noticing how the flicker of the lamplight cast shadows over her skin, and how her hair turned to different shades of fire in the dim light.

And here he was again, letting his thoughts go places they shouldn't. He gave Leo a small pat, and the babe stirred against him, then wriggled his fist into his mouth and started sucking.

"All finished." Keely pushed herself away from the desk. "What did you...? Wait. Shouldn't you be at church?"

"If I'm at church without you, it might cause questions about where you are. Figured if I stay here, people will assume I'm working."

"But you went to church last week."

That was before the stranger had arrived on Monday and tried to tack posters of Keely up around town.

He'd debated telling her about the man with the posters but

had decided it would only worry her. She was falling into a rhythm at the ranch and starting to seem comfortable, and he didn't want to ruin it.

Besides, his Pinkerton agents were still guarding the ranch, and they hadn't turned up anything unusual after finding that one campsite four weeks ago. Keely was as safe as she could possibly be, given the situation.

"Well? Are you going to explain why you went to church last week and not this week?"

Leo started to squirm again, and Wes bounced him on his arm. "I just don't think I should go every week without you. People might start to wonder why they never see you, and those kinds of questions won't do us any favors. It's been five weeks since you gave that information to Marshal Redding, I'm hoping we won't need to worry about the Wolf Point Ring for much longer."

Keely bit the side of her lip. "I'm worried it will take more time than that, be more complicated."

"And it could be as simple as finding and arresting whoever is snitching on the marshal's office in Chicago. It could be the entire Wolf Point Ring was arrested yesterday, and we just haven't been told yet."

"Maybe." Keely shifted some papers around the desk. "Was this what you wanted to tell me? Is that why you came to the office?"

He couldn't help the small smile that tilted the corner of his mouth. "It's my office, Keely. Believe it or not, I still have work that I need to do here." He scanned his desk. "Though it might take me until supper to unbury my desk from all the papers you have on it."

"Oh, I'm so sorry!" She started stacking the papers. "I can take some of this to my room so it won't be in your way. Will you be needing the arithmometer or should I put it back on the shelf?"

"I can move it, but I'm curious to know what you've spent the morning working on."

"Oh." She glanced around again, searching for one paper amidst the mess. "This right here, though it's not finished yet. I was looking at the prices you got last month when you took the cattle to market. If you sell thirty percent of what you sold this year, which seems likely since you had to sell off more of your herd than you wanted, and if the cattle price holds, then I estimate you'll make...

"Well, here." She shoved the paper at him and pointed to a figure. "Again, this is if the price holds. But the price of beef has increased from anywhere from three to seven percent over the past five years. So this is what your earnings next year will look like if beef increases."

She pointed to another row of figures at the bottom of the page, one for each percentage increase in the price of cattle. "On the off chance the price decreases by three percent, I calculated that sum here. I was just starting to figure how much you can expect from the prime stock you've been breeding. Didn't you say you wanted to sell a thousand head?"

"I did." He looked at the sheet, at the neat column of numbers and clear way she'd laid everything out, and had the sudden urge to pull her into his arms and drop a kiss atop her head.

It wasn't that her information was terribly valuable. In fact, her exact figures were all close to the estimates he'd already done in his head.

But that Keely would take the time to add everything up and make her own projections made something warm trickle through his chest.

He glanced at her, his gaze involuntarily sliding to her lips. *Maybe that's what I should kiss instead of the top of her head.*

He forced his gaze back to the paper and cleared his throat. "Thank you, Keely. This is very helpful."

She smiled at his compliment, and he had to stifle a groan, because the smile only made her lips look more appealing.

He took a step away from her. "I should probably—"

"I don't know where you keep a list of expenses for the ranch." She spoke at the same time. "So I can't estimate what your overall profit will be."

He took another step away, just to put more distance in between him and the kindhearted, helpful woman he'd somehow married. "Expenses usually total around four thousand dollars. That includes paying the house staff and cowhands, but it doesn't include investments I might make in my stock, like the purchase of a new bull or some calves."

"But if your expenses only run four thousand dollars..." She looked at him, her eyes widening as she realized just how much profit the A Bar W brought in every year. "You're richer than I thought."

A laugh rumbled from his chest. "My father used half our wealth to buy into a railroad this summer, remember?"

"Yes, but..."

Leo let out a little cry and pulled his drool-covered fist out of his mouth, then scrunched up his face.

"Oh, dear." Keely glanced at the clock on the wall. "I worked for longer than I realized. Here, let me take him and get his bottle."

He handed Leo over, but the moment she took the babe, his arms felt achingly empty, and the little spot where Leo had been snuggled up against him seemed cold.

When had he gotten so used to holding a babe?

When had he started to like it?

Keely wasted no time turning and heading for the door, but Wes stood in his office, staring at the empty doorway long after they'd disappeared.

When he finally turned back to his desk, mounds of papers and ledgers greeted him. He'd need to spend forty-five minutes organizing everything before he could sit down to work, and he wasn't even mad about it.

He rubbed the back of his neck. Abigail had never helped him in the office. She'd been content to ride the ranch with Charlotte on occasion, but she'd spent most of her time working on the menu with the cook or redecorating rooms of the house. More than anything, she'd wanted to be a mother.

Keely wanted... what?

To survive, of course. To see the Wolf Point Ring brought to justice. But did she want anything beyond that? Charlotte had assumed Keely would want children and a family. Keely had never said anything to him about wanting those things, yet she was so very good at caring for Leo and so very happy when he spent time talking to her after Leo was asleep for the night.

Did she want more than just food to fill her belly and a place to sleep without fear?

Wes blew out a breath.

He'd promised himself to never put another woman at risk the way he'd put Abigail at risk by getting her pregnant. Even if Keely wanted a family, he couldn't let her hopes and desires sway him.

But what if Leo was the answer? God had given them a child out of the blue, and despite Wes's best efforts to find his mother, she might not come back for him.

If Leo stayed, then he would have an heir, someone to pass the A Bar W down to. And Keely would have a child.

Could that be enough for her?

Could that be enough for him?

## 17

K eely felt like she was going to explode. Never in her life had she eaten such a feast. She'd always loved Thanksgiving, but when a renowned French chef was cooking dinner, the food was too delicious to refuse.

"I shouldn't have had that second piece of pie," Anna Mae muttered from where she sat on one of the chairs across from the sofa in the parlor.

"Or that extra helping of mashed potatoes," Ellie groaned from her place on the sofa beside Keely.

Keely let out a similar groan and patted her overstuffed stomach. "Someone is going to need to roll me off the couch and upstairs later so I can go to bed."

The parlor filled with laughter, and it sounded good. Leo was already asleep upstairs, but everyone else was gathered here, Daniel and Charlotte, Anna Mae, and Sam and Ellie Owens—with all eight of Ellie's siblings. They filled the room beneath the warm glow of the chandelier, turning the parlor that had once felt ridiculously ornate and large into a comfortable, homey room. A fire crackled in the stone fireplace, just enough to take the chill out of the cooler air that had descended on the desert that week, and the contented chatter of Ellie's younger siblings came from the back of the room.

"Ellie, my tummy hurts." Jeff—or was it Joe?—trotted over from where he had been playing jacks and patted his protruding belly, then the little boy climbed onto Ellie's lap.

"It's because you had too much pie." Ellie stroked a thatch of wayward hair off his forehead. "I bet if you go run around the outside of the hacienda four times, your tummy will feel better."

"And how is your tummy feeling?" Sam used the arm that had been resting on the sofa above Ellie's shoulders to squeeze his wife close to him. He rested his other hand on where the round mound of a coming babe protruded from her stomach.

Ellie smiled up at him, the look on her face so tender that Keely felt something dip in her own stomach.

"Sometimes the two of you are so sweet on each other I can hardly watch," Anna Mae said with a roll of her eyes.

"I agree," came Wes's wry voice from where he leaned against the wall by the doorway.

Sam shot a glare at Wes. "As though you have any room to complain now that you're married."

"I'm not cozying up to my wife in front of an audience."

He wasn't. In fact, he stood on the opposite side of the room from where Keely sat. And while she didn't expect him to kiss her cheek or toy with the wayward strand of hair that hung from her cheek, she wouldn't complain if he at least came and sat by her.

"Maybe not," Sam answered. "But I remember how dead set you were against me marrying Ellie."

"You were against Sam and Ellie marrying?" Keely sat up a little straighter, looking from Sam to Wes and back again. "Why?"

"He hasn't told you the story?" Charlotte glanced at her brother, then smirked.

"No, and why would I?" Wes scowled back at his sister.

"You should have seen the fit Wes pitched when he found out about Ellie coming." Sam sent Wes a wink. "He was over at my place, looking at my house, which I'd finished building by myself when he was on a roundup. I told him I had to get to town to meet the stage, and he picked up on how my clothes were all clean and I'd left a flower on the bed and whatnot."

"You left a flower on the bed?" A smile crept across her lips at the image of a single flower lying on a bed. "That was sweet."

And something Wes had never thought to do for her.

"Well, Wes had a conniption once I told him I was going into town to meet my future wife. He said it was because she could have murdered me in my sleep and taken my land, but I think it had more to do with the fact that I didn't ask for his approval first. Wes here likes to have a say in just about everything."

Keely couldn't help the laugh that burst out of her.

"I do not." The scowl was back on Wes's face, and part of her was tempted to walk over and tease him until his frown disappeared—if only she could roll her overstuffed body off the couch.

"That's not even the best part of what happened when Ellie arrived." Daniel leaned forward, his eyes dancing with memories. "Sam might have finally confessed Ellie was coming and he was planning to get hitched, but he didn't tell either of us about the young'uns. There were only supposed to be three, you see. But he didn't say a word. So the stage finally shows up, and out pops one little redhead, then a second redhead, then another and another. Here I was thinking Sam must have gotten the day wrong, that this couldn't be the stage that had his wife. Then Ellie comes out, and Sam squeaks out something about all the young'uns being with Ellie.

"You didn't know they were coming?" Keely looked at Sam.

Sam looked down at Ellie, his face wreathed with tenderness. "I was ready to strangle Ellie when she stepped off that stage. She'd told me three siblings were coming, not all eight."

Ellie slapped Sam's arm. "The letter explaining my aunt couldn't take anyone had gotten lost! That wasn't my fault. And then you wrote me back saying you were looking forward to seeing everyone, which I thought meant I could bring all of us."

Ellie turned to Keely, her eyes radiating a vibrant green in the firelight. "I still remember Sam coming up to me, no smile on his face, and asking if we could have a word in private. I thought I was going to be sick, but instead he agreed to take everyone in. Sweetheart that he is."

"Sam's always been too soft," Wes grumbled.

"But it worked out for the best now, didn't it?" Sam dropped a quick kiss onto Ellie's lips. "I can't imagine life without you, love."

"Do the two of you need to use one of my spare rooms?" Wes's dry voice rang through the room. "I have plenty."

"Stop acting jealous." Sam bent down and gave Ellie a kiss that lasted long enough that Keely felt heat rising in her cheeks.

"If you think Ellie's arrival makes for a good story, just wait until you hear about the marriage pact they made when they were twelve." Anna Mae leaned forward in her chair.

"A marriage pact?" Keely found herself sitting up straighter despite her engorged stomach. "What kind of twelve-year-olds make a marriage pact?"

Daniel let out a bark of laugher, then launched into a story about Wes being upset after his ma died, Cain antagonizing him, and a blood promise that involved the three of them pledging to get married before they turned thirty, and Cain and Harrison swearing they wouldn't marry before thirty.

It would have been the most outlandish story she'd ever heard, if it wasn't so adorable. Keely glanced around at her room full of friends, then tucked her stockinged feet up beneath her on the sofa and let the story swirl around her.

She couldn't remember the last time she'd felt this content, which was a bit crazy. After all, the Wolf Point Ring was still on the loose, she was wanted in Illinois for a double murder she hadn't committed, and there were wanted posters with her face plastered all around Texas.

But her situation only made her more determined to soak up every moment she could with her friends. Something told her if she ever left Twin Rivers, she'd have to search the world over before she found another group of friends like this—or a man as good as Wes.

~.~.~.~.~

SHE WAS TOO good at being a wife.

At being *his* wife.

Wes stood against the wall, watching as Keely sat with his friends, laughing and talking and enjoying herself. A bout of laugher burst out as Sam took over the story of their marriage pact, explaining how Daniel and Cain had nearly come to blows while arguing about whether men needed wives. But Wes wasn't in the mood to laugh.

His gaze drifted back to Keely. First, she helped with the ranch paperwork, then she took care of Leo, all while still overseeing the running of the house.

Now she sat here laughing with his friends and hearing their stories, acting like she'd been the one to grow up in Twin Rivers rather than him.

It should all be wonderful.

So why did his heart feel so heavy?

Wes slipped out of the room and headed down the corridor to his office. He needed space, a bit of air, some distance between himself and Keely before he ended up even more confused.

The second he stepped inside the familiar room, he saw the blanket Keely would spread on the floor for Leo and a pile of toys in the corner.

And was he crazy, or was his office even starting to smell faintly of the lilac water she wore?

Wes sat down at his desk. He'd look over reports from his foreman, that would keep his mind away from the way Keely's face lit up when she smiled, or the gentle manner in which she cradled Leo during one of his tantrums.

Grabbing a stack of papers, he picked up a pencil, only to realize that the paper on the top was the business projection Keely had done for his prime cattle.

"Why are you so agitated?"

Wes looked up to find his sister standing just inside the door. "You wouldn't understand."

Her brow drew down, marring her forehead. "It's Thanksgiving, of all times. Can't you find a reason to be happy?"

"It's not that I'm unhappy."

"So what's the problem?"

"No problem." He was lying, and she'd be able to see right through him. He had the urge to lick his lips that suddenly seemed far too dry.

"Is it your feelings?" Charlotte took another step inside the room. "That you're falling in love with Keely?"

His head snapped up. "I am not."

Charlotte stopped beside one of the tall wingback chairs, her eyes pinned to him. "I watched you fall in love with Abigail. I lived in this house with you for the three years you were married. I know what my brother looks like when he's around a woman he loves."

Wes shook his head. "Don't go down this path, Charlie."

She just stood there, watching and waiting.

He blew out a breath, then raked a hand through his hair. "I might... admire Keely, yes. And there are certainly things I appreciate about her. But..."

"But you're too afraid of losing her to let yourself love her."

"Yes. And I'm not sure whether it's for her own good, in that I don't want her to die in childbirth, or if it's because I don't want to open myself up to the pain that might come if I let myself love her—only to lose her later."

"Keely has feelings for you. Do you realize that?"

Did he? Wes moved to the window and looked out over the desert, where the hills shone silvery beneath the gleam of the moon. "What Keely feels... what I feel... I can't let it matter."

Charlotte came up beside him and tilted her head. "Keely's lost everyone and everything she loves in an attempt to bring criminals to justice. Outside of you, she has no one. And here you are, falling in love with her, but still so hurt you're determined to keep yourself at arm's length. Keely doesn't need a roof over her head. She's got enough gumption she could find a roof and a meal no matter where she runs. She needs someone to love her, utterly and completely."

Wes shifted awkwardly from one foot to another. Was his sister right? Did Keely need someone to love her that way?

If so, could he be the person to provide that love?

Something twisted in his stomach, and he stared out the window—at the landscape that was just as dark and desolate as the place inside him that had once felt love and laughter.

"I have news." Charlotte straightened beside him. "That's why I followed you to your office, not to talk about Keely."

Wes drew his gaze away from the desert to find his sister standing with her hand splayed over her belly in a way that could only mean one thing.

"I'm pregnant." Her words were soft, barely discernable

above the ticking of the clock on the wall and the sound of voices filtering down the corridor.

All he could do was stare. He'd known when he stood beside Daniel as the best man on his sister's wedding day that children would follow. He'd even told himself he'd find a way to be happy for her.

And he probably would feel happiness. Eventually.

*If Charlotte lives through childbirth.*

"I figured you would want to know now, before Daniel announces it to the others." Charlotte sniffled, a single tear trailing down her cheek. "I... I hope you can find a way to be happy for me and Daniel. We're terribly excited."

"Don't cry, Charlie. Thinking about having a child shouldn't bring you to tears."

"That's not why I'm crying."

"Why then?"

"Because you're not happy for me."

He groaned. "It's not that I'm not happy. It's..." *That I'm terrified.*

"I swear, Wes. I don't understand you. Not even a little."

"My previous wife died in childbirth," he snapped. "What's so hard to understand about that?"

"Did you ever stop to think that maybe, instead of trying so hard to control everything around you, you just need to step back and let God handle things?"

*What?* He looked down at his sister, his mouth falling open, then closing, then opening again before he spoke. "I don't try to control everything around me."

"Then what do you call your response to what I just told you? I'm pregnant, but instead of being happy for me like everyone else, all you feel is fear because you can't control what will happen during the birth."

He stiffened. "There is nothing wrong with me wanting you to survive the birth."

"No." She looked down to where her hand still rested protectively over her stomach and took a few steps away from him. "But there's something wrong with you wanting to control every facet of it. You're the same way when it comes to the lawsuit with the Mortimers."

"Again, there is nothing wrong with me wanting the A Bar W to stay in the family," he growled. "If I don't try to get the ranch back, it will go to a family who's done nothing to work for or deserve this ranch after I die."

"Except there is something wrong. 'Be careful for nothing; but in every thing by prayer and supplication with thanksgiving let your requests be made known unto God. And the peace of God, which passeth all understanding, shall keep your hearts and minds through Christ Jesus.' Don't you remember that verse from church?"

"I remember it, all right." Though he didn't have the first clue what it had to do with him getting his ranch back.

Charlotte raised her eyes until they met his. "Then you realize that all you ever are is careful and anxious and worried? You've been that way since Abigail's death. In response to your worry and fear, you try to control everything around you. Two women put you in uncomfortable situations that you couldn't control earlier this year, so you decided to up and marry a stranger for no other reason than that you could control that relationship."

*That's not entirely true.* But the words died on his tongue, because there was a whole lot of truth to the statement, even if he wasn't ready to admit it.

"You couldn't control a baby being left at your door, so you've been trying to control when and how the baby goes back to his mother."

"I'm only doing what's best for Leo." He fully believed that.

But there was still truth to her words, and it made the spot between his shoulder blades suddenly itch.

"You couldn't control the contract Father signed before he died, but you're trying to control it now by getting rid of it."

"It's a horrible contract." He threw up his hands. "It goes against every inheritance law in the country."

"Maybe so, and maybe it's something you should fight, but I'd feel a whole lot better about it if you started by praying for God's peace, like the verse says, rather than putting all your energy into controlling a situation you don't like."

*Peace.* It was such an odd word, almost foreign.

"Do you realize peace is the one thing you don't have in all of this?" Charlotte reached out and squeezed his hand. "And you should have it, at least looking at things from the outside. You have more money and prestige than anyone else in the county, but when was the last time you let yourself trust in God? When was the last time you had God's peace in your heart?"

Something sharp sliced through him. He opened his mouth to argue, to tell Charlotte that he was perfectly content with his life, that he had God's peace.

But his lips fell shut.

"That's why I'm not fond of you taking the Mortimers to court, because if you and Keely end up having children, everything in that contract will be void, and you'll have wasted hundreds of dollars that could be used for something better. But you're too busy trying to control things to stop and ask God what He thinks or what His plans for you might be." Charlotte drew in a breath, her chest heaving. "Maybe you'd have more happiness in your life right now if you just let the feelings between you and Keely grow and trusted that God would take care of the details."

Tears were streaming down Charlotte's face in earnest. She wiped them on her sleeve before he thought to offer a handkerchief. "I need to go. Daniel's waiting to tell the others about the baby, and I said I'd only be a few minutes."

She backed away from him. "Do you want to come back to the parlor for the announcement?"

"I've got work to do here," he managed.

She turned and walked out of the room, her dress swaying around her ankles.

He watched her until the last bit of blue fabric disappeared down the corridor, then he turned toward the window.

But the barren landscape and silvery moonlight had lost its calming effect. Was his sister right? Was he trying to control too much?

Oh, he could justify every decision he'd made over the past six months, in asking Keely to marry him, in trying to find Leo's ma, in filing a lawsuit against the Mortimers, in a hundred other choices he'd made. A ranch didn't grow to be the size of the A Bar W without careful planning.

But somewhere along the line, had he gone too far? Had he started trusting himself and his own decisions more than trusting God?

Wes wasn't sure how long he kept himself closed inside the four familiar walls of his office. At some point he heard the others say goodbye, but he didn't go out and speak to anyone.

Instead, he surrounded himself with reports, mounds and mounds of them. He went back and pulled the earliest reports from the ranch, then searched through his grandfather and father's records, looking for times the ranch had been strapped for cash and had to sell off an undesirably large amount of cattle.

He read until the words blurred on the page and his eyelids grew too heavy to stay open. But even then, he couldn't quite force his conversation with Charlotte from his mind.

*Dear God, am I really trying to control too much? Is that why I can't be happy for Charlie? Is that why I can't see myself loving Keely?*

He pushed his chair back from the desk, only to slump deeper into it. It was all so confusing.

A glance at the clock on the wall told him it was nearly two a.m., far too late for him to still be thinking clearly. Maybe he'd be able to make better sense of things in the morning.

He stood and turned off the lamp, then headed down the corridor toward the stairs. He would have gone straight up to his room, but the parlor door was open and light filtered out, spilling onto the tile floor.

Wes stepped inside to extinguish the lamp, only to find Keely asleep on the sofa. A pile of hairpins lay on the table beside the couch, and her curly red tresses fanned out over the deep blue of the cushions. She looked peaceful lying there. Peaceful and delicate and... lovely.

He swallowed. Some men couldn't find even one pretty woman in their lifetime, and here God had given him two beautiful women to wed.

And there was no denying Keely's beauty.

Most days he refused to let himself think about it. But at two in the morning, when she'd let her hair down, and her creamy skin contrasted with the deep blue of the couch...

He took a step toward her, then another and another until he found himself kneeling beside her. Her chest rose and fell in an even rhythm, and her breath puffed little plumes of air against his cheek.

He took a strand of hair and twisted it between his fingers. "Keely, wake up, angel."

She didn't move.

"Keely, sweetheart." He rested his hand on her cheek, intending to stroke it until her eyes fluttered open. But at the soft feel of her skin beneath his palm, he stilled.

Charlotte had said Keely had feelings for him, but Keely had never given him any indication that was so.

Or maybe she had, but he'd missed them? Her soft smiles,

the way she asked if he needed anything when he'd been stuck in his office for hours. The way she curled next to him on the couch every evening and told him about her day.

What if her feelings were evident, but he'd not wanted to see them?

He leaned forward and placed a kiss on her forehead.

She shifted, her eyes blinking open. "Wes?"

"I was trying to wake you." His hand still rested on her cheek, and he moved his thumb to stroke across the soft skin again. "You fell asleep in the parlor."

"I was waiting for you. Leo was already asleep upstairs, and we usually talk after he goes to bed." She sat up, but that only brought her nearer to him, so close that her breath once again puffed against his cheek. "I knew you were working in your office. I just figured I'd sit down and... well, never mind about me. You left the parlor early. Did you have fun this evening?"

"I..."

She looked straight at him, waiting for an answer, but all he could see was the deep green of her eyes, the soft pink of her lips, the rise and fall of her chest, which suddenly seemed to deepen.

Then she leaned forward, and he bent his head the slightest bit, causing their lips to brush.

He drew in a breath, and she paused, their mouths still touching, as though not quite certain whether they should keep kissing or pull back.

He found his hand reaching up to cup her cheek, then his other arm wrapping around her back and bringing her closer.

He moved his lips against hers, the scent of lilac water swirling around him and her soft sigh filling his ears. She tasted like candied yams and coffee and pie, and something else he could describe only as "Keely."

Her lips were tentative at first, but the longer he held her, the more relaxed she grew in his arms. The feelings all came back to him. The rightness of having a woman in his arms, and the warmth that came from two bodies pressed closely together. The desire to lay her back on the couch, kiss his way down her neck, and show her just how special things could be between a husband and wife.

*Bong! Bong!*

The sound of the clock chiming two in the morning jolted him out of his senselessness, and he pulled back.

"Keely, I'm so sorry," he rasped, his heart thundering against his ribs, his chest rising and falling in hard, quick breaths.

"Don't apologize." Her words came on a breathless whisper, and a fresh stain of red appeared on her already flushed cheeks. "I liked it."

"No." He scrambled farther back, then pushed to his feet. "I can't. We can't. I... I never should have done that."

He turned and strode out of the room before she could say anything more.

## 18

"Let me hold him for a bit."

Keely looked up from where she'd been sitting with Leo to find Anna Mae was setting down the tiny yellow sweater she'd been crocheting. Anna Mae pushed herself out of her chair and walked across Charlotte's parlor.

Keely, Charlotte, Anna Mae, and Ellie had decided last night that both Ellie and Charlotte needed more clothes for their babies, so they'd decided to gather for a clothes-making party.

Keely gave Leo a little squeeze, then handed him over and picked up the pink bootie Leo hadn't let her work on.

Leo let out a small burst of giggles when Anna Mae took him, which only caused Anna Mae to hold him high in the air, then bring him down to touch her face. Another fit of giggles followed.

"He's the happiest baby." Ellie rubbed a hand over her protruding stomach. "I hope mine is that happy after he's born."

"Me too." Charlotte sighed and leaned back against a pile of extra cushions on the sofa, her own hand finding her flat stomach.

After Daniel had announced Charlotte was expecting last night, the four of them had decided to meet twice a week to make clothes for the coming infants.

"Having a baby feels so very far away right now," Charlotte said on a sigh. "Tell us, Keely, what's it like being a mother?"

"I... um..." Keely had the sudden urge to squirm. "I'm not really his mother."

"Don't be silly." Anna Mae clasped Leo's hand and jiggled it, causing his entire arm to wobble and producing a happy squeal from the child. "You've been caring for him for two months. You're the closest thing he has to a mother."

Two months. Had it only been that long? It felt like four months, or maybe even four years. Leo had become such a large part of her life that she couldn't imagine living on the ranch without him.

"It's wonderful." She didn't try to stop the smile that spread across her lips. "I mean, there's work involved, but to have a happy little baby greet you every morning or curl his hand in your hair and not let go, well, it's the most wonderful thing."

But what would happen if Leo's mother returned? The question haunted her mind far too many times a day. There'd been a time when that was all she hoped for. A child should be raised by his mother, not a stranger. But she was far from a stranger to Leo now, and the thought of his mother returning caused her stomach to twist.

Would she be able to give Leo up?

She bit the side of her lip. Oh, how had this turned into such a mess? When she'd told Wes she'd come to Twin Rivers and marry him, she'd known she was agreeing to a situation that didn't involve any love or feelings—at least initially.

But she hadn't known she'd end up wanting children anyway.

Hadn't known she'd end up caring so deeply for a man who didn't want her affection.

She shook her head, then blew out a breath, but she still couldn't clear Wes's image from last night out of her mind. When he'd taken her in his arms and held her against him, she'd felt safe, like nothing could happen to her as long as he kept his arms wrapped around her.

Then they'd kissed, and that had caused a whole different host of sensations to tumble through her. She'd wanted to fall into the kiss, to live inside of it for hours, or maybe even days. She could have lain on the sofa with him all night, snuggling and kissing and feeling the warmth of his body against hers.

And then he'd pulled away, and the tender man who'd just held her had morphed into a hard, cold shell.

That kiss had been the most wonderful five minutes of her life, yet he'd been insistent they never should have kissed.

Moisture welled in her eyes. What was she going to do? Her feelings for him had grown too strong, and now she wanted children too—with him.

She didn't even know if she could stay in Twin Rivers, and there hadn't been any news about the Wolf Point Ring in weeks.

But if she stayed, and she loved Wes with all her heart, that didn't mean he'd ever love her back.

"Keely, what's wrong?" Ellie's voice sounded like it came from far away. "I thought we were talking about happy things, like marriage and a family."

Keely looked up to find all three women watching her. "We were, and those things would probably be happy for most people, but my situation is different."

"Different, yes, but not hopeless." Charlotte set her knitting down and reached for her hand. "Wes has feelings for you."

Keely shook her head. "No, he doesn't." He'd probably been imagining she was Abigail the entire time they'd kissed last night. "I'm nothing but a giant inconvenience to him, Leo and me both."

"Don't be cruel." Anna Mae jiggled Leo on her side, but a stern look had replaced her smile. "It's true Wes probably should have waited to get remarried, but he doesn't think of you as an inconvenience, not even given what you're running from. Daniel told me he hired six guards who could pose as ranch hands to protect you."

She looked down at her forgotten pink bootie. "He did, yes."

"You know how we were laughing about Wes being opposed to Sam and me getting married last night?" Ellie rubbed a hand absently over her belly. "Well, we were all against him marrying you, Keely. Not because we thought ill of you, but because every one of us knew Wes wasn't ready for another marriage. I know from my own experience how much heartache having different expectations of a marriage can cause."

"We didn't have different expectations. I knew exactly what he wanted of me before I spoke my vows."

"Maybe, but that doesn't mean his expectations are realistic." Charlotte stood and crossed to the table, where she poured herself a glass of lemonade. "You love him. It's plain to everyone in this room."

Keely stared down at her hands. Did she love him? She hadn't allowed herself to think about her feelings that much. She cared, yes, but had it grown into love? "It was supposed to be so simple. Just live with Wes, in what I thought would be a small ranch house, and help with things. It didn't sound difficult when I answered his ad."

"You can't live in the same house with a good man like my brother and not develop feelings for him." Charlotte's voice was soft as she spoke. "What's happening to you would happen to any of us, and you shouldn't feel guilty."

"He's so kind to me," she whispered. "I know he can seem

all serious and official, but if you get him away from his office, the real Wes comes out."

"He's always been that way," Anna Mae said. "Even when he was a boy."

"What am I going to do?"

Charlotte sighed. "Give it time. Wes is already upset that I'm pregnant and—"

"No." Ellie's eyes rounded with horror. "How could he be upset about something like that?"

"Because he looks at pregnancy like it's a death sentence," Keely answered.

A heavy silence descended on the room, and once again she looked up to find all three women staring at her. The ticking of the clock sounded from the corner, and the wind rustled the shrubs outside, but no one spoke for far too long.

"You can't be serious," Anna Mae finally whispered.

"It's true." Charlotte swirled the lemonade in her glass. "He was upset for weeks after Ellie and Sam made their announcement last summer."

"But parenthood is of the Lord," Ellie protested. "The Bible says to be fruitful and multiply!"

"What happened to Abigail isn't all that common." Anna Mae stroked a hand over Leo's downy head. "Most women handle pregnancy just fine. If every woman died in childbirth, then humanity would die off in a single generation."

"I think he knows that, which is why I said my brother needs time. Deep down, he realizes his position is ridiculous, but he's not ready to open his heart to the kind of risk that loving again means just yet." Two splotches of red marred Charlotte's cheeks.

"Do you remember that verse Preacher Russel preached on a few Sundays back?" Anna Mae said. "The one about being of good courage because God is with you and won't fail you?"

Keely nodded. She went back to that passage of scripture far too often, especially since she'd not been back to church.

"Well, I think this is a time for courage. God is the one who brought you and Wes together, even though the rest of us had our doubts. The more I see you and Wes with little Leo, the more I wonder if God is using this situation to heal Wes. So be strong. And remember that God won't fail you or forsake you. He's with you right now, even though it feels like Wes is as far removed from you as Chicago is from Twin Rivers."

Keely swallowed the sudden lump in her throat. "Thank you, Anna Mae. I needed to hear that."

"Try to be patient with my brother." Charlotte's voice took on a pleading, almost desperate quality. "When Ellie here comes through childbirth unscathed, maybe he'll start to see how ridiculous he's being."

"Patient," Keely repeated, then picked up her crocheting hook. "Yes, I can be patient." She had little choice, really.

But as the others started talking about motherhood, she couldn't quite bring herself to join in the conversation.

What if time didn't erase Wes's fears about childbirth?

Would she ever be able to have the type of family she wanted with her husband?

~.~.~.~.~

"You going to tell me why you got a bee under your bonnet?" Sam said from where he rode beside Wes.

Wes slanted a glance at his friend. The sun sat in the sky high above them, touching everything in sight with its golden light, but the cold spell they'd been having meant that its rays weren't overly warm. The Rio Grande sputtered and gurgled beside them, filling the Mexican desert with the rare sound of moving water.

"I'm not wearing a bonnet," he muttered.

"Maybe not, but you're about as aggravated as you would be if a swarm of wasps decided to sting you."

Wes pressed his lips together. He could see the Mexican weaving shop up ahead, the building looming on the desert beside the Rio Grande. "Nothing's bothering me."

"You're lying."

"I am not." He just couldn't stop thinking about the kiss. The kiss, and the way Keely had felt in his arms, and the way her soft sobs had drifted into the corridor when he'd walked away from her.

He'd left the house before she'd woken that morning, and he didn't plan on going home until well after dark.

When he did return, he hoped to have Leo's mother in tow.

He pulled Ares to a stop in front of the large adobe building that had once been falling down and crumbling. The sound of the looms clacking as the workers inside spun rugs and saddle blankets echoed out the open windows.

Wes swung off Ares and tied him to the hitching post beneath the shade provided by a woven ocotillo mat suspended between four posts.

"You sure you don't want to tell me what's got you all bothered before we go on in there?" Sam tethered his horse beside Ares and sent him another glance.

"Not bothered by anything, just looking for some answers." Wes entered the building with Sam only a step behind him.

Sam let out a low whistle as he surveyed the inside of the shop that resembled more of a factory than anything. "Been a while since I visited here. You've added on."

Wes looked around the building. Looms filled every last foot of space, and beside each loom sat a Mexican woman, weaving brightly colored strands of yarn into anything from a saddle blanket to a rug to a bedroll. The building did look rather impressive these days, more like a factory than the rundown adobe hovel Charlotte and their former housekeeper, Consuela, had talked Pa into buying a decade earlier.

His family had acquired the shop when Consuela's cousin on the Mexican side of the river had just buried her husband, and she'd been in need of a job. Even more, Consuela's cousin knew several other women in Mexico who needed work. So Charlotte and Consuela had talked Pa into buying the dilapidated old building and turning it into a weaving shop. The Mexican women made the goods, and each year when Wes went on the cattle drive, he took several wagons full of textiles to sell for top dollar in Austin.

It would have been a good business investment, but Wes could never manage to take any profit from the shop's account. Instead, he put every last penny he made right back into it. The building had been added on to four times and now held sixfold more looms than they'd started out with.

"Mr. Westin." Consuela's cousin, Marina, called to him from the other side of the building floor, then threaded her way through the maze of looms. She had been promoted to manager eight years ago, after the first addition had been completed and four more looms had been added.

"Did you come for more rugs?" She stopped in front of him, her brightly colored skirt swishing around her feet. "Charlotte was just here last week, and I gave everything to her. I only have a few new ones finished."

"No, I'm not here for rugs." Wes nodded toward the open door that led to the office. "I need to talk to you."

Her gaze drifted over to Sam before she turned toward the office. "Come then, let us talk."

Wes followed her into the small room, where an equally small desk sat filled with papers. "I'm sure by now you've heard that a baby was dropped off at my house about two months ago. Do you have any idea who the mother might be?"

Marina shuffled some of the papers on her desk. "You sent one of your hands here after it happened asking that same question. I told him then that I didn't know anything."

"A lot can change in a month. Are you sure you haven't heard of anyone missing a child? You know every mother on this side of the border for fifty miles. Surely you must have some guess as to where the baby came from."

The woman raised her hand in an empty gesture. "I'm sorry. I know nothing."

"Do you mind if I question the workers?" Of the fifty women who worked there, certainly someone knew of a woman who'd had a baby one day and no baby the next.

Marina frowned. "Mr. Westin, they are busy working. I'd hate to distract them."

"I won't be that much of a distraction."

"We really need to find the child's mother, *señora*." Sam leaned forward in his chair. "Or at least find out what happened to her. It's important."

"Very well." The woman didn't smile, only made a shooing motion with her hands.

Wes rose from the chair and went onto the shop floor, speaking to the woman who worked the loom closest to the office door first.

She didn't know anything. Nor did the woman after that, or after that, or after that. Sam followed him around the shop, mostly listening to the conversations. Every so often he asked a question of his own.

Three hours later, Wes stalked outside to Ares, untethered him, and swung into the saddle. No one seemed to have a clue where Leo had come from. Sam sauntered out of the building behind him and lazily climbed astride his horse, then gave his reins a small flick.

Wes glared at his friend, who seemed to move extra slowly, never mind that he was ready to race across the desert.

"The manager—Marina, was it?" Sam gave his reigns another small flick. "I think she knows more than she's telling you."

Wes stared at the desert ahead, barely resisting the urge to dig his heels into Ares and see how fast his horse could carry him. "How do you know?"

"When you asked about Leo's mother, she didn't answer any of your questions, she just distracted you with questions of her own. She never looked at you when she gave her twisty answers either."

"If she knows something, why won't she tell me? I've helped them for years."

Sam scanned the mountains to their south, his face grim. "This might be a lot more complicated than just a mother not wanting her child anymore."

"What do you mean?"

"I mean, I got the impression several of the other women you questioned knew things, but they'd been instructed not to say."

Wes's grip on the reigns tightened involuntarily. "Who would instruct them to keep a child away from its mother? That's the most ridiculous thing I've ever heard."

"Pieces of this story haven't fit from the beginning. That's why I'm saying something else is going on. Think about it. Most women who need to give up their babies will see if a relative can take it, and if not that, they'll go to an orphanage."

"But the orphanage where you were raised has been closed for years. It's not like there's a place in Twin Rivers for a woman in a difficult situation to drop off a child."

Sam directed his horse around a large rock sticking out into the trail. "No, but if a woman really wants to give up her baby, she would make the trip to the orphanage in Midland."

Maybe. All he knew was that each day Leo was in his house, he and Keely and the babe seemed more and more like a real family.

They weren't, of course, and they never could be. But Leo made it too easy for him to feel close to Keely.

Too easy for him to want a family of his own.

Maybe that had been what led him to kiss Keely last night. The feeling that they were already a family, the notion that she might have feelings for him, the—

"You all right?" Sam drawled.

"Fine," Wes snapped.

But he wasn't fine. He needed to find the child's mother.

If Charlotte knew what he was up to, she'd probably claim that he was being controlling again. But he was only trying to protect Keely, just like he was doing by hiring the Pinkerton agents. Charlotte had pointed out that Keely had already lost too much. The last thing Keely needed now was to come to love the child, only to have Leo taken from her.

Yes, saying goodbye to the baby now would be far easier than if he stayed with them for a year or more.

Wes adjusted his hat against the bright sunlight.

So why did he feel like such an oaf for trying to find Leo's mother?

## 19

"There, there. You have sweet dreams." Keely laid a drowsy Leo in the crib for the second time that evening, then covered him with a blanket. He instinctively snuggled down against the tick, and she began humming the song that she hummed to him every night since he'd arrived on their doorstep, "Abide with Me."

The babe blinked once, then twice before his eyes closed in slumber, but she still stood by his crib to finish the song. Even then, there was something so precious and vulnerable about him that she had a hard time stepping away.

Had Leo's mother stood over his crib every night and watched him fall asleep too?

She shook her head. Where had that thought come from?

"Keely."

She turned and found Wes standing in the doorway. His clothes were covered in dust, and subtle lines of weariness etched his face.

"I didn't realize you were home."

"Just got in. Do you have time to talk before bed?"

She looked down at herself, clad only in a nightgown, and her face heated.

She'd put Leo to bed once already, then had spent nearly two hours reading in the parlor, fully dressed and waiting for Wes to come home. But the hour had grown late and Leo had woken and started fussing, so she'd readied herself for bed.

Had Wes seen her in a nightdress before?

She didn't think so, and she was likely to remember something like that.

"Well? Can we talk?" Wes walked across her room, opening the inner door that connected her room with his.

She swallowed. Perhaps it was the thin fabric of the nightgown and the knowledge that she wore so little underneath it. Or perhaps it was the memory of last night's kiss and the way Wes had cradled her against him. Or her conversation with Charlotte earlier, when her friend had claimed that Wes only needed time before he'd take her to wife in full.

Or perhaps it was the door itself. It was the first time the one separating his room from hers had been opened since she'd come to live there. Even now, she could see Wes's bed.

"Keely?" Wes raised an eyebrow at her. "Are you coming?"

"Of course." She forced her bare feet forward, moving through the doorway and heading to one of the two chairs by the empty fireplace.

Rather than take the chair opposite her, Wes started pacing, scattering tiny flecks of dust from his clothes over the pristine floor.

"Is everything all right?"

"No, nothing is right. It's all wrong. Just plain wrong." He kept pacing, the clacking of his boots against the Spanish tile the only sound in the room.

She shifted in the chair, trying to maintain a dignified and ladylike position, though the soft cushions tried pulling her into a comfortable slouch.

Should she try to guess what was bothering him? "Are you worried about Charlotte? With the pregnancy, I mean."

Her question stopped his pacing, but she wasn't sure that was a good thing, not considering how the muscle on the side of his jaw pulsed.

"Please don't worry overmuch." She stood and went to him. "Motherhood is a wonderful thing, a blessing from God. Just because Abigail..."

"Stop."

She could see the fear in his eyes, lurking just beneath their warm brown color. She wrapped her arms around him and leaned her head against his chest. "You shouldn't let this fear control you. Can't you see the suffering you bring upon yourself?"

He stayed stiff in her arms for a moment, but then he drew in a breath and his arms came around her, strong and warm.

She nestled her face against the soft fabric of his shirt, drawing in the scents of sunshine and wind and bergamot. His hand found her hair, and he ran his fingers down the loose locks.

She wasn't sure how long she stood there, with her head resting against him and his fingers stroking her hair, but when she looked up, she found his face just above hers and his eyes soft.

Like they'd been last night, just before they'd kissed.

She pushed up onto her tiptoes and would have touched her lips to his, but Wes dropped his arms from around her and stepped back. "We can't."

She wrapped her arms around herself, though the sensation wasn't remotely close to the feeling she got when Wes's arms were around her. "We need to talk about last night."

"No, we don't."

A lump lodged in her throat, but she forced her tongue to work anyway. "I know I wasn't supposed to develop feelings for you, and I've spent the past few weeks trying to tell myself that I hadn't, or that my feelings weren't genuine, or that I was only attracted to you because you've been kind to me. But after we kissed last night, I realized—"

"It was a mistake. We never should have kissed."

She sucked in a breath. "Don't say that."

"I told you what happened to Abigail. I told you about the promise I made to myself on the day of her funeral." The muscle on the side of his jaw clenched and unclenched in a rhythmic, pulsing motion. "I will never touch you that way. I will never put you at risk of dying from childbirth."

"I wasn't asking you to take things that far!" She flung her hand toward the large bed taking up the opposite side of the room. "All I wanted was a kiss!"

"I can't. Don't you understand? I'm a grown man. I can't spend my days with you, watching you care for Leo and help around my office, then take you in my arms and kiss you at night and not want you in every way."

"You can't?" she whispered, unable to keep the thread of hope from her voice.

"Of course not," he growled the words, terse and mean, and yet they made her feel light.

"So there's part of you that... that wants to take me to bed?" Warmth crept up her neck and onto her cheeks. "Because when you say our kiss was a mistake, it makes me feel as though you don't want me like that."

He ran his gaze down her, and her entire body flushed. She'd never been more aware of what she was wearing—or rather, what she wasn't wearing—as he stared at the thin fabric shielding her body from his gaze.

"I want you too much. That's the problem." His gaze left her body, and he turned his back to her. "Having Leo here, watching you care for him, watching you tend the hacienda, it makes me desire things I can never have."

"But what if you can have them?"

"I can't, not without putting you at risk."

That dratted lump popped back into her throat, and she couldn't tell whether it was from anger, a breaking heart, or maybe a little of both. "I've got news for you, Wes. One day, I'm going to die."

He turned, bringing his gaze back to hers, but rather than the warmth that had filled his eyes before, hardness radiated from them. "That's enough."

"One day, you'll die too."

"I said stop."

"One day Charlotte will die and Daniel will die and every other person you know will die. We will all die. No one has ever escaped death, save Christ."

He pressed his eyes shut and looked away from her again.

"I don't know when I'll die or how I'll die, but God does. In fact, He says, 'It is appointed unto man once to die,' in Hebrews chapter nine. That means my death is already planned." She drew in a breath, her voice quavering.

Wes was completely silent as she spoke, the muscles of his body coiled tight. But at least he didn't try to stop her from saying more.

Maybe, just maybe, some of what she said would filter through the stubbornness and pain he used to shield his heart. "That means there's nothing you can do to stop my death from coming. Not with all your money and land and cattle. I could die tomorrow, or I could die seventy years from now, or I could die in nine or ten months, trying to bear you a child.

"The same was true for Abigail." Keely's throat tightened, the quiver in her jaw now matching the quiver in her voice. "Abigail was going to die when God wanted to call her home. That's all there was to it. If she wouldn't have died in childbirth, maybe she would have died of a disease or an accident with a horse. Maybe she would have been shot by rustlers. I don't know. But I do know this..."

She paused and drew in a breath, her lungs heaving for air inside her chest, even though she'd done nothing that should make her starved for air. "You're not God, Wes. You can sit in your fancy office behind your fancy desk and try to control your little empire, but you can't control the entire world. You can't control life and death."

"Who are you to talk?" Wes flung a hand in her direction, his eyes burning with fury. "You're just as afraid as I am. You ran all this way, you married a stranger. You lied about your name, and why? Because you were trying to stay alive. So here I am trying to make sure I don't kill you, and you're telling me I'm wrong for it?"

She closed her eyes and swallowed. When she raised her eyelids again, the moisture she'd been battling for the past ten minutes finally filled her vision. "It's not death that I fear. It's... it's what they'd do to me first."

~.~.~.~.~

WES BLEW OUT A BREATH, the tension that had wound his body tighter than a barbwire fence draining from him. He was an oaf, an utter and complete brute. What had possessed him to say such a thing? Of course she was terrified of what the Wolf Point Ring would do if they got ahold of her, especially after seeing what had been done to her brother's fiancée.

"I'm sorry." He stepped closer and reached out to take her hand, but her fingers were limp and cold in his palm. "I misspoke. I said what I did out of anger, without thinking about my words first, and it was cruel of me."

"It's long past time I went to bed. If you'll excuse me."

She turned for the door, but he didn't release her hand.

"Please. I just want to go to bed and be alone, and you shouldn't have any objections, seeing how you don't want to be with me anyway."

"That's not true."

She looked at him through wet, tired eyes. "It's true in the way that matters most."

Hang it all. Did she have to say that? Did she have to look at him with such hopelessness? Hold such weariness in her voice? She wasn't even trying to understand his reasons for not touching her.

And they made sense.

A whole lot of sense.

He released her hand. "Fine. But before you go, I spent the day searching for Leo's mother. I've decided to strengthen my efforts to find her, and I wanted you to know."

"You what?" She stared at him, her body suddenly stiff.

"I went to Mexico today looking for information about who Leo's mother might be. That's what I asked you in here to say. I don't want you to be surprised if his mother returns for him in the next day or two."

"How could you?" Accusation dripped from her voice.

He held up his hands. "The child needs his mother, and last time we went searching for her, you came with me, remember?"

"That was weeks ago! A lot has changed."

"No, it hasn't." Wes held up his hand, then raised his fingers as he ticked through a list of Leo's circumstances. "We still don't know where his mother is, what's happened to her, or why she left him here." He showed Keely his three fingers before dropping them back to his side. "I may not know a lot about parenting, but I know that the absolute best place for a child is to be with the woman who bore him."

"What if she's in some kind of trouble?" Keely shook her

head, and one of the tears that had been brimming in her eyes streaked down her cheek. "It made sense to look for his mother when he first arrived, but he's been with us for two months. It's not your place to meddle any longer. What if Leo's in some type of danger by staying with her? You know nothing about her situation. Nothing!"

"Nor do you, and until we find out more, it doesn't do you any good to get too attached."

"I'm not getting attached, I'm caring for him, that's all. He's a babe. He needs comfort and love and support."

But that didn't mean Keely should become his mother. "I'm only attempting to protect you. Leo is doing unhealthy things to your emotions."

"There is nothing unhealthy about loving a child!"

"There is when he's going to leave." He kept his voice flat, though Keely paced around the room the way a newly captured bear might pace his cage.

If she would just calm down, if she would try to treat this like a business transaction and keep her emotions out of the conversation, maybe she'd see reason.

"This isn't about my growing too attached, is it? It's about you." She jabbed an accusing finger at him. "You're the one who's afraid. You're growing to care for Leo too, aren't you? And instead of loving him and giving him what he needs, all you can think about is what will happen if he's taken away from you. And so you'd rather get rid of him now than risk losing him."

Wes drew in a shaky breath. It wasn't about him. Was it?

No, he was only thinking of Keely. If she had this much trouble merely talking about Leo leaving, then she'd find handing him to his mother impossible.

"You're a fool, Agamemnon. Every person who has ever walked this earth has experienced loss. It's part of living. But here you are, thinking you're above it. That losing someone you love one time means you should never love again."

She stopped pacing and met his gaze, her eyes burning with green fire. "I wonder, would you even go back and marry Abigail? Clearly you loved her. But knowing how she died, knowing the loss and the pain you would feel, would you choose to go back and do it all over again? To have all the good memories, all the wonderful moments? Or would you be so afraid of the grief, that you'd choose to give up all the happiness Abigail brought into your life?"

"How dare you." His voice came out quiet, but even he could hear the deathly warning dripping from his words.

"How dare I? I'm not the one who thinks he's God. How dare *you!*" Keely whirled around and stalked through the door that separated their rooms, slamming it behind her.

~.~.~.~.~

WES RUBBED at his bleary eyes, then refocused on the Bible passage in front of him. *To every thing there is a season, and a time to every purpose under the heaven: A time to be born, and a time to die.*

The passage went on to talk about time for all kinds of things. A time to plant and a time to pluck up what had been planted, a time to mourn and a time to dance, a time to love and a time to hate.

But he kept coming back to the first phrase. *A time to be born, and a time to die.*

Had God appointed a time for Abigail to die? Would she have died on July 29, 1884, no matter whether she was pregnant or not?

No matter what he did to try to prevent her death?

He shook his head and stared at Ecclesiastes 3 again.

Lamplight flickered across his bed, creating an uneven light for him to read by, and he could just make out the faintest hint of light gray on the horizon above the mountains to his east.

He didn't know how long he'd been sitting there, his Bible splayed on his lap as he rested in bed with pillows propped between his back and the headboard.

He'd tried to sleep after his conversation with Keely, truly he had. At first, he'd blamed his inability to fall asleep on Leo, who had woken when Keely slammed the door. But after the babe's cries had stopped, he'd still been unable to calm his mind.

Keely's final question from earlier kept coming back to haunt him. *Would you even go back and marry Abigail...? Knowing how she died, knowing the loss and the pain you would feel, would you choose to go back and do it all over again?*

He wanted to say yes, that he didn't even need to think about it. That he valued the love he'd shared with Abigail so much he'd be willing to experience it all over again, even if it ended with unbearable pain.

But he couldn't say yes. Not if he was being honest.

*God, what's wrong with me?* He tilted his head up and stared at the ceiling. *Am I really so hard and unfeeling that I'd choose to have never met Abigail? Am I really so concerned about myself and my pain that I'd leave Abigail out of my life entirely if given the option?*

He stared back down at his Bible. *A time to be born, and a time to die, a time to mourn and a time to dance, a time to weep and a time to laugh. A time to love and a time to hate.*

He squeezed his eyes shut in an attempt to rid them of the moisture trying to gather. He knew it wasn't a time to hate. But what time was it?

A time to mourn?

Maybe. He still missed Abigail, but he'd been mourning her for almost a year and a half.

Part of him wanted to say it was a time to weep, but what if it was a time to laugh instead? What if it was a time to dance and a time to love?

What if God was giving him a second chance to have a family... and he was too busy mourning and weeping to notice?

"Dear Father, I don't know what to do," he whispered. "I can't just forget Abigail. I can't just stop being afraid that Charlotte or Ellie might die in childbirth. I can't just take Keely to bed and pretend the notion of her conceiving doesn't scare me."

And yet, he couldn't go on this way either. His actions were bringing Keely pain and hindering him from moving forward with the wife he now had.

Thanksgiving night, Charlotte had talked about having God's peace. She'd even quoted a verse that said God's peace would surpass all understanding. But God's peace felt as far away from him as the ocean did from Twin Rivers.

*I want to trust you, God. I want that peace you promise. But what if... what if I don't know where to start?*

Except he did know where to start. He'd start by not returning to Mexico to look for Leo's mother. He'd let God bring her to them when God was good and ready.

And if he grew too attached to Leo in the meantime, if Keely grew to love the babe even more than she already did, then he'd trust God to heal their wounds.

Or at least he would try.

He could only take things one day at a time, but he could use each day to give God more control and trust himself less.

## 20

"**Y**ou'd better clear your plate, or the big bad bear is going to get you."

From her position drying dishes, Keely looked over her shoulder at the Owenses' table, where Sam's declaration had produced a fit of squeals from Ellie's younger siblings.

"I'm getting my plate. I won't forget this time," Joe shouted as he hurried into the kitchen and dropped the plate into the murky water Ellie was using to wash dishes.

"I already cleared my plate," Janey shouted. "You can't get me."

"Oh yes, I can," Sam growled, a giant smile plastered to his face. He took a couple quick steps and hooked the small girl with his arm.

She let out a squeal, followed by a fit of laughter. "Joe, Henry, save me!"

"I'm coming," Joe cried. The small boy rushed to the rug in front of the sofa, where Sam had carried his twin sister, and climbed on his adopted father's back.

Sam pretended to eat Janey, making loud chewing sounds as he tickled her neck.

Two of the boys who had been helping to clear the table put their dishes back onto the table and rushed over to join the fray.

"Come on, Susanna," one of them shouted. "We need your help too."

"I'm holding Leo." But Susanna got up from where she'd been sitting at the table, entertaining Leo with a rattle, and handed the babe over to Keely. "I'll be back in a minute."

Keely couldn't wipe the smile from her face as she watched all but the oldest boy pile onto Sam in the center of the Owens's house. They tried to tickle him. They tried to pin him down. They crawled on top of him and rolled him over and back again. Shouts and giggles and laughter filled the entire space.

"Sorry," the oldest boy—Leroy, was it?—carried an armload of forgotten dishes to the sink. "It can get kind of loud in here sometimes."

"I don't mind." She watched as Janey launched herself onto Sam's back, only to have him buck her gently onto the sofa. In truth, she'd never seen anything quite like the pile of bodies on the living room floor. Was it normal for fathers to play with their children like this? Hers certainly never had, and Wes...

A hard knot formed in her stomach. She was not going to start thinking about Wes. That was the entire reason she'd decided to ride over to Sam and Ellie's earlier. She'd figured all the commotion around their place would be a distraction from the awkward silence that had filled the hacienda for the first half of the day.

She hadn't said a word to Wes since their argument last night, and he'd seemed perfectly fine with that. He'd holed himself up in the office the entire time she'd been at the A Bar W. It had seemed a bit odd, since he'd said he planned to go to Mexico to continue looking for Leo's mother, but she hadn't asked about it. If she tried to open her mouth around him, she was rather certain only one question would emerge.

*Why do you want to send Leo away so badly?*

But she already knew the answer he would give—that the best place for a babe was with his mother. The trouble was, his answer wasn't the full truth—that Abigail's death had wounded him so deeply he refused to let himself love again.

Not anyone, and not for any reason.

She blinked away the sudden rush of heat stinging her eyes. If only she could find a way to stop the situation from hurting so much.

Keely looked back over at the rug, where Sam still tussled with Ellie's siblings. Did he ever complain about them? Did some part of him feel overwhelmed by taking on a family of this size?

What had made him decide to legally adopt all of them, even though they weren't his?

Part of her wanted to ask Ellie, but although the two of them were friends, asking whether Sam felt burdened by her siblings seemed too sensitive of a question.

"You look sad." Ellie set a dish in the drying rack and turned her way. "What are you thinking?"

*That if Sam has room in his heart for so many adopted children, why can't Wes make room in his heart for one?*

She shook her head. "I'd rather not say."

"Are you having more trouble with Wes? Is that why you rode over?" Ellie gave her arm a little squeeze before turning back to the dishes. "Try to be patient. He's a good man. He'll come around."

"But what if he doesn't?" She bit her lip. "He went into Mexico yesterday and offered a reward for news of Leo's mother. And I... I..."

"Oh, Keely," Ellie's arms wrapped around her in a gentle hug.

"I just don't understand." She sniffled. "Why doesn't he want a family? Why doesn't he want to keep Leo? Is there something about him that makes him undesirable? Because the longer I care for Leo, the more I wish he were mine."

And the more she wished Wes wanted her to be his wife in every way.

Oh, she never should have let things go so far with him. Never should have let herself think about how handsome he was or be flattered by his desire to protect her.

Never should have let herself... *care about Leo?*

No. Babes needed love and mothering. She refused to regret an ounce of the affection she'd shown Leo.

Of course, she'd known all along that Leo's mother could return. But Wes actively trying to find her?

It felt like a betrayal.

"There, there." Ellie patted her back. "Don't cry."

But she was crying. Again. For the second time in less than a day.

*I just want a family, God. I promise that's all I want. If you give me one, I'll never ask for anything again. I'll never complain. I'll never... never...* She didn't know what else she wouldn't do. She only knew what she wanted more than anything else.

After being on the run for so long, she felt it more keenly. Most people had a family and saw nothing special in it, but she only wanted a husband who loved her and a child or two of her own. Was that really so much to ask for?

If there'd been any question over how she felt about Wes, it had been answered last night. Her feelings for him went far beyond caring. She loved him.

Loved him but couldn't have him.

And it hurt almost as bad as losing James.

At least losing her brother was done and over, but how was she supposed to stay at the A Bar W for the rest of her life, seeing the man she loved but never receiving a drop of love from him in return?

Her heart wasn't going to survive it.

~.~.~.~.~

WES COULDN'T SAY what woke him. Perhaps it was that he'd been sleeping so lightly, tossing and turning as thoughts of Keely and Leo swam through his mind. Or perhaps it was that he hadn't been sleeping very long.

He glanced around the dark room, his body still while his eyes searched for anything unusual.

There. Near the door.

Out of the corner of his eye, he spotted a figure bathed in shadow.

He slowly reached his hand under his pillow and gripped the pistol that he'd placed there when he'd first learned Keely was running from the Wolf Point Ring.

His heart pounded in his ears, and sweat beaded along his hairline.

He sucked in a slow breath. He needed to stay calm and steady, needed to think.

He could make out the movement better now. The moonlight from the window didn't quite reach where the intruder stood, but he knew where to aim his pistol.

He pointed the barrel and cocked the hammer. The unmistakable clack of metal against metal echoed in the room. "Don't move."

The shadow stilled for a moment, then came a familiar voice. "Agamemnon, it's me, Consuela."

Consuela?

Wes propped himself up higher in the bed, still keeping his pistol trained. Had his former housekeeper come back to work at the A Bar W?

If so, what was she doing in his room? And in the middle of the night?

"Step over to the foot of the bed. Slowly. I want to see you."

"I swear it's me." Her footfalls sounded as she moved her portly form across the room.

Sure enough, the moonlight filtered over the planes and angles of the face that had become more familiar to him than his mother's.

"Do you know how long I've been looking for you?" He lowered the gun to his lap, disengaging the hammer before tucking the gun back under his pillow. "How many times I've sent people into Mexico to find you? Your position is still waiting for you."

"I didn't come to take back my old position. I came for the babe."

"Leo?" Wes swung his legs over the side of the bed and shoved his legs into the trousers that were laying over the chair beside it. "Why? He's not your child."

"His mother is standing outside your door."

Something twisted in his stomach. He looked toward the door, which had been left open a crack. Was the child's mother truly outside? He raked a hand through hair already messy from sleeping. That was supposed to be good, right?

But why had she come in the middle of the night? And with Consuela, no less?

And why did his chest feel suddenly hollow at the notion of sending Leo away?

Only because Keely would be devastated. Certainly not because he was going to miss the infant.

"Well," Consuela asked, looking about the room. "Where is he? Don't tell me you put him in the bunkhouse. I figured you'd hire a maid for him."

Wes shook his head. He'd forgotten how long Consuela had

been gone. She wouldn't have the first clue about him marrying Keely.

"Leo is safe, I assure you. But I want to meet his mother before anything else."

"Please, Wes." Exasperation etched Consuela's voice. "Don't drag this out. We haven't much time."

"Is she in some kind of danger?" He padded to his dresser, where he lit a lantern and tugged a shirt out of the drawer.

"You know she's in danger. The note when we left him for you said as much."

Wes pulled the shirt over his head, then carried the lantern into the corridor without bothering to tuck his shirt in.

Sure enough, a woman leaned against the wall beside his door. As soon as she saw him, she straightened. *"Dónde es Leo?"*

She looked around him toward the door, clearly waiting for someone behind him to emerge with the child.

He used the moment to study her. She had a long face with high eyebrows and prominent cheekbones. Glossy black hair flowed down her back and framed her slender shoulders. She was pretty in the usual way of young women, but he wouldn't call her either striking or beautiful. And yet, she was familiar somehow. Where had he seen her?

"Your son is somewhere safe for now." Wes spoke in English, wanting to see if she could understand him. "What's your name?"

She looked at him. Fear swam in her large brown eyes, but she kept the rest of her face and body so composed he would have missed it had he not been looking. "Hortencia."

Hortencia. That's where he knew her from. Not because he'd seen her in person, but because she was the woman in Cain's sketch.

Wait. Cain's informant who had disappeared... was Leo's mother?

That would explain why she was in danger, but why had

Cain said nothing to him about Leo? Did he not know what she'd done with her child? Wouldn't he have been able to surmise what had happened when a babe showed up on his doorstep around the same time Hortencia's child disappeared?

He bit the side of his lip to keep the questions from spewing out and settled for the one that was most important. "Tell me, Hortencia, if I give you Leo, will you be able to keep him safe?"

She shrank back against the wall, her eyes moving from him to Consuela. "I will try."

"If she can't keep him safe, the fault is yours," Consuela snapped. "We all thought bringing the babe here would be best, even Cain. That's why he dropped Leo off."

Cain had been the one to drop off Leo? Since when? Cain had pretended like he knew nothing about Leo when he'd shown up at the ranch the day after Leo had arrived.

Wes's hands clenched into fists at his side. He could only assume Cain had known where to find Leo's mother at first too, but he hadn't said a word.

As soon as the sun was up, he had a visit to pay to a former friend.

"I should have known you wouldn't leave things alone." Consuela jabbed a thick, pudgy finger into his chest. "If you just could have kept him and been quiet about it, everything would be fine. Instead, you had to go searching for his mother. You were going to give her away! You and your search and your reward money."

"Everything I did was perfectly logical." Yet somehow Consuela had a way of making him feel like he was ten again. Ten and in trouble for stealing Mrs. Costner's petticoat off her clothesline. "Had you still been working here and known nothing of Hortencia's situation, you would have demanded I search for Leo's mother too."

"It matters not. Now everyone is wondering why you are looking for a Mexican woman who just had a baby." Consuela made a slashing motion with her hand. "Everyone is wondering why you have her baby. Do you realize how this has hurt Cain? The rustlers are quiet now, not talking when they go to the cantina. They are suspicious of everyone, and Cain's information has all but dried up."

"You've been helping Cain?" Wes stared at the housekeeper as the bigger picture started to form in his head. "Is that why you haven't come back to the A Bar W?"

Consuela shook her head and muttered something in Spanish he couldn't quite make out. "Hortencia was helping him. I still can if I return to Mexico."

"You're not staying? I'm still in need of a housekeeper."

"I'm needed in Mexico." The way she said the name of her country, with gentleness and care, made her seem even more removed from him.

"Is it safe for you there?" He reached out and laid a hand on her shoulder. "Because if it's not, I—"

She shrugged his hand away. "As long as they don't find out what I'm doing. Everyone knows I once worked here. Everyone knows I got angry and left. They don't assume we're friends."

Wes drew in a breath. Evidently the cruel way his father had treated Consuela had led to something good. And now he knew why he hadn't been able to find her despite months of searching.

"Hortencia needs to go." Consuela gave him a stern look. "Where is Leo?"

Wes looked over at the woman who had shrunk back against the wall, her dark hair falling in waves that hid half her face. "Where do you plan to go once you leave here?"

Hortencia opened her mouth to reply, but Consuela answered before her. "It's safer not to say."

"But she has somewhere she can go? Somewhere that's safe, where the rustlers won't find her?"

"She has a plan," Consuela quipped. "If it works, both her and the babe will be safe."

"Has Cain offered men to escort her?"

"He doesn't know I'm here." Hortencia spoke this time, her voice soft, yet laced with a fierce determination. "Any contact with him would be too dangerous. Now please, just give me my son so we can go before daybreak. The farther we get tonight, the better."

Crossing the desert alone couldn't be any less dangerous than going to Cain. "I have trained men, guards that I hired to pose as cowhands. Let me send a couple of them with you."

Consuela looked to Hortencia, then spoke in rapid Spanish. Hortencia answered her just as quickly, and back and forth the two went.

He could understand most of what they said, debating between themselves whether it would be better to have some men on the journey for protection, even though the men would be strangers to them.

Consuela finally turned back to him. "Do you trust these men you hired? Can you assure me they will keep her safe until she reaches Albuquerque?"

"Albuquerque?"

Consuela crossed her arms over her chest and humphed. "Yes, Albuquerque. If people come after her, they'll take the trail to San Antonio. She will go opposite."

"I see." It was a good plan. By the time the rustlers realized she wasn't on the trail to San Antonio, she would be halfway to her destination.

He looked at Hortencia again, sweeping his eyes down her and then back up. Just how well did he know his hired guards? They were being paid handsomely to protect Keely, but were they honorable enough to send over the desert with a young woman? If the rustlers decided to offer more money than what he was paying, would one of them turn Hortencia over?

Likely not. But Hortencia had already done much to help Cain, even going so far as to give up her child for a time. If he had to send Charlotte or Keely over the desert, he'd choose two of his longtime cowhands to accompany them, not one of the agents he barely knew.

"I'll ask Dobbs and Bruce to go."

Consuela looked at him for a moment, and even in the dim light from the lantern, he could see the approval in her eyes. Then she turned to Hortencia and laid a hand on the other woman's shoulder. "Those are his two most faithful hands outside of his foreman. They'll protect you with their very lives."

"They will. Now wait here for a minute. I have something more for you." Wes took the lantern back into his room and set it atop his dresser, then reached for the picture above it. Leaning the painting against the wall, he dialed the combination to the small safe hidden behind the picture. The larger safe in his office downstairs held his important papers and more money, but after selling Harrison that railroad stock, he had enough cash on hand to ensure that Hortencia's and Leo's needs would be met for several months.

He took two stacks of bills, then closed the safe back up, rehung the picture, and stepped into the corridor. "This should see to your needs long enough for you to get established elsewhere."

Hortencia reached her hand out, then pulled it away. "It's... it's too much. I didn't help the rangers for money. I helped them because... because..." She gave a small shudder and wrapped her arms around herself. "The rustlers, they are evil. Friends of *el diablo*."

"Helping Cain put your life in danger and separated you from your son. This is my way of helping you in return." He held the money extended toward her.

"Take it, Hortencia." Consuela nudged her shoulder. "It's

enough you can go to California. It might even be enough to start that restaurant."

"Yes, take it. Please."

She looked between the two of them, then reached out her slender hand and picked up the bills. "Gracias."

"Now all we need is the babe." Consuela turned to him. "Where is he?"

Wes drew in a long breath, then looked at Keely's door. "You and Hortencia go to the office and wait. I'll bring you Leo, then go wake Dobbs and Bruce while Hortencia gets reacquainted with her son."

Consuela frowned. "Is everything all right?"

Wes swallowed, then met Hortencia's eyes in the lamplight. "Leo's a delightful child, and he was well cared for here, just as you'd hoped. But I'm afraid it's going to be hard for the woman who's been tending him to say goodbye. She'd appreciate some privacy."

Consuela glanced at Keely's door. He could see questions in her mind, but instead of voicing them, she wrapped an arm around Hortencia's shoulders and guided her toward the stairs, their shoes clacking overly loud against the tile in the otherwise silent night.

Wes drew in a breath, then pushed it out in a giant rush and reached for Keely's door handle. *Dear God, I thought I wanted Leo's mother to return. It was supposed to be for the best. But now... give me wisdom. Give Keely the strength she needs to say goodbye.*

He pushed open the door, but the glow from his lantern didn't reveal a sleeping Keely. Instead, he found her already sitting on the bed with Leo cradled in her arms.

She shook her head when he entered the room, and a tear fell from her watery eyes to streak down her cheek. "I don't know if I can do this."

"Keely." He set the lantern down, then climbed onto the bed beside her. Instead of taking the babe, he wrapped his arm around her shoulders and drew her against him. "He belongs with his mother."

"But I love him." Her words were soft, yet they had a way of filling the entire room more fully than if she would have shouted them.

"I know. But sometimes you have to say goodbye, even to people you love." *Even though you don't want to. Even though you'll spend the next year of your life dreaming about them and waking with an ache in your chest where your heart used to be. Even though tiny, little things will remind you of them all day long and heat will prick your eyes at the worst times. Even though your heart will never be the same.*

The words rested on his tongue, but he refused to open his mouth and let them spill.

"I heard you through the door," she sniffled. "His mother was helping Cain. That's why she had to send Leo away."

"Yes."

"She could have tried to escape with Leo. When it got too dangerous, your housekeeper could have brought both of them here and said they needed to leave Mexico, and you would have given her money and sent men to escort her."

"Yes."

"But instead, she sent Leo away and stayed in Mexico because she thought she could help Cain more."

"I assume so, though I don't know all the details." Something he was sure to remedy when he visited Cain in the morning.

"His mother..." Keely looked down and stroked a hand over Leo's cheek. "She sounds like a good woman. Sounds like she'll do her best to care for him."

Wes scooted a little closer to Keely, then guided her head down so it rested in the crook of his shoulder. "Hortencia wants to go to California and open a restaurant."

"And you gave her enough money that she'll be able to do that?"

"I didn't know about the restaurant when I gave her the money. I'll give her more before she goes."

Keely wiped another stray tear from her cheek. "You're a good man, Wes."

"And you're a good woman." He kissed the top of her head. "You took in a strange child and treated him as though he was your own. You cared for him, you provided for him—you loved him. Not many women would have taken to mothering an abandoned child as well as you did."

"But now I have to say goodbye." She squeezed her eyes shut, but more tears leaked down her cheeks, and her shoulders began to shake.

"Oh, Keely." He stroked a hand down the hair tumbling down her back. This was why he'd gone into Mexico, even though Charlotte had said he was being too controlling. This was what he'd tried to avoid. This pain and heartache.

Why hadn't Hortencia come for Leo within a week? Then none of this would need to have happened.

But if he asked himself that, then maybe he should ask himself why his relationship with Abigail had lasted more than a week.

"You just said that Leo belongs with his mother. That the only reason she gave him up was so that she could help Cain," he spoke softly against her hair. "Surely you realize that saying goodbye is the right thing, even if it hurts."

"Do you remember when I went to church a few weeks ago?"

"Yes."

"The preacher brought a sermon on having courage. There was a verse, Deuteronomy 31:6, about being of good courage because God won't ever fail you or forsake you."

"I remember." He rubbed her shoulder.

"What am I supposed to do if it feels like God is failing me?"

"I think..." He released a small groan. He didn't know, and he was the last person she should be asking, because these were the very same questions he had regarding Abigail's death.

Keely sniffled again. "It all just hurts so much."

He stroked her arm, up and down, up and down, in a soothing motion. "I understand."

And he did. All too well, he knew what it was like to love someone and then be forced to say goodbye.

## 21

She couldn't stay in Twin Rivers. Not without Leo.

Keely grabbed an armful of clothes from her dresser and stuffed them into her carpetbag. The sky outside was black as ink, and somewhere downstairs, Wes was sending Leo, his mother, and his two most trusted ranch hands out into the night.

She could understand why Leo's mother had sent him to the A Bar W, and she no longer faulted her or begrudged her for it. Saying goodbye to Leo, even temporarily, must have been the hardest thing Hortencia had ever done.

But the longer Leo had stayed, the more comfortable she'd become with the notion of being his mother. But now...

Maybe saying goodbye to Leo wouldn't be so hard if she'd one day be able to hold her own child, if she'd one day have a husband who viewed her as a wife rather than a housekeeper. But when she thought about what the next fifty years of her life would look like in Twin Rivers—no child of her own, no love from the man she'd married...

She sniffled back a fresh round of tears as she stuffed more clothes into her carpetbag.

She couldn't stay. It felt too hopeless. This house might be grand and ornate, but there was no love inside it. No hope. No reason anyone would want to live here for a day, let alone decades.

When she'd come to Twin Rivers, she thought she'd known what she wanted. A place to put the past behind her and start again. The day she married Wes was supposed to have been the first day of the rest of her life.

Now she just wanted to leave.

No. That wasn't quite true. She didn't want to leave as much as she wanted a baby. And a husband who loved her.

A husband who wanted to have a family with her.

She bit the side of her lip, letting her teeth sink in hard enough to chase away the new round of tears threatening her eyes, then turned back to her dresser.

At least she hadn't been in Twin Rivers very long. She and Wes could still file for an annulment on the grounds he'd committed fraud when they'd married.

In fact, they could probably file for an annulment on the grounds she'd committed fraud too. After all, she'd gotten married using a fake name, she was under investigation for a crime in Chicago, and there'd been a warrant out for her arrest that she hadn't disclosed before they'd married.

Either way, Wes was smart enough to figure out how to get an annulment without her. And fortunately, it was Tuesday, which meant the weekly stage would arrive just after lunchtime. She fully intended to be on it.

A knock sounded at her door, but she ignored it and stalked to the wardrobe, throwing the doors open.

"Keely?" Wes stepped inside.

She turned with her arms full of clothes.

He scanned the room with its open dresser drawers and wardrobe. "Why are you packing?"

"Why do you think?" She headed toward the carpetbag.

"You can't leave." He said it matter-of-factly, as though he was discussing the current cattle price at market.

She stuffed more clothes into the bag, not bothering to fold anything. "No? Give me one reason why I should stay."

He trailed her over to the bed, then stood behind her, giving her no choice but to face him when she turned around. "I can give you ten, starting with the Wolf Point Ring. You're safer here than you will be anywhere else."

She shook her head. "You're wrong. I kept myself safe for eight months before coming here. But you're too well known, and I've been here too long. They probably know where I am and are just waiting for a time to sneak in and take me."

He glanced around the room, almost as though expecting a man in a red bowler hat to pop out of the shadows. "You think they've tracked you to Twin Rivers?"

"Not really. No." She pressed her lips together and looked away, even though he still kept her stuck between him and the bed. "But it doesn't change my mind about leaving."

Silence lingered between them, heavy with unspoken words. Wes kept his gaze on her, the heat and weight of it causing her to remain nearly frozen.

"Was Leo really the only thing keeping you here?" His words were quiet, yet they felt sharp, as though they'd been shot out of his mouth the way an arrow would when drawn from a bow.

"Yes. No... Oh, never mind. It's not something you would understand."

"Try me."

She felt suddenly tired. As though all the life had been sucked out of her and she'd been strung up to dry beneath the blistering desert sun. "I already have."

"You haven't, or I'd know what you were talking about. Leo wasn't the reason you came to Twin Rivers. It makes no sense for him to be the reason you're leaving."

"It's a family, you dunderhead!" She shoved at his chest. "I want a family. I didn't realize it when I first arrived. I didn't realize it until after Leo came and I got to know you more. I didn't realize it until..."

*I fell in love with you.* No, she wasn't admitting that, not to the man who kept his heart shuttered so very tight. "I did you wrong. I thought when I came here that all I wanted was a roof over my head and a place to hide from the Wolf Point Ring. That's the deal we agreed to. But I... I didn't know..."

She shook her head, tears threatening to choke her once more. "I can't do it. I can't spend the rest of my life married to you but living as your housekeeper. It's like I said. I want a family. Children. A husband who loves me. Those are things you will never give me, and that's why I can't stay. Because at least when I'm running from the Wolf Point Ring, I have a hope that one day they'll be caught. That one day they'll stop chasing me and I can go back to living a normal life. But with you... I'll never have the thing that I want most. And I can't spend the next forty years of my life living like that. It's too dark."

"It doesn't have to be like that." He reached out and rested a hand on her shoulder, the warmth from his skin seeping through the thin fabric of her nightdress.

"Not for you." She turned her head, refusing to look at him, yet his gaze burned the side of her face. "You're content to live the rest of your years without a family to love and be loved by. I don't understand it. In fact, I thought you were lying at first. But you really believe that this is the best way to live your life. I can't be part of a life like that, because I... I...

"Oh, forget it." She pulled away from him and turned back to the wardrobe. It wasn't empty, not considering the dresses he'd had made for her, but she had nowhere else to put her things without her trunk, and something told her Wes wouldn't be too keen on digging it out of the attic.

She grabbed a green dress to change into before leaving.

"What if I don't want a life like that anymore?"

She stilled, the dress frozen in her hands and she stared at the wardrobe. "What did you say?"

He came up behind her, and she could feel him again, the heat of his chest against her back, the ruffle of his breath on her hair.

Why did her body have to be so sensitive to every last thing Wes did?

"I said, what if I don't want a life like that, where I don't love anyone, and no one loves me in return. What if I want more?"

She spun around. He was still too close. She could see the ring of dark brown around his irises and the faint lines at the corners of his eyes. And each time she drew in a breath, her chest brushed against his. "What are you saying?"

He swallowed, his throat muscles working tightly. "I'm saying that I didn't uphold my end of our marriage bargain either. I'm saying that somewhere over the days and weeks you've been here, I fell in love with you."

She sucked in a breath but forgot how to release it. The air stayed in her lungs, bottled up tight.

"Do you mean it?" She searched his face. Sincerity etched the lines around his mouth and warmth radiated from his eyes. "You really love me?"

"I do." He stroked a strand of hair behind her ear, then let his fingers linger there, in the tender spot where her ear met her neck.

She felt another round of tears brewing, but not because she was sad. She threw her arms around his neck. "Oh, Wes. I love you too. I've loved you for weeks. I was just too afraid to say anything. You were so insistent about not wanting a family, about wanting any "romantic entanglements" as you called them in your letters."

He wrapped his arms around her and chuckled, the sound low and deep. "It's a little too late for that."

Then he leaned down, and his lips claimed hers.

She felt light enough to float, like the only thing pinning her down were Wes's arms around her. Then Wes tilted her head, making the kiss seem somehow more intimate, and his hands came around to anchor her against him. The dress slipped from her fingers, falling to the floor in a soft heap as he brought her body flush against his.

There was nothing restrained about the way he held her, nothing controlled or calculating about how he moved his mouth against hers. If anything, she'd call his movements desperate.

And yet somehow, they were tender too, almost worshipful.

She sank into the kiss, wanting to stay like that forever, wrapped in his arms, kissing him until the sun came up.

But Wes pulled away after another moment, then cradled her against his chest. "I'm sorry about Leo, sweetheart. I know how much it hurts you to let him go."

She burrowed deeper against his chest, letting his strong arms hold her so tightly the pain in her chest over Leo seemed to lessen.

"Maybe one day we can go to California. Just to see how he and Hortencia are doing."

"Count on it." He planted a soft kiss on the top of her head, then released her and stepped to the bed. "Let me move this carpetbag so you can get in."

He hefted the overly stuffed bag onto the floor, and she couldn't stop the giggle that burst from her chest.

"What?"

"It's just, that's the worst packing job ever. I needed my trunk, but I didn't want to ask you to get it. And... Oh goodness. My clothes are going to be wrinkled if they sit there all night. I need to hang them up."

She took a step toward the bag, but Wes snaked an arm out

and caught her around the waist. "I can hire someone to iron your clothes. Let's go to bed."

Together? Did Wes intend to fully make her his wife right then and there?

He must have sensed her questions, because he spoke into the quietness between them. "I just want to hold you for a bit. I'm not ready for more yet, but will you let me hold you?"

She nodded, her throat suddenly too thick to speak.

He went back to his room to change into his nightshirt, giving her time to slide beneath the covers. A few minutes later, the door opened, and Wes climbed into bed behind her. When he opened his arms, she snuggled into his warmth. The last thing she remembered was the feel of his breath against her head before she drifted to sleep.

~.~.~.~.~

WES KNEW she was there before he fully woke. It was impossible to miss the warmth of her body pressed up against him, or the way her silky hair lay in riotous curls over his shoulder and her head snuggled against his chest.

He drew in a breath, long and deep and content. He couldn't remember the last time he'd slept so deeply.

Keely shifted beside him, and he angled his body toward her, pulling her closer.

How many nights had he thought of going into her room? Of tucking her up against him and holding her close through the night?

He'd always banished the thoughts as soon as they popped into his head, but now he was here, curled into bed with her, and holding her as though he never wanted to let her go.

*Dear God, thank you for giving Keely to me.* He stroked his fingers through her hair. *Now help me keep her safe.*

He'd told her he loved her last night. The moment he'd seen her packing, he couldn't help but blurt out his feelings.

*She loves you too.* He'd known for a while, hadn't he? Known, but hadn't wanted to admit it because he'd been afraid it would make things between them too complicated.

Keely shifted again beside him, and her eyes fluttered open. "Wes?"

"Good morning, angel." He gathered her closer and pressed a kiss to the top of her head.

"Angel?"

"Yes, angel. That's how I think of you, as my angel sent from God."

She blinked up at him, her green eyes soft in the dim light of dawn. "I don't think I'm a very good angel, but I'm glad you stayed."

"Of course I stayed."

"I figured you'd only hold me until I fell asleep, then you'd go back to your own room."

"I wanted to be near you." He stared down at her, soft lips and mussed hair and creamy skin, then stifled a groan. She was far too tempting to be lying in bed beside him.

"Did you mean what you said last night?" Her voice was quiet against the stillness of the room. "When you told me you didn't want me to leave? Did you mean that... that...?"

"That I love you?"

She drew in a breath, watching him carefully.

"Yes, I meant it. I love you, Keely."

A slow smile spread across her face, and she reached up and laid a hand against his cheek. "I love you too."

And then she kissed him. Her lips were soft and gentle against his, the skin of her face smooth beneath his touch. Part of him wanted to haul her closer and deepen the kiss, to feel every last curve of her body pressed against him. But he pulled away and gulped in a breath.

"I love you, Keely, but the rest... it's going to take time. I know you want children, but I'm just..."

An oaf, that's what he was. Because even though he was lying in bed, holding his wife in his arms, he still wasn't ready to make love to her.

She blinked up at him, her eyes soft with understanding. "I can wait. As long as we're taking steps in the right direction, I can be patient."

He pressed her closer, coaxing her head to the spot between his arm and shoulder that seemed as though God had carved it just so Keely could snuggle with him. "Thank you for understanding."

*And thank you, Father, for giving me a patient woman.*

She gave him an absent nod, her eyes drifting closed in the predawn light.

"I need to go into town and talk to Daniel and Cain, see what all Cain knows about Hortencia and tell him she came for the baby last night." He stroked his hand absently through her curls.

"This early?" She yawned but kept her eyes shut. "Can't you stay a little longer?"

He chuckled, then shifted her so that she lay even closer to him. "I suppose."

It didn't take long for her to doze back off, but he held her the entire time, watching the shadows of early morning creep across her creamy skin and her eyelids flutter ever so softly against her cheek. The sun was just peeking over the mountains when he climbed out of bed, dressed, and headed out to the barn.

As soon as he reached Twin Rivers, he turned Ares down O'Reilly Street and headed for the sheriff's office. It was closer than the ranger encampment by the river, and something told him Daniel would be plenty interested in coming with him to talk to Cain.

Both Sam's and Cain's horses were already tethered to the hitching post despite the early hour. Wes tied Ares to the wooden post and climbed the steps before opening the door.

Three bodies filled the space, but he narrowed his gaze at the lanky form with long, wavy hair that stood by the table with coffee and biscuits.

He moved across the office in three long strides and jabbed a finger at Cain. "You deserve a fist to the jaw."

"For what?" Cain drawled.

"For what you did to Keely and Hortencia."

"What's going on?" Daniel straightened from where he'd been leaning against his desk.

"He was the one who dropped Leo off at my house." Wes glared at Cain. "He knew where his mother was the whole time, why she needed help, all of it. But he never said a word."

"Keep your voice down," Cain growled. "We can't afford for people to overhear you."

Both Daniel and Sam start talking, probably asking Cain more questions, but all Wes heard was the sound of blood roaring in his ears. "So you don't deny it? Don't even have an excuse?"

"You've seen Hortencia?" Cain raised his coffee cup to his lips, but there was nothing laidback about the gesture. He held Wes's gaze with his own, his eyes like two pointed spears. "Is she safe?"

Wes felt one of his hands involuntarily clench into a fist. "Don't pretend to be concerned about her safety. You're the one who put her in danger by asking her to snitch on the rustlers."

"I didn't force her to be an informant. She agreed of her own volition."

"Really? When she had a child on the way?"

"The baby's father is one of the rustlers. He forced her into his bed."

Wes stared at Cain. Was that why Hortencia had been willing to act as an informant?

"She came forward about four months ago." Cain set his coffee down and crossed his arms over his chest, but once again, there was nothing relaxed or careless about the gesture. Every inch of him radiated barely controlled fury. "She worked in a cantina that the rustlers often stopped by. Those rustlers are just as despised in Mexico as they are on this side of the border. They don't treat women right. They don't treat farmers right. They run roughshod over anyone who gets in their way or refuses to give them what they want. But no one was brave enough to speak up, except Hortencia."

"Because one of the rustlers had forced her," Wes muttered, the situation finally starting to make sense.

"Enrique thought he had a right to visit her bed each time he passed through town. He was well aware the babe was his, and he wasn't making any plans to care for it." Disgust twisted Cain's face. "When we finally caught up to him, I made sure he was shot, not captured. I have to think God saves a special place in hell for men like that."

Yes, Cain of all people would think so, considering Cain's father had treated his mother in much the same way. She hadn't been forced that Wes knew of. But she'd been a cantina girl with eyes for Cain's pa. When she'd ended up pregnant, Cain's pa had wanted nothing to do with her or the babe.

It was why he'd been named Cain. Both Cain's parents had always thought him a curse—just like Cain in the Bible.

"That still doesn't explain why she sent Leo to Wes's," Daniel said. He'd taken up his position leaning against the front of his desk again, while Sam stood beside him.

"She was worried she wouldn't be able to care for him, and she certainly wouldn't be getting information to pass on if she wasn't working at the cantina. So I suggested having the baby stay with Wes until she figured out what she wanted to do, and Consuela agreed it was a good choice. I dropped him off when you were at church, then went to check on him the next day."

"And somewhere in the meantime, you learned my wife was wanted for murder," Wes muttered.

"Hadn't rightly seen that coming." Cain rubbed the back of his neck. "The plan worked for a few weeks, and Hortencia kept passing information. But then she disappeared, and I was worried enough to start looking for her discreetly. That's why I showed you and Daniel her sketch. I didn't realize she'd gone to Consuela for help."

"And you did every last bit of this without consulting me," Wes snarled.

Cain leveled his gaze at him. "You would have said no."

"Of course I would have said no!" He threw up his hands. "Do you know what this has done to Keely? Did you ever stop to think how much saying goodbye to Leo might hurt her? Did you stop to..."

He clamped his mouth shut before he gave away anything Cain might one day come back and use against him. Cain wouldn't have stopped to think about the effect this would have on anyone. The man had about as many feelings as a rock.

"Hortencia and Leo are on their way to Albuquerque," he said instead. "I sent Dobbs and Bruce with them, so they should arrive safely. And from Albuquerque..." he shrugged. "Let's just say I gave her enough money she should be able to start a restaurant in California. She can tell everyone Leo's pa died, which is true enough, and the folks out there will all assume she's a widow."

"Be mad at me if you want, but I knew you would help." Cain leaned a shoulder against the wall, an awfully carefree stance for a man that had spent the last month meddling in other people's lives. "Figured it would give your new wife something to do. And I figured that if Hortencia came back for Leo, you would send her away with enough money to get resettled."

"Congratulations, Cain." Sarcasm dripped from his voice. "Looks like you were right."

"I don't get why you're so all-fired angry. You just helped a shamed woman escape a band of outlaws and gave her a new start. That's something a man should be proud of."

Was he serious? The man really did deserve a punch to the jaw. "I'm mad because you didn't ask! I'm mad because you took what you knew of me and used it to your own advantage. I'm mad because you hurt Keely. Do you realize how many people she's already lost? How many times she's already had to say goodbye? And now she's had to say goodbye to Leo too."

Cain pushed himself off the wall and ran a hand through his hair. "I miscalculated there. I was gone when she got here. I only knew that she was supposed to arrive, and I didn't know anything about her situation when I offered to bring Leo to you. I didn't intend to cause her any pain. I just forgot to think that far through."

"You would," Wes snapped.

Cain's gaze shot to his. "What's that supposed to mean?"

"It means you don't have the first clue about women. You don't know how they think or what they feel, and you don't even try to understand. They're different than me or you, Cain. They feel things more keenly. Making a woman give up a baby that she loves is nothing short of despicable, and you somehow managed to make two women do it in the span of a few weeks."

"Hang it all, Agamemnon. If it's a babe your wife wants, then give her one. It's not that all-fired hard."

Wes swung his fist, and it connected with Cain's jaw in a sickening crack.

"Enough," Daniel roared. "Wes, you strike Cain again, and I'll lock you up for assaulting a lawman—which is a criminal offense, even if the lawman deserves a punch or two. Cain, just because you're a ranger doesn't mean you can manipulate or use the people of Twin Rivers however you see fit. I'm the chief law officer in this county, and what you did to the Westins was both unfair and manipulative. If you think someone in Twin Rivers can help with some aspect of your mission, you clear it with me first, and then you talk to the people you want to help. These are people's lives we're talking about. You don't get to turn them into pawns in your game of chess with the rustlers."

"How very kind of you, Sheriff," Cain sneered. "Thanks for lending a hand."

He shoved off the wall and stormed toward the door, stopping only to grab his hat before slamming the door behind him.

The moment he was gone, Wes slumped into the empty chair behind the desk the deputies shared. "This is all such a mess."

"How's Keely?" Daniel asked.

"She's..." He shook his head. "She wanted to leave. You should have seen her last night. Throwing things into that carpetbag, saying she couldn't bear to stay without Leo."

Sam shifted to look out the window. "She's not outside waiting for the stage, is she?"

Wes scrubbed a hand over his face. "I told her I wanted her to stay. Said I loved her."

Daniel tilted his head. "You weren't lying, were you?"

"No." Wes looked down, letting the memories from last night play in his mind. The anger and hurt in Keely's eyes when she told him she was leaving. The crack in her voice when she said she couldn't spend the next forty years living with someone who wasn't willing to be her husband in full. The way she'd melted into him when he said the three words he probably should have told her weeks ago. *I love you.*

"She... she said she loves me back," Wes rasped.

"Then what's the problem?" Sam drawled. "Sounds like the way things are supposed to be between a husband and wife."

Wes clenched a hand into a fist, then forced it open, its tendons stretched white against his palm. "What if I lose her? What if God takes her from me the way he took Abigail?"

Sam slapped him on the shoulder. "Then you trust God to get you through the hard times. Remember that sermon Preacher Russell gave a few weeks back? There was a verse. 'Be strong and of a good courage, fear not, nor be afraid of them: for the LORD thy God, he it is that doth go with thee; he will not fail thee, nor forsake thee.'"

"Yes, I remember." How could he forget when half the town kept quoting it at him? "I know that verse says God isn't going to fail me or forsake me. The problem is, I feel like that's exactly what God did when Abigail died."

The words landed in the room with silent thuds, large and heavy and leaving a searing silence in their wake.

"You're thinking about things wrong." Daniel leaned against his desk, where his coffee and biscuit sat forgotten. "Abigail's death wasn't God failing you, it was part of God's plan. I know you weren't ready for her time on earth to be done, but the Bible says it is appointed unto man once to die. There was a reason God called her home. You don't understand that reason now, and to be honest, you might never understand. We aren't called to understand all of God's workings, only to accept them and trust God through them."

Wes scrubbed a hand over his face. Keely had said as much when she'd told him that everyone suffered loss, and that he was a fool for trying to escape it. But when he looked at Abigail's death, he didn't see any good. He only saw pain and sorrow, heartache and despair and...

...And God guiding him through it?

He stilled. No. He'd felt completely abandoned and

forsaken, the exact opposite of what the verse from Deuteronomy said.

But what if he'd been mistaken? What if God had been there, and he simply hadn't realized it?

He'd been so blinded by grief he hadn't wanted to get out of bed in the morning.

But he had.

And how many times had Daniel or Sam or both of them shown up at his house and dragged him to church or about town?

Charlotte had been there too, making sure Marceau cooked a breakfast or supper that smelled so good he'd had to eat at least a few bites, even though he'd not felt hungry for months on end.

And Preacher Russell had come to his house every week for months, not to lecture or sermonize, but simply to pray with him.

Had that all been God? Sam and Daniel, Charlotte and the preacher? He hadn't seen it as God helping him, just as people he knew finding ways to show they cared. But what if God's hand had been in all of it, and he'd missed it?

He still didn't understand why Abigail had died.

But was that where trusting God came in?

Maybe he had to trust that there was good somewhere, even if he couldn't see it.

"You can't control life and death, but I'll tell you what you can control." Daniel rubbed the back of his neck. "How you respond to it. We all know you didn't have a choice about losing Abigail, but you had a choice—still have a choice—about how you respond to her death."

Wes looked at the man who'd been his best friend since the cradle, at the familiar planes and lines of his face and the sincerity radiating from his deep blue eyes, and swallowed.

"But what if... what if I let myself love Keely, and God takes her too? You still haven't given me an answer for that."

"Sure, we did." Sam took a slurp of coffee. "You keep trusting God. You'll pray and read your Bible and believe that God had a reason for taking her from you."

Wes swallowed. Yes, he'd resolved to start trusting God more after his fight with Keely two nights ago, but he'd done that by not going into Mexico to look for Leo's mother. He wasn't yet sure he'd come to the place where he could trust God with Abigail's death. Not when it still hurt so very much.

"'Perfect love casteth out fear.'" Daniel crossed the room and stopped in front of the deputy's desk, bringing himself only a handful of feet from where Wes sat. "And that verse isn't talking about love between a man and woman, it's talking about God's love for us. His love is so perfect that we have no need to fear the future."

"I'm not gonna lie." Sam rubbed the back of his neck. "The future's gonna have some valleys and bleak spots from time to time."

"Sam's right," Daniel said. "But we can always rest in the promise that God loves us wholly and completely, and because of that, we have no need to fear."

Wes had the sudden urge to squirm. That verse seemed to be one of Preacher Russell's favorites, but he'd never thought too much about what it meant, never realized it could apply to Abigail and what came next in his life.

If he could bring himself to trust that God might have something good in store for him with Keely, could he be the husband she deserved? Give her all the parts of marriage that she wanted?

"Sheriff!" The door to Daniel's office burst open, and in rushed Pablo Diez, waving the small slip of a telegram in his hand. "It came! The telegram you've been waiting for."

Daniel took the paper and glanced at it. "It's from J. R. Says 'The situation will be under control by next week.'"

"Is that good news?" Pablo asked. "Is it what you've been wanting to know?"

Daniel clapped Pablo on the shoulder. "I reckon it is. Thanks for bringing it over, but do me a favor. If you get another telegram from J. R., can you bring it to me right away?"

"Sure will. You're going to want confirmation that the situation gets dealt with, right?"

"Something like that, but remember what we discussed? Any telegram coming through the sheriff's office is to be kept confidential."

"*Sí*, Sheriff. I remember."

"That means no one can know about the telegram I'm holding right now."

The man scratched his head, his gaze drifting over both Wes and Sam. "But..."

"I was the one that read it aloud, and I was the one that told them because they are affected by it. This is different than telling Mrs. Miller or the Widow Perez. *Comprendo?*"

"*Sí, sí.*" The man nodded, then turned for the door.

"Thank you," Daniel called.

"*De nada.*"

As soon as the door shut behind Pablo, Sam let out a hoot. "Boy howdy, that's the best news I've heard in a month of Sundays. Sounds like the Wolf Point Ring is going to be caught!"

Wes stood. "I don't know. The telegram doesn't say very much, just that the situation should be taken care of in another ten days. We don't even know for sure what situation the sender is talking about. Does 'taken care of' mean arrested?"

"That's what I would assume, yes." Daniel looked back down at the telegram. "Marshal Redding can't go into too much detail. Any telegraph operator from here to Austin to Chicago can eavesdrop on a telegraph line. If I were in his shoes, I'd send a message pretty similar to this one."

Wes reached for the telegram. "I still don't feel like it's very clear."

Sam slapped him on the back. "Would it kill you to smile? Your wife isn't going to need to look over her shoulder in a few more days."

He sighed, letting his eyes run over the telegram again. Was it really as simple as Sam made it sound? They'd been waiting for word of the Wolf Point Ring's arrest, yes, but he'd been half expecting a band of men to show up in Twin Rivers searching for Keely. "What if the telegram is wrong? How do we even know Jonas sent this? What if a member of the Wolf Point Ring knows Keely is here and is pretending to be Jonas?"

Daniel narrowed his gaze at him. "Do you have any reason to suspect the telegram might not be authentic?"

Wes shook his head.

"Have your guards found something unusual around the ranch?"

"No, just those travelers who passed through over a month ago, and they just mistook one of the trails through my ranch for the Chihuahuan Trail."

"Then I see no reason not to take that telegram at face value," Daniel answered. "But we won't drop our guard either, not until we have confirmation that every last member of the Wolf Point Ring is behind bars."

Sam gave his head a shake. "Sure seems like this is an answer to prayer. Is there a reason you're worried, Wes?"

The only explanation he had was that it seemed too good to be true. That it seemed like the Wolf Point Ring was supposed to show up and fight for Keely, that it seemed like something was bound to go wrong.

But the telegram did appear an awful lot like an answer to prayer. And hadn't he just decided he needed to trust God more? If God was giving him something good, who was he to doubt it?

Wes glanced back down at the telegram. For the first time in over a year, he was going to ignore the twist of worry in his gut and trust God to handle things.

## 22

K eely stared at the words on the page in front of her, trying to concentrate. Oh, she could spot words like *the* and *came* and *tall*, but to have them all in the same sentence? And to understand what they meant? She just couldn't force her brain to focus on the book for more than two seconds at a time, not with Leo gone and Wes still in town.

She sighed and glanced at the page number. Twenty-one. She'd been reading for three hours. What a waste. She plopped the book down on the table in front of the couch and stood.

If Leo were here, she wouldn't be able to sit around and read like this in the first place. He always seemed to need something, and even when he was perfectly content, she'd much rather play with him than read.

Had Hortencia and Leo run into any trouble on their way to Albuquerque? Were rustlers on the desert searching for her even now? Or did they not realize she'd been an informant?

Keely shook her head, then stood and walked to the window. She'd drive herself crazy if she sat there wondering about Leo. Eventually Dobbs and Bruce would return, and then she'd learn what had happened to Hortencia.

But thinking about Wes was another matter entirely. The way he'd held her last night, the way he'd whispered comforting things in her ear, the way he'd looked at her when he said he loved her.

He should be back soon. How would he treat her when he returned from town? Would he go into his office and say he needed to work, acting as though nothing special had transpired between them?

Or would he sweep her into his arms and kiss her like he had in bed that morning? Tell her that he loved her again?

Her body felt warm just thinking about it.

Hopefully they could go on a picnic for supper, but that was still hours away, and even if he did greet her with a kiss when he returned home, he'd have work to do.

She sighed. Maybe she'd leave a note for Wes about the picnic, then ride out and visit Charlotte, tell her that Wes had slept in the same bed as her last night. That he'd said he loved her.

The far-off clomp of horse's hooves drew her attention out the window. Wes was riding up the mountain. She could tell it was him even from this distance, and not just because she recognized Ares. Wes had a way of carrying himself that always seemed to command her attention.

She was out the front door and down the steps before she even realized what she was doing.

Wes smiled at her as he came into the yard, then swung off his horse. "Hello, angel."

Warmth rushed into her cheeks. "I keep telling you I'm not an angel."

He hooked an arm around her waist and pulled her close. "Could have fooled me."

His lips brushed hers, and she started to melt against him.

"You want me to stable Ares for you, boss?" A voice sounded from somewhere behind them.

Keely jumped away from Wes.

"Just take him to the corral." Wes kept his eyes on her as he answered. "We'll be headed out for a picnic in a bit."

"Sure thing." The cowhand led Ares away, but Wes still didn't pay any mind to what the other man was doing. He had eyes only for her, and the smile he'd been wearing when he first rode up had only grown wider.

"Why are you so happy?" Was it the time they'd shared together this morning? The things they'd said to each other last night?

"Daniel got a telegraph from Marshal Redding." He fished a piece of paper from his pocket and held it out to her. "The marshal expects the Wolf Point Ring to be arrested by the end of next week."

She took the paper from him and stared at it. "Is that really what this means?"

"Yes. I'm keeping the Pinkerton agents on until we know for sure that everyone who wants to hurt you is behind bars. But I wanted you to know the most recent news."

Tears pricked her eyes, and she heaved in a breath, then threw herself into Wes's arms. "This is so close to being over I can almost taste it."

"Me too." Wes's arms came around her, warm and strong. "I couldn't be happier for you."

"Thank you."

"Don't thank me. You're the reason they're about to be caught. You're the one who turned over information to the marshal's office."

"And you're the one who hid me and made sure I was safe."

He pulled back enough to look down into her eyes. "I can't promise you're safe just yet, but I'll let you know as soon as we have word that everyone has been arrested."

"The telegram says it should be done by the end of next week. That's ten more days." There was a time where she didn't even think the Wolf Point Ring would ever be captured, where she'd given up on ever getting justice for James or Cynthia, where she'd thought she'd have to hide for the rest of her life. "After I've been running for over ten months, I can wait that long."

~.~.~.~.~

THE SCENT of beans and spices invaded Daniel's nose as he opened the back door to his parent's house and let himself into the kitchen.

"Hello, son." Ma smiled at him from where she stood at the table rolling out dough for tortillas.

"Hi, Ma." Daniel gave her a quick peck on the cheek. "Is Pa here?"

"In the parlor, I think. Or maybe he's in the bedroom." She jutted her flour-dusted chin over her shoulder in the direction of the parlor.

Daniel headed down the hallway of the house he'd lived in for almost thirty years, passing his former bedroom and Anna Mae's current one before stepping into the parlor.

Sure enough, Pa sat at the writing desk, his head bent over the Bible and a thick commentary.

How many times had he seen Pa in such a position since his leg had been amputated?

How much would he miss it after Pa was gone?

How much would he miss this house? The constant smell of Mexican food drifting from the kitchen. The memories of him, Sam, and Wes crammed into his small room for the night, bedrolls sprawled across the floor while they stayed up telling ghost stories.

Good grief. He'd been sitting in this very room when Anna Mae had suggested he teach Charlotte how to flirt—a ploy that had ended up with the two of them married.

Daniel looked back over at his father, who was so caught up in whatever he read that he still hadn't realized he had company.

"I don't want you to leave Twin Rivers." His voice filled the silence of the room.

Pa was slow to raise his head.

"You don't..." Pa blinked. "Oh."

"I want more than anything to beg you not to go to seminary." Daniel hung his head, digging the toe of his boot into one of the grooves in the floor. "When you first asked about it, you were so excited, but my main thought was that I didn't want you to go."

"I sense you've had a change of heart...?" Pa looked at him, his blue eyes soft with understanding. Something told Daniel that look would prove useful once his father was a pastor.

He cleared his throat. "Wes has been through a lot, first with losing his ma and baby brother, then with Abigail and his daughter dying, then his father..."

"I agree." Pa's brow furrowed. "But what does Wes have to do with my going to seminary?"

"I told Wes this morning that he can't let his life be controlled by fear. That God loves him and has good things planned for him, that God won't fail him or forsake him." Daniel looked down at where his toe still dug into the floor. "But when Wes came to my office this morning, I realized that I wasn't doing that with you. It was one thing to tell Wes to trust in God's goodness. But here you are, wanting to go to seminary, and I didn't want to support you. I wasn't looking for God's goodness like I should have been. I wasn't asking what plans God might have for you or how He can use you in spite of your leg."

His throat grew tight. "I'm sorry, Pa. I think you should go to seminary. Or rather, I think God wants you to go to seminary. And I was wrong for not encouraging you from the beginning."

Pa leaned back in his chair. "Thank you, son. Having your support means everything to me."

Daniel walked over, knelt beside the wheelchair, and clasped his father in a hug. "I have to admit, the notion of not being able to bring my first child here to crawl around your living room or chase the scorpions that get into the house makes me sad. But I still think you'll make a wonderful pastor."

After Pa left, he wouldn't be able to stop by and get his advice about tracking rustlers, hiding fugitives, or figuring out which ruffian had been the one to instigate trouble.

But the promise that was true for Wes and Pa was true for him too. God wouldn't leave him, and he'd find strength in that.

# 23

---

es dug his heels into Ares's side as the horse raced over his property towards Daniel's house. Dawn was breaking behind him, but the yellow and pink rays of morning only lit the eastern edge of the sky. Dark indigo painted the western sky in front of him.

"Come on, Ares. Giddy up," he muttered.

If he was fast enough, he'd be able to catch Daniel before he left for the sheriff's office. He couldn't say what had prompted him out of bed quite so early, especially not when he'd been snuggled up next to Keely. But he'd woken before dawn and hadn't been able to sleep, so he'd headed down to his office. There'd been a book on ranching on his desk, which he'd thought odd, since Keely hadn't done any work in his office since Leo left. When he went to move the book back onto the shelf, a piece of paper was under it.

He'd instantly recognized the handwriting as Consuela's, and it had a location in Mexico written on it.

There'd been no other words, no reason for why the location was important, no date or time.

Why hadn't she just handed him the paper? Because of

Hortencia? Had she been trying to give the other woman time to get away from Twin Rivers before the rangers took another trip across the border?

The sooner this information was in the hands of a lawman, the better.

Wes frowned as Ares crested a hill and raced toward the bottom. Were those tracks from a large group of cattle in the valley below?

The farther Ares moved down the hill, the clearer the tracks became. It looked as though a few thousand head of cattle had been moved through the bottom of the valley. And it certainly wasn't his doing. The only time his men moved that many cattle around the A Bar W was during spring and fall round up.

The cattle could have come from a ranch to the north, but why would anyone drive so many cattle into Mexico? And why through his property rather than on the Chihuahuan Trail?

His stomach twisted. Cain's presence had scared most of the rustlers off. There'd been very little activity on this side of the border over the last five months.

But what if the tracks were from his cattle being taken over the border?

*Not this, God, please.*

As soon as he uttered the prayer, he regretted it. If not his cattle, then it would be someone else's, and losing a few thousand head wouldn't hurt him the way it would hurt someone with a smaller ranch, like Sam Owens.

He slowed Ares to a stop and jumped off to examine the tracks. They were recent enough to hold their shape in the rocky soil, which meant the cattle had likely been moved sometime during the night.

He surveyed the valley, then imagined a map of the A Bar W in his head. These tracks weren't well hidden, not like the rustler's trail on Sam's property had been. Sure, if he hadn't been cutting across his land to visit Daniel, it might have taken another day or two to discover the tracks, but it wouldn't have taken long.

Would a gang of rustlers known for using hidden trails decide to make a trail this blatant?

He shook his head. Did it matter? He needed to get back to the ranch and tell his hands to count the stock.

He swung back up onto Ares, then paused. The valley where he'd been keeping his prime stock was near here. What if...

*No.*

The rustlers had tens of thousands of cattle to choose from. They wouldn't just happen to take his best beef, would they?

They shouldn't even know where that herd was being grazed.

But he had to know for certain. Wes turned Ares north and dug his heels in. The Arabian stallion took off over the desert, retracing the path the cattle had taken.

*Please, God, not my best cattle. I've been breeding them for four years.*

He followed the tracks up the valley for about a quarter mile, and then the path veered sharply to the east, in the exact direction where his prime herd had been.

He didn't bother praying again or asking God to keep the inevitable from happening. He just followed the trail as quickly as he could, the lead ball in his stomach getting heavier and heavier until Ares crested one of the hills that surrounded the small valley with a creek running through it. A few calves straggled around, but otherwise the landscape was empty. Every last mature cow was gone.

Wes scrubbed a hand over his jaw and blinked away the stinging sensation in his eyes.

*God, why?* Here he was, trying to trust that God was good, trying to trust that God wouldn't fail him. And now his best cattle were somewhere in Mexico.

He wanted to shout, but instead he sat there with his teeth clamped together so tightly his jaw ached, dragging ragged breaths into his lungs.

He needed to look for the good. Wasn't that what he'd decided yesterday with Daniel and Sam? He couldn't just get mad, couldn't just turn his back on God the first time something went wrong.

There had to be good somewhere... like in how he'd discovered the tracks so quickly. And how Cain was in Twin Rivers with thirty rangers at his disposal.

But what if God didn't bring his cattle back?

What if he had to start over, breeding his prime herd from the very beginning?

Wes swallowed. Then he'd handle that too. At least he had enough stock that he could start again. It wasn't as though his entire ranch would be ruined by the loss of his cattle.

But first he planned to do everything in his power to recover his livestock.

~.~.~.~.~

KEELY TOOK A SIP OF COFFEE, then stared out over the valley. From her position on the balcony outside of Wes's room, she could see all the way to the Rio Grande and the giant wall of cliffs that rose from the Sierra Madres just beyond it. She wasn't complaining about the view from the window in her own room, which looked out over the Bofecillos Mountains to the east, but Wes had a corner room, affording him views of both the east and the south, and the landscape to the south was magnificent.

A gust of wind blew up from the desert, and she wrapped

her shawl tighter about her. She could sit out here every morning, drinking coffee and watching the sun rise.

It would be better to drink coffee with Wes, but she'd woken only to find a note on his pillow rather than his warm body beside her. *Ran to Daniel's. Be back for breakfast,* it had said.

And so here she was, sitting with the most beautiful view she could imagine, feeling utterly and completely safe. For the first time in over ten months, she didn't scan the desert for a rider in the distance or worry if a member of the Wolf Point Ring would jump out from behind a boulder. They were about to be arrested, and she fully intended to enjoy her morning without worrying Lester Mears might arrive in his unmistakable red bowler hat.

Now if only Wes would return, they could spend the morning together.

As if knowing she'd been thinking of him, a rider came into the yard, but not from the direction of Daniel's house. She could tell right away that it was Wes—a horse like Ares was impossible to mistake—but he'd come from the direction of the bunkhouse.

He swung off Ares, then turned and spotted her on the balcony.

She smiled down at him. "Good morning."

He didn't smile back. Instead, he raced up the steps and into the hacienda, more determination than usual in his stride.

She rose and moved into the bedroom, where she set her coffee mug down on the dresser. She was about to go downstairs to meet him when the door burst open.

"Rustlers have taken some of my herd."

She put a hand to her mouth. "Are you sure?"

He gave her a hard look.

"I'm so sorry." She went to him and wrapped her arms around his chest. "Do you think Cain and Daniel can recover them?"

"I hope so." His voice sounded rough and uneven, as though he'd swallowed a mouthful of desert sand and was now trying to talk through it.

"Is there anything I can do?"

His arms came around her, and he gave her a squeeze. "I wish there was. The cattle, they were my prime herd from the valley I showed you." Wes released his arms from around her and took a step back. "I need to go. I've already gotten the men. We need to do what we can to save the cattle."

She pressed her eyes shut for a moment, just long enough for the sudden burning sensation in them to subside. "Will you be going into Mexico?"

"We'll have to. We need to at least try to follow the trail."

"Be safe." She gave him a final squeeze, then dropped her arms and stepped back.

He was out the door and swinging back up onto Ares in a matter of seconds.

She stood on the balcony until Ares galloped out of the yard with a group of fifteen other horses. "Dear God, please keep them safe."

Was there something she could do? Wes had said no, but she couldn't just sit around and worry for hours on end. Wes had a topographical map of the A Bar W somewhere in his office. And didn't he have one of Mexico too? Maybe she could study it, see if she could determine the natural trails cattle would follow. That way if they came back to the ranch empty-handed later, she'd have some ideas of where the men could search next.

At the very least, studying a map was better than sitting around and worrying.

She turned and headed back inside the room.

"Well, well, well."

The sound of the rough male voice caused the hairs on her arm to prickle.

Slowly, she turned her head toward the direction of the voice. A large man stood in the door—wearing a red bowler hat and holding a pistol.

"Mears," she breathed, her breath clogging in her chest.

It couldn't be. The telegram had said he was about to be arrested.

"Look at you, Nora." His voice was deep and gravely, and it caused a chill to sweep through her. "Went and got all fancy on us, I see."

She took a step back, her heart hammering against her ribcage. "What... what are you doing here?"

"Looking for you, of course." He raked his gaze down her, and the leer in his eyes made nausea churn in her belly.

"I thought the marshals... that you..."

"That I was going to be arrested? Probably would have been, had Stevens and I been in Chicago yesterday and not in Mexico."

Mexico? "How did you know where I was?" She licked her lips and shot a quick glance around the room.

Maybe Wes had forgotten something, and if she could keep Mears talking, Wes would return and...

*What?* Come all the way up to the bedroom? Even if someone returned to the yard and she screamed loud enough to be heard, Mears would have her shot before anyone reached the room.

"Did you really think you could marry the owner of a ranch like the A Bar W and not be discovered?" He took a step toward her. "Rumor is they're talking hanging for the mayor and harbormaster and chief of police."

"The mayor's been arrested?"

"He has." Mears's eyes narrowed. "Good thing I know exactly who needs to pay for that."

He took another step, and she turned, searching for something, anything she could use as a weapon against him.

Sweat had slickened her hands, but she grabbed the pitcher from the basin on the washstand then whirled back around to throw it at his head.

But he was already on top of her, the butt of his gun coming straight for her head.

"No!" she screamed.

Pain shattered through her skull, and her world went dark.

## 24

W es raced Ares over the desert, not caring that he outran his men. He'd sent one cowhand to Daniel's house to let him know about his cattle. But the sooner he and his riders got to Cain the better. Hopefully the trail could be followed in Mexico. Hopefully the rustlers hadn't snuffed it out somewhere or set up an ambush. Hopefully...

He crested the final hill before town, then looked at the valley below. Cattle. There were thousands of them. They filled the area to the west of Twin Rivers while rangers wove in and out of the herd, trying to keep the beasts together.

But were the cattle *his*? Even from a distance he could see the medium build of the beasts and well-proportioned muscles, both characteristics of his prime herd. But they could still belong to a rancher farther north.

"Giddyap." He flicked his reins and dug his heels even harder into Ares's side.

A holler sounded from behind him, followed by a chorus of hooting. His men must have just crested the ridge and seen the cattle.

Wes rode up to the first cluster of beasts, his heart hammering against his chest. There, on the left shoulder of a heifer, was the familiar AW brand with a bar that ran through it. He glanced at the steer beside it to find the same brand. The cow next to it was facing the wrong direction for him to see the brand, but a quick scan of the herd told him the cattle facing east was all his.

He let out a breath he hadn't realized he'd been holding. *Dear God, thank you.*

"Mr. Westin." One of the rangers approached on a horse.

"Are they all here? Do you know how many cattle have been recovered?"

"I don't have an exact count for you just yet, but we're estimating around four thousand head." The man reigned his horse to a stop in front of Ares. "The sheriff had a note left at his office saying what trail the cattle would be on. We didn't know where the cattle stolen would be from, or we'd have asked to set up a watch on your property. Instead, we set up an ambush just over the border."

"Are we missing any?" His foreman Jeb rode up, eyes scanning the herd.

"Not that the rangers can tell." Wes drew in another breath, his lungs light and free. "If the rangers don't need them for anything, let's get them back to the ranch where you can do an official count."

"You can take them whenever you're ready," the ranger said. "I can send a couple men to help if you want."

"Yes, thank you." He wasn't going to rest easy until this herd was back on his ranch in a valley that was hidden better than the previous one, and with men guarding it.

The ranger called to a couple of the other men, then turned back to Wes. "Captain Whitelaw and the sheriff are in the sheriff's office. I assume they'll be wanting to talk to you."

Wes looked over his shoulder at Jeb. "You got things under

control here?"

"Sure do. Go talk to the law."

Wes flicked Ares's reins, and the horse trotted off. *Thank you, Father,* he prayed again. Here he'd been so worried he would lose everything, but God had other plans. He might not have been a shining example of faith like Moses or Abraham when he'd stared at the empty valley that was supposed to hold his prime herd, but he hadn't turned his back or railed at God either. It felt like progress.

*Thank you, God, for your goodness to me, and for your grace. I'm trying to trust you more. Truly I am.*

Could God tell? Would it make a difference that he was trying to do right, even if he wasn't perfect at it?

He hoped so.

But regardless of whether he could have done better at trusting God, he knew one thing: God had been good to him that morning.

Even though he hadn't deserved it.

~.~.~.~.~

CHAOS. Absolute, complete chaos. Daniel stood in his office with Cain while Spanish curses and angry voices rose from the rustlers locked in the jailhouse.

They'd caught the outlaws and recovered all the cattle, though he still wasn't quite sure how it had happened other than God had helped them.

The second he'd seen the familiar brand with an AW and a bar stretched between them, he'd understood just how devastating the rustlers' actions would have been had he not gotten another note.

"You're sure I ain't goin' to hang for this iffin I talk?" one of the rustlers—Mervin—asked from where he sat tied to a chair in the middle of the office. His shirt rode up over his large stomach to show a patch of grimy skin speckled with a dusting of hair.

"That one there looks like he wants me to hang." Mervin jutted his chin toward Cain.

"The offer I made stands. I've got both of our signatures here to prove it." Daniel held up the plea agreement the man had signed before he'd been bound to the chair. "If you give us information that leads to the capture of *el jefe*, we'll make sure that you get a lighter sentence."

Likely life in prison instead of a noose, but that would be decided based on how helpful the man's information ended up being.

Mervin had been the only American riding with the Mexican rustlers, which was why Daniel nabbed him and offered a plea agreement rather than tossing him in a cell with everyone else. Call it a hunch, but with Mervin already being a bit of an outsider, he had a feeling the man would be far more willing to talk than any of the Mexicans.

"Who's your boss?" Cain asked.

The man shrugged, or at least he tried to shrug, but with how his hands were tied to the chair behind him, he only succeeded in raising his too-tight shirt higher on his belly. "Don't know."

"How do you not know?" Cain leveled a steely glare at Mervin. "Who your boss is seems like a rather important piece of information."

"Never seen him. Just get his instructions." The man answered in twangy English. "I hired on for a job moving cattle around Mexico. Saw the advertisement outside a bar. It's good pay, and I get money every week, not just when a job's finished."

The man had already said as much earlier. The first question Daniel had asked was how he came to be the only American working with a bunch of Mexicans.

"Who gives you the instructions from *el jefe*?" Cain asked.

The man looked toward the jailhouse to his left, causing the layers of fat beneath his chin to jiggle. "Hugo or Edwardo or Raul. One of the usuals."

The door to his office opened, and Wes entered, a look of relief on his face. He extended a slip of paper to him. "Consuela left this the other night, but I'm assuming it was about what happened to my cattle last night."

Daniel looked down at the note. It was nearly identical to the one he'd received yesterday morning, except it didn't have a time or date on it like his note had.

"You assumed right, but thanks. I'll put this in the file." He set the note on his desk, then turned back to the portly rustler.

"What were the instructions for last night?" Cain took a step closer to the man, his eyes growing colder with each question he asked.

"To get cattle off that fancy ranch just over the border. Knew exactly where the cattle were and the precise number. Even got a map."

Daniel slanted a glance at Wes, who had moved to the corner, watching the interrogation with a hard jaw. Either the rustler didn't know Wes was the owner of the ranch, or the man hadn't seen him come in.

"So you got hired on to move cattle around Mexico, which isn't illegal. But when you were asked to rustle cattle from the Texas side of the border, you didn't up and quit?" Daniel turned back to the outlaw.

The man tried to shrug again, but at least this time his shirt didn't move any higher. "You seen how big that ranch is? The man won't miss a few cattle."

Cain crossed his arms over his chest. "Did you get everything you were instructed?"

"Well, everything but the girl. Hugo wasn't too happy, sayin' we'd already been paid to nab her. Figure the American won't be none too happy either."

Daniel stilled. "What girl?"

"You know, on the ranch. The rich man's wife. Curly red hair. Can't miss her."

"Someone paid you to take my wife?" Wes stepped forward, his voice deathly quiet.

Sweat beaded along the outlaw's hairline, and he tried to shrink back into his chair, but his large girth made shrinking impossible. "Like I said, we didn't get her. Too many men around the ranch. Hugo called us back."

"Who asked you to take her?" Wes balled his hands into fists.

The man squirmed despite his bindings. "I already said. It's the American. Came clear down her from Iowa or Indiana or some such looking for her."

"Illinois." Wes took another step closer, his voice hard as steel. "Did he come from Illinois?"

"Yeah, think that's it. But we didn't get the girl, so I don't see what the problem is."

"Is Keely at the ranch?" Cain asked.

"Yes. Or rather, she was when I left her." Wes swallowed, his face turning white.

His friend didn't need to say more for Daniel to know what was running through his mind.

"Where was this American staying?" Cain grabbed the outlaw by the shirt collar and yanked him as far up as the rope tying him to the chair would allow.

"I... I won't hang if I tell you, right?" Mervin rasped. "That's part of the deal?"

"Right," Wes answered, never mind that the man had no authority to make any kind of plea agreement.

"You tell us where the American is, and you won't hang. I'll have it added to the agreement you signed." Daniel tapped the plea agreement sitting on his desk.

"Where in Mexico is the outlaw staying?" Cain tightened his grip on the man's shirt collar.

"About three miles south of Ojinaga," the man sputtered. "There's a small farming town—Cantarrecio, or something like that. His place is about a mile past that, on the other side of the mountains."

"Draw a map." Cain released him, and he fell back into the chair.

"Do you think Lester Mears has her?" Wes met Cain's gaze.

"Only one way to find out." Cain settled his hat atop his head. "I'm sending a group of men to the ranch and another into Mexico."

"I'm going with you," Wes strode toward the door.

"To the ranch, yes. To Mexico, no." Cain's voice invited no argument.

Wes whirled on Cain anyway. "If he has her, he'll take her into Mexico. She's my wife."

"Which is exactly why you can't go." Daniel stepped between the two of them. "This is a job for trained lawmen."

"But what if..."

"If he has her, I'll get her back." Cain jerked open the door and strode outside.

Wes stared after him for a moment, then turned back to Daniel, frustration and worry etched across the lines of his face.

Daniel rested a hand on his shoulder. He couldn't promise Keely would be returned to him unharmed—no matter how badly he wanted to. But there was one thing he knew to be true. "Remember that verse from yesterday? God hasn't forsaken her, Wes. Wherever Keely is and whatever she's enduring, God's with her."

## 25

P ounding. Something beat inside her head, and she couldn't stop it, nor the pain that thrummed through her body.

Keely groaned and opened her eyes, only to have light sear her vision. She slammed her eyelids shut, but that didn't stop a hundred tiny knives from jabbing at the inside of her skull.

Where was she? What had happened?

She moved to stretch her arms but couldn't. Something was keeping them in place.

She let out another groan, then peeked a single eye open and glanced at her hands. Bound in front of her.

Her breath shuddered. Why couldn't she remember anything?

She tried to think back, sifting and grasping, hoping to find a memory to cling to. Something that would make sense of things. She remembered sitting on the balcony at dawn, remembered Wes returning home. He'd told her rustlers had taken the cattle, and he needed to go get Cain. Then he and his cowhands had left, and...

Mears.

Her heart thundered against her ribs, and a scream built in her lungs. She nearly loosed it but somehow stopped herself.

Lester Mears had probably been inside the house when Wes had told her about the missing cattle. He'd told her at the ranch that he blamed her for the arrest of the mayor.

What kind of revenge was he going to exact now that she was his captive?

Images of Cynthia's body flashed in her mind. Bruised and bloody. Broken.

Keely heaved in a jagged breath, and another scream climbed into her throat.

But no, she couldn't scream. What if that brought Mears?

She forced herself to take a small, controlled breath, then another, and looked around the room. It was small, with a dirt floor and a single table against the wall near the tick where she lay. But at least it was empty of her kidnappers—for the moment.

She heaved in a breath and pressed her eyes shut. *Why this, God? Why now?*

She'd been through so very much, from losing Cynthia and James to hiding for eight months on her own, to coming to Twin Rivers and making friends and meeting Wes. She'd built an entirely new life for herself, one with a husband who loved her.

Was God going to dangle all that in front of her, only to take it away?

*Be strong and of a good courage, fear not, nor be afraid of them: for the LORD thy God, he it is that doth go with thee; he will not fail thee, nor forsake thee. And the LORD, he it is that doth go before thee; he will be with thee, he will not fail thee, neither forsake thee: fear not, neither be dismayed.*

The verse promised that God wouldn't fail her, but it sure seemed like He'd failed her, otherwise she wouldn't be trussed up like a calf and at the mercy of Lester Mears.

Footsteps sounded outside the door to her room, then the door handle jiggled.

She slammed her eyes shut, fear rising in her chest. This was it. Mears was going to come inside the room, realize she was awake, and do unimaginable things to her.

Except the door didn't open.

Talking sounded outside it, Mears's low voice mixed with the higher voice of another man. Then footsteps sounded, heading away from the door.

She drew in a breath. *Thank you, God.* At least He'd kept her safe for a few more minutes. *And thank you for giving me the chance to know Wes before I died, to be a mother to Leo for two months, and to become friends with Anna Mae and Ellie and Charlotte.*

There were certainly worse ways for a person to spend the two months before her death. So much of her time in Twin Rivers had been good. There'd been heartache too. The pain of having Wes kiss her only to tell her he'd made a mistake, and then go searching for Leo's mother. The agony of watching Wes carry Leo from the room, knowing he was about to place the babe in his mother's arms.

But she wouldn't trade the time she'd had in Twin Rivers, not any of it. She'd still gotten to hold and cuddle Leo, to sing him lullabies and see him grow stronger and bigger. She'd still gotten to kiss Wes and hold his hand and smile against his shoulder.

Still had gotten to hear him say he loved her and spend two nights wrapped in his arms as she slept.

Lying in a strange room, with her hands and feet bound and at the mercy of terrible men, it almost seemed like God had forsaken her.

But He hadn't, not really.

*Forgive me for not seeing it sooner, Father. Please give me strength to face whatever Mears has planned for me. Give me the strength to trust you no matter what comes.*

Because trusting God meant more than just trusting Him when things were easy. She had to trust Him even when facing death.

*Like Daniel from the Bible.*

She blinked. She didn't have the first clue where that thought had come from, but Daniel's situation seemed awful similar to hers. He'd faced death, going to the lion's den not for something as dangerous as running afoul of opium smugglers, but for something as simple as his faith in God.

Of course, Daniel had lived, but he certainly hadn't known that when he'd been thrown into the pit of hungry lions.

Then there was Shadrach, Meshach, and Abednego. They too had faced death, thinking they'd be burned alive for their faith.

Maybe she could face her death with the same calmness and faith as Daniel and his friends.

*And maybe God will deliver you.*

She blinked. There was another thought, seemingly out of nowhere. It wasn't as though someone was coming to rescue her, not with Wes and Cain and Daniel tracking the rustlers. No one even knew she was gone, and she was bound in a way that prevented her from so much as standing, let alone running.

But that didn't mean she couldn't at least *try* to escape, didn't mean she had to lie here and just accept whatever Mears did to her. After all, she'd escaped Chicago and hid for over ten months.

Keely inched her way into a sitting position, which was no easy feat considering her feet were bound along with her hands. A hammer pounded on the inside of her skull, but she forced herself to focus on the room around her instead of her ragged breathing.

She'd already discovered she'd been placed atop a tick on

the floor with a dirty blanket heaped at the foot of it. The room itself was small, with only the tick, a low table, and a wooden chair. But a window was positioned high over the bed.

She blinked up at the clear view of sky it afforded. Was the window open? It sure appeared that way.

Was Mears so confident she wouldn't run that he'd stuck her in a room with an open window?

If so, where had he taken her? The middle of the desert? Too far away from water for her to survive if she tried leaving?

In order to see out the window, she'd need to stand, and she couldn't do that with her ankles bound. But if she could use her hands to pick the knot on her ankles, maybe she could escape.

A scraping noise sounded from the next room, and she glanced at the door.

Footsteps followed, growing louder behind the door.

She scooted back down onto the bed, slammed her eyes shut, and tried to calm her breathing. *God, please let him think I'm still unconscious.*

A creak sounded, then more footsteps, louder and clearer. She didn't need to open her eyes to know he was in the room with her. She could almost feel the evil of his glare.

Her breath wanted to hitch, and her heart ached to pound against her ribs. Yet she forced herself to relax, to take one calm breath after another as she lay completely and utterly still.

More footsteps, even closer now.

He knew she was awake. He had to. Why else come into the room and stare at her for so long?

She was going to endure unspeakable things, and she'd have to trust God would get her through it.

Something nudged her shoulder. The toe of his boot, perhaps.

"Hey, wake up."

She forced the muscles of her face to stay relaxed, her body to remain limp as she let her shoulder jiggle with the movement of his boot.

He withdrew his boot a few seconds later, and the footsteps receded. Then the door thudded shut. "Still unconscious."

"Told ya you shouldn't have given her that chloroform," another voice said. "Bet she's out for another hour or two."

"We can wait. I want her awake before we start."

A chill traveled down her spine, but Keely held herself in place for another minute or two, just to make sure Mears didn't return.

When the footsteps from the room outside hers grew more distant, she propped her eyes open, scooted into a sitting position, and bunched her knees up against her chest.

It would be difficult to pick the knot on her feet with her hands bound, but if she twisted her wrists just right, she could reach the rope that tied her feet together.

~.~.~.~.~

THE DOOR to his office opened, and Wes stopped his pacing long enough to see his sister step into the room. Not Daniel. Not Cain. Not anyone who might have news of Keely.

She made a beeline straight for him and wrapped him in a hug. "I came as soon as I heard."

"Thanks." He gave her a half-hearted pat on the back, then pulled away.

"How are you?"

"How do you think?"

"I'm so sorry."

"I try so hard to keep people safe, try so hard to make good decisions for my ranch, but I'm not guaranteed of anything, am I?" Wes blew out a breath and tried to blink away the burning sensation that kept returning to his eyes. "I'm certainly not guaranteed of another day, let alone a moment with Keely."

"None of us are guaranteed anything." Charlotte reached out and gripped his hands, her palms so warm they almost burned his icy fingers. "I'm married to a lawman who nearly died this past summer, remember? I'm aware that God has a plan for my life that's bigger than what I can see or understand."

"Sometimes God's plans hurt." Like now, when his heart felt like it had split in two inside his chest, and he was helpless to put it back together.

"Maybe the plans that hurt the most are the ones that make us strongest," she whispered. "I would have given anything not to have Daniel injured this summer. Doc Grubbins had to drill a hole in his head to save him, and even then, he almost died. But do you know what I did the entire time he was unconscious?"

"You asked God to spare his life." He well remembered the agony Charlotte had gone through when they'd thought Daniel might not wake up. He'd held her in his arms and prayed with her, even though he hadn't expected their prayers to do much good.

"It was more than just that. Daniel almost dying drove me to my knees in prayer, not just for his recovery, but for all kinds of things. My foolishness, my stubbornness, my pride. God uses situations like this to show us what's truly valuable."

Wes pulled his hands away from hers and turned toward the window. "Losing Abigail didn't draw me closer to God. It pushed me away from Him."

"I know."

"I'm sorry."

"I'm not the one you should be apologizing to."

He raked a hand through his hair. "I've already apologized to God."

It's all he'd done since returning to the ranch to wait for word of Keely. He'd told God he was sorry a thousand times for not trusting Him when Abigail died. For allowing himself to grow bitter. For refusing to look for the good that God had kept in his life during the hardest times.

It felt like he had a thousand more apologies to go before God would even think of forgiving him.

"If you've apologized, and you meant it, then you're already forgiven," Charlotte said.

"I don't feel forgiven."

She reached out and wrapped him in a hug. "The Bible says God separates your sins as far as the east is from the west. I guarantee God has forgiven you, whether you feel like it or not."

"I suppose even forgiveness is another area where I need to trust God more. I mean, I know God says he'll forgive me, but I've messed up so much, I'm reluctant to believe it."

Charlotte's brows drew together, her forehead pinched with a pained expression.

"Whatever happens with Keely, I won't let it push me away from God again. I've spent the past two hours either on my knees or pacing, and praying the entire time. This time, I'm going to trust God, even... even if He takes her from me." His voice broke, and tears obscured his view of the cacti and yucca and hills.

"I used to think that God had already been good to me," he whispered. "That he'd already given me one woman to love, and that I'd never be able to replace her. But when I look at Keely... she's not a replacement. She's different, so very different from Abigail, and yet I love her just as much, and we've only known each other two months. With time, I can see myself coming to love her the same way I loved Abigail."

"Don't give up hope yet," Charlotte whispered. "Cain is out searching for her."

"I know, but if Cain doesn't bring her back..." He shook his head. "I'm such a fool. Two months. God gave me two months with her, and I spent that time pushing her away rather than loving her like I should have."

He bent his head. *Dear God, forgive me for all the time I wasted with Keely. I know I don't deserve to have her back, but if you choose to return her, I promise to love her, to cherish her, to be the husband I'm supposed to be in every area of my life. I won't waste another moment you give me with her.*

The prayer left him, and it felt as though the heart that had been irreparably broken in two shattered into a thousand jagged splinters. He'd done everything he could to protect Keely, even going so far as to sell railroad stock so he could afford guards for her. But what had those guards done to protect her once the Wolf Point Ring came?

He'd been afraid to love Keely fully because he didn't want to lose her in childbirth, but here he was with the very real possibility that he could lose her anyway. As much as he tried to manage the things around him, as much as he tried to protect the people he loved, there were limits to his protection.

It was as Keely had said that night they'd argued. He wasn't God. He couldn't control life and death.

But there were no limits to God's protection, just like there were no limits to His love.

He was finally ready to trust the God who controlled the things he couldn't—even if it meant facing the pain of losing someone he loved yet again.

But somewhere deep inside, he still couldn't help but hope and pray that God would return the woman he loved to him.

Even though he didn't deserve to have her back.

## 26

F ree.
    Keely stared down at her feet that were finally free of the rope. A breath of relief rushed out of her, and invisible pinpricks poked at her skin as the rope fell away. She wiggled her toes through the prickling sensation, then stretched her legs.

It had taken far longer than she'd hoped to pick the knot, but she hadn't heard any more footsteps outside her door. Hopefully Mears had gotten distracted, and it would be a while before he checked on her again.

Keely pushed herself to a standing position on the tick, braced her elbows on the high window, then paused. Rolling hills covered the desert. In the distance, shadowed mountains loomed, but they didn't look familiar. Was she still in Texas, or had Mears taken her to Mexico?

It didn't matter. She had one chance to escape, and this was it.

Except the ground fell away below the window. She'd assumed she was on the first floor of the house, but the house looked to have been built on a hill, and while some of it was a single story, the window where she stood had a second story drop.

With her hands still bound, she'd hardly be able to catch herself when she jumped. But what other choice did she have?

Movement caught the corner of her eye. Was there an animal in one of the bushes? She scanned the desert, her breath stopping in her chest. There, the bush moved again, and...

Was that a man?

He moved from a crouch to a stand. His cowboy hat shadowed his face from both the sun and her view, but she recognized his long blond hair and lanky form. It was none other than Cain Whitelaw, the ranger she'd first thought an outlaw.

Cain looked straight at her and gave her a nod. How had he found her? Wasn't he supposed to be in Mexico somewhere, recovering Wes's cattle?

He made a motion with his hand, and several of the nearby bushes rustled.

She scanned the desert again, her gaze pausing on each scraggly shrub that was big enough to hide a man. How many rangers had he brought with him?

Cain started toward her, his gun drawn, his legs covering the wide expanse of the desert with nary a sound. When he reached the side of the house, he held his gun by his face, peeked around the corner, and crept toward her window.

He'd nearly reached her when she heard a chilling sound from inside the house—footsteps.

Keely glanced over her shoulder. The door was still shut, but for how much longer?

"Push yourself out the window," Cain whispered from below her. "I'll catch you."

"He's coming." Her jaw quivered and her lungs burned. "I can hear him."

"As soon as you're clear, I'll send my men in. This place is surrounded, and we want nothing more than to put a bullet in those lowlifes' chests." His voice was calm, almost gentle as he spoke. "But first I need you to push yourself out. Can you do that?"

She nodded, then pressed her eyes shut and heaved herself forward.

The window was too high. Even though she was standing on the tick, without being able to use her hands, she only made it about halfway through.

The creak of the door sounded behind her.

"Now," she croaked, wriggling her hips and legs desperately to get the rest of the way through. "Send the men now."

Cain didn't ask any questions. He gave a sharp whistle, and the shrubs around the house came alive with hidden rangers.

"Hey," Mears shouted from inside.

The metallic click of a pistol's hammer echoed through the room, then a gunshot rent the air. The bullet whistled past her cheek as more gunshots ricocheted through the desert, first from outside, then from inside the house.

She wriggled the top of one leg through the window, then let gravity pull the second leg through as she plunged toward the ground.

She wasn't in the air more than a second or two, but it seemed like an eternity as she barreled toward the ranger waiting below. He caught her head down, just like she had fallen, his arms banding around her just below her shoulders.

"Are you all right?" Cain shifted here so that she lay over his shoulder, her legs against his back and her hips bent over his shoulder.

Then he ran. The ground was uneven and bumpy, causing her to bounce against his shoulder. She couldn't see anything with the way her head was pressed against his stomach, but no bullets whistled past them, and each step carried her closer to safety.

After several minutes of running and just when she was starting to get a headache from being held upside down and jostled, Cain scrambled into a gully that held about fifteen horses.

He lowered both of them to the ground, his chest rising and falling as he positioned her on his lap.

His gaze instantly fell to where her hands were bound. "Let me take care of those ropes."

He reached toward his belt and pulled out a knife that gleamed sharp in the sunlight. He had the blade through her bindings in a matter of seconds. "There you go."

She just sat there, listening to the sound of the wind and voices shouting over the desert. The gunshots had stopped. Did that mean Mears was dead?

Almost as though he'd heard her question, another ranger scrambled down into the gully. "Got 'em, boss."

"He alive?" Cain shouted back.

The other man shook his head. "The first one's alive, but Mears took one bullet to the neck and three to the chest. Sorry we let him get a shot off though."

Cain pressed his lips into a grim line. "We need to do better next time."

"It's all right. The bullet didn't hit me." Keely's voice trembled, along with her hands and her feet.

"But it could have." Cain rubbed a hand up and down her arm, the motion bringing a bit of comfort.

"Is Wes here?" It seemed like her entire body was shaking now.

"Back at the ranch." Cain shifted to see her better. "Did the outlaw hurt you while you were inside with him? Answer me true. I need to know."

The question brought a sting of tears to her eyes, and she shook her head.

The stroking motion continued on her arm, up and down,

up and down. She didn't know how many women Cain had rescued from similar situations, but he certainly knew how to calm her nerves.

"My hands were tied in front of my chest, not behind it," she blurted as several more rangers appeared at the top of the gully. "I picked at the knot on my feet. That's how I was able to get out the window."

"You did right good today, Keely. Right good."

She sniffled, her breaths coming hard and fast. The shaking was growing worse, and she couldn't seem to stop it. "I just want Wes."

"I'm sure you do. But first I need you to blow out a breath of air, long and slow. Let's see how long you can blow for."

It felt as though her lungs couldn't get enough air, not that they had too much. But she did as Cain said, and sure enough, the breath rushed from her.

"That's good, real good. Now try to breathe easy. Take long, slow breaths in and out."

She drew in another breath, long and slow like he said, then blew it out.

"You keep breathing like that, and I'll take you home." Cain picked her up, and took her to his horse...

And carried her to the one place she wanted to be more than anywhere else.

## 27

K eely's eyes fluttered open to find morning sunlight wrapped around her. She stretched, then rolled to the side and snuggled back into bed. The place Wes had occupied in bed beside her last night was cold, though the scent of bergamot drifted from his pillow. She pulled the pillow closer, inhaling the familiar smell. Her eyes had just drifted closed when the door to the bedroom opened.

"Good morning, angel." Wes stepped inside carrying a tray with tea and toast. "How are you feeling?"

Her lips curved at the question. It was one he'd asked nonstop yesterday after Cain brought her back to the A Bar W. *How are you feeling? Are you sure you haven't been hurt? Do you need anything?*

He'd not been able to go five minutes without asking her one thing or another, all while he'd paced nervously around the bedroom.

He'd only calmed down after the sun started to set and he'd slid into bed beside her.

Wes set the tray on the table beside the bed, then bent over her and smoothed a strand of hair back from her brow.

Something inside her melted at the gentle touch.

"You didn't say how you were feeling."

She smiled up at him. "Better now that you're here."

"That's not what I meant." He scanned her with serious eyes. "Is your headache gone?"

She would have touched a hand to her temple, but Wes placed his fingers there first and massaged with gentle, circular motions.

"It's gone, yes."

She'd had the worst headache yesterday after Cain had returned her. The ranger had said it was normal considering she'd been pistol-whipped, drugged, and held hostage, as was the trembling that she couldn't get to stop. It hadn't helped that a storm had popped up on the desert on their ride back from Mexico. She'd arrived at the hacienda soaked and cold.

Wes had taken one look at her sitting in front of Cain in the saddle, swept her into his arms, and carried her upstairs where he'd built a fire.

Still, it had taken the rest of the day to get warm and stop shaking.

"How did you sleep?" Wes moved his hand from her forehead down to her cheek, the heat of his palm seeping into her skin.

It seemed he was determined to pepper her with questions again today. She reached up and laid a hand over his on her face. "Not as good as I would have slept had you still been in bed when I woke."

The corner of his mouth tipped into a half smile. "Is that so?"

"It's a problem that can be easily rectified." She scooted toward the center of the bed to make room for him, then patted the empty sheet.

"You want me to get into bed now?" He glanced at the clock on the wall. "It's ten o'clock in the morning."

"Just for a bit, please?"

He toed off his shoes, then climbed in beside her. He was fully dressed for the day, including his belt and the butter-soft leather vest he wore over his shirt. He smelled of hay and sunshine—and bergamot, of course. "You've already been outside."

"The day's half over." His arms came around her, and he pulled her against the warmth of his chest, but his eyes still held a trace of worry.

"You know, you spent the entire day yesterday asking me how I was doing, but I never once asked how you are."

"I'm fine."

"Are you really?"

Rather than answer, he tucked her head beneath his chin, and the steady thump-thump of his heart filled her ears.

"Wes?" She trailed a finger up his chest, stopping to toy with the button right over the center of his heart.

"I'm going to drop the lawsuit against the Mortimers."

"What?" She attempted to look at him again, but he coaxed her head right back down to his chest. "I thought you wanted to give the ranch to Charlotte's children? Don't you have to file a lawsuit to do that?"

"I changed my mind."

Her breathing hitched. "So you're just going to let the Mortimers have it?"

"I'm not going to do anything of the sort."

"I don't understand."

He let out a shuddering breath, then pulled her fully against him, his arms so tight around her that she could barely draw breath. "That's because I should probably start by apologizing."

She blinked at him. "For what?"

He ran his hand down her hair. "For not making you my wife in full."

"I... um..." Had he just said what she thought? She searched his face for some sign he'd meant the words that had just come out of his mouth. His eyes were warm and soft, his lips curled into a tender smile.

And somehow it all made the breath still in her lungs.

"Before yesterday, I couldn't see the future God had given me with you, but now I see it. When you were gone, I had no choice other than to trust God to bring you back, and I promised God that if He returned you to me, I would be grateful for it."

"So does that mean..." She glanced down at the bed, then swallowed. "That you want to have a child with me?"

He rolled her onto her back and slid deeper into the bed. His breath brushed her ear, then the side of her face, before he planted a kiss at her temple. "It does."

"But what if something happens to me or the baby? What if..."

"God promises not to fail me or forsake me, even in hard times, even when things seem impossible. If something bad happens to you, I'll have to trust that it's part of a bigger plan I don't understand." He planted a kiss on her jaw, then another at the soft place where her jaw met her ear.

"So, does this mean you want to get me with child... now?" She squeaked the last word, her heart suddenly thudding against her chest. "It's the middle of the day!"

A chuckle rumbled from somewhere deep inside him. "Now, tomorrow, the day after that. I don't know how long we'll have together, so I'm going to spend every minute loving you and caring for you and being the best husband I can possibly be. And that includes loving you in the bedroom and outside of it."

"Oh, Wes." Something about his words caused her heart to stop thudding quite so hard. She'd thought the day she'd married Wes was going to be the first day of her new life, but it wasn't. If there was a day when her life started anew, it was today, after she'd faced Lester Mears and Cain had brought her back to the A Bar W.

It was the day Wes told her he was ready to be her husband in every way.

She moved her hands up to frame his face, meeting his deep brown eyes. "I love you."

"I love you too, and it's time I show you how much." He smoothed a strand of hair away from her cheek, then rained kisses on her face, her neck, her collarbone.

And her heart swelled. With love for her husband, with thankfulness to God, and with the hope of a thousand happy tomorrows waiting for her and Wes.

# EPILOGUE

**Three Months Later**

Keely sucked in a deep breath as her eyes fluttered open. Alone again. She shook her head. Why did her husband insist on getting up at the crack of dawn and going to work? It had been three months since she'd been captured. Three months since Wes had told her to move her things into his room. Three months of him climbing into bed with her every night and treating her as a husband was supposed to treat his wife.

Now if she could only get him to sleep in with her so they could wake up together every morning.

She stretched her arms over her head and yawned, then pushed herself out of bed and headed for the balcony. Maybe Wes hadn't left the yard yet, and the two of them could at least have breakfast together.

Sure enough, Wes was in the yard talking to Dobbs. A moment later, Dobbs headed toward the bunkhouse to the left of the ranch, and Wes went into the barn.

Turning, she headed to the wardrobe, where she pulled out

a dress and quickly slipped it over her head. She double-checked that Wes hadn't come back out into the yard as she took a brush to her hair and wound her unruly tresses into a messy bun at the back of her head. Then she jabbed a few pins in her hair and rushed out the door and down the stairs.

She couldn't say quite what she planned to do other than surprise Wes, but when she crept into the open barn door and saw him standing in Ares stall at the far end of the barn with his back toward her, she knew exactly what to do.

She grabbed a handful of straw and crept down the aisle, crouching so that he wouldn't be able to see her over the stalls unless he came into the aisle himself.

"Charlotte says it's time to breed you with Athena, boy," Wes murmured as she drew closer. "What do you think of that?"

Keely crept through the open stall door, then made a mad lunge for her husband. Quick as a rattler striking, she shoved the straw down the back of his collar.

He jumped back, then hollered after her, but she didn't stay put long enough for him to catch her.

She darted into the aisle, ran like lightning, and then ducked into a stall.

"Keely dear, where are you?" Wes's voice was just a little too sweet, and she grinned into her palm. He'd have a handful of straw ready for her by now—or maybe something worse.

He'd be able to get the straw out of his shirt by unbuttoning it and shaking it out, but if he managed to shove a handful of straw down her dress, she'd have to go upstairs and change out of both her dress and corset.

Though that might not be so bad if Wes insisted on helping her change...

"Is this your way of paying me back for getting out of bed before you woke up?" Wes's voice sounded closer than farther away.

A stall door creaked, and she peeked over the stall where she was hiding.

Wes stood in a stall in the middle of the barn on the opposite side of the aisle, still not looking in her direction.

Keely glanced at the open barn door, which was only three stalls away. But Wes started to turn, and she ducked back inside her stall.

"Keely, I know you're in here."

Did he? Or was he just saying that? How did he know she hadn't escaped outside?

If she made it back to the house, she could be sitting down and eating breakfast when he came in and pretend like she'd never even been in the barn. Her straight-laced husband wouldn't have the gall to bring straw into the dining room.

She waited until she heard the creak of another stall door, then she made a dash for the front of the barn.

"Hey!" he shouted after her.

She didn't look over to see where he was as she fled into the morning sunlight. A laugh burst from her as she started for the house.

She didn't get more than a handful of steps from the barn before she stopped.

Two riders stood in the yard beside their horses, both of them looking at her.

Wes rushed out of the barn with a handful of straw. "You're going to pay for that, angel."

He stopped too when he spotted the men, his chest heaving against a shirt that was untucked and unbuttoned.

Keely felt heat rise in her cheeks as she looked from her disheveled husband back to the men.

"Marshal Redding." Wes straightened, then started forward, acting as though it was completely normal to strut around the yard with his shirt open. "Good to see you again."

"Yes, good to see you," Keely muttered, trying to ignore the way her cheeks burned as she started toward them.

She recognized the marshal, of course—how could she forget the man who'd questioned her for over an hour about the Wolf Point Ring?

But who was the man with him? He looked familiar. Extremely familiar. Almost like... like...

James.

She shook her head. It couldn't be. Her eyes must be playing tricks on her. James was dead.

But there was no mistaking the red hair peeking out from beneath the second man's hat, or the way he stood with his hip cocked and head tilted to the side, or how his shoulders looked too wide for his long, narrow frame.

The man turned his head from Wes to her, and their gazes locked across the dusty yard.

"James?" she croaked, her eyes filling with tears.

He took a few steps toward her, then held his arms open.

She rushed into them, his familiar arms coming around her, holding her so tightly her lungs couldn't fully draw air. She sank into the feel of him, the leanness of his body, the pattern of his breathing, the familiar scents of coffee and aftershave. They stood there for several minutes, arms wrapped around each other, holding tight.

Finally, she pushed back far enough to search his face. "How are you here? I thought you were dead."

"Not dead. I was working as an informant for the marshals. It was too dangerous for me to stay working for the mayor, not after what happened to Cynthia."

"So you went into hiding, but you left your sister to face the Wolf Point Ring alone?" Wes said from behind them. The glare he sent James looked cold enough to freeze the Rio Grande.

"It was never supposed to be that way." James kept an arm wrapped around her shoulders as he turned to face Wes. "I went to give information to the marshal I'd been working with one evening after finishing at the mayor's office and was told I'd been followed and I couldn't go back to my apartment. The marshals had plans to go in and get Keely later that night, but when they arrived, she was gone. She'd taken all of the information I had stored at home with her—including a list with names I'd forgotten when I went to meet the marshal."

James looked down at her, his grip around her shoulders tightening. "We searched everywhere for you, half pint."

"So did the Wolf Point Ring," Wes muttered.

Marshal Redding stepped forward. "I assure you, the U.S. Marshal service was looking for your wife just as hard as the Wolf Point Ring was."

Wes whirled toward the lawman. "Do you mean to tell me that when you came here in October, you knew James was alive? Who Keely was? all of it?"

The marshal raised his hands in a gesture of innocence. "I did, yes, but—"

"Why didn't you say anything about my brother being alive when you were here?" Keely shrugged off James's hold. "Or about how you'd been searching for me? You... you let me think my brother was dead when you knew full well he wasn't. That's cruel."

The marshal heaved out a breath, then rubbed the back of his neck. "I had to talk to my superiors before I could say anything about James. And there was a lot I didn't know about the situation. Sheriff Harding had given me the file on the Wolf Point Ring as soon as I arrived in town. I already knew who Nora O'Leary was and that she was missing, but I didn't know for certain that she'd been the one to give this information to the sheriff. When you walked into the room for breakfast, it was all I could do to keep a straight face. The Wolf Point Ring was still at large, and James had forgotten the list of names that you had taken. We couldn't tie the mayor and chief of police to the smuggling without it. As soon as I had your papers, we started planning the arrests. I also made the decision to let you keep the assumed identity you'd created until the arrests were made."

"You didn't arrest Lester Mears or the man who was with him. Someone named Stevens." Keely wrapped her arms around herself, trying to ward off the shudder that traveled through her every time she thought of Mears.

"Did Daniel fill you in on the trouble we had down here with Mears?" Wes asked.

"Yes," Jonas answered.

"No," James said at the same time.

"Turned out Mears wasn't in Chicago like we'd thought." Marshal Redding repositioned the hat on his head, shading his eyes from both the morning sun and her. "When we arrested the man we thought to be him, we learned he was an imposter. It would have looked strange to have him gone from the mayor for several months, and so a similar man in a red bowler hat was acting like him."

"He came down here looking for me." Keely resisted the urge to shudder again and looked up at her brother. "It's not a fun story. I'm all right, but maybe this should wait until after breakfast. Have you eaten?"

"Just trail food. Hard tack and jerky."

"Come on. Cook should have breakfast on the sideboard by now." She took James's hand and would have led him inside, but he used his grip to pull her back into another hug. "I don't need food. I'm just happy you're safe. When I learned you'd been found, I wanted to rush down to Texas immediately, but the marshals wouldn't let me."

Keely pulled back from James long enough to glare at the marshal. "Why wouldn't you let my brother come to me? Or at the very least tell me he was alive?"

"Too much risk." The man's voice was brisk and businesslike. "Like I said earlier, since we had enough information to start making arrests, I thought it best to let the cover you'd already created stand rather than remove you, which could have tipped off the Wolf Point Ring."

"Remove her?" Wes stepped closer to the marshal, his jaw hard even though a bit of his intensity was lost due to his shirt still being untucked and unbuttoned. "She's my wife, not a vase. One doesn't simply remove her. Marshal or not."

Marshal Redding met Wes's gaze without flinching. "We will if it's in the best interest of the U.S. Government."

"Not here, you won't."

The marshal gave Wes a retort, but James pulled her away from the two arguing men, then bent close so only she could hear.

"Are you happy here, married to this man?" His eyes searched hers. "If you married him under a false name, we should be able to get the marriage annulled, and you can go back to Chicago. It's safe there now."

Chicago. She blinked at her brother. It had never occurred to her to return, even though she missed the children at the orphanage. "Are you still living in the apartment? Have you gone back to the way things were before?"

"Actually..." James reached into his pocket and produced a tin star. "I'm working with the marshals. Turns out they liked the information I was able to uncover in Chicago. I'm headed to San Francisco next. Already got my 'job' as an accountant at the port there lined up."

The marshals and her brother. She tilted her head to the side, taking in the familiar lines and planes of the face she never thought she'd see again. It seemed a good fit somehow. Sure, James had a head for numbers and made a fine accountant, but she'd never been able to picture him sitting behind a desk for the rest of his life. "When you say accountant, does that mean you'll be looking for signs of smuggling, like you did in Chicago?"

"Exactly."

"Your brother is an excellent informant." Marshal Redding stepped up beside her. "We're looking forward to having him work with us."

He and Wes must have stopped arguing, because Wes came to stand on James's other side.

"So do you want to stay? I know you got married because you felt like you were out of other choices." James raised his eyes to survey the land surrounding them. "And I have to say, I don't see what you like so much about this place. The desert is awful desolate."

But it wasn't. Sure, the landscape was sparse, but the town was filled with her friends, and her home was filled with love. She couldn't think of a single place she'd rather be—or a different man she'd want to spend her life with.

"I'm sure I want to stay." She stepped away from James, then went and wrapped her arms around Wes, laying her head against his heart. "I might have come to Twin Rivers as a way to escape, but this is my home now. There's not another place in the world I'd rather be."

"Are you sure?" James looked between the two of them. "I don't want you to settle for a situation that will make you unhappy just because you got tangled up in my mess with the Wolf Point Ring."

"Completely sure." Keely pushed up onto her tiptoes and placed a kiss on the underside of Wes's jaw.

She'd never been more sure of anything before in her life.

*A Note from Naomi...*

Wow! Aren't you glad Wes and Keely found a way to work

things out and have a house filled with love and happiness? I'm so happy Wes realized he was trying too hard to control everything around him and decided to start trusting God. All admit, even though I wrote the story, part of me was also sad when Keely needed to give up Leo.

But there's another part of me that's happier for the peace Keely and Wes found together after Leo was gone. I think the happy couple is in an excellent place to start their new life together—and I also think Keely and Wes just might have several children of their own in their future...

I don't know about you, but I'm ready for that horrid rustling ring to be caught! If you're thinking the same thing, then you won't want to miss Alejandra and Harrison's story, *Love's Steadfast Prayer* (coming in 2022).

Hint: If you're curious about who's been giving Daniel those notes about the rustlers' activities, you may have already met her!

I don't have a sample chapter available quite yet, but I do have the first paragraph...

*She knew too much. Everyone had their secrets, but as Alejandra Loyola stood over the still body of Preston Rutherford, watching his lungs struggle for breath, she didn't wonder whether her secrets would end up killing her. No, of that, she was certain. She only hoped she'd be able to see her sister provided for before she died.*

# PREORDER TOMORROW'S STEADFAST PRAYER ON AMAZON!

*If you're looking for something to read while waiting for* Tomorrow's Steadfast Prayer *to release, turn the page for a peek at* Love's Unfading Light, *the first book my USA Today bestselling Eagle Harbor Series. (You might even get a glimpse of Ellie and her siblings before they moved to Texas...)*

https://naomirawlingsbookstore.com/

# LOVE'S UNFADING LIGHT

Eagle Harbor, Michigan, June 1880

"I said no." Tressa Danell scowled at Finley McCabe, whose rancid breath wheezed across the bakery counter that stood between them.

He wore faded doeskin trousers and a shirt so old and sullied she could only guess what color the fabric had originally been. "But Tessa—"

"Not Tessa, it's Tressa." The mere sound of her first name on his lips—or at least its mispronunciation—nearly made her wince. "I'm Mrs. Danell to you."

Mr. McCabe's lips twitched into a frown beneath his droopy gray mustache. "Now see here, it isn't fitting for your betrothed to be calling you by your surname."

Becoming his betrothed was about as likely as ice forming on the harbor in June.

The door opened, dinging the little bell that sat above the entrance to Tressa's bakery. Good. Maybe Mr. McCabe would leave her alone if she had a customer to attend. She looked over the display of bread, muffins, and cookies toward the front of her shop.

Except it wasn't a customer. Mr. Ranulfson, owner of Eagle Harbor's one and only bank, stood just inside the doorway.

Her shoulders slumped.

Mr. McCabe moved to the side of the counter and gripped her hand with his dirt-encrusted one, then dropped down on one knee. "Reckon I need to clarify my intentions a bit."

She glanced at Mr. Ranulfson and tried to tug her hand away, but the wizened trapper had a grip as tight as a sprung bear trap. "Mr. McCabe, if you could kindly—"

"Tessa Danell, I'm asking you to be my wife. I promise to love, honor, and cherish you for the rest of my days. Plus I'll leave you my cabin to settle in after I'm gone. And old Nellie. I know my Nellie girl don't look like much, but the nanny goat's good for milking."

Heat started in Tressa's chest and worked its way up her throat. She stared down at the top of Mr. McCabe's head, bald with little flakes of skin waiting to fall off the moment he scratched his scalp.

Behind him, Mr. Ranulfson cleared his throat and took a few steps farther into the bakery, his polished three-piece suit declaring him a regular dandy amid the rough and tumble town of Eagle Harbor, Michigan.

"We could be hitched by tomorrow night." Mr. McCabe spoke as though the other man wasn't in the bakery. "What do you say, Tessa?"

"It's Mrs. Danell. And my answer is the same as it was yesterday." And the day before that, and the day before that, and the day before that. What had she done to make this man think she'd marry him? "No."

"Now see here, a man's only going to ask so many times."

"It doesn't matter how many times you ask; I'm not going to say yes." Which he should well understand considering this was somewhere near the thirtieth time she'd turned him down. She tugged on her hand again, but he still wouldn't release it.

Mr. Ranulfson pretended to examine the crack in the mortar above the window. Why was he acting as if this was a private moment between her and the trapper? Surely he didn't think she should consider the offer.

Or accept it.

"The way I understand things, you don't have much choice." Mr. McCabe drew her hand to his mouth. His chapped lips scraped against her skin as he forced a kiss. "You're needing a man now that Otis is dead. I'll make you a good husband. I promise not to go down to The Rusty Wagon and gamble or head up to Central and visit girls the way yer husband—"

"That's enough." She yanked her hand, finally getting Mr. McCabe to release it. The entire town might know of Otis's indiscretions, but there was a difference between knowing and speaking.

"I'll gladly take the boy in too, might even teach him some trapping." Mr. McCabe's knees popped as he stood.

"No." The word emerged rough and raspy.

"Well then, I'll be seeing you tomorrow."

Tomorrow? She rubbed at her temples, which had started throbbing the moment Mr. McCabe opened the door to her bakery.

He offered her a tight smile and a glimpse of teeth yellow enough to match his tobacco-stained beard—teeth inside a mouth he'd expect her to kiss if they wed.

A shudder ran down her spine.

He squashed his hat atop his head and headed toward the door, the cheery bell tinkling behind him as he left.

She rubbed her temples again and turned to Mr. Ranulfson. "I'm sorry for that..." *Display. Fight. Misunderstanding.* What word to even use?

The banker took a strawberry pie from the shelf. "You should consider his offer, Mrs. Danell."

Why did everyone assume she needed another husband? She'd made the mistake of getting trapped in a marriage once, and she wasn't fool enough to make it again. "I don't need anything Mr. McCabe has to offer."

"Have you recovered your money then? Did Sheriff Jenkins find who stole it?"

A hard lump formed in her throat, and she shook her head. She hadn't even bothered to tell the sheriff about last week's robbery. If the man hadn't lifted a finger to find who had taken her money the first two times, he wasn't going to help with the most recent robbery either. Was it good or bad that she'd only had eight dollars taken this last time? If there was one benefit to having no money, it was that whoever robbed you couldn't steal very much.

Mr. Ranulfson dug around in his pocket for some change and set two dollars' worth of quarters on the counter beside the pie. "Do you have the money to pay your mortgage?"

"I can pay this month's, but I don't have enough to catch up, no." Though the eight dollars that had gone missing last week certainly would have helped.

Mr. Ranulfson sighed so hard he almost ruffled the curtains on the opposite side of the storefront. "I'd like to work with you, Mrs. Danell. Truly I would. I'm not in the habit of turning people out of their homes the moment they fall on hard times, but neither can I ignore your situation forever. Another month has passed, which means you now owe me another ten dollars for June's payment. You haven't paid on your mortgage since February, so that brings you up to fifty dollars even."

"If not for being robbed, I would have been able to pay you." She wouldn't let tears flood her eyes. She wouldn't.

"But I still need you to make back those payments, and it's

time we set a date. Say August first? That gives you two months
to get things caught up."

Where was she going to come up with so much? She wrung
her hands together, keeping them behind the counter so Mr.
Ranulfson couldn't see. "And if I don't have the money by
then?"

"I'm sorry, but I'll have to take back your building." His
voice was gentle, understanding even. Like he'd done this
hundreds of times before. Like he'd perfected just how to
deliver such news while keeping the person indebted to him
from flying into a panic or rage.

She glanced down at the tips of her boots, peeking out from
beneath a faded mourning dress she'd purchased secondhand.
If it weren't for her son Colin, she might just let her building go
to the bank and start again elsewhere.

Of course, having a little money saved to leave town and
buy a bakery somewhere else might be a good idea, too.

"You should know that Byron Sinclair has been spouting off
about the fishing boat Otis bought last year." The banker stuck
a hand in his pocket and jingled some change as he spoke. "You
do know about the boat, don't you?"

She'd kept from getting teary earlier, but she couldn't stop
her cringe now. It happened automatically, much like a yawn at
bedtime or a deep breath on a crisp autumn day. Yes, she knew
of the fishing boat Otis had lost in a game of whist at The Rusty
Wagon a week after buying it. She had no money to pay what
was owed on that either.

The change jingled again—probably just some spare coins,
like the ones he'd used to pay for the pie. Never mind that those
very coins could make the difference between her keeping the
bakery or losing it.

"I wish I could tell you Sinclair had forgotten all about the
boat, but I assume you're better off being warned. He'll try
wringing money out of you one way or the other."

"Thank you for the warning." She forced the words over her tongue, though she couldn't think of much to be thankful for at the moment.

Unless the fact that Mr. Ranulfson wasn't turning her out of her home this afternoon counted.

"I best be off then." He picked up the pie and turned for the door.

"Wait." She grabbed the money box beneath the shelf, retrieved eight dollars, and scooped the quarters he'd just given her off the counter. "At least this can cover June's payment."

It was probably better to give him the money before the robber returned. Because after three robberies, there was no point in telling herself that he wouldn't be back or that next time she'd find a hiding spot he wouldn't find for the money.

Mr. Ranulfson held out his hand for the meager pile.

"I'll get more, I promise."

The slightest hint of compassion glinted in his gray eyes, and he sighed again, softer this time. "I hope you do, Mrs. Danell. I'd hate to turn you out of this building, but I don't see any other way."

"I understand." And she did. It was a business decision. Clear and logical. She made them every day when dealing with her bakery. It only made sense that a banker would do the same.

Oh, how had she ever gotten to the point of becoming the poor business decision? The liability rather than the dependable asset?

"Good day." Mr. Ranulfson turned and walked to the door.

"Good day," she mumbled, though there had been little good about it. Or any other day over the past three months since she'd been robbed and Otis had died.

Then again, there hadn't been much good about her days before Otis's death either—except for their son, Colin.

She rubbed her throbbing temples once again. How was she going to come up with forty dollars by August first?

No, it would be fifty dollars by then, because she'd owe the bank for July's mortgage too.

She blinked her tired eyes, eyes she wasn't about to let grow moist with something as useless as tears.

The bell above the door tinkled, and in came Mrs. Fletcher and Mrs. Kainner. She plastered a smile on her face as the women each picked out a muffin and left. If only the two dimes they paid was enough to appease the bank. But if nothing else, they would help purchase more flour.

Wiping her hands on her apron, she headed back into the kitchen. A glance inside the flour sack that had once held fifty pounds told her she only had enough left for two days of baking.

She squeezed the flour in her hand and watched it drift back into the sack. This two-story bakery was supposed to guarantee her a place to sleep and some income. Not a lot, but enough to provide a living for her and Colin since the wages Otis had earned logging disappeared quickly after he returned from the woods every spring.

Now she had little hope of putting a decent meal on the table and giving her son a dry place to sleep come August.

But what was she to do? Stop baking?

She reached for the sourdough rising on the counter, plopped some into a clay mixing bowl, then sifted some flour.

Maybe Mr. Ranulfson was right and she was a fool for turning away Mr. McCabe. The old trapper would be dead in another decade, two decades at most, and that would give her time enough to raise Colin and see him situated.

Unless Mr. McCabe got her with child.

She dropped the sifter into the mixing bowl with a clunk. Even if she had to work twenty-hour days until her fingers were raw and her back ached, she'd find a way to provide for her son that didn't include a yellow-toothed man's bed.

"Is Colin here?" The back door to her bakery sprung open and in bounded Leroy Spritzer, his face streaked with dirt and his dirty blond curls hanging into his eyes.

"Yeah, where's Colin?" Martin Spritzer followed his older brother inside, his bare feet padding across the floor of the bakery.

Tressa wiped her hands on her apron. "I thought he was at the beach with you."

Leroy shook his head, which allowed his bangs to flop enough she could almost make out the green of his eyes beneath. "He never came."

"We stopped by the general store to see if he was sweeping the porch, but he wasn't there neither." Martin blinked up at her, his overgrown bangs were parted to one side and didn't obscure his eyes.

"Perhaps Colin's playing with someone else?"

Leroy shrugged. "I s'pose."

But that didn't make sense. Colin wouldn't go off and find other friends if Leroy and Martin were waiting for him. She walked to the door and peeked into the alley.

No sign of Colin. Where could he be?

"Can you tell him we'll be at the beach when he gets back?" Leroy tromped up behind her.

"Are you certain you didn't see Colin somewhere about town?"

Both boys nodded, their too-thin faces earnest as they watched her.

"All right then." She wiped her suddenly sweaty palms on her apron once more and attempted to focus—on Leroy and Martin, not her missing son. "You said you're going to the beach? You know not to go into the water without an adult there, right?"

"Ma says Cliff's old enough to watch us." Martin scuffed his big toe against the bakery floor. "She don't let us go in the water without him."

Yes, the oldest Spritzer son was nearly an adult now. "That's fine then." Tressa scanned the alley once again before bringing her gaze back to rest on the boys. "Oh, before you go, I've got some extras for you to take."

It'd make more sense to send the food with the boys now rather than walk to the Spritzer house later. If one could even call the weathered shack with quarter inch gaps between some of the wall planks a house.

Leroy spread his fingers and held his hands up. "Ma says she don't want no more of your extras."

Tressa ran her eyes down the boys' thin faces, arms, and legs. Their shirts hung loosely on their shoulders, and if not for the strings tied around the waists of their short pants, both pairs would fall to a puddle on the floor.

Everyone in town knew Ruby Spritzer struggled to keep food in the bellies of her nine children. Or maybe it was ten children? Eleven? The handful of times she'd stopped by the Spritzer house, she'd never gotten a good count. The children popped in and out of everywhere, never still long enough to count. Perhaps lack of food was only part of the reason why the children were all so thin and the other part lay in Ruby not remembering which ones had eaten and which ones hadn't.

But why would she tell her children not to take any more food? "Well, I suppose it's always best to obey your ma."

The boys looked at each other and then nodded slowly, their eyes as round as dinner plates.

"But I'm wondering if you two are hungry for a snack. Did your ma say anything about eating snacks at the bakery?"

They looked at each other again before Leroy shook his head. "No, ma'am."

"It just so happens that I've got some leftover bread and a little jam."

~.~.~.~.~

SHE SERVED three customers during the time it took the boys to eat in the kitchen, and in the end, Leroy and Martin left with a loaf and a half of bread, her last jar of jam, and a dozen cookies minus however many they'd scarf down before they made it home. Tressa scanned the back alley once more as they disappeared around the side of the bakery. Still no sign of Colin. Had he found another job to do around town in exchange for a coin or two?

Most likely.

She walked around the back of the bakery, then along the side, before coming out to the front on Center Street. No sign of her auburn-haired boy anywhere. She'd go back inside for a minute, mix up the bread dough and set it to rising, then look for him.

She hastened through the storefront and back to the kitchen. He couldn't have gone far, could he? And in a town the size of Eagle Harbor, someone had certainly seen him.

Unless he'd gone into the woods by himself. Or down to the lakeshore without anyone watching him. The beach stayed busy enough that someone would probably see him, but what if he'd climbed out onto the rocks by the lighthouse? No one would be watching him there, and those rocks could get awful slippery.

But no, Colin knew better than to do either of those things.

Once she knew where her son was, she'd laugh about how

worked up she was getting. But at the moment, her hands were so damp they struggled to hold the flour sifter.

She reached for the wooden spoon in a canister with her other utensils and yanked it free.

*Crash!*

The entire canister toppled onto the counter, sending spoons and whisks flying while the rolling pin clattered to the floor.

Just what she needed. She gathered the spoons and forks and a wire mesh strainer off the counter and shoved them back into the canister, then she stooped to pick up the whisk off the floor.

Where had the rolling pin gotten to? She dumped the dirty utensils into the sink and got down on hands and knees. Traces of flour from that morning's baking dusted the floor along with a glob of muffin batter she must have spilled earlier. The rolling pin had managed to settle against the back wall beneath the counter. She dodged the stickiness and crawled under the countertop before grabbing the pin.

The back door burst open. "Ma!"

Her head came up—*thump!*

"Ouch!"

The mixing bowl teetered precariously on the edge of the counter. She shot out a hand, but—*smash!*

A cloud of fine white flour plumed into the air, the glob of sourdough landed on her lap, and chunks of broken pottery clattered across the floor.

She might as well take the rolling pin and beat herself on the head for good measure. Except her head already throbbed where she'd smacked it against the counter.

"Ma, what happened?" Colin crouched down and peered at her, his hair mussed from running and his forehead drawn into a furrow of little wrinkled lines.

"You're here." The pounding in her chest slowly lessened. "Leroy and Martin said they couldn't find you."

"'Course I'm here. Where else would I be?"

"Is everything all right?" An unfamiliar voice filled the kitchen. Then footsteps thudded against the uneven floorboards and a pair of man's boots appeared beside Colin.

Tressa ran her gaze up, up, up. Past the man's legs and waist and shirt and neck until she stared into a face with a faint golden beard lining its cheeks and chin. Her eyes finally met a pair of light brown ones filled with laughter.

Her cheeks burned. Of all the ways to meet someone.

She scrambled up from her place on the floor, which only sent a fresh plume of flour wafting from her apron and the blob of sourdough tumbling to the floor with a splat.

A booming guffaw filled the small kitchen, followed by her son's tinkling laughter.

"Did you hear that, Ma? It splatted like a mud pie."

Perhaps so, and a ten-year-old boy would probably think that funny, but did the stranger have to laugh? She took a step back from the muck at her feet and bumped into the counter behind her. Her elbow collided with the bag of flour, which slumped toward the edge.

She reached for it, but the stranger grabbed the sack before it fell.

Wedged between a chest that seemed too wide to belong to a living, breathing person and the counter, Tressa looked up at a man tall enough to reach up and touch the ceiling. "Ah... thank you."

He smiled, and faint lines wreathed his eyes—lines that indicated he still wanted to laugh at her. "You're welcome."

A warm puff of breath feathered across her cheek, much different from Mr. McCabe's sour exhalations. Then the man reached across her and placed the bag of flour on the counter against the wall, seemingly unfazed by how his chest pressed into her side.

The small movement gave her room enough to step away from—

*Squish.*

Another round of laughter filled the kitchen.

She didn't need to look down to know what she'd just stepped in.

Cheeks burning again, she clamped a hand to her hip and glared at the man. "Who are you, and why are you in my kitchen?"

"I, um..." A chortle choked off his words.

"He's Mr. Oakton." Colin spoke through a snicker, one that died quickly when she turned her glare on her son. "The lightkeeper."

"Oh." After living in Eagle Harbor for a year, most of the townsfolk had wandered into her bakery at one time or another, but not this man. She would have remembered, what with the way he towered above them like an oak tree.

"Assistant lightkeeper," Mr. Oakton managed. Then he pressed his lips together as though doing so could somehow hide his urge to start laughing again. "But not for long. Got a shipyard down on Lake Huron my friend and I are buying."

Colin wiped at the flour that had settled onto his face. "He walked me home."

"Walked you home?" She narrowed her gaze and ran it down Colin. Red cheeks, slightly mussed hair, bright eyes, working arms and hands and legs. Why did her ten-year-old boy need someone to walk him home?

"Here, Ma. Remember how I said I'd bring you a quarter for sweeping the porch at the general store? I got two." He held the coins out, his eyes shining. "Maybe we can buy a chicken from the Markhams, or a rabbit from Mr. McCabe next time he comes 'round?"

Something large rose in her throat, and she glanced at Mr. Oakton. What kind of mother did this big, hulking man think she was, sending her ten-year-old son off to work?

But she hadn't sent him. He'd found work on his own.

*Because he feels the strain of my debts.*

She rubbed at her head, the ache growing worse rather than lessening. What a terrible mother she was turning out to be.

"What's wrong? Should I give the quarters to Mr. Ranulfson instead?" Colin looked at the coins she'd yet to take, then back at her, the joy in his eyes starting to dull. "You can do whatever you want with them, I promise."

"I..." She took the money. The stranger still stood by the counter, his tall form and broad shoulders taking up too much space in a room that had never seemed small before. "I think we best give it to Mr. Ranulfson."

Or maybe use it for flour. Yes, that's what she'd use the money for, flour so that she could keep baking. She simply wouldn't think about how long it had been since she'd tasted chicken, or even a rabbit.

"Did you sell a lot of stuff today?" Colin spun on his heel and dashed into the storefront. "I've been praying you would."

She'd sold some, yes. But not as much as she would have at this time last year, and not enough to pay off what they owed by the beginning of August. Her customers had certainly tapered off this winter after Otis died and news of his numerous debts and swindling attempts had floated around town.

"Well, did you?" Colin called from the other room.

"A handful of people stopped by." She simply wouldn't confess the majority had spent a nickel or dime rather than several dollars.

"Oh. It kind of looks like there's lots of bread and muffins left."

And cookies. Plus a pie.

She took a step toward the storefront, only to have the heel of her ankle boot squelch against the floor. How could she have forgotten her shoes were coated in sourdough? She bent and undid the trio of tiny buttons at the top of her worn shoes, feeling Mr. Oakton's gaze on her back all the while.

Oh well. The stranger had already seen her sprawled on the floor and covered with flour. There was little reason to stand on ceremony. She set the shoes aside, leaving the mess of flour, sourdough, and broken pottery to clean up later, and proceeded into the storefront in nothing but her stockings.

If the back of her neck burned a little while he watched her, it was hardly the worst thing that had happened today.

"Sure looks like you've got lots to choose from." Mr. Oakton's boots clunked against the floor behind her. "I was just thinking how we need a couple loaves of bread back at the lighthouse. And maybe some muffins for breakfast in the morning."

Colin turned from where he stood in front of the display counter and sent the lightkeeper a smile that caused his freckles to scrunch up on his cheeks. "Really?"

"That's all right." Tressa twisted her hands together. "You don't need to..."

But the man was already moving to survey her shop's goods.

Had Colin's questions about money given their situation away? She'd worked hard to keep news about them being robbed and owing money to the bank from circulating. The stories about Otis's swindling caused her enough trouble by far. Would people still come to the bakery if they knew she was in danger of losing it?

She stared down at her apron, covered in wasted flour and soiled from the sourdough blob. She'd sunk her every last penny into this bakery. If she didn't make things work, she had nowhere to go and nothing to offer her son...

Except for a blanket on the floor of Mr. McCabe's cabin.

~.~.~.~.~

MAC PLUCKED his hat off and held it against his chest as he looked around the bakery hewn of rough planked lumber and pitch. Though a few shelves sat empty, baked goods filled a good portion of the storefront, and what he saw looked delicious. Scents radiated from every crack and crevice of the room, a whiff of ginger here, a touch of cinnamon there. And didn't it beat all, the woman had a strawberry pie sitting smack in the center of one of the shelves. His mouth was already watering, and that was before he stepped close enough to see the large grains of sugar sprinkled on top and a fancy curlicue design cut into the flaky dough.

A line of people should be wrapped around this building waiting to purchase that pie alone, not to mention the gingerbread cookies and loaves of fluffy looking bread. So why was no one here? This was strawberry pie, after all.

"Are you really going to buy some bread?" The boy looked between him and the bread uncertainly.

"I said I was, didn't I?"

The doubt didn't leave the boy's eyes.

He'd found Colin crying in the woods. After drying his tears and giving him a quarter to make up for the one a couple bullies stole, plus a second for good measure, couldn't the boy trust him to do as he'd stated?

But then, the child was Otis Danell's son. Having had Otis for a pa, the boy likely had a hard time trusting anyone.

He knew about those kinds of pas far too well—and how their pungent reputations seeped into their innocent son's pores until the entire town thought his little boy stank as bad as his skunk of a father. His own pa had left twelve years ago this summer, and he still couldn't manage to entirely cleanse the stench of his father's deeds off himself, at least not in the eyes of a few townsfolk.

He lumbered toward the loaves of bread stacked neatly onto the far counter. He probably shouldn't spend much, what with how he'd been saving every spare penny for his move to Port Huron. But the woman seemed in need of a customer or two, and he had enough money put by to give himself a good start after he moved.

Three loaves were discounted to half price. He snatched the lot of them plus the two fresh ones. He reckoned Jessalyn Dowrick could use a loaf of bread, what with three little ones to look after and her husband up and gone to the gold fields Out West.

And word around town was the minister's wife had taken a fall and was hobbling about with a turned ankle. Her husband would probably appreciate some bread. Heaven only knew what Finley McCabe ate save for the muskrats and possums he managed to trap. And Ruby Spritzer had so many young'uns running about the place she probably worked twelve hours a day just to keep them fed and clothed.

And there were the Cummingses. Something hard fisted around his chest at the thought of stepping into their cabin now empty of the man who'd taken him in and raised him as a son after his pa ran off, even if he was just to deliver bread. Last he'd heard, Mabel still wasn't faring well and certainly wasn't up to baking.

"That's an awful lot of bread, mister. Are you sure you can eat it all?" Colin's eyes had gone from wary to wide.

So maybe he wouldn't be depositing any extra money in the bank this week. "And the strawberry pie."

"No! I mean..." Mrs. Danell's voice held the softest accent. Not the blunt, forceful sound of the Cornish, nor the rolling lilt of the Irish, but something altogether different. Something so subtle most people wouldn't notice. The woman tucked a falling strand of hair behind her ear and raised eyes as tawny and rich as maple syrup to meet his. He'd seen her around town a time or two, but why hadn't he ever taken notice of Otis Danell's widow before now?

Of course, she hadn't exactly been a widow all that long, and he'd been a mite busy at the lighthouse of late.

Did she realize how much flour was sprinkled through her hair? Or that her forehead was dotted with little white splotches?

"That's too much." Again, the faintest accent tinged her voice. "You can't possibly need five loaves of bread and a pie."

It was little surprise the woman had half a shop full of unsold goods if she went about telling customers not to purchase her food.

"My ma makes the best pie in Keweenaw County." The boy pulled the pie off the display shelf and set it near where his ma stood with the money box.

"Colin, hush now." The woman's cheeks had turned a faint rose color despite the flour dusting them.

"I'm sure she makes a right fine pie." And buying it would be money well spent if for no other reason than keeping the smile on the moppet who beamed at him.

He just might come 'round again tomorrow too. It wouldn't hurt to buy a few cookies to see the boy grin again. Maybe if he was lucky, he'd even get a smile out of his ma.

He might be departing town in two weeks, but there was no harm in leaving a handful of dollar bills and a couple smiling faces behind him.

# THANK YOU

Thank you for reading *Tomorrow's Constant Hope*. I sincerely hope you enjoyed Wes and Keely's story. I'm so very excited to be writing a series set in Texas, and I hope you come to love the rugged town of Twin Rivers as much as I have. The next full-length novel in the Texas Promise Series is Harrison and Alejandra's story, *Tomorrow's Steadfast Prayer*. To purchase: https://naomirawlingsbookstore.com/

Want to be notified when *Tomorrow's Steadfast Prayer* releases? Sign up for my author newsletter: http://geni.us/AqsHv

Also, if you enjoyed reading Wes and Keely's story, please take a moment to tell others about the novel. You can do this by posting an honest review on Amazon or GoodReads. Please note that to leave a review on Amazon, you need to go directly to Amazon's website. Your e-reader may ask you to rank stars at the end of this novel, but that ranking does not show up on Amazon as a review. I read every one of my reviews, and reviews help readers like yourself decide whether to purchase a novel. You might also consider mentioning *Tomorrow's Constant Hope* to your friends on Facebook, Twitter, or Pinterest.

# OTHER NOVELS BY NAOMI RAWLINGS

**Texas Promise Series**

Book 1—*Tomorrow's First Light* (Sam and Ellie)

Book 2—*Tomorrow's Shining Dream* (Daniel and Charlotte)

Book 3—*Tomorrow's Constant Hope* (Wes and Keely: releasing 2021)

Book 4—*Tomorrow's Steadfast Prayer* (Harrison and Alejandra)

Book 5—*Tomorrow's Lasting Joy* (Cain and Anna Mae)

**Eagle Harbor Series**

Book 1—*Love's Unfading Light* (Mac and Tressa)

Book 2—*Love's Every Whisper* (Elijah and Victoria)

Book 3—*Love's Sure Dawn* (Gilbert and Rebekah)

Book 4—*Love's Eternal Breath* (Seth and Lindy)

Book 5—Love's Christmas Hope (Thomas and Jessalyn)

Book 6—*Love's Bright Tomorrow* (Isaac and Aileen)

Short Story—*Love's Beginning* (Elijah, Gilbert, Mac, Victoria, Rebekah)

Prequel—*Love's Violet Sunrise* (Hiram and Mabel)

**Belanger Family Saga**

# AUTHOR'S NOTE

When I first started planning Wes and Keely's story, I had no way of knowing the world was going to fall apart. But within a few weeks of writing the opening scene of this novel, COVID 19 errupted and the world stopped. I was stuck at home (which probably gave some people extra time to write), but I was with my children and my visiting parents trying to find something to keep everyone occupied.

On top of that, we were alsyo fixing up our house and moving!

A year and a half later, I am sorry it took me so long to write Wes and Keely's story, and I thank you all for waiting for the novel to release. I also hope each and every one of you are safe and well. I'm sure some of you have suffered the loss of loved ones due to COVID, and I am so very sorry.

Okay, I'm going to get a little honest here. Wes's part of the story was hard for me to write. In some ways, he might be the character that most closely reflects who I am as a person. While I haven't suffered loss to the degree Wes has, I very much like to have a plan for everything. Wes struggles with balancing wise planning and trusting God. People say a square peg can't fit into a round hole, but I'm the type of person to go out and buy a chisel and chip away at the corners of the wood until I can shove the peg into the hole where it's not supposed to fit. Only after I'm done do I remember to stop and ask God whether He wanted me to buy a chisel, whether He actually wanted the square peg in the round hole in the first place and me to go through the trouble of making the peg round.

So yes, Wes and I are similar, and I have a feeling some of you might be the same. The truth is, it can be hard to trust a God you can't see, when everything around you is going up in flames. It can be hard to trust a God who promises to love you when trials come and hard things happen.

But at the end of the day God is good. His mercies are everlasting. And perhaps most important, He is there to carry us through trials—if we let Him.

I'm so very glad you took the time to read Tomorrow's Constant Hope. And I hope Wes's story inspires you to live out your faith every day. Even when it's hard. Even when you are failing. Even when you feel like living the Christian life is pointless.

Because it's not pointless in the end. There's always a loving God waiting with open arms to cherish and love and help you.

Thanks for reading!
Naomi

# ACKNOWLEDGMENTS

Thank you first and foremost to my Lord and Savior, Jesus Christ, for giving me both the ability and opportunity to write novels for His glory.

As with any novel, an author might come up with a story idea and sit at his or her computer to type the initial words, but it takes an army of people to bring you the book you have today. I'd especially like to thank my editors, Roseanna M. White and Melissa Jagears, for pointing out ways to make this book stronger. Also, thank you to Judy at Judicious Revisions for helping with the finer details of this novel.

Many thanks to my family for working with my writing schedule and giving me a chance to do two things I love: be a mommy and a writer.

And thank you to the wonderful, flexible staff and parents at Copper Country Christian School in Chassell, Michigan, for letting me find time to finish this book while also working at the school.

Finally, many thanks to the hospitable people of Terlingua, Texas and the staff at Fort Leaton for answering my numerous questions and helping me make the Texas landscape come alive. Thank you to Janelle at Lajitas and Big Bend Stables (https://www.lajitasstables.com/) both for the tour on horseback and for answering my many questions. Thank you to James at Big Bend River Tours (http://bigbendrivertours.com/) for a memorable trip down the Rio Grande. My only complaint was that the trip was too short. Thank you to the wonderful park ranger at Fort Leaton who answered my numerous questions on two separate occasions. I'm so sorry I don't remember your name. I thought about calling Fort Leaton to see if I could learn it, but figured that might seem rather stalker-like.

And finally, thank you to Curt Swafford of Tarantula Ranch for hosting me and my traveling companions in your guest cabins. Your stories and detailed explanations brought my Texas experience to life and gave me a deeper understanding of the Big Bend. Also, you win the award for hot tub with the best view ever. Seriously, I'm talking mountain vistas at sunset. How many people with hot tubs can claim that view? You also win the award for having the most memorable driveway ever. I never knew it could take fifteen minutes to drive a half mile. Fortunately, the spectacular hot tub views and quintessential stories made up for the driveway.

Tomorrow's Constant Hope: © Naomi Mason 2021

Cover Design: © Clarissa Yeo 2018

Cover Photographs: Shutterstock.com

Editors: Roseanna White; Melissa Jagears

# ABOUT THE AUTHOR

Naomi Rawlings is the author of over a dozen historical Christian novels, including the Amazon bestselling Eagle Harbor Series. While she'd love to claim she spends her days huddled in front of her computer vigorously typing, in reality she spends her time cleaning, picking up, and pretending like her house isn't in a constant state of chaos. She lives with her husband and three children in Michigan's rugged Upper Peninsula, along the southern shore of Lake Superior where they get 200 inches of snow every year, and where people still grow their own vegetables and cut down their own firewood—just like in the historical novels she writes.

For more information about Naomi, please visit her at www.naomirawlings.com or find her on Facebook at www.facebook.com/author.naomirawlings. If you'd like a free novella, sign up for her author newsletter.